SO-DTC-713

shelterbelt

also by tricia bauer

Hollywood & Hardwood

Boondocking

Working Women and Other Stories

st. martin's press ᴁ new york

shelterbelt

tricia bauer

www.stmartins.com

Book design by Victoria Kuskowski

Title page and part title image courtesy of Photodisc.

Library of Congress Cataloging-in-Publication Data

Bauer, Tricia
    Shelterbelt / Tricia Bauer.—1st ed.
        p. cm.
    ISBN 0-312-26647-2
        1. Teenage girls—Fiction.   2. Teenage pregnancy—
Fiction.   3. Voyages and travels—Fiction.   I. Title.

PS3552.A83647 S48 2000
813'.54—dc21   00-040234

First Edition: October 2000

10 9 8 7 6 5 4 3 2 1

For Bozzone

With thanks to the Fundación Valparaíso

Mojáca, Spain

contents

one

two

three

four

one

I

january

*My world was flat. It had always been flat. A huge expanse of wheat-
and corn- and sorghum-colored work smoothed across the land's
slightest dip and curve. Life stretched out in front of me as if it would
run on forever at one level. Except for the band of trees—the shelterbelt—that protects the place where I used to live, its farmhouse,
barn, and pastures, events in my life have been one horizontal line:
the view from my bedroom, the gray glaze of highway emptying into
the future, the beds of my mother and father and my brother. My
belly. And then everything changed.*

Ellis and Vivienne sat side by side on the soft olive sofa in
the living room of the little house with its covered porch butting
up against the main street of Paradise, Nebraska. The boundary
between the town's property and the landlord's was highlighted
by a dirty, crusted band of week-old snow.

Jade watched her father and Vivienne, but was distracted
every time someone walked past the house. The passersby reminded her that no matter what happened—or didn't happen—
inside the house, the world clicked on in footsteps just beyond
the front door. Since the move to town, since her mother had
left, Jade had a hard time forgetting how tightly everything fit

together. Sometimes she didn't think she could get a full breath of air without taking in something someone else had left behind.

"He's not late yet, sweetheart. If it gets to be seven o'clock, then you'll have reason to worry," Vivienne said, her voice high and sugary.

Ellis humphed and turned to look at Vivienne. A jagged scar wriggled from under the bridge of his thick, black-framed glasses and down the side of his nose.

"Wonder what route he took," Vivienne said.

"I'm not worrying about Rory," Jade said, punching the "worrying."

Vivienne squeezed Ellis's hand. When he humphed again, Jade saw his hand tighten in return. Jade's girlfriend Sara said that all newlyweds "displayed." Jade had protested that they weren't even married because Ellis hadn't divorced Rexanne. But there had been a ceremony in the fall with lots of doves and cakes afterward, all arranged by Vivienne so that her church, Holy Light Christian Fellowship, wouldn't object to the living-together arrangement. "We're married in the eyes of *my* Lord," Vivienne had once said to Jade. That remark was the first time her voice hadn't sounded like the beginning to a song, but made Jade think of a squeaky door being slammed shut.

Jade picked up the paper to block her view of the lovebirds, and studied the headlines. Most of page one was devoted to a story on the 4-H banquet honoring the county's youth and yet one more follow-up report on the fall crop harvesting. She skimmed a piece on the Retired Teachers' Club entertained by the Blue Cows, a local jazz band, and announcements of an RV expo, a scout-o-rama, a fiddling workshop, and some guy giving a talk on the history of rural mail service. A small boxed ad announced au pair work in New England. The news of her own body was more interesting than anything right here in print, but that was a story that couldn't be told.

"Some feed you put on for just the three of us," Ellis said to Vivienne. "Wasn't it, Jade?" Jade had heartburn, but she nodded at her father.

"Ate like there was no tomorrow," he said. Vivienne shifted and smiled with pride.

Jade was surprised Vivienne hadn't tried to force the ham into their crock pot. Nearly every other day she scooped some bland concoction from the cooker, its exterior the color of pea soup.

"Come here, baby," Ellis said. Jade was ready to gag at all the cutesy talk until she noticed that the remark was directed at Butterbean. Ellis was patting the sofa. When the big yellow-and-white cat jumped onto his lap, he stroked her until she started to purr.

Jade looked back at the paper, but she couldn't concentrate on the story entitled, "Pizza Hut Announces Winners of Coloring Contest." Last summer, for the few months after Rexanne left but before Vivienne came into the picture, Jade had cooked for her father. She liked the feel of flour on her fingers and the way it dusted the air around her as she worked on a recipe; she squeezed ground beef into patties and meat balls and loaves until her fingers were coated with a light layer of grease. Sara said it was weird that Jade preferred slicing fresh vegetables, mincing onion, garlic, and celery into mounds, to talking on the telephone.

Jade could remember when kneeling on a kitchen chair made her the perfect height to help Rexanne stir and pour. When she got older, Jade prepared the meats, eventually taking on that part of the meal exclusively as Rexanne became an increasingly committed vegetarian. By the time she left, Rexanne wouldn't touch meat of any kind. Jade knew that Ellis saw her mother's refusal of meat as a major reason that his farm had failed. In one of their last fights, he yelled that a man without the whole-hearted support of his wife couldn't be expected to beat the high odds of surviving in his own business. Rexanne had responded that a man who'd listen to a banker's promises over his wife's good sense got what he deserved.

Jade didn't look up when Vivienne made a kissing sound on some part of Ellis's body. Sara said Ellis was handsome, but Jade couldn't tell; her father's looks didn't normally concern her. He was tall with a thick broad chest and a full, mostly dark-brown beard, which hid his more subtle facial expressions. He wore a camouflage outfit nearly every day and T-shirts announcing "Special Forces" or "American Made." When Jade assembled the quirky parts of him into an objective picture, she thought a stranger might find him more frightening than good-looking: the "Sine Pari" tattoo on his forearm; his thick glasses, which had kept him out of the real military; the scar pressing out across his nose into a tiny tributary, the only clue that a river once coursed with rage inside him.

"I don't know why we had to get the spiral ham," Jade said, though she had been surprised at how easily the slices pulled loose from the bone.

"No waste, honey," Vivienne said.

"What's spiral ham?" Ellis asked.

Jade could have pursued an argument, but Ellis was rapt by Vivienne's explanation of the precut meat. Even though she didn't eat it herself, Rexanne had never wasted a morsel on a regular ham, which could be gotten for less than half the price. Under Rexanne's direction, Jade could strip every mouthful of meat from whatever configuration of bone supported it. But now, forbidden from mentioning Rexanne's name in the house, Jade couldn't effectively argue against the special ham.

Vivienne was asking Ellis if any of his friends were going to watch the Quack Off, a local duck race on ice. She said competitors could bring their own duck or rent one. Ellis laughed. Jade had to admit that her father talked more and laughed more than he had in years, particularly since losing the farm in July, and the previous December losing Benjamin. Those days all their lives felt sucked down a huge drainage system. Broken apart, the family sloshed away with the huge accumulation of discarded liquids and solids. Despite the way Vivienne had improved Ellis's temperament, Jade considered the woman a scathead.

Vivienne was blonde, blue-eyed, and slender. She was younger than Ellis, but not so young that it was easy for her to conceive a child. Jade had heard her on the phone in a lowered voice telling a friend how badly she wanted to become pregnant and how uncooperative her body was. And then there was Jade's body, cooperating all too well to make for a situation she didn't want any part of. None of it made much sense to Jade. Nothing had since Benjamin's accident.

"You have all your lessons done?" Ellis asked sternly, while gently pulling at the cat's ears and the back of her neck. Butterbean's eyes were closed and she was drooling.

"Of course," Jade lied and mumbled how she'd completed a social studies report on world hunger. Ellis took an uncharacteristic interest in Jade's life now that he had only one child. When Vivienne's concern collaborated with his, Jade felt totally claustrophobic.

Maybe Vivienne was well-meaning, but she pushed her frilly tastes all over Jade's closet. If clothes were the extent of it, Jade could have handled the intrusion. There was something creepy about a grown woman whose dresser drawers were stuffed with pink, who wore oversized bows in her hair and at her waist, who accessorized flowered dresses with rickrack and lace. But Vivienne's flouncy exterior hid a political agenda. She tried to enlist Jade to promote the cause of Plains Babies Right-to-Life as if she were holding a new outfit she wanted Jade to slip into ("Go ahead and try it, sweetheart. It will look adorable on you.").

The thought of Vivienne's cause spreading through county after county, state after state, as if the patterns of blooms on the cutesy dresses had seeded themselves and produced real flowers propagating fiercely as dandelions made Jade panic. She stood up suddenly, unconsciously touching her belly, then instantly dropping her hands. No one knew.

"*Now* maybe Rory's on the late side," Vivienne said.

Jade made for the stairs.

"Anything the matter, honey?" Vivienne called. Jade pictured the woman turning toward Ellis and beaming her concern.

"Can't I go to my room without something being the matter?" Jade snapped.

"Hey," Ellis said softly. Jade wanted to scream. But by the time she made it to the second floor, she felt more like crying. They meant well, trying their best to be parents to her, and yet they didn't have a clue.

Jade's room was the only one in use on the third floor of the skinny Main Street house. The other room with a matching dormer window was filled with unpacked boxes and paraphernalia no one used. Jade thought of it as the one room in the house that had died. Beyond Jade's window, beyond the house itself, lay the town of Paradise with half its storefronts empty. From her window, Jade could spot one of the town's old mansions, a remnant of the days when oil was discovered beneath farmers' pastures. The once elegant structure now housed a number of professional offices, including a lawyer's and chiropractor's and the real estate agency where Vivienne worked.

Beyond town were the farms. Field after field that in a few months would show soybeans, wheat, sorghum, but mostly corn. The even rows of crops met with unpredictable weather, uncontrollable prices, and surely growing designs of corporations. The land determined lives, and it destroyed them. Her father had shown her that much.

So many times Jade had wished to be done with taking the cows down to pasture before she left for school and retrieving them each evening, with walking beans and picking rock, and canning corn from early July until it was done. She tried not to consider that her collective wishes had any part in the way the family's farm life had come to a disastrous halt.

The scarred wooden floor creaked beneath Jade's feet. Posters of endangered animals—red wolf, sea otter, peregrine falcon— which Ellis had given her soon after they'd moved in, hid the cracks and gouges in the old plaster walls. During the weeks before Ellis met Vivienne, Jade and her father had watched televised nature shows regularly.

Jade opened the book of blank pages her mother had presented her with seven months earlier. Its leaf-textured cover featured a black-and-white inset drawing thick with trees. Jade couldn't distinguish what type of trees they were; the trunks bent into some strong abstract wind that jumbled the tiny leaves into a blur. Maybe it was the remarkably fast-growing cottonwood. Or it could be an oak.

Rexanne had told Jade that their shelterbelt had started with oaks, transplanted more out of nostalgia than practicality by east coast ancestors who'd settled the Nebraska land. Jade had no idea how her mother knew so much about their distant past.

Rexanne was big on history. She'd pointed out ruts worn into the land by the oxcarts carrying early settlers west. The night before Rexanne took off, Jade had dreamed those ruts all along the Platte River were furrows for trees. A shelterbelt that straightened out, and grew thick and out of control.

That book was the last she'd seen or heard of her mother, though she suspected Ellis had gotten word and wasn't letting on. Jade had rewrapped the book in its white tissue paper and retied the purple bow, her favorite color. Then yesterday, after she'd taken the second home pregnancy test and watched the small white window darken with a deep pink positive line, she reopened the gift.

"Some day you'll be glad you kept a record of things," Rexanne had said. She'd taken a quick breath, avoided looking at Jade when she added, "Or maybe your kids will be." Rexanne could have had no idea the "kids" mentioned would become relevant so soon. The other comment Rexanne had made after presenting the book was, "You don't have to tell everything," emphasizing the word "tell," and sounding as though this were a discovery she'd just made herself. Jade didn't know if she meant you didn't have to write all the details down or if you could write things down instead of talking to people about them.

Staring at the page, she had no idea of how to express the secret way she felt. She didn't want to write about the sensations of pregnancy. She wanted to speak to her mother in person about that. She studied the blank rectangle until its edges became fuzzy and then disappeared as the book dropped from her hands.

Jade jolted awake at Vivienne's voice curling up two flights of stairs.

"Jade," she called, making two syllables of the name. "Come look at this."

From the second floor, Jade spotted Vivienne in a pale pink leotard and matching tights, a stiff veil of white skirt at her waist.

"Let me show you my routine for the recital, hon," Vivienne said. "Since you won't be able to make it to the actual performance," she added.

Close to forty, the woman took weekly ballet classes with a group of ninth-and tenth-grade girls. Jade was both astounded and disgusted at the image of Ellis sitting proud and oblivious in the audience of *mothers* younger than Vivienne watching their daughters stretching their growing arms and legs into the music. Jade wanted to appeal to her father, "Make her stop. This is too strange. She's acting like a little kid and *I'm* the one going to be a mother," but she held back.

As soon as Jade got to the bottom of the steps, Vivienne reached out to affectionately touch her shoulder-length straight black hair. Jade turned, knocking a stack of Christmas cards to the floor. "Who's Robert?" she asked.

The name was beautifully signed inside a unique card. The abstract evergreen stood out among the ordinary realistic holiday bells and wreaths and nativity scenes.

"Thank you for reminding me," Vivienne said. "I have to put those away." She explained that next Christmas she would use the cards to make a decorative collage. "Robert's a cousin I haven't seen since I was twelve," she added. "But he sends me a card every year." Vivienne had the largest collection of holiday cards Jade had ever seen.

Jade sat on the bottom step and endured the preview of Vivienne's dance routine until she heard a rap on the front door. Rory's familiar four thumps.

"Jesus Christ," Jade said, jostling Vivienne on the way to the door.

"Watch that language, young lady," Ellis said in a monotone.

Jade grabbed a jacket and slipped past her father, then quickly pulled the door closed so Rory couldn't see Vivienne in the ridiculous outfit. The awkward escape felt like changing clothes in the front seat of a car.

"Ten-thirty, Rory," Ellis called through the front door.

"It's Friday, Ellis," Jade called back.

"Ten-thirty," Ellis repeated.

"They're driving me right out of my skin," Jade whispered to her boyfriend, though in truth she knew the problem was more hers than theirs.

Rory squeezed her hand, winked. To the door he said, "No problem, Mr. Engler." She couldn't hear him, but Jade was sure Ellis humphed at the promise.

Rory strode ahead to his pickup, swung open the passenger door, then, without waiting for Jade to catch up, went around to his side of the truck. As she pulled herself onto the bouncy seat and slammed the door, she wished she could have shut the front door to the house with the same intensity, blocking out all her conflicting feelings about Vivienne and Ellis.

She knew Vivienne and Ellis watched them through the front window, peered with concern until the two red taillights disappeared over the railroad tracks like cigarettes that had burned out. And then the couple would return to their places on the sofa, her thoughts flipping back to the fluid movements of dance routines, his fumbling around in secret spots stockpiled with dried foods and ammunition, preparation for an invisible threat. Silently they would worry about the possibility of Rory drinking and driving. If Jade told her news, maybe it would jolt them back to the actual world, the way she'd seen on TV how the impact of a lightning bolt had enabled a blind man to see, for a couple of months anyway. Suddenly Jade realized how exciting it was to hold news powerful enough to disrupt other lives or simply to change her own.

"Thought we'd go up to the Dairy Queen," Rory said without looking at her. He mentioned that he'd planned to take her to the Red Carpet for smothered steaks and mashed potatoes, but Gil hadn't paid him yet.

A year and a half out of high school, Rory made residential and commercial deliveries for a local oil company. The times when Gil paid the supplier usually required Rory to wait on his own weekly wages. Gil said he was diversified; he sold RVs on the side. But in the middle of January, business on that end was way down.

Rory drove straight at the D.Q. Despite the fact that Jade wasn't particularly hungry, she liked Rory's decisiveness, unlike so many of the other boys she'd gone out with who bantered about where they should go, what they should do. "I don't care," "It doesn't make any difference," "What do *you* want to do?" were thrown back and forth enough polite times to make Jade nuts.

Rory told her the Paradise D.Q. was the only one open the entire winter. She thought she'd seen one lit up over in Trackson, and she could have mentioned parts of California where the cold weather never brushed snow against a dairy stand, but she didn't normally challenge Rory's bullshit stories. It was part of his personality to talk a lot in order to pretend he knew things, just as it was her father's business to be silent and offer the same impression.

Rory kept the heater running while he stepped out to order the food. She watched his tall thin body, his sagging pants, moving away from her. She entertained the fantasy of telling Rory, then the two of them going off together to start life again in a new place where no one would know their histories.

"Ice cream," he said and shook his head at Jade's choice as he handed over the cone and then started in on his hamburger platter. The greasy meat odor filled the cab of the truck.

"What I'm really in the mood for is some mountain oysters," he said, his mouth half full of the burger. A twang of nausea poked at Jade's stomach, then shot up to her mouth.

"God," she said. She fought the feeling. An odor, a sound, sometimes merely a mental image could make Jade gag these days.

Rory began a story she'd heard him tell once before, how his father served his cousin from back east the seasonal delicacy each time she made her yearly trip to Paradise. Jackie ate fried bulls' balls for twenty years before she discovered what they were.

"OK, Rory," Jade pleaded when he'd gotten just a few phrases into the graphic story.

Her story, the absolute real one about her "condition" would be one she could shock him with. Two words would do it. No embellishment necessary. She wanted to tell him, to tell anyone, but at the same time it felt all hers, a predicament she'd have to make decisions about and then deal with.

Before she'd even wiped her mouth of the ice cream, Rory put the truck in gear and headed over to the construction site of an expensive housing development. He reminded her that the place would be home to the management of a major food producer, which, in a complicated scheme, had bought up a number of small area farms that had slipped into foreclosure. Building had stopped for the winter months, the bulldozers stilled, the echoes of hammering and hauling interrupted. The foundation of a couple of the homes lay open like giant graves. A light snow coated the ground.

The first time Jade and Rory had made love had happened

right here during an unseasonably warm December night. Jade had been impressed with the way Rory had planned the whole seduction, picked out the exact spot for their lovemaking. He'd retrieved his father's old army blanket from behind the driver's seat and spread it over a cement surface, which, he explained, would be some rich person's patio by the following summer. It thrilled her to think that she'd have this one secret on everybody when all the patios were finally in place.

Rory had even brought a half-burned-down candle, which he lit afterward, and then in turn they lit cigarettes from it and sent their smoke into the sky thick with clouds. She and Rory had been going out exclusively during the three weeks since Christmas.

Rory engaged the parking brake. "It's too cold to get out tonight," he said. Jade nodded in the darkness. After wrestling with a six-pack behind his seat, he handed her a can of Bud and then pulled off one for himself.

"Come here, you," he said, for the first time all evening really concentrating on her. He set the beer on the dashboard, he took her dark hair between his fingers. He stared into her green eyes. His were blue, though Jade couldn't really tell it now; in the darkness even his fair hair looked dark.

"Jade," he said on an exhale. "My Jade."

She took a swig of the beer though she didn't really want it. Overnight her tastes had changed. She thought the pregnancy would make her feel differently toward him, too, want him less. But as soon as he kissed her, she bent into him. Instantly, his hands were all over her. He was pushing past her coat, her sweater. "Rory," she said softly, weakening, ready to tell him what was happening to her body.

He could drive her off, way beyond the boundaries of Vivienne's political meddling, to get an abortion. She imagined they'd have to travel hundreds and hundreds of miles to find a doctor who didn't fear the ramifications of her stepmother's cohorts. Maybe they'd have to drive all the way to New York.

"What's the matter, babe? You don't seem like you're into it," he said. His perceptiveness could amaze her. He'd be doing his male things, like watching football games all Sunday afternoon, and then say something to make her think he'd been watching *her* all along—"Try another book if that one's no good"—or at least for the last ten minutes.

Jade tried to imagine telling him about the pregnancy. But she couldn't. Such a revelation would set off a string of actions that would take the predicament completely out of her hands. First she needed to think this all out for herself.

"It's my parents," she lied. As if she were telling him of some strange disease with a name he couldn't pronounce, Rory instantly sympathized. Though he occasionally griped about his mother's nagging or his father's pushing him to get a better job, his family was solid. His dad owned the grocery store in town; his mother headed up the PTA. Rory had an older sister majoring in elementary education and a younger brother on the football team. The most discord the family experienced was the week before Christmas when his dad twisted his ankle and couldn't drive to the mall. Jade didn't ignore the fact that part of her appeal to Rory was her broken family, which must have been exotic to him with its eccentricities and its genuine tragedies. Sometimes, to win his support, she even played up her disagreements with Vivienne.

Her lie was only a small one. She thought Ellis probably owned camouflage underwear he was so into arms preparedness. Even though he hadn't farmed seriously in over eight months, he still got up at 6 A.M. and listened to the farm report. Then all day he sat around the house, watched television, and practically memorized the day's paper. In the late afternoon, he drank beers with some of his pals as they got off work. "Dropping the neck yoke," the men with jobs in town called the end of their workday. The group of militiamen talked about the time when they'd need the dried food and canned goods, nine-millimeter semiautomatic pistols, assault rifles, and countless rounds of stockpiled ammunition. They planned weekend maneuvers, excursions, and told stories of training attacks they'd staged. They referred to "the big day" as if it would be the one after tomorrow. But as far as Jade could tell, they only discussed the *possibility* of not paying their taxes or not registering their cars. She thought Ellis surrounded himself with plans and strategies and stories because he didn't want to talk about them himself. He simply humphed at the other men's words.

Another of Ellis's distractions was feeding the squirrels. Tossing handfuls of stale bread out the front door, he watched until every crumb had been whisked away. He did this often enough that the squirrels grew fat and fearless. Before he lost the farm to the bank, Ellis never had a minute of unaccounted for time. His farming schedule seldom allowed him to help Jade with her homework or pick her up from some after-school activity.

Vivienne filled her days with nonsense, too. Though she'd have Jade believe she spent whole afternoons showing Paradise homes to prospective buyers, Vivienne was seldom busy. The times Jade stopped by the office, Vivienne was paging through catalogs. Her favorite featured religious items or tiny china figurines holding plaques with sayings like "Guardian Angels: Don't Leave Home without Them." Jade wished there was a little gnome displaying "If you're rich, I'm single," like the bumper sticker on Sara's mother's car. Last week Jade had come on Vivienne studying a catalog of militia paraphernalia. "Your father looks so handsome in his uniform," she'd said. A few minutes later Vivienne had pointed at a teddy bear photographed in camouflage. Ellis's birthday present, Jade guessed.

And yet for Christmas the two of them surprised her with an expensive leather jacket, a dark brown coat Vivienne would never have selected for herself. Jade could almost see them paging through racks of clothing to try to please her. She wished she'd thought to wear the jacket, which probably wasn't even paid for yet.

"Let me help you forget about all that stuff," Rory said, his voice husky, pleading. He lifted her beer gently, waggled it to gauge how much she'd drank.

She gave his advances another try, but images kept sliding to the foreground to interrupt the sensations Rory's fingers evoked. If she told them about her pregnancy, Ellis might grow so quiet he'd be reduced to grunts, and Vivienne for sure would go into her hyper mode, pulling at the ends of her shoulder-length brassy hair until it became frayed as the fringe of an overly washed bedspread.

"Sorry, Rory," she said as she butted her head into his chest.

He sighed, jerked at the front of his pants, and turned the key in the ignition. "Forget about it," he said, finishing off his beer.

He backed the truck up but didn't turn on the headlights until they hit the main road. As they drove past the frozen fields, he uncharacteristically said nothing. The moon was nearly full. Although the heater pumped at full blast, just beyond the warm cabin the air was frigid; the world felt breakable outside their doors. Rory lit a cigarette.

"Gil's got a beauty of an RV out back," he finally said as they drove by his workplace.

"Really?" She tried to feign interest.

At her voice, he slowed the truck, did a quick U-turn on the empty street, and turned into Mitchell's Oil Company lot. Rory followed a bumpy one-lane road past the huge oil tank in the direction of a sign announcing, Gil's RV World.

"Let me show you this baby," he said. He surprised Jade both by using the word "baby" and then by producing a handful of keys. "They're not hooked up," he explained, as he gestured toward the RVs then leaned over her and grabbed a flashlight from the glove compartment.

The mobile home was huge. Moonlight glanced off its exterior and sent shadows across the snow. After following Rory up the portable steps, she waited while he tried different keys. She watched her breath, visible with each exhalation.

"Last week a guy from the Big O was checking this out. He must have been packed with dough. He said he wants to take his family to the capital of every state in the country. Imagine that. Every summer they'll do a few states."

Momentarily forgetting that she was pregnant, that she was to graduate in five months, Jade got caught up in Rory's enthusiasm.

"Maybe he won the lottery," she said.

"Maybe," he said.

She wondered what it would have been like to grow up with a family that took off for unknown places instead of remaining rooted to one spot with the crops.

Rory sent the light over the vehicle's interior picking out the cabinets and faucets, the kitchen benches, which converted into an extra sleeping area. "Sometimes I just come out here and sit in the dark and imagine this is where I live," he said. She considered how she might go about sneaking into the few homes Vivienne showed, walking through strangers' kitchens and living rooms, falling asleep in their beds. If you slept in anonymous beds long enough, would you lose track of who you were?

"What if Gil catches you?"

"I'm careful," Rory whispered. "Just can't smoke in here." Fanatical about smoking, Gil was reported to have snatched a cigarette right out of a stranger's mouth in a restaurant.

Rory took her arm and coaxed her onto the couch. "This is a little more comfortable than the truck," he said directly in her ear.

"A hell of a lot colder though," she said.

"Come on, babe." He produced the blanket he kept in his truck; she hadn't noticed him bringing it in.

She went with him then. Putting herself totally into her body, she closed off all her worries. She fantasized that this was where she lived. With Rory. They had their own bathroom and faucets, small refrigerator and stove. Every appliance and utensil was brand new, not a patched-up piece of somebody else's past or a reminder of her own.

Jade clearly remembered the first day Ellis got the combine. As a girl, she'd been impressed with the novelty of the machine, its glassed-in cab equipped with air-conditioning. Her happiest times with her father were riding in his new combine at night and early in the morning with Beatles' songs playing full blast. Sometimes Benjamin rode between the two of them. With the air-conditioning, Benjamin's allergies didn't kick up. The crop dust swirled around them like snow that wasn't cold, that couldn't catch up under their tires and hold them in place.

Unable to feel the heat outside or breathe the dust of the separating crops, Jade had sensed herself removed from every difficulty. As the grain and seed were pulled from the brittle husk and stalk and pod, Jade was drawn out of the dusty work-aday life that had owned her family for generations. Then, she couldn't have known that one day she would think of herself separated from her family by some force far larger than a top-of-the-line combine.

Rory offered her another beer, though she hadn't finished the first one in the truck. She took the can more out of politeness than any taste for it. Rory began kissing her again. And this time she let herself fall into what he wanted. She slowed his fingers so that the little journey out of herself lasted as long as possible. Her lips on his neck, she cooed with the rhythm of a far-off train. Then she lay still as he moved against her and moved her, the way her father's crops once bent with the wind.

"Great place," he said afterward. She kissed his neck lightly instead of answering.

"It would be something. Just to take off whenever you wanted to leave. Never have to worry about forgetting a bottle opener," Rory said.

"I'd like to travel," she said, remembering her sixth-grade class and their trucker pen pal. Mr. Tremain had sent photos of his silvery-blue rig with its self-contained bedroom, and himself in the driver's seat, his forearms tanned deeply as her father's. His letters told of adventures in Kansas City and New York City, and described Utah landscapes where mountains bloomed red and pink as flowers. The class followed his progress across the country on a large tan and green map at the front of the room. He sent menus from his favorite diners and rocks from areas that particularly impressed him. Even then Jade knew her responses made for bland news in comparison, with their ordinary details of school cafeteria food fights and classmates' quibbles. She dreamed of going off with the trucker, although she had no idea what she could offer him in return for showing her the world with all its dimensions beyond her flat-as-fact farm.

Spectacular outcroppings like Scotts Bluff and Chimney

Rock disturbed the monotony of the land. But from Jade's vantage point, the world mostly stretched along at one level.

"It would be cool," Rory said again, his wishfulness already tinged with resignation that it would never happen. Jade felt the cold creeping through the blanket he'd thrown over them.

Jade suddenly saw as clearly as she witnessed the bright light of the nearly perfectly round moon that for all Rory's determination, if she were to tell him she was pregnant he'd insist on marrying her, then settling on some street with the same telephone exchange as both their families. His regular family wouldn't be so easy to leave behind. And Ellis and Vivienne liked Rory, primarily because he had a job that usually paid steady. After a few crisis sessions they would sanction a marriage, welcome a grandchild. Jade would be the holdout, unable to accept that her life began and would end right here.

She wasn't even positive the baby was Rory's.

When Jade turned to adjust her clothes, she bumped her arm on the table.

"Shit," she said.

"Let me rub that for you," he said, but Jade stood up and moved away from him.

Rory didn't drive straight home. He swung onto the old country road the locals called Number One, edged with the frozen memory of last season's crops. Despite the darkness, Jade could make out the volunteer corn and the boundaries of fencing. Grain elevators bunched together formed the most of a city scape Jade saw these days.

She was glad she couldn't really distinguish the distant pale yellow farmhouse and matching outbuildings of the property that used to belong to her family. The nearly eight hundred acres. The cows and pigs and chickens. The sod house with exposed roots dangling from the roof, a curious remnant of the days the land was first settled. Jade didn't imagine Rory was aware that he was driving her past the outpost of so much trouble. The place wasn't as overtly tragic as the scene of a highway accident with every passing driver turning to catch a glimpse. In daylight the family farm simply looked like an average spot to live and work. A passerby wouldn't be able to tell that a family had been shattered on those grounds.

Because Jade wasn't in the mood to talk anymore about her parents, she hoped Rory was oblivious to the old farm and concentrated solely on the fact that he was driving without the congestion of traffic lights and stop signs and pedestrians.

"What are you so quiet about tonight?" Rory asked, startling Jade. Instead of answering, she reached over and put her hand on his thigh.

"Quiet as a cat," he said softly, then turned on the radio. It crackled like the crushed stone in Sara's driveway.

Jade didn't want to become as silent as Ellis had and then lose it. Hearing about heredity in science class had terrified her. But Ellis had been headed in the wrong direction for a long time, according to Rexanne. Despite her warnings, with every setback he extended himself further, buying too much new farm equipment. When the grain prices went down dramatically one year, he purchased an adjoining field. Rexanne said he was like a man with a gambling disease. "He keeps shooting his wad, then shooting himself in the foot," Rexanne liked to say after it had become obvious that she no longer had any influence on the situation.

Ellis worried Jade those months before the bank took steps to claim the farm. He became more and more quiet, unexpectedly coming in from the field and sitting for hours in the living room before a blank TV screen. The entire room would smell of alfalfa and impending disaster. Ellis could be silent for hours on end and then suddenly stand up and punch his fist through a window. Even though the genetics stuff concerned her, Jade didn't think she was more than 20 percent Ellis.

"OK, babe," Rory said. "I can see I'm going to have to shake this stuff out of you."

They turned onto Black Pond Road. Barb-wired fields lined either side. Just beyond the reach of headlights, the road was black as Jade's hair. And then Rory cut the headlights and simultaneously punched the gas. Jade screamed. When she stopped screaming, she was excited and wide-eyed, as Rory, speeding through what she remembered was an intersection, took the chance that no other car would be coming from another direction at precisely that moment. The truck rushed the darkness like a sudden wind across the prairie.

When Rory flicked the lights back on and turned to her, she noticed moisture at her underarms. She loved Rory's unexpected rash moments, when he recklessly stepped outside of his usual self to test the world. She loved the deep breath of daring before he buried himself in details that didn't matter.

Jade wished she and Rory could keep driving across time zones so it never got any lighter as they went even farther from home and all the trouble that now stuck to her. But soon Rory was back in town and turning up Jade's street. He didn't get out and come around to open her door like she knew he would if she were seven or eight months pregnant. Instead, he kissed her lightly on the lips, then leaned over her and pushed her door open. He waited until she got to the front door, lightly tapped his horn, then drove off.

Jade turned on the kitchen light. Two cages sat against the far wall—one housing a small black bird with a broken wing, and the other a squirrel with a bandaged leg. They were her father's wards.

It was eleven-thirty. Ellis and Vivienne hadn't waited up. Jade made herself a plain cheese sandwich on white, fed the squirrel a balled-up piece of the bread the way she'd seen Ellis do, and headed upstairs turning on lights ahead of her, turning them off behind. With Ellis and Vivienne's door slightly ajar, Jade could sort of make out her stepmother's face and the unmistakable chin holder she wore to bed each night in order to "strengthen her profile." The stretchy band pressing at her chin and the top of her head made Jade think of a sweater with a too-tight neck band.

When everything fell apart last year, Jade had wished she could somehow contain her emotions, her own impulse to bolt, her fear that her every phrase and thought was flying away from her. She *had* spoken to a counselor but that, itself, had turned into one more piece of craziness.

Now Jade wanted a band big enough to contain her whole body, hold back the changes happening to her belly, something simpler than "the options" Sara was sure to discuss with her. "The options" that Vivienne raged against.

Jade listened to Vivienne, on her back, puffing softly into the darkness. When she heard Ellis turn in the bed, she quickly started for her attic room. But by the time she reached the top floor, he was snoring loudly.

At first Vivienne was all surface to Jade—phony sweetness— but just last week Jade had caught her weeping at an afternoon soap opera. Vivienne pronounced most television programs unhealthy entertainment, and when Ellis was around she stuck to classic movies or game shows. But as soon as Jade had entered the room, Vivienne had clicked off the television and pretended to dust Ellis's bowling trophies.

Despite the woman's ability to irritate her, Jade recognized that Vivienne had rescued Ellis, at least temporarily. He hadn't

shot anyone, thrown any of the grenades stockpiled in the basement, tasted the rations of food as practice for the day when it
would become part of his lifestyle. He hadn't proved to be the
"loose cannon about to go off" that their neighbor Carlsen had
predicted.

The men had started coming to the front door of the farmhouse just as Ellis's faith in the place was leaving him. Benjamin
always stayed in his room when the men arrived at the back
door. Later Jade realized some of the men only looked foreign
because they wore weird shirts and serious expressions. She recognized a few of her father's cohorts as area farmers she'd known
since she was a child. Jade categorized the different men in her
father's life as dogs or wolves. The dogs didn't frighten her, but
she knew not to startle them when they ran in a pack. The
wolves, she was glad, made themselves scarce.

The morning Ellis missed milking and Jade had to skip school
to help her mother, Rexanne asked what he thought he was
doing. Ellis had replied that he and his friends were making
plans to lead an independent life without the confines of government. Even the pastor of the Baptist church owned a gun
shop, Ellis argued. Ellis quickly lost the smell of dirt and crops
and milk and began to reek of gunpowder.

And then, when Benjamin died suddenly, Ellis gave up on
the farm entirely. "He dropped the whole ball of wax," Rexanne
had said.

The days of the auction, Ellis and Jade stayed in a motel in
Russ. Jade swore she could hear the auctioneer calling out prices,
repeating bids, and describing every piece of furniture, every tool
she'd grown up around. That sad, lonely song trailed all the way
into the bathroom of the motel unit. The final day when the
property itself was auctioned, Ellis watched *Giant* on TV and
later took Jade over to Burger King.

When Ellis came to the real estate office to rent a new place to live with Jade, Vivienne promptly recommended a rental without trying to push him to buy. A week later, they went to the annual fashion show and tractor pull together. Vivienne's high voice seemed to calm Ellis, dull him against the old rages he'd trampled through right after Benjamin died. Her bows and rickrack distracted him from all the losses. And her meetings and rallies cemented his own commitment to take a stand against what he saw as injustices.

Jade couldn't understand either of their rabid stances on issues—he on the right to bear arms and live independently and she on the right of babies to be born. Jade had never felt so impassioned by something she couldn't see. Just when she'd been starting to give her imagination free rein—considering joining up with Sara, who wanted to be a singer—the farm had gone into foreclosure. Jade had even sent away for course information on running a hotel. A classy hotel in a big city with Sara the entertainment.

Rexanne told Jade that one of their ancestors had opened an inn on the pathway of the Transcontinental Railroad. Ellis had laughed and said yes, she started one of many "inns"; in fact she'd "gone whoring all the way to Utah," moving her bed as the train tracks were laid. Despite Ellis's comments, Jade thought hotel/motel management could be an exciting career.

Vivienne might have been successful with Ellis for the time being, but she couldn't save Jade. Jade wasn't sure that Vivienne truly cared when she came home; maybe Vivienne only worried because Ellis was concerned. And she might have fretted over a rule (ten-thirty on Fridays) being broken. Vivienne never struggled in the gray area between right and wrong; she had strict lines for every behavior.

Jade wished that she could talk to someone about the long

list of troubles that made up her life and had come to one hard
kernel of truth that now grew inside her and could press up
against the flat surface of her middle. Jade wanted her mother.
Rexanne with her long dark brown hair pulled back in a ponytail
that nearly reached her waist, her hazel eyes and small strong
hands. And her strong opinions.

Jade had grown up watching calves weaned. She'd heard the
cows cry for their babies, bellow their loss at the little ones.
And when the calves found themselves in a new place and realized what had happened, they cried, too. Until lately, Jade had
never given much thought to what all the noise was about.

Jade told herself she should have paid attention—no,
listened—to the trees standing tall, the wind rushing through
them with a rumor that all was not leveled to the height of
crops. She'd looked at that stretch of trees each night with Rexanne before going to bed. The shelterbelt that had years ago
been transplanted from the east could have been a row of people, including her brother and mother before they'd walked off
from her and everything they knew by heart.

2

february

Rain made my father nervous. He said if he could control it, he could grow a perfect farm. But there was either not enough or too much, especially when the mature crops needed to dry out. Even in a good year he had problems. Then our excess was heaped beyond the boundaries of our land into elevators where he paid for it to wait the winter.

"Good for the corn," he said about sunshine, about rain, about most any kind of weather. But that statement was more prayer than fact.

Trouble was predictable. You could read about it. When the Paradise headline said, "The Harvest of Fall Crops Is Complete," it wasn't talking about something that was over. It meant a pause only. The minutes in a day it takes to read a paper.

The daily is four pages long, eight if you count both sides. A vehicle backing into a school zone sign; a disorderly pancake feed; nighttime hay bale fires; missing hogs; a black male cat available for adoption. In the classifieds for three months, somebody's needed a personal assistant to a "developmentally disabled adult." A couple of weddings, a column of deaths a week.

People in this part of the country live to be ninety and a hundred. It's no big deal. They blend into the land; its fields and pastures move with them like an essential body part, color their meals, then spread over their dreams with nightfall.

In spring my parents smelled so strongly of soil I imagined they lay in the damp clumps and grains, rolled the dirt through the spaces between their legs and fingers, counting the days until it would bury them.

Walking off into first light is like slipping into worn denim. In one way or another a few people have always picked up and traveled beyond their given place. They're talked about briefly before being shuffled off into rumor. I think about the land that holds its spot the way a family is supposed to. And I think about faces the color of dust that have headed out.

Shit shit shit. "Shit," she said out loud when she reached her bedroom. Jade's condition felt more real when she voiced it.

Sara sat on Jade's bed and paged through *Cosmopolitan*. It was Saturday and the two were alone in the house. "How many times are you going to take that stupid test?" Sara asked without looking up from the glossy pages of ads.

"This is the fourth," Jade said.

"Save your money," Sara said.

"Who says they cost money?"

Sara lifted her head, stared at Jade a second before smiling. Jade explained that she didn't steal the tests, not from the pharmacy anyway. Vivienne kept a storehouse under the basement stairs. It was all part of the organization's campaign to befriend pregnant girls and women, then to convince them to carry their babies to term. Jade had discovered the cartons of stick tests one afternoon when she'd been curious to sample a package of her father's emergency dried food.

Now Sara wanted to have a look at Vivienne's and Ellis's various underground supplies, but Jade wasn't in the mood.

"What am I going to do?" Jade pleaded. Although the predicament felt frighteningly new to Jade, she recognized it was a familiar one—the ignorant country girl in trouble. She was angry that her own life had become part of the cliché.

"Two options," Sara said.

"Thanks a lot. But I'm not sure I have two."

"What?" Sara said. "They've got this pill now. The abortion pill."

"Fat chance they have it within a five hundred mile radius of Paradise," Jade said. She took a deep breath, then added, "How can we find out?"

Sara shrugged her shoulders. Behind the frame of her dyed blonde hair and all her makeup, she had a pretty face. She was five feet tall and overweight. Because two of her four sisters had gotten married before they turned eighteen, Sara wasn't panicked by Jade's condition.

"Maybe I'll have a miscarriage," Jade said, then immediately thought of Vivienne whose crying woke her one night, and the tearful laundry scene the following morning when her father's bed was stripped of all its bedding, including the mattress cover.

"Molly thought it would disappear," Sara said. "She jumped off the stone fence at St. Bartholomew's. If that doesn't jar things loose, nothing will."

Sara lit a cigarette. "Just get married to Rory, Jade." She exhaled. "He's cute."

Jade stared at her friend, her plump hands and flabby arms, and realized Sara envied the situation. A life selected for her. The future laid out into a walkway of symmetrical stone pieces, all leading to a destination everyone told you was the one you wanted to reach.

"I could be your maid of honor." Sara blew a cloud of smoke away from Jade. "I'd wear black," she said and laughed. Jade had never known Sara to let a boy upset her. She knew for a fact that Sara wasn't nearly as promiscuous as she pretended to be.

"What about the plan?"

"Don't know," Sara said.

"What do you mean you don't know?" For as long as Jade had been her friend, Sara had wanted to be a singer in a fancy hotel. Without any ambition herself to perform, Jade had decided she'd be the ancillary to the performance. Not the warm-up, but the one who made the audience comfortable, saw that the show was advertised, served good food and drinks. She fantasized herself a behind-the-scenes wizard. Even though she couldn't afford it, Jade had sent for application forms for the ACC (Associated Correspondence Campus) hotel management course program.

Before Jade had come up with "the plan," Rexanne had said that was the problem with kids today. "They don't have any dreams."

"What's to dream about?" Jade had answered.

All her life Jade had set her sights on just getting by the next hurdle in front of her. Rexanne said in that respect the farmer's life was bred right into her. Ellis argued that dreams were what got Rexanne to thinking crazy, eventually abandoning instead of supporting him. "Where did dreaming get her in the end?" Ellis had asked Jade last summer. And Jade didn't know, except that it had taken Rexanne away. If Jade had a baby, she'd be trapped here for the rest of her life.

"Mrs. Moyer said my voice was mediocre," Sara said.

"No way. When?"

"The day before yesterday."

"Mrs. Moyer is a big fat jackass."

Sara laughed. "Belinda said it, too," Sara said.

"Belinda Big Mouth?" Jade asked, adding the qualifier the two of them always tacked onto their classmate's name.

"If it wasn't for the cigarette and the heavy bag I was carrying, Belinda's ass would have been down," Sara said.

"Say it's true," Jade said. "Say Mrs. Moyer is absolutely right. You can still sing in a Chicago hotel with a mediocre voice. It's not like you want to be on MTV."

"Chicago's probably got a thousand out-of-work jazz musicians." Sara paused. "Black singers."

"Well, maybe it'll be Indianapolis where you'll sing." Here Jade was consoling Sara when *she* was the one who needed the support. Jade heard the familiar click of the mailbox. "I'll be right back," she said, but Sara followed her downstairs.

In her search for a letter from Rexanne, Jade always rushed to the mailbox when Ellis and Vivienne weren't around. She couldn't believe her mother wouldn't try to get in touch; she suspected her father of intercepting the mail. Or Vivienne. Though that possibility irked her, she guessed they thought they were protecting her.

Vivienne had used Comet on the dresser in which Rexanne's underwear and shirts had once sat in regular piles. She layered a mattress cover and two mattress pads on the bed where Ellis and Rexanne had slept. And she didn't speak Rexanne's name. Doing everything she could to eradicate "Rexanne" from their vocabulary as well as Ellis's memory, Vivienne for sure wouldn't share news of her whereabouts.

Jade paged through the drugstore flyer and four envelopes. She longed for the sight of her mother's childlike handwriting, news of where she was, the writing paper still holding the scent of whatever distant state Rexanne now called home.

"How long has it been?" Sara asked.

Jade looked over at her friend. Sara could do that, hone in on exactly what Jade was thinking as if she'd been in Jade's skin all along.

"Almost eight months," Jade said. "I think Vivienne's destroyed the letters."

"Wouldn't she want to reach Rexanne so Ellis could get divorced?"

Jade paused, sighed. "I just think I would have heard something by now." Jade set the mail on the scarred living room coffee table.

All Jade knew was what Ellis had told her. Last week she'd tormented him until she feared he'd explode. But finally he'd spoken very softly, as if Vivienne were not at work but in the kitchen a few yards away. He said he thought Rexanne had gone east, maybe Massachusetts. Rexanne had an aunt near Springfield that before now Jade had known nothing about.

"Do you think she left for a man?" Sara asked, offering Jade a cigarette.

"Don't know," Jade said, though lately she'd wondered as much herself.

The morning the auctioneers were to arrive, Rexanne had helped Jade pack, allowing her only two small suitcases worth of belongings. It was dark in the room as Rexanne hurried her to select among sweaters, books, hair ribbons, cosmetics, shoes, and jewelry. Rexanne had been in such a rush, so determined to leave, Jade hadn't asked where they were going or why. She'd figured Ellis was packing, too, in another part of the house, the three of them preparing to steal off with all they could carry like people you saw in old movies whose homeland was being invaded.

As Jade had zipped the luggage, she spotted Ellis in the doorway, backlit by a harsh kitchen lightbulb. He had a gun in one hand. Rexanne screamed that he'd lost it. "Simply lost it," Jade remembered, had been Rexanne's exact words.

Ellis had gripped Rexanne by the hair, then pressed the gun

to her temple. He told her she could leave if she wanted, but there was no way she was taking his little girl. He wouldn't have everyone he loved leave him. Rexanne became gentle, then angry, then pleading in an effort to "talk sense" to him. Ellis didn't budge. "Nothing's going to happen to my little girl," he'd said practically in a trance.

By the time Rexanne drove off, he was crying and holding Jade. She loosened his fingers from the hard body of the gun. The weird thing was, in the instant before she pulled at his hands, she'd wanted to die, too, to be done with all the screaming and crying, to be with Benjamin on a huge wheat-colored blanket floating in warm air.

"Jade," Sara said. "I'm talking to you."

"Talk."

"How long has it been since your period?"

"I didn't think you were going to show," Jade said to Sara, who was out of breath as she stood by the door to the gymnasium.

"Are you kidding?" Sara said. She wore a bright pink sweater and black leggings, her jacket flung open.

"Let's get out of here then," Jade said, quickly looking around, then walking off.

"Slow down," Sara called.

"Try not to make a spectacle of yourself," Jade said as she waited for her friend to catch up. Jade kept her hand in her coat pocket, fingered the key to a nearby house, which was one of Vivienne's exclusive prime listings. The house was especially interesting to Sara because it was where her latest crush lived.

"We don't need the world knowing we're cutting school," Jade reprimanded.

"Who's telling the world?"

The two walked in silence. They rounded the back of the gym, then crossed over to Second Street and into the network of residential streets. The winter air was crisp, and when the wind kicked up, Jade's ears ached with the cold. Plus she had to pee. "Damn," she said. "Are we almost there?" her words practically visible in the brisk air.

"It's just ahead. One forty-five," Sara answered.

The older but well-maintained house sat in the middle of the wealthy section of town, which now comprised less than a dozen individually owned houses. Rexanne had told her that when oil had been discovered in the area fifty years earlier, rich people from back east had indiscriminately bought up acreage and then built lavish homes in town when their investments paid off.

Now one forty-five was owned by Sean Mueller's married brother, a dentist who'd just gotten work in his wife's hometown of Milwaukee. As soon as the couple found a place to live, they planned to move their furniture and the rest of their belongings. Vivienne routinely relayed the stories of people in town buying and selling real estate as if they were close friends. At nearly every meal, she shared the details of lives in transition.

Jade walked cautiously along a patch of icy sidewalk carelessly shoveled. A large porch encircled the entire first floor. She slid the key into the door.

"How'd you get this by Vivienne?" Sara asked. She'd pestered Jade for two days to see the house where Sean now lived alone.

"She was out of it this morning. There was some problem with the car pool into South O." Jade didn't let on how easily the ploy had gone. When Vivienne left for the big rally near Omaha, Jade had simply taken the key from the collection on the dresser.

Carefully Jade pushed the door open. Although she'd done all her research, there was still the possibility that someone else might show up or that Sean had cut school himself.

"You know, I just found out my cousin went to school with Vivienne."

"Really?" Jade said, though she wasn't so much paying attention to Sara as to the beautifully decorated living room. The floors of waxed hardwood looked shiny. Jade lightly stomped her feet on the green-patterned foyer rug.

"Ellen said Vivienne was a real wild ass."

"Vivienne?" Jade said, then "Shhh." She stepped gingerly into the room with its beige leather sofas and glass-topped end tables.

"You don't want to hear about Vivienne?" Sara said. "I can't believe this."

"In a minute," Jade said. She picked up a bronze ashtray.

"Are you nuts?" Sara said. "Leaving your fingerprints all over the place."

"Relax," Jade said.

"What if somebody gets murdered in here? What if . . ."

"Shhh," Jade said again, this time more emphatically. Sara watched too much TV; she was constantly working her life into the plot of a highly dramatic mystery.

Maybe because it was daytime, because this was a real house and not some RV, Jade couldn't let herself go the way she had when she'd sneaked into the trailer with Rory. Not even for a second could she pretend this was where she lived.

"They must be so rich," Sara said. "And they look like they're only my brother's age." Sara glanced at a family portrait of a handsome young couple with a baby between them. For a full minute she stared at a small framed photo of Sean.

The kitchen was totally white—its ceiling and floors, walls, appliances, and cupboards. The room looked as if it belonged in California. Jade hadn't known such homes existed in Paradise, and couldn't imagine who would be able to buy them. Vivienne told clients the Muellers were related to the Bakers who'd been one of the original families to tap into Paradise oil, but Jade wasn't sure that story was reliable. Vivienne was known to embellish facts in order to make a house more appealing. "Saleable" was Vivienne's adjective to excuse deception.

Deep in the house, glass shattered. The sound instantly brought Jade back to herself, her body. She wondered if the moment the tiny thing, which couldn't even be called a baby yet, was siphoned from your body there was a sound like something breaking. She wondered if it would hurt.

When she was a little girl, Ellis was the one to console her when she fell off a rafter in the barn, when she sprained her finger in the screen door. Rexanne was less effective in fighting physical pain, but she paraded into school with Jade the day she was falsely accused of cheating on a geography test.

Jade found Sara in the bathroom cleaning up a broken drinking glass. "Jesus, Sara."

"Don't worry about it," Sara now said, having already forgotten the imaginary murder plot.

"That's easy for you to say." Jade took a deep breath. "I've got everything in the world to worry about."

Don't worry about it. Every time she'd given her delicate brother that very advice, he'd responded as if she were speaking a foreign language. Then when he'd finally put his guard down, he'd ended up dead.

After Sara finished picking up the shards of glass, wrapping them in a tissue, and sliding the package into her handbag, she put her fleshy arm around Jade. "Come on. Let's find Sean's room." For an instant, Jade wished her mother was this close. Rexanne taking one arm and Ellis the other, the way she'd always hoped to be protected.

They mounted the wide wooden stairs that were impeccably

clean. A glass chandelier hung above their heads. Sara went off to look for traces of Sean as Jade stepped into the master bedroom. "Who needs that many pillows to fall asleep?" Jade asked aloud. Every detail of the bedroom was either white or beige. The room was larger than the entire upstairs of their rented house on Main Street. Jade sat at the dressing table to check herself out in the oversized mirror, used the bathroom, then went on to another room, though smaller, still larger than her own bedroom; it was a baby's room.

The walls were painted the palest green. A narrow band of roses decorated the juncture along wall and ceiling. Drawn to a wooden crib positioned at the center of the room, Jade touched the small green and pink quilt lining the bed. She briefly imagined a baby in the center of her life, a beautiful infant who would depend on her for everything, make her dream of places she'd never gone, feel emotions she'd never before experienced.

"Don't go getting crazy," Sara said behind her.

"What?" Jade asked, quickly turning around.

"This is the easy part," Sara said. "Don't forget the shitty diapers. The crying." She paused, sniffed emphatically. "There's no smell of baby puke in here."

Jade laughed. She knew she laughed as a distraction, the way Butterbean began licking herself frantically when confronted with a new situation.

"Plus there's this stuff like motor oil that comes out their butts in the beginning."

"Wow," Jade said. "I thought you *wanted* me to get married."

"I wanted to calm you down." Sara paused. "You need to look at the whole picture."

Sara's succinct advice startled Jade. She considered that maybe Sara was jealous of a life that was possible with Rory. But if she settled down in Paradise with Rory, for sure, she wouldn't be living in a house anything like this one. A trailer would be more like it. In any of her plans for the future, Jade was always the backup for someone else.

"Sorry," Sara said. "Just wanted you to hear what my mother told Molly before she got married. And my mother's big on babies."

"If I wanted to hear that, I would have called your mother," Jade said.

Sara launched into a discussion about a friend two years older who'd gotten pregnant and then given the baby up for adoption. "That's another option if you don't want to marry Rory." Sara lit a cigarette. "Or he doesn't want to marry you."

"Sara, are you crazy? Put that out." They looked around, but there was no ashtray in sight.

"Sean smokes," Sara said, but obediently flushed the cigarette. She went on to explain that the friend had interviewed eighteen different sets of potential parents. "She got to call the shots," Sara said. "They all wanted that baby so bad they would have given her anything."

Jade tried to picture someone desiring that much of her. And she being able to give it.

"The lawyer couple especially," Sara said. "They would have emptied their savings account for that cute healthy little baby." She went on to explain that ultimately the young mother made an arrangement with a couple who lived in a working-class neighborhood of Detroit. Jade heard a thunk, but Sara went on. "You've got the upper hand with people ten or fifteen years older than you are. The people cry and beg. It's absolutely unbelievable."

"What's that noise?" Jade asked.

"It's Sean."

"What?"

"Kidding," Sara said. She reported that Sean's room was nothing special. "I think you heard the wind."

Jade whispered, "Let's get going."

"I haven't told you what I found out about Vivienne yet."

"Tell me on the way back."

The two left and locked the house. As they walked in the cold air, Sara told the story her cousin had recently revealed: Vivienne had been the first person in the class to sleep with a boy. She was fifteen with long dirty-blonde hair that touched the back of her knees. Jade immediately thought of Rexanne's hair always secured in a ponytail.

She didn't even know what was happening at first, Vivienne told the cousin. Vivienne and the boy were in a car, then a field at night. Vivienne had described the incident as darkness. A kiss in the night became so big you couldn't tell your own mouth from the one that was kissing you. The kiss took over your whole body.

After that, Vivienne and David went steady. Almost always with David, Vivienne spent little time with her girlfriends. She and David went steady right up until the senior prom when he suddenly asked someone else to be his date. After the dance, Vivienne went a little nuts. Whenever there was any talk about babies or reproduction or something vaguely related to love, Vivienne would suddenly retreat to the bathroom to cry. Though she had no proof, Sara said she suspected Vivienne had an abortion at some point.

Jade thought it would have been better for Vivienne to have had the kid. Then she could have turned her neuroses toward one person instead of making half the world crazy.

Mr. Donnelly, the guidance counselor, leaned back and sat along the edge of the desk, his arms folded across his chest. He wore a navy blazer, ugly checked pants; his loafers looked varnished.

Jade wouldn't have come to him again voluntarily, but he'd called her into the office. Looking down at her clasped hands, she felt him staring at her. At her dark hair and delicate face, at the skirt just starting to tighten across her middle, at the black tights she'd carefully slid up her legs two hours earlier.

Twice she'd slept with him. In December when she was angry and remembering how Benjamin had died. Before she'd gotten so close to Rory.

He brushed by her now, making her blue sweater crackle as he moved toward the door then closed it gently. When she looked up, he was smiling. He put one palm against the door. It was as if he'd touched her, pushed a button to stimulate her memory: his open palms against the wood as he pressed into her, practically grinding her against the hardness until she felt a part of the door, that barrier to the routine goings-on just inches away. Boys and girls innocently flirting with one another, rustling papers, dropping books.

"How have you been, Miss Jade?"

"Fine," she said and looked away.

"Good holiday? I haven't seen you since before Christmas break."

She'd avoided him, ducking into bathrooms, catching up to a group of girls and blending into their chatter. Evading his eyes, deep blue and never still when he looked directly at her and tried to take every bit of her in.

In December she'd come to him for simply the word emblazoned on his now-closed door—guidance. She'd needed an adult to pull her out of her confusion and anger and fear, and point her in a new direction. Ultimately, he'd done just that, though the course of their relationship had improved his life more than hers. She knew that now.

His hand was cold when he touched the side of her face. She pulled away and started for the door. In her rush, she dropped a pencil and quickly bent to pick it up.

"Whoa, whoa," he said. Ellis had once used that confident and calming tone of voice with a cow that had strayed, a hog due to be butchered.

Mr. Donnelly's lips were smoothed into a smugness she despised. As if he knew her better than she knew herself. And understood what she wanted.

She was cornered.

"I think I might be pregnant," she said. There it was—out in the air between them. She'd thrown the remark at him like a weapon. He was the only adult she'd confided to because she knew he'd tell no one.

He dropped his hand, brusquely walked to the back of his desk, placed his hands on the office chair as though taking someone by the shoulders.

"Do you think or do you know?" he asked, looking down at the papers arranged in seven tidy piles on his desk. A glass paperweight in the shape of a turtle sat atop the paperwork nearest his hands.

"I think I know," she answered.

In the long silence, she sensed the air in the room making way for Mr. Donnelly's anxiety. It touched her and her face reddened.

For a moment she felt sorry for him with his thinning hair, hands nervously squaring off the stacks of paper, thirty-five, divorced and no children. He seemed to have only his job of guiding students into futures all potentially more interesting than his own, and now even that could be in jeopardy.

"Does this have anything to do with me?" he asked.

She looked directly at him. The brightly lit room felt harsh, in collusion with him.

"It has everything to do with you." She could have gone on—and Mike and Carl and Rory. . . . The ands.

The thing inside could give her away, end up resembling any of the men or boys from December. Dark hair, blonde hair, blue eyes, brown eyes.

"They got tests," she imagined Sara saying. A woman would have an easier time forgetting a certain man if she could be sure he wasn't forever welded to her in the form of a child. But Jade wasn't sure she wanted to know. This baby would be a reminder of *all* the mistakes she'd made in the weeks before Christmas, a year after Benjamin's death. A year it took for her sadness to turn into an anger so strong at times she didn't recognize herself.

"OK, OK," Mr. Donnelly said. When he suggested a local doctor, she briefly told him about Vivienne. He touched two fingers to his forehead.

As she spoke, she realized she was telling him about her predicament precisely because he wouldn't want to marry her or possess her in any way. He'd want to help her get her life back on track so that her mistakes could be forgotten as easily as this morning's breakfast. "Come see me at the end of the week. I'll work something out," he said, his voice low, the coffin-sized desk between them.

When he said, "Maybe we can go to Chicago together," he almost sounded fatherly. But then she pictured the long ride with him, and the nondescript clinic at which they'd park. She imagined a waiting room of women, with her looking as though she were accompanied by her father. The examination room would be bright with shiny instruments clinking against one another in a sound nothing like love. The groan and whoosh of a tiny vacuum cleaner would echo inside her for days.

What concerned her more than any of these physical details was the very real possibility that she'd cry afterward. She'd heard reports of young girls, and even women who'd already had several children, breaking down after the procedure was completed. Mr. Donnelly couldn't see her cry.

What if what happened at the clinic made an opening for all her sadness to rush through—all the crying she hadn't done for Benjamin or her estranged mother? What if she couldn't stop?

When she left, he didn't kiss her like the two other times, putting his lips to his forefinger then touching it to the tip of her nose. He remained behind the desk, arms folded, intensity spread into his expression penetrating as heavy rain.

He'd given her a note to excuse her tardiness for math class. The corridors were empty, teaching and learning going on in muffled tones behind each closed door she passed. She walked slowly on the pale linoleum, scuffed and dull, and paused at the bulletin board. There among the notices for a pep rally, a bake sale fund-raiser, an invitation to purchase numerous magazines at a student discount, beneath the hand-lettered "Employment Opportunities for Seniors" area was the ad she'd first spotted in the newspaper.

"A room of your own," the announcement read. "Young women from the heartland needed for au pair work with lovely New England families. Salary, room and board, transportation included." Jade copied the 800 number into the front of her notebook.

As she closed the book, Jade envisioned a pretty white room in a big white house surrounded by hundreds of trees. Mountains in the background. She imagined the liberal states, the liberal mother and father not too far from a clinic where no one would have heard of Vivienne and her crusade to save little lives the size of beans just beginning to sprout.

Jade could get ahold of her life without Mr. Donnelly or Rory. She could locate Rexanne, who would take her hand, lead her into a clinic where no one would ask questions or take names. Every male from December would be flushed right out of her system. How hard could it be to find her mother in a part of the country where all the states were squeezed together into an area smaller than the entire state of Nebraska? Even considering that big hunk of Maine.

Sara was the one to tell Jade the states might be smaller, but so tightly packed with people that without an address, you couldn't find a person any easier than picking out your favorite hog at the slaughterhouse. Sara went so far as to get her cousin to ask Vivienne for Rexanne's address. If she knew, Vivienne was steadfast in protecting the secret; she said she had "no idea where that woman might be keeping herself."

Sara didn't always show it, but she was pretty good about figuring out things. And even though she admitted to not having a clue as to why Jade wouldn't want to marry Rory, she at least tried to understand Jade's perspective. Just be up front with Vivienne—make some deal—was Sara's advice. It took Jade a day and a half to come up with an offer to present her "stepmother."

Now Vivienne sat across from Jade at the corner table in Em's, the popular diner on lower Main Street. Jade had borrowed ten dollars from Sara, stopped by the real estate office, and invited Vivienne to lunch.

"Well, if you aren't the considerate one," Vivienne had said twice before they'd taken their seats. Vivienne wore a peach suit with a peach bow at the back of her hair. Her fingernails were painted a frosty white.

As soon as she ordered a hot dog and Vivienne had decided on the meat loaf special, Jade excused herself and went to the ladies' room. She was always going to the bathroom these days. After she finished, she splashed cold water on her face and prepared to come right out and tell Vivienne about her plans to leave Paradise. Focused on the mission, Jade looked straight ahead at Vivienne's table as she closed the bathroom door. She didn't even check to see if Sara's sister Molly was waitressing.

"There's something I want to tell you," Jade said. Vivienne sucked at her cherry Coke. "Actually, I was hoping *you* could tell Ellis."

At the mention of his name, Vivienne widened her eyes.

"I was thinking I'd like to take this au pair job," Jade said.

"What kind of job, honey?"

"You know, baby-sitting. Live-in." Jade started to explain just as lunch was set before them. Twice Jade had spoken with a friendly woman at the 800 number. Carrie said that her clients wanted responsible, respectable young women who'd graduated from high school and loved children. When Jade had hedged at the word "graduated," Carrie said maybe they could work something out.

"Well, that's nice." Vivienne stuck her fork into a cloud of mashed potatoes. "Who's using such a fancy word for baby-sitter?"

"Someone in Connecticut," Jade answered.

"*Mmmm*," said Vivienne on her first bite of the meat loaf. Unsure of whether the sound was a comment on the food or Vivienne trying out the Connecticut scenario, Jade quickly elaborated on the particulars of the job as well as its benefits.

"Connecticut," Vivienne said. "That's so far away." Then she told Jade that cousin Robert was the traveler in her family, for a long time sending a Christmas card with a new address nearly every year. "He's settled in California now," she said. Vivienne sighed. "It's terrible there's no work in town for young people after they graduate."

"Oh, I don't want to wait 'til I graduate," Jade said. "I want to start now." Before Vivienne could protest, Jade unraveled the details of going to school nights in Connecticut, sending part of her salary home. She asked Vivienne to convince Ellis the job would benefit everyone.

Jade couldn't bear to tell him herself, reveal that he wouldn't witness her graduation. Just remembering how tightly he'd held her minutes after Rexanne went off could fill her with guilt thick as muddy water. No way could she up and leave Ellis the way her mother had.

Vivienne's heavily made-up eyes filled with tears. "You know he thinks the world of you. You're all he's got left of his old life." She paused. "Family's so important to that man."

Jade nodded. "But he can start a new family with you, Vivienne." Jade could hardly believe how easy it was to tell Vivienne exactly what she wanted to hear. "You don't need a leftover part of his past in the way," Jade added. Vivienne was quiet and kept her eyes on the meat loaf.

In fact, since Vivienne had moved in with them, Jade didn't feel as smothered by Ellis. He was still on her case every chance he got, and the two of them often teamed up to torture Jade about school work, but he'd begun to temper his over-protectiveness with food and injured animals and with Vivienne herself.

Vivienne dabbed at the corners of her eyes with the rumpled paper napkin. Maybe she was fantasizing about becoming fertile with Jade out of the picture temporarily. Jade's instantaneous sincerity would have impressed Sara.

"I need to get away," Jade said, more urgently than she'd meant to sound. Vivienne didn't have to know about Jade's abortion plans. "Sometimes it's just too sad around here."

"Oh, honey," Vivienne said, and for an instant Jade thought she saw in Vivienne what Ellis did, the need to reach out and envelop you with a sweetness not natural to the real world. "What about Rory?"

"I don't know. I think I'd like to get away from him for a while, too." She bit into her hot dog. "Just until fall." Fall. Before today she hadn't considered how long she'd be gone, how long she'd stay at the New England job after she got what she wanted from it.

Vivienne ate in silence for a few minutes. Then she cleared her throat. "Sometimes a man can swallow you right up if you're not careful," Vivienne said, and Jade wondered if Sara's cousin's story about Vivienne's early sex life was true.

Vivienne said, "I'll bet you're thinking of your mama, too. Am I right?" Vivienne's perceptiveness so surprised Jade that she nodded agreement. Like a child found out that she'd swiped a piece of cake.

"How did you know?"

"On account of your eyes. The eyes always give a girl away."

"Everything all right?" Audrey, the waitress, asked.

"Just fine," said Vivienne. Then she turned back to Jade. "Honey, you maybe should pick up some of those Stri-Dex pads." Jade ignored the suggestion. Since she'd become pregnant, her complexion had gone out of control; she hadn't had such a breakout on her chin since she was fifteen.

"Hi, ladies," Molly called from behind the counter. Jade

waved and Vivienne simultaneously lifted her empty Coke glass.

Sara's oldest sister was twice as heavy as Sara and had colored her hair black. She lived in a tiny one-story house with brick-colored linoleum flooring. The two folding chairs on her front porch looked as if they might have been stolen from the school auditorium. Molly had two children and a husband now. A couple of times when Molly wasn't waitressing, Jade had seen her wearing a skirt patterned with a map of the United States. Sara said that was funny because Molly had never been anywhere outside the state. Karen, Sara's other sister, who'd found herself pregnant just after finishing high school, lived with a grade-school daughter who already wore an expression that nothing would shock her. Karen was on welfare.

When Audrey left the check and tucked her pencil into the stiff curls above her ear, Jade said, "Tell me where she is, Vivienne."

Vivienne slid the check from beneath Jade's hand. "You know I can't do that." She sucked loudly at the melted ice in her drink. "You know where my loyalties lay."

But two days later on the floor outside her bedroom, Jade spotted an empty envelope from a personal letter. The return address was definitely Rexanne's handwriting—a post office box in Massachusetts, right next door to Jade's new Connecticut family.

In February, the men in Paradise, Nebraska, were updating their books in preparation for filing income tax returns. And they were selling calves and envisioning their fields green beneath the patchy snow. Although Ellis no longer observed this routine, he sat with his friends while they talked farming and Jade made dinner. In the lull between the holidays and spring planting, the men frequently spent Saturdays together at one another's houses.

The weekly winter get-togethers reminded Jade of earlier times when the farming families would return from church, eat a big Sunday dinner, and then go visiting. The conversations mostly began and ended with comments about the weather. Only then, the wives were included as well. Recently Ellis had suggested that spouses be invited, but the others had voted him down.

Today four men had come for dinner and Jade had volunteered to cook because Vivienne was off at a planning meeting of the Plains Babies Right-to-Life. Two fat loaves of corn bread sat warm on the counter as Jade prepared a stuffing to pack into the middle of the thick-cut pork chops Hank had brought.

Jade liked to change recipes, to make them uniquely hers, adding different spices, today substituting mushrooms for celery in the stuffing. Her mother never used a cookbook, and amazingly remembered precise amounts of different ingredients each time she prepared a dish. Rexanne's food was delicious standard fare. Jade preferred to start with someone else's instructions then vary them. She'd had her share of culinary disasters; the venison omelet was disgusting. Yet, she'd gotten raves from Ellis on many of her "experiments." But, unlike Rexanne, Jade couldn't always remember proportions and could seldom duplicate her efforts unless she thought to keep a record.

The size of a professional wrestler, Hank stood in the doorway to the kitchen and stared at the corn bread. He let out a grunt of pleasure. "Want me to taste test anything for you?"

Jade handed him a beer and shooed him out of the kitchen the way her mother had once dismissed Benjamin when she baked. Her brother had made a game out of raking a fork or finger through whatever cake or casserole Rexanne was cooking.

On his way back into the living room, Hank asked where Kirk was hiding. Jade heard her father explaining that Kirk was trying out his hand grenades, a Christmas gift that hadn't arrived in time for the holiday. She was glad Kirk hadn't shown up. Being so close to the noisy farm machinery, Kirk had gone deaf; the other men now screamed around him. Jade didn't mind the loud voices so much as the reminder that any one of them, her father included, could suddenly succumb to that occupational hazard.

"Did he get the lemon or the baseball style?" Hank asked.

"Don't know. They're those practice grenades," Ellis said.

"No guts," Hank said, launching into a story about what was supposed to be a replica actually exploding in a school yard in New York.

Jade didn't dislike Hank, but he was the kind of person who instigated a person to talk, asking questions just to have a launching pad to tell a bunch of stuff about himself. As he droned on into another story, she stopped paying attention to his specific words and concentrated on cutting kernels from the frozen ears of corn. Substituting turnips for limas in the succotash, she pictured the New England map she'd been studying for days.

Blue Field, Connecticut, the site of her new home, was located just north of the indent in the state's western border. When she looked at a map of the entire United States, that head of an uncompleted arrow pointed out her future location. Massachusetts appeared close enough to Connecticut to be the next farm in a state like Nebraska. Crystal, the town where her mother now lived, was northwest of Worcester, a short angled line from Blue Field.

Ellis had accepted the fact that Jade was temporarily leaving Nebraska. Jade wasn't sure how much Vivienne had influenced his odd resolve that right now Connecticut was a safer place than their hometown. Maybe his friends were planning to turn some practice maneuvers into reality and he wanted to know that Jade was far away from danger. In any case, she felt bad not sharing the whole truth about leaving. For sure she hadn't revealed how a field representative for the au pair agency had interviewed Jade and videotaped her responses one afternoon when she arranged to be at home alone.

Brad startled her when he passed by on his way into the small bathroom located under the stairs to the second floor. Brad was the oldest of the men, probably close to fifty.

"Didn't know a man could shit without something to read," Hank called. A muffled reaction echoed in the living room followed by Hank's voice again. " 'Cuse me, Jade." It was only a matter of minutes before he launched into his well-rehearsed theory of why men read papers and magazines in the toilet.

Jade didn't think the Sturgeses, who would be her employers and new family, would discuss anything so crude. The New Englanders she'd seen on TV were quiet and a little stiff, every aspect of their lives laid out just so, including what everyone said so that a voice never interrupted or talking over another.

Ellen and Ted Sturges had sent a photo of the three children she would care for: a son Jesse, nine, and four-year-old twin girls, Vicky and Carolyn. The Sturgeses had express-mailed a plane ticket for the flight in four days. Jade had never been on a plane before and she'd never gotten an envelope from Federal Express either. When the driver had come to the door for her signature, Jade hoped he'd think she was someone important. He was about twenty-five and definitely good-looking.

After Brad closed the bathroom door, he peeked into the kitchen. He focused not on the bread and stuffed chops, but on

Ellis's menagerie of wounded wildlife. In addition to the injured bird and squirrel, Ellis had secured two more cages. One housed a pair of chipmunks and the other a large gray rabbit he'd named Jackhammer.

Brad was pale, broad-faced, a follower. His son, Johnny, whom Jade had dated briefly, was a replica. "Fattening him up for Easter, Ellis?" Brad asked.

"He's big enough to play with the Huskers," Hank hollered from the living room.

Now Dillon looked into the kitchen to view the new patient. Short and wiry, Dillon had black hair and wore a camouflage shirt while the others had on flannel shirts or long-sleeved thermals.

"Sure you don't take a lead pipe to these things just so you can fix 'em up?" Dillon called.

"Shut up," Brad said, laughing.

Ellis humphed. He'd told Jade that Dillon had a small-man complex. Dillon rented storage space in his silo when his own crops didn't perform as expected. His largest field had been polluted by a suspicious fertilizer accident, supposedly staged by a food conglomerate when Dillon failed to sell them his land. Jade understood that he had reason to be angry, but he was the only one of Ellis's friends who frightened her on a one-on-one basis.

Most of Ellis's other acquaintances were almost fatherly when she met them in town or greeted them individually at the house. But when they assembled for maneuvers or for beers, they could become frightening with their plans and demands. Even the young men in her class at school worried her when they hooted as one at football games. With the insulation of fellow men, a man might do the kind of damage he'd never think of on his own.

As the food cooked, the men settled into a rehash of the

Huskers' season, then talk of their taxes. Jade had heard the complaints before—the money went to the UN; this would be the last year any of them would be paying for other peoples' problems. Dillon brought up Nebraska becoming its own country.

"That's choppin' in tall cotton," Hank replied. Then Brad asked who he thought they'd sell their corn to.

Dillon interrupted as a couple of the men laughed. "You must be confusing me with somebody who gives a shit."

Ellis coughed loudly. Even without seeing her father, Jade was certain he was giving the guys the high sign, pointing in her direction in the kitchen. Always protective of her, Ellis routinely discouraged the men from going too far with their Rufus and Liza jokes when she was around.

"Got a tough one for you guys this weekend," said Hank, who usually orchestrated the obstacle courses and suggested maneuvers.

Cassidy wondered if they might focus on a family event one weekend. "Like hide-and-seek," he said.

"Hide-and-seek?" Hank asked. "Hide-and-seek," he repeated.

"It's on account of Donna," Brad said. "His wife's ridin' him about not being home weekends."

"He married it," Dillon said and let out a guffaw.

When Jade called the men to eat, Hank said, "Put on your dinner jacket, Ellis." They all laughed, though Jade knew Hank, at least, coveted the Bundeswehr jacket. The regulation uniform of the German armed forces sporting a small camouflage pattern in brown, olive, and tan, a scattershot of natural colors, was a present from Vivienne.

The men talked about guns and handed the serving bowls of food around the table. Dillon said the scent of gunpowder was an aphrodisiac to a real man.

Jade said, "Would somebody please pass the corn bread?" Five men looked up at her. Then the conversation turned to an upcoming farm and home show, an ag program, a meeting of the Future Farmers of America that some of their kids would attend. Hank bragged that his daughter "could cowboy with the best of them," pulling calves, loading forty head of cattle on a truck. Jade thought that Matilda even looked like a cow.

Brad salted his chops heavily. In an accident eight months earlier, he'd struck the side of his face hard enough to lose his sense of smell completely. He couldn't tell garlic from onion. Jade wondered if she would be able to cook with such a handicap.

Cassidy started in on how he was using the computer to do his taxes. The youngest of the men, he was ruggedly handsome, proud, and wore sunglasses ("Gargoyles," he corrected anyone who mentioned them) almost constantly. He'd started life as a mechanic, but when his father died he took over the old man's farm rather than sell.

As Cassidy kept on about taxes, asking why the Federal Reserve Board didn't get audited, Ellis quietly complimented Jade on the meal. What little money Ellis made these days doing odds and ends was off the books. Checking on ranchers' cattle, roping and hauling out the sick ones, fixing farmers' fencing and machinery, he was paid under the table. Jade felt bad that her father didn't even have the aggravating obligation to the IRS to weld him to the other men. She watched Ellis put a few kernels of corn aside; later when everyone was gone, he would feed the squirrel. She'd caught him presenting treats before, the leathery rodent fingers touching Ellis's own. And Ellis making such a soft humphing sound in his throat it might have been a burlap sack dropping to the floor.

"Got in touch with some Freemen yesterday," Cassidy bragged.

"Freemen," Dillon said. "Sounds like a Jewish name."

"Shut up," Brad said. "Freemen's on our side."

The men had had extensive discussions about the name for their militia group. They'd considered N Troop, with the N standing, not only for "Nebraska," but also "neighbor" and "new solution." Hank eventually squashed the idea when he said his wife thought the name sounded too much like a TV show to be taken seriously.

Normally, no one paid attention to Loreen. Whenever she had too much to drink, she'd go off, saying, "Maybe you can tell me what I saw scootin' all over the sky twenty-five years ago. Hank and me were on our way back from the drive-in."

The group finally settled on ESSOP, the backward spelling of "posse."

Cassidy took seconds of nearly everything that was on the table as he explained about his computer's fonts and proposed putting out a newsletter.

"What in the hell do we need a newsletter for?" Hank asked, his mouth full of the corn bread.

"To recruit more members," Brad said, but went on to suggest Cassidy get approval from the organization's higher-ups.

"We're twenty-two strong," Cassidy said.

"Twenty-one," Hank said and laughed. "Donna hasn't let Cassidy here out of the house for the last two maneuvers."

Cassidy ignored the comment and suggested they contact Terry, Sara's brother-in-law, to join the ESSOP.

"Born on the third and thinks he hit a triple," Hank said of the absent man. Ellis humphed agreement.

"You should see the babe I downloaded yesterday," Cassidy said. He put his sunglasses on for emphasis, then quickly took them off. "Forgot to bring it."

"What does Donna think of it?" Brad asked.

"What Donna doesn't know won't hurt her," Cassidy said. "You can move the people all around on the screen. Hell, I got this little lady to bend over right. . . ."

Ellis cleared his throat and Cassidy immediately went quiet. "Jade's got a job," Ellis announced. She was amazed that in this company he talked almost as much as humphed. Outside of his group of friends, he seldom volunteered an opinion without being asked directly.

"That's what everybody wants. Jobs," Cassidy said. Jade could tell he wanted to go on with his downloading story. Jade saw, too, with the mention of "jobs," and the way they looked at one another, that they knew how to keep Ellis's wound open. Not even allowing it to go to scar.

"Girl's got a head on her shoulders," Brad said. Jade wondered if he had any idea that she'd once slept with his son.

"And can she cook," Hank added. "Unlike her daddy," he said and laughed. Ellis shook his fist halfheartedly.

"Why don't you wait 'til June?" Hank asked, passing the chops to Dillon.

Ellis answered for her. "Opportunity might be gone by June."

Jade saw the five faces—the children from the photograph, and the parents from her imagination.

A discussion followed concerning rich people who hired illegals to watch their children and later got in trouble, especially if they were politicians.

"Nothing illegal about Jade," Hank said, "even *with* that name." Several times Hank had teased her because her hair was darker than that of either of her parents.

"She's made in the USA," Brad said. The two younger men said nothing, though they looked over at Jade, then back to Ellis.

The Sturges children were smiling in front of a huge Christmas tree. The boy stood between the two girls with his arms around them as someone, probably the mother or father taking the picture, must have instructed. For a moment, she missed Benjamin intensely though it had now been over a year since he'd been found dead.

She'd found him dead.

"Is John Deere still U.S. made?" Dillon asked.

A brief argument ensued, which led directly to a discussion of foreign-made equipment and parts, importing and exporting. Jade wondered if Ellis was as out of place in this discussion as she, if thought of the mechanics of farming still hurt him. One of the men, usually Hank, let the talk go so far before guiding it back to a place where everyone could participate.

Jade half paid attention as the conversation shifted to how many head of cattle someone was running, then to a new combine someone else needed. The miracle machine that could separate the grain and seed from its stalk and protective outer layers still impressed Jade. Now she saw how she and Ellis and Rexanne had been torn apart from the one unit that they'd once called a family. She wished she felt like the valuable grain the machine had gone to all its trouble for. Instead, most of the time, she imagined herself the husk, discarded and unusable on its own.

In the old days, eastern girls who'd "got in trouble," were sent to aunts and uncles in the Midwest who hid them out until a baby was born and put up for adoption. People in town dropped off pregnant cats or kittens at farms where a warm barn was supposed to absorb them. Most people unfamiliar with the workings of a farm had a romantic picture of how a small family-run operation could be salvation. Rexanne had said all that thinking was just garbage.

And now Jade was doing the reverse—heading east with her

secret, defying her ancestors who'd set out for the west from Massachusetts way back when the country was new. The day she'd received the airline ticket, she'd dreamed about her Yankee ancestors, Rexanne's side of the family. They were people she'd never met. Would they have thought she and her mother were cowards, retreating to the point from which the family had originally departed?

"What do you call this dish?" Ellis asked, pointing up her creative cooking to the other men.

"Risotto."

"Who?" Cassidy laughed.

"No matter what you call it, it's damn good," Hank said. "And I don't even know what these little red things are."

"Sun-dried tomatoes," Jade explained.

"Long as you don't slide no ants or worms by me," Hank said.

"Put the leftovers in a sack for Hank," Ellis said, turning to Jade.

Brad said, "Hank, you going to play Santa again next year? You're eating like you're in line for the position."

Though his mouth was full, Hank laughed. In December, the ESSOP gave out candy canes in front of the post office. Hank swallowed. "I thought I'd turn the reins over to Ellis."

"Santa, hell," Cassidy said. "Let's nominate him for the Big Posse." The men called the organization that presided over their local group, "the Big Posse."

When Jade noticed that Ellis had some corn bread caught in his beard, she discreetly motioned for him to brush it out. She was glad the men had been in a good humor all afternoon and hadn't mentioned anybody's "God-given rights." When they talked like a group, she imagined they lost their dog qualities and became wolves, creatures you could hear but not always see stalking the outer boundaries of property lines.

As Ellis blushed at the nomination and took another helping of the risotto, Jade saw how the men pulled him in and bent him to their will. When Benjamin died, they'd formed a protective circle around him instead of letting him alone with his grief. Making sure they were close at the most vulnerable time in his life, they'd never be forgotten.

Last spring, Brad had thrown the testicles of a gelding onto Ellis's barn roof. They stuck, which meant good luck. Ellis said he didn't believe he'd found any of that luck until nearly six months later when he met Vivienne.

The ESSOP coerced Ellis the way salesmen with state-of-the-art farm equipment and machinery to sell gave demonstrations. The times the salesmen served hamburgers and iced tea as enticements, the farmers called parties. Sometimes hats or T-shirts were handed out.

Normally Ellis helped her clear the table, even doing the dishes on occasion. But when his friends were over, he never tried to assist. Jade remembered how Benjamin's interest in the kitchen seemed to frustrate Ellis. Cassidy stacked the dishes for her, at least. He and his wife Donna had four children under the age of ten.

Jade sliced a pan of lemon bars Vivienne had made the night before. After starting coffee, she went back to arranging the dessert on a flowered plate that Rexanne had used for company. Jade had smelled the lemon last night as soon as she'd gotten home from her date with Rory. Her last date. She'd told him she was leaving, but only Sara and Mr. Donnelly knew the real reason. Mr. Donnelly had sent on her school records so that she could graduate if she decided to attend night school. She knew her decision to move to Connecticut had relieved him.

Rory had been confused that she hadn't included him in her

plans. He'd said maybe he could use one of Gil's RVs and drive east with her. Then he'd mentioned a friend who'd driven to the east coast in less than twenty-four hours in a customized RV. Thinking out loud, Rory had suggested stealing one of the vehicles, but a few minutes later she saw how this idea embarrassed him. In the end Jade had spoken two words that made him let go, that differentiated them as much as their sex—"my family."

Then Rory told her that the only reason he'd gone out with her the first time was that he knew she was likely to sleep with him right off. That confession almost made her reveal the truth. Right there in the truck in front of the D.Q. with the pimply kids filling their faces. But she'd held onto her secret, taking deep breaths, as he touched her breasts, tender to his rough groping and pulling.

"Ellis said the paper was in here," Hank said, poking into the kitchen. Jade pointed toward the space between the refrigerator and the wall where she stored old grocery bags and newspapers that Ellis would eventually use to line his animal cages.

"Here it is," Hank called out and set the open paper on the table as if it were a map to a hidden treasure. The men pushed back in their seats and gathered around the picture—the weekly Mystery Farm Contest. An aerial shot of a local farm highlighted the page of newsprint. To the right of the black-and-white photo was an entry blank, which included a space for contestants to guess the farm's identity. Jade didn't know why the men made such a big deal of the contest. There was only one twenty-five-dollar prize, the correct guesses all thrown into a drawing. She wasn't sure the men had ever mailed in a single entry form.

"Looks like Walker's barn," Dillon said. He sipped his coffee.

"Walker's barn isn't white," said Cassidy.

"Who's not white?" Hank asked.

"How can you tell what the hell color anything is in this?"
Dillon answered, slapping at the paper.

Last week's had been easy. With the main road bypassing a
smattering of livestock and a circular driveway to the farm's
main house, Ellis had gotten it right off. Now as the men quibbled over the details of the farm, Jade concentrated on the
snapshot-sized reproduction. She looked over the miniature hog
houses, pens, grain bins, and outbuildings, the pasture nearest
the house. Forgetting for a minute what her family's farm had
looked like, she imagined that this purposeful arrangement of
wood and stone could be it. Without the people and their problems, the picture was the backdrop for something that should
work. Like a beehive. Or a whole village. But the orderly crop
rows were nothing like the lives of the men who planted them.

Beyond the buildings and fenced areas, lay a light-colored
field, which Jade imagined as the end of the corn. The top of
the picture featured a huge expanse of land delineated with the
broad regular strokes of machinery curving into the farm's handwriting. No, this couldn't be Ellis's. She'd almost forgotten the
pride of the farm. The big bowl of a lake set on this immense
table. Ellis had dug it out with a backhoe, filled, stocked, and
maintained it. He'd visited the lake almost daily the way he
checked the cows and pigs for beginnings of trouble. And later,
after Benjamin died, he'd walked daily to the site as if it were
a gravestone, a fluid marker mirroring the changes in the sky.

The buildings might still be standing, but nothing was the
same. The farm had died and the secret of a baby would end
inside her.

"Time to get a move on," Cassidy said.

Simultaneously, Hank said, "Got it."

"What?" Brad said.

"Carlsen," Hank said, identifying a farmer who six years earlier following his divorce, had bought the farm bordering Ellis's.

The men's faces went dark; foreheads wrinkled with anger. It felt as if a severe storm had blown up suddenly to cross the plain from the west while everyone was looking in the opposite direction.

"That little faggot," Dillon said.

The men looked at Ellis, then immediately looked away.

When Ellis suddenly began talking about cowbirds, nobody interrupted. He explained how the cowbird laid its eggs in other, smaller birds' nests; the cowbird hatched first and grew faster and larger than the parents' natural babies. Out of duty, out of ignorance, the parents continued to feed the big bird even when it had surpassed their own size. The mother stuffed large bugs down the huge baby's mouth.

"The birds' real babies wither and die before they can become songbirds because the cowbird, the freeloader, has such an immense appetite," Ellis said. "I saw it on one of the animal shows on TV," he explained. When he finished his story, the men were quiet.

Finally, Brad said, "A lot of adopted babies turn out bad. Look at the Graff boy."

The men went silent again. Jade was thinking now of herself as a cowbird, glad to be on her way out of Paradise. Away from that cold rainy day in December just over a year ago that still sat right in front of her.

"Sometimes the strong look monstrous," Ellis said and went into the kitchen. He came back with his Jim Beam and a deck of cards.

"Sweetheart," he said turning to her, "can you bring the boys a few glasses?"

3

december

I moved him.

In December when the color of stale sun spread across our brittle cornfield, I found him. The ground hard as slate, I walked out beyond the yellow house and its tall shelterbelt, through the stubbled remains of crops past harvest time. I'd come home right after school without waiting for Sara to finish cleaning out her locker jammed with books and papers, socks without mates, makeup, peanut-butter crackers half-wrapped in cellophane that she'd forgotten about.

I'd left on time because Benjamin and I had been planning something dangerous. Two cigarettes in my coat pocket. We were going to smoke and work out the details of how to leave the farm. For the summer. Maybe longer, I said, though Benjamin worried about school. Even when I told him school was no big deal, they have schools in Chicago—schools without bullies—he bit at the sides of his fingers. Unlike me, Benjamin was an A student.

We wanted to hitchhike to Chicago, to our Uncle Conroy and Aunt Ethel, who owned a bakery. We planned to work for them, making money to take back home to Ellis and Rexanne to stop their fighting. To stop the men with strange clothes and names from coming to our house.

Even as I walked toward the lake to find my brother, I must have known Chicago wasn't far enough, that we'd never make the money necessary to save our family. But Benjamin thought we could; he thought together we could do anything. I was simply content to know we'd get away, if only for the long green growing months that teased us into believing our lives were improving. To escape the boys who hurt him and our parents who hurt each other, that's what I wanted.

We were supposed to meet at the house. And even though Benjamin could always be counted on to follow my instructions exactly, and I was surprised that he wasn't in his room when I returned home, I knew he'd be at his favorite spot at the lake. I just knew. Sometimes you can smell rain at a distance despite there not being a cloud in sight. I guessed he'd gotten upset at school again. One of the other boys had teased him or hit him.

Deep in my coat pocket, I fingered the cigarettes as I walked, careful not to bend them. With my legs breaking through the tall weedy grasses, my new jeans rubbed out a sound even louder than the residue of summer plants crunching beneath my feet. The unwanted corn that would grow from these remains is called "volunteer." If not pulled out, the corn grows again, starting a landscape of its own instead of obeying a farmer's planned rotation.

I saw my brother's red coat first. The color spread across the water into a sunset that had gone all wrong. It was too bright and too delineated. Too early for the end of the day hues. Too real.

I stopped. Then I ran at the shallow water, knelt in the cold that didn't feel cold. His face rested on a rock and was turned to one side, away from me. His tiny silver earring—a triangle

I'd given him for his birthday—glinted in the fading light. I moved him.

Without thinking anything but *Benjamin,* I reached under his arms and pulled his body up and out of the water, his feet dragging dark lines across the ground. His black and white flannel shirt was soaked. Turning his face to mine, I wiped his hair away and saw a tiny bump on his head beneath a bright spot of blood that had already hardened. And his eyes. His blue eyes were wide open, but he couldn't see a thing.

He was cold so I hugged him. Then I took off my jacket and put it around him, over his wet jacket.

I called his name again and again, soft at first until it became a rhythmic song. Then I stood up and screamed it across our flat frigid land.

Benjamin would never have thought to leave on his own. He loved every inch of our farm, even when it was in trouble. He loved the broad fields, the shadows of the shelterbelt, not the people all around it. I wish I could have connected with the scenery that way, but I couldn't. I was the one who wanted to take off. Now, I think I was wanting to protect him, too. To make up for betraying him.

I remember Benjamin before he was born. Rexanne told me how wonderful he would be as he grew bigger and bigger. She held my four-year-old fingers to her stomach so that I could feel his tiny feet bumping against her belly. Picturing him the size of one of my dolls, I was anxious to dress him in the little socks and hats and pants stored in my doll wardrobe with its miniature hangers and cardboard drawers the size of butter boxes. One time

I held Ellis's transistor radio to Rexanne's stomach so the baby could hear just what I was listening to—"I Go Out Walking after Midnight."

The night Benjamin was born, Hank's wife, Loreen, came to stay with me after Rexanne and Ellis had left for the hospital. I remember that afternoon, too, Rexanne vacuuming every room of the farmhouse with me following behind. I held a square of terry cloth and tried to help her dust the furniture in preparation for something I didn't truly understand. Then she baked two loaves of bread and chocolate chip cookies. Even after she and Ellis had sped off in the truck, the aroma of her baking hung in the house until I went to bed.

I sneaked into Benjamin's bed that night, the crib with the new pastel quilt that would be all his. When I woke with the bars of wood surrounding me and Loreen smiling down, simultaneously laughing and chastising me for mussing the baby's spot, I grew afraid of all the alterations in our house. Bottles and toys and rattles and bibs had moved into my bedroom. And the crib, just feet from my own single.

Shortly after my brother was born, when helping Rexanne change him and feed him became routine, I stopped eating. I don't remember consciously deciding to spite anyone by refusing food, but that's what I did. I turned away from my favorite chicken noodle soup, even cookies, finally milk itself. At first, Rexanne tried to cajole me by making an occasion out of each meal, setting dolls around me, their little dishes lined beside mine. Later she dispensed my food in the toy china dish set belonging to my dolls. The covered casseroles held peas and potatoes; the tiny platters were heaped with chicken or hamburg instead of my imaginations of food. But I couldn't consume anything set before me. The family doctor, who was the size of a small outbuilding, prescribed a bright red tonic, which Rexanne stored in the egg compartment of the refrigerator. In time, I came to hate the taste of that liquid more than chewing her macaroni and chicken and potatoes.

Benjamin always woke first, sometimes in his crawl position pushing back and forth until he got up the momentum to butt his head against the foot of the crib. When he grew old enough to stand, he'd lob blocks or stuffed animals, whatever had gone to sleep with him, at my bed. I lay still as long as I could, pretending I couldn't feel his efforts or hear his shrieks. Sometimes I turned away toward the cold wall, the covers pulled tight across my head.

I'm a smiling, chubby baby in the photos of me, Ellis, and Rexanne mounted in their album and filed among the stacks stuck in large manilla envelopes. In some of the photos taken after Benjamin was a couple of years old, my brother and I are dressed in outfits Rexanne made from the same bolt of material, my dress matching his suspendered shorts. My face is wrinkled with anger, lips pursed in a pout. His is pretty as a doll's face, staring at me with a look of idolatry.

Benjamin rode in the combine practically as soon as we got him. Back then Ellis not only worked our nearly eight hundred acres, but had shares on other farms as well. During long harvest days when Ellis could easily fall asleep from working eighteen or twenty hours straight, Rexanne set me and Benjamin beside him in the combine. With the two of us so close, she knew no matter how tired Ellis became, he wouldn't allow himself to drift off to sleep, the machine then wandering on its own course to endanger the lives of his children.

Though I didn't know all the words, I tried to imitate Rexanne's lullabies and sing them to Benjamin above the combine's roar and the flurry of dust and chaff and insects. My attempts at song did more to keep Ellis awake than put Benjamin to sleep. "Let's hear that one about the bear again," Ellis would say, his lids thick and heavy. And I'd belt out the tune a second and third and fourth time above the rushing of corn, Benjamin quietly staring at me all the while. He never fussed in the combine, not that I can remember.

The way other kids recited the names of dinosaurs, differentiating the creatures by their necks and tails and weird appendages, Benjamin learned the different types of corn. Ellis coached him. Paymaster, Super Cross, Pioneer, Coker, Jacques. . . . Ellis coaxed him to perform for the other farmers, "What are we putting in this year, son?" "*This* season what are we testing?" "Benny, what are we cropping?" The names tumbling from Benjamin's tiny voice were met with knowing laughter. And when he grew older, you could blindfold him and he'd know whether corn or soybeans were being cut and flushing through the machinery.

Benjamin must have gotten his love of animals from Ellis. The only trouble was, he thought of all the animals as pets who could be taken in, stroked, and fed by hand. He didn't differentiate as Ellis easily could the animals that were part of the business. Benjamin gave the pigs names—Sammy, Tully, Sniffer. . . . Just the word "Omaha" we learned to associate with death. When the pigs and cows were sent off to be butchered, Benjamin transferred their names to his growing collection of stuffed animals that eventually overflowed his bed and lay in neat lines on the floor beside it.

Ellis believed leaving the radio on in the hog houses calmed the animals. Usually he had it turned to easy listening. Whenever Benjamin checked on the animals, cleaned their quarters, or helped with the feeding, he'd flick the radio off; he didn't want it covering the grunting, stirring, chewing. When he left the building he preferred to switch the channel back on to NPR—classical music. The ESSOP guys say the government uses public TV and radio to spew left-wing propaganda; they believe that the tote bags are membership cards. The only thing I know is that animals like their music.

Back before he started kindergarten, Benjamin stood with me when Ellis released the calves that had been born over the winter months into the spring pasture. The babies shook their ropey tails, butted into one another, jumped and bolted across the fresh green. The mothers lolled behind and called to their calves. Benjamin said to me, "They don't know what grass feels like." He sensed something I'd never thought about before— why the calves were happy.

He pointed out animals that easily got by me—the coyotes and foxes keeping their distance behind the combine, waiting for the fields to be spotted with rushing mice. But he wouldn't look when the predators bounded forward to pounce on small rodents fleeing in all directions. Benjamin gestured at hawks, eagles, prairie dogs, and snakes. Milkweed and morning glories. He brought a romance to farming that no actual farmer could afford to entertain.

It was Benjamin's idea to pretend the two sticks the size of pitchfork handles could be horses. Galloping across our yard, I saw the beautiful black horse of my imagination bloom beneath me. I called my fantasy Midnight after the song I'd shared with Benjamin before he was born. My brother never told me the name of his horse or what color it was.

I went along for curiosity more than moral support the Saturday Ellis led Benjamin from our house and pointed toward the starlings nesting in our barn.

"Benny," Ellis said, "we've got to protect our hogs." He proudly presented his rifle to Benjamin. "Time you learned how to use this thing, son."

The glossy dark birds with their bright yellow beaks didn't scare when Benjamin screamed for them to leave.

"Won't do no good, Benjamin. Here take this." He pushed the gun at my brother. Benjamin ordered the birds a second time and Ellis said, "Now you've got the pigs squealing." When Benjamin refused, Ellis took off his seed cap and threw it to the ground. "They pass all kinds of diseases onto the livestock. There's nothing else to be done." My father understood both the hard and the soft business of animals.

"No," Benjamin said, tears coming to his eyes.

"Don't be such a sissy," Ellis said.

"Don't call my son a sissy," Rexanne yelled from the doorway.

The starlings called their *whee-ee* as if taking sides with her. But Ellis said, "They're laughing at you, Benjamin."

"Come on inside with me," Rexanne said to Benjamin. She whisked him off with her, the sounds of gunshot following them into the house. Ellis held open a burlap bag, shaking his head all the while I picked up the warm birds.

"That's my girl," he said when we finished.

Benjamin liked to watch Rexanne fixing dinner, retrieving flour or salt or sugar as she needed the different ingredients. My favorite times back then were the few days every harvest when Ellis and Rexanne had to run the combine practically nonstop to get all the crops in time.

Benjamin would assist me in preparing sandwiches, then carrying them out to the field for our parents' lunch, and later making dinner. I roasted meats and baked muffins and steamed carrots, peas, or beans. Once I made bread, rolling fried onions and sausage pieces, which Benjamin had cut, into the dough. Ellis loved the warm slices of my concoction that dusty evening with the combine drowning out the sounds of insects welcoming night. I made a pie of spinach and cheddar cheese, as well as chicken topped with a dark gravy of olives and dried prunes, and London broil marinated with garlic and Dijon mustard. My deviations from the standard fare delighted Benjamin, too. He preferred helping me to the men in our fields rushing to take the harvest.

The day I defrosted venison from the deer Ellis had shot the November before, I flavored it with fresh basil and Parmesan cheese and capers. It was Benjamin's idea to trail me into the field with a tablecloth and real dishes instead of paper ones. The silverware clinked against china in his basket lined with a rose-colored tablecloth. Ellis even turned off the machinery after announcing, "This is an occasion." Our special preparations had coincided with his optimism about the crops. The four of us sat in the field and laughed and ate as night came on, Benjamin dishing up seconds. I think, now, that was the happiest day of my life though even then I didn't anticipate it lasting much longer than the sunlight.

If Benjamin didn't want to touch the machinery Ellis fiddled into working, if he hated repairing fences, oiling machine innards, and the monotony of picking rocks off a field, if he wanted no part of disking, which didn't even require him to steer straight, or driving the corn picker, he loved the overall picture of the farm. With his camera, he captured the ripe fields the way a hostess might photograph a special meal just before it was eaten. He understood that the colors of our fields indicated exactly when to plant and when to harvest. Soybeans were ready at a certain shade of yellow, not too bright, not too faded. He had a barometer in his head for when a field looked too wet or the corn held too much moisture. Ellis came to use him almost the way a few of the neighbor women depended on a fortune teller for guidance.

Sometimes Ellis became exasperated with Benjamin, not over his advice, but over his unique approach to usual things. Carefully holding a bag of nitrogen fertilizer, my brother sprinkled my name on our unused pasture. The letters grew thick and green above the other grasses, a shaggy handwriting Ellis dismissed as shenanigans.

"What do you think, boy?" Ellis would say of the land that stretched off in every direction.

"I think the beans will be ready Wednesday," Benjamin said.

"That a boy," Ellis would say of Benjamin's suggestions the way others might congratulate an athletic son. "We'd better turn in early then. Rest up while we can."

Benjamin contributed to our farm by feeling it—without dirt ever banding under his fingernails. And when the farm began to collapse, that wasn't because Benjamin guessed incorrectly or Ellis slacked off on the manpower. We had no way to *try* to fix what we couldn't see—prices, weather, loans called in, conversations whispered in boardrooms. Ellis, at least, adapted to Benjamin's softness the way the boys at school never would.

At first Benjamin agreed with my plan to leave because of the boys. I think he trusted me because, though he loved the patterns of the land, the habits of both its wild and domesticated animals, had memorized every dip and turn of our fields, he knew the people who surrounded us would never let him be himself.

Ellis took us to Chicago to visit Uncle Conroy and Aunt Ethel in February. On the drive up, we got caught in a blizzard, snow thrown at us like the storm of chaff the combine blew during harvest. We passed hours slicing through landscapes so white or gray that the slightest detail of color stood out like a flag. A person's coat or hat, a highway sign in yellow. At places the land lost its flatness, but there wasn't always a way to distinguish between actual hills and snowdrifts.

It was the first time Benjamin and I had been to the city, and when we approached, neither of us could take it in. Everything appeared concrete and glass and unnatural light. The three nights we were there I couldn't sleep; the sky never grew dark enough, the streets quiet enough.

Ellis made himself scarce most of the day, following Uncle Conroy around and lapsing into hushed arguments. I think, now, he was probably begging his brother for money to pull us out of our difficulty back home. Maybe in reaction to the tense discussions passing between Ellis and Uncle Conroy, Aunt Ethel focused on activities having nothing to do with farming.

Our second morning in the city, Aunt Ethel announced that she'd be taking us to the art museum. Wearing a soft brown felt hat and stylish wool coat, she led us onto the streets of the city. The number of people walking on the sidewalks and crossing the streets, the sheer multitude of strangers clipping along in all directions amazed me. I'd seen crowds before at meetings of the farming association Ellis belonged to, at the summer fair, at the school science project week, but I'd never walked among so many people without seeing a familiar face. Although the winter wind howled down the city street as if blown from a huge horn, I hardly felt it. Aunt Ethel chattered and identified buildings, the El, pointed out streets where events of historical importance had taken place. She said the skyscraper was invented in Chicago. Benjamin held my hand and I held Aunt Ethel's.

With its stately entrance and high ceilings, and particularly the whispered conversations going on all around us, the museum resembled a church. The dialogue we heard had nothing of the urgency of Uncle Conroy's and Ellis's. Instead, the voices were respectful and full of puzzling phrases and references. People mentioned light and texture and intention. I had no idea how to bring words to the rectangles of color laid out in room after room. Benjamin followed me, mesmerized, camera hidden deep in his coat pocket.

Back at the bakery, our aunt showed us the kitchen with its immense ovens and containers of flour and other ingredients. She spoke kindly to the women shoveling buns and breads in and out of the oven, its hot breath warming the entire room. And in the store fronting the building, Aunt Ethel introduced us to a few of her customers. "They've got the hard job," she said to a pretty red-haired woman. "Their father grows the wheat." When I specified, "Corn mostly," the women laughing friendly-like made me blush.

When we got home, I decided our father's job was *too* hard. For weeks I fantasized about living in Chicago, being an apprentice to the women wearing funny nets on their hair while baking the wonderful pastries. I imagined improving my stuffed bread, wrapping exotic bits of foods and spices into the dough and surprising customers with the tasty contents. Finally, I told Benjamin I wanted to bake for Uncle Conroy and Aunt Ethel. I wanted them to be our parents.

One day Sara would join me in Chicago. She could sing at a club and maybe we'd share an apartment. My brother and I discussed possibilities until planting time when, with our many chores, we became too busy and too tired by nightfall to even think. We helped Ellis all we could, but still he worried that our debt was too big to overcome. It was as if the farm were terminally ill and no matter what we did, eventually it would die.

Ellis spoke less and less; Rexanne screamed more. Benjamin became as upset with them as he'd been with the taunts of his classmates.

After harvest I suggested to Benjamin that we make a move. I lied to him. I told him I had a job at the bakery, which I insisted he not talk about with our parents. They fought enough already and we didn't want to instigate more outbursts. I think he believed Rexanne and Ellis had sanctioned my plan to move away because we'd be less of a burden to them, and we'd be sending my salary home. Benjamin always assumed whatever I did I'd gotten permission to do.

Benjamin became obsessed with Chicago. He studied maps of the city and a broader map of the states between Nebraska and Illinois. He wrote down instructions, naming the roads that we'd take to get there. He memorized the streets surrounding our aunt and uncle's bakery and their house, and could recite the names of the ones between the two locations the way he'd once ticked off varieties of corn.

He studied the Monopoly game card for Illinois Avenue. It was one of the red cards. "Rent is twenty dollars," he announced, as if where we were going was affordable. Later, he called the title deed card "our ticket to Chicago." He asked me what mortgages meant and when I put the questions to Rexanne she did something she seldom did. She started to cry. "We're mortgaged out the ass," were her exact words.

My mother cried the evening Benjamin died, too. She didn't wail, but cried softly, almost whimpered, as if she'd expected the tragedy. The next morning, though, she was totally lost.

She and Benjamin had this ritual. Because the kitchen sink was equipped with a spray attachment, she'd take her blouse off and wash her hair right there in the open. Benjamin routinely kept watch in case anyone came to the door and should spot her in her bra. The morning after he died, I woke to find my mother standing at the kitchen sink, totally naked, her long wet hair dripping down her back and onto the linoleum floor.

"I never should have sent him to the little garden," she said.

"You sent him there?" I asked. "You sent *him* to the little garden?"

The "little garden" was the term she and I used for a concealed bit of land, the only piece of her magnificent vegetable garden remaining after Ellis put the lake in and drowned all of her efforts. He'd plowed up a larger square for her special plantings closer to the house, but she never pursued the new garden the way she had the first. She transplanted her parsnips and raspberry bushes to a secret spot just beyond the man-made basin of water.

In the late summer, she sent me on missions to retrieve the tasty fruit that even the birds didn't seem able to find. Rexanne loved raspberries, and, bringing them to her by the handfuls, I felt I was presenting her with a gift. In the late fall, she'd ask me for the parsnips. She said she'd rescued them from Ellis's lake just for me and had been feeding them to me since I was little. Rexanne said they were an acquired taste.

The parsnips were best after a frost when their starch turned to sugar. She helped me cut them in thin strips and sauté them in butter with onions. Then I turned the heat down and covered the mixture with large spinach leaves. My mother and I had shared these treats for years. So I was shocked that she'd send my brother to do my special job. I thought she'd shown the remains of her hidden garden only to me. I thought, something is definitely wrong with this picture.

. . .

The militiamen came even before the police. That was weird, too, because Wednesday had never been a meeting night. Hank and Dillon were the only men I recognized. The men thumped through our house, their boots and shoes rumbling like something was about to happen. I had to remind myself that the worst had already happened. Like the time our beans were lost in torrential rains that lasted ten days. When the sky finally cleared to reveal the flooded fields, a few grumbles of thunder lingered on.

Ellis's sneakers were untied. The hard plastic tips of the laces bounced against the wood when he went upstairs and when he came back down. The house was quiet except for the laces ticking like a clock that had gone all out of whack. As he reached the rug, the noise was silenced. Then the men talked, none of their voices or words standing out enough for me to figure out what was being said.

The men started to argue. A stranger shouted. His teeth were huge and yellow. Rexanne took my hand and led me into her bedroom, then covered my ears. We waited there until the men left. A few minutes later, the police and an ambulance arrived. "My gentle son," Rexanne said softly.

Later that night Ellis said he was going to Carlsen's, the farm that bordered ours. Dean Carlsen was from Missouri and he'd bought Henderson's land in addition to some of Ellis's acres. For spending money, one afternoon a week Benjamin got off the school bus at the neighboring farm and cleaned Carlsen's house. Sometimes he'd make a simple dinner for Carlsen before coming home to eat with us. Carlsen was thirty-eight and lived alone.

When Ellis finally tied his shoes and prepared to leave, Rex-anne took me aside and whispered, "Go with him." She took a deep breath. "So there's no trouble."

I don't remember much except how black it was that night, the moon nowhere to be found. Ellis didn't say a word the whole way there.

I can't recall what Ellis said to Mr. Carlsen. Only Carlsen weeping. It was the first time I'd seen a man cry.

I'd seen my brother cry plenty. The first time he'd appeared with a bruised face and scraped elbows, Ellis went wild. The deep scar down Ellis's nose grew more pronounced than ever as he demanded names from Benjamin, who stopped his crying intermittently to sniff in long gasps. Rather than squeal out the names of his classmates, Benjamin stared at me the whole time Ellis raged.

When my brother next came home beaten up, Ellis calmly said that Benjamin would have to learn to stick up for himself. "Get tough, boy," he said, and patted Benjamin on the back, maybe reminding himself as much as advising Benjamin. Maybe he was trying to discourage Benjamin from participating in fe-male activities like canning corn. Maybe he wanted to teach Benjamin to do things *to* girls instead of *with* them. Ellis was beginning to hang with the men who called themselves the ESSOP.

All I could think of was the time our chickens had ganged up on one chicken in particular, pecked away at it until it died. For weeks, the image of bloody feathers haunted me. I tor-mented Ellis with whys until he finally told me that nature had its own way of handling situations that we were in no position to question.

In time, Benjamin came to me in secret with a sprained wrist, a kicked leg, an elbow that needed bandaging. He wouldn't confess abuses that didn't show up on his body—kisses blown on the school bus, names tossed down the long hallway stretching between classrooms. In private I did my best to nurse him through the difficulties that had begun to shame him, but I had no idea how to stop them. Even when I could, I didn't.

A month before he died, Benjamin accompanied me to a high school football game; it was *the* event that fall. Having just gotten my license, I insisted on driving. The moon was huge and the sky so bright you almost didn't need headlights. I drove carefully, trying not to wiggle the steering wheel.

Boyfriends and girlfriends huddled together over cups of coffee they normally didn't drink. The parents sat off to themselves, their unattached kids spun off in all directions in separate cliques. Breath and hot coffee made a horde of little clouds against the chilly air.

Benjamin left our bleacher seats for a snack. As I watched him making his way through the crowd, Sara came up beside me, then took his seat. She leaned in close. "You're never going to meet a guy if you hang out with your brother." She offered me one of the orange peanut butter crackers she'd bought and whispered, "Look at Lenore. She's so big it's easier to jump over her than walk around."

Before my brother died, I was a virgin. I had listened to Rexanne who confided one night after a couple of beers past her normal two that even though she was part of the sixties generation, she didn't sleep with anyone until she married and got on the pill. Instinctively, she'd known that a pregnancy could tie her to a man forever, even a guy she didn't particularly like. In the beginning she'd thought that sex itself was just as powerful and refrained longer than anyone she knew. A man could hold your freedom over your head like a carrot, she believed. I accepted what she said for a while, but shortly after Benjamin died I didn't give men that much credit.

Sara talked about a couple of guys she wanted to go out with and when she mentioned Ray Cooper, I caught sight of Benjamin down behind another set of bleachers, a group of boys surrounding him. Some of the boys were from my class and a couple were older than me. They taunted him. He stood alone at the center of their circle disoriented as a dog abandoned on the highway with predators sensing his confusion, honing in to take advantage. One of them unzipped and peed on him.

I swear I heard the word "faggot" and my brother's scared-boy face looking around for protection. For me. With all my friends and classmates and potential dates buffering me, I couldn't identify myself as the sister of someone who didn't belong.

At the end of the game I found him in our car sniffling and bleeding, smelling of urine, his small broken body curling in on itself. "What happened? Where were you, Benjamin?" I asked over and over as if I didn't know.

There are some people, if they knew my condition, would say I got pregnant intentionally to have another brother. Rexanne might even agree; she said everything had to do with him for a long time afterward. But then I wasn't consciously considering consequences any more than a coach who gets drenched with a bucket of Gatorade by his winning team. He's focused on the game down to the last second.

I only wanted to sleep with every boy I knew. Maybe so I wouldn't get attached to any one as strongly as I had my brother. Or I might have been afraid for the first time that I would die, too.

I sort of liked Alvin. He was one of the few people at school who would have anything to do with me right after Benjamin died. Most kids actually seemed scared of me the beginning of that winter. Never mentioning my brother's name, Alvin and I had long conversations about issues like breaking horses and how to approach different writing assignments.

I went with Eddie because somebody told me he was gay and I didn't believe it.

But ultimately, I think I just wanted to hurt them all for what they'd done to Benjamin. Six months after I found Benjamin in the water, I began to sleep with one after another of them. At first, I didn't really know what to do. I had only what Sara had told me of her sisters' exploits as guidance.

All of the boys brought me gifts of alcohol. After the first couple of times, I refused their beer and whiskey and cheap wine. I had my own, I'd tell them and smile. A pint of apple juice camouflaged as Jim Beam. I wanted to be in control every inch of the way.

The ones I let finish would call me. I'd refuse them a second date. Break their hearts sometimes. Tell them they didn't satisfy me. Tell them they were small, laughing at the little bouquets in their pants laid bare to me.

Alvin, the first, I led to a corner of our barn and gave myself to while "Another Pleasant Valley Sunday" poured into the ears of our pigs. Others I took out to the lake, the very spot where Benjamin had died. Though I suspected in some way they were all to blame for the trickle of red that ran a rivulet across his forehead, and maybe one of them in particular had chased him into falling, none of the boys seemed squeamish about the place where my brother found an end to all their taunting.

I had my first orgasm with Mr. Donnelly. I didn't intend to sleep with *him*, only to ask him to help me stop myself. He told me I was angry and then *he* had sex with me. Up against the supply closet in his office. Door locked. After hours. Pounding me against the doorway to all the official forms that paved the way to my classmates' futures—job applications, college brochures, four-page forms with each copy a different color, one for everyone's office. He was slower in sex than the boys though no less urgent. He demanded it a second time. The second time right during school hours against the door labeled with his name and title, guidance counselor.

In between the first and second times, he gave me information, telling me what men and boys really say about girls in private. The most obviously politically correct among them were the worst offenders, according to him. He told me no one was to be trusted. He told me to be careful. "You can tell a man who's been deprived of sex," he said. "It's all he talks about when he's alone with another man."

With him, I don't know which confused me more, the sex itself or the talk of it.

I didn't stop myself until I met Rory. Rory was different, confident with sex. He told me his "pleasure package" had nothing to do with size, and then he proved it to me time after time. His determination to reach me, his insistence, gave a form to my confusion. The anger blew away, then guilt came flowing in, too much rain after months of ground so parched with deprivation it couldn't hold the needed moisture.

. . .

There was no investigation of the scene. One of the policemen who came to our house just as the day's light drained from
our fields said, "There's not a damn thing more we can do. I'm
sorry. She moved the body."

They found nothing on him but the game card to Illinois
Avenue tucked in his shirt pocket. No one had any idea why
the card was there. Even I hadn't noticed it when I moved him.
The band of red at the top of the card, the exact color of his
jacket, paired me with the crime.

two

4

march

The town I left is called Paradise, and I can't think why in the hell that's so. Either things were way different years ago or else people less demanding of heaven. Maybe Paradise just meant stopping.

Getting out of the wagon, off the horse, out from under the sweat-soaked blankets after weeks of trudging west. Arriving at a stretch of genuinely empty land—no fences or stores or trees to mark owner-ship, no roads to indicate any outpost of interest beyond that spot— you could leave every mistake in the past and start again. That idea of beginning must have been wild.

When I was a little girl, Rexanne shared that story of the begin-ning of our town. But I could never picture anyone I knew living in the wilderness.

Before I reached my new home, I was overwhelmed with details. Everything looked like something else. Once the plane was in the air, I spotted a grouping of prefab homes that at first I thought were gravestones. Trailers in a semicircle could have been a congregation of railroad cars. I imagined I noticed Carlsen's farm, but the pilot announced that we'd already left Nebraska. As we got above the clouds, the rectangles of empty fields went out of focus. If I pictured where I actually was, I could have panicked.

The woman who sat next to me on the plane was huge; she'd brought her own seat belt extender, which she snapped into place with one movement as practiced as zipping a pair of pants. She talked nonstop, describing a bottled water convention she'd recently spoken at. But after a pretzel snack was served, she went silent and read a book for the rest of the trip. In front of me, two women wore identical ponytails high on their heads.

As we neared New York, a basketball score was announced. And then I saw the lights of the city at night. The slight cloud cover made them dull, then brighten as if they were being adjusted. Bridges draped with lights resembled pieces of Christmas decorations. Traffic lights snaking along the highway looked alive.

The father and three children met me at the airport, then waited with me until my two suitcases, one brand new peach-and-white flowered one courtesy of Vivienne, spun down the carousel. They looked like a family, but nobody touched me or asked about the place I'd just left. Ellis might be quiet, but he gives hugs. Big ones.

On the hour-and-a-half drive to the house, the children were silent. Eventually the father made comments, pointing out towns, apologizing for his wife's absence, and overdoing it with anecdotes. But all I could concentrate on were the trees. I'd never seen so many trees.

They were everywhere—lining the highway, their branchy extremities mixing in with the dark sky. Maybe the whole state is one big protective band of trees.

The house was white and enormous. Seven windows stretched across the second floor. Bay windows were set on either side of the front door, and a thick stone fence below, which looked to have been there as long as the earth itself.

This morning, the apple trees were coated with ice and bent toward the ground. The slender twigs clinked together and the thick bodies of the trees groaned in the cold like a giant saddle beneath a rider. They sparkled.

In Paradise soon the men will be preparing the fields, the upturned *ground filling the air with an aroma of fertility. They come home at night, their hands and faces and jeans streaked with shades of earth, their entire bodies exhausted yet hungry. And though they've gone through the seasonal routines all their lives, in spring they somehow remember their ancestors settling the land when everything was new. They'd paused, smiled, and if only for the second it took to say, "Paradise," thought themselves lucky.*

"Laborers, please take your shoes off when working in the house," Jade carefully lettered on a piece of paper. Too embarrassed to verbalize Ellen Sturges's instructions, Jade taped the note on the door. The issue of the workers' shoes was the only discussion Ellen had had with Jade the night before. Vivienne, at least, made an effort.

Ellen was blonde, extremely skinny, and although she wasn't particularly pretty, she was so impeccably groomed that her overall appearance was pleasing. Jade thought she'd be more attractive if she put on a little weight; the woman's facial features weren't delicate enough for the chiseled-down size of her face.

Jade's idea that the Connecticut wife would be a confidante sympathetic enough to offer good advice about how to deal with the pregnancy vanished almost immediately. A corporate lawyer, Ellen was seldom at home. Even when she was, she avoided speaking with a person directly. She stuck Post-it notes on the refrigerator, the phone, the toilet, and not just for Jade. Jade had found a pale green note on Mr. Sturges's pillow—"No snoring tonight, please." Jade hoped her employer had been making a joke.

The house was quiet, its rooms sunny and still now that the family had finished Jade's French toast breakfast and gone off. The rooms of the Sturges house were spacious, the appliances and floors shiny, the large windows spotless. And Jade had thought the house she and Sara sneaked into in Paradise had been a big deal. That cold day felt like years ago now.

The chocolate-covered sweet corn that Jade had presented to the family her first morning in Connecticut two weeks ago was still wrapped. Buffalo steaks would have been a better gift from Nebraska, but she couldn't have dealt with carrying them on the plane. Plus Sara told her that people in Connecticut didn't eat much meat.

Jade's hands were deep in the soapy clatter of breakfast dishes when she heard the truck bumping down the road and then crackling along the circular, crushed-stone driveway. And when she opened the door on the men, the house immediately filled with noises—tools and buckets clanking up against one another, drop cloths swishing and swelling with air, heavy man boots ignoring the sign and thunking across the thick carpeting, then becoming more distinct when they hit the hardwood floor. The men's joking voices carried through the rooms.

Jade prepared coffee and presented it to the two workers along with the list of jobs that needed completing. The prioritized list had been prepared in triplicate—one for Mrs. Sturges, one for Mr. Sturges, and one for an attorney in New York, who handled the family's finances.

Freddie, the taller and heavier of the two and the one in charge, quickly looked over the list, then scratched at his curly red hair. He touched two fingers to his brow.

"Looks like we've got a couple days' work ahead of us, pal," Freddie said to a younger, darker complected man.

Jade said to Freddie, "What's the other guy's name?"

"Mario," Freddie said.

" 'The other guy' is fine," Mario said at the same time.

Mario appeared eager to begin, but Freddie sat on a kitchen

stool and sipped at his coffee. Leaning back in her chair, Jade unconsciously crossed her hands on her stomach, caught herself pointing out her vulnerability, then sat up straight.

"What does the husband do for a living?" Freddie asked. Before Jade could answer, he said, "No, don't tell me. Let me guess."

Mario shook his head and rolled his eyes at Freddie, then opened the closet door. Stuck to the inside was a list of emergency numbers nearly as long as his forearm. The first eight listings were Ellen's and Ted's different office numbers, car phones, and beepers. Mario closed the door with exaggerated care.

"Mrs. Sturges said it should take twelve hours," Jade said softly.

"To guess what her old man does for a living?" Freddie asked.

"To finish," Jade answered, pointing at the paper in his hands.

"Dickhead," Mario said.

"Watch your mouth," Freddie said to his partner. He glanced in Jade's direction.

Studying the full page of typed instructions, Mario said, "Mrs. Sturges is up her own ass." Mario's edginess made her think for an instant of Ray Cooper, the guy she'd once wanted to notice her at the football game.

At a knock on the door, Freddie stood up. In another minute he introduced a third handyman. Juan lowered his eyes and nodded. Though small, he appeared strong; his hair was black. He stood in stocking feet, a hole at each big toe.

As Jade left to start the laundry, she heard the men dividing up the tasks. Normally the housekeepers handled the sheets, but Ellen had left a note asking Jade if she wouldn't mind "pitching in" now that one of the women was sick. The housekeepers were Czechoslovakian and never spoke to Jade.

"How about you shingle the playhouse roof and I'll paste down the wallpaper along the windows in the master bedroom," Freddie said.

"OK, but you replace the toilet seat in the powder room," Mario said, accenting the last two words. "Also, oiling the squeaky door." He paused. "They even want us to put one of their file cabinet drawers on track."

The men were still debating over the list when Jade returned from loading sheets in the washer. Start the van in the garage and affix recycling sticker; replace ceiling panel in guest room; hook up new VCR; install dead bolt on kitchen door; paint the dining room. . . . Then Freddie and Mario quibbled over whose assistant Juan would be.

Freddie would stop in the middle of a conversation with Mario to pronounce one or two words in Spanish for Juan. Following this commentary, far less detailed than subtitles, Freddie repeated an English word as if he were a foreign language teacher. The procrastinating reminded her of how Jesse, the Sturgeses' son, put off his homework by spending more time figuring out the fastest way to do it than actually completing the assignment.

"Here's my favorite," Mario said, pointing to number nine, which involved constructing twenty-six stakes to line either side of the driveway. The bottoms were to be painted gray to match the driveway stone, and the five inches from the top the same deep red as the house's front door. "They're going to look like giant cigarettes," Mario said and laughed.

"Not if you paint them gray," Freddie said. Freddie went along with some of the shenanigans, but underneath, unlike Mario, Jade could tell he respected people with money and the social standing that came with it.

"Not computers," Freddie said to Jade. "That kind of guy

usually has one huge computer set up like an altar." He paused. "Idea man. Is Mr. Sturges what they call an idea man?"

"Sort of," Jade said. She didn't mention that Ellen was an attorney.

Before Freddie left to buy materials, he said to Juan, "Go with the *hombre*," and indicated Mario. The two trailed Jade upstairs to the library to start on what Ellen had named "touch up" on the job list. The room's walls were infested with pale green, one-and-a-half-inch-by-two-inch Post-it notes.

"Jesus H. Christ," Mario said as he examined a couple of the spots, many no larger than the size of a dime. "Why doesn't she just have the whole room repainted?"

Jade shrugged. When Mario turned and stared at her, she felt he saw through the white sweater the darkening nipples that had recently surprised her. But he began talking about Blue Field residents.

"I don't know how you do it," he said, shaking his head, looking away.

"What?" Her voice came out in a squeak, but he didn't answer. Jade asked if he'd like more coffee.

He shook his head and told her that the week before, he'd painted the interior of a wealthy woman's house. "She said she needed to get away from the smell of the paint, so she went to France. Can you believe it? She told me to call her when the job was done and she'd jump back on the Concorde." He looked around. "These people."

As Ellen Sturges had instructed, Jade suggested that the men not use the upstairs bathrooms. But not long after Freddie returned, she heard a toilet flush. Though it wasn't always easy to hear over Mario's boom box, she eavesdropped on their conversations. She figured out that Freddie and a partner operated a dry-cleaning business in town. Mario, too, did the handyman work as a secondary source of income. Because he worked evenings at his brother-in-law's liquor store, Mario knew what everyone in Blue Field drank and how much. And he knew which residents bought lottery tickets regularly.

Jade offered the men lunch, briefly entertaining the idea of preparing a tasty specialty the way she'd once fed her father's friends, but Freddie, Mario, and Juan had brought their lunches. Although Mario wanted to eat in the truck, Freddie convinced him to pull up a chair in the kitchen. Jade set out dishes and napkins before leaving the room. Juan ate and smoked in the garage.

Despite his lowered voice, Jade heard Freddie telling Mario about a young model who'd brought a leather G-string into his shop.

"She wanted it cleaned," Freddie said, punching the last word. He went on to explain that word got out along the strip mall where the dry-cleaning business was located. "I could have charged the guys just to touch it," he said.

Jade pictured the local merchants in a tight circle around the exotic piece of leather. Jade wouldn't impress anyone in a bikini these days. Her body had thickened and tightened, her new shape obvious only when she stripped down.

"They paid me in coins," Mario said, referring to a recent handyman job he'd done solo. "Like I was seven or something."

"Why?" Freddie asked.

"I know exactly why," Mario said. "They rolled these coins and didn't want to turn them in at Blue Field Savings, which now charges one dollar for every ten dollars you want to change to bills."

"They charge now?" Freddie interrupted.

Ignoring the question, Mario said, "They didn't want to pay that dollar."

"How much was it?" Freddie asked.

"Forty-five," Mario said. "Four and a half rolls."

"They didn't give you half the roll as a tip?" Freddie said and laughed.

"Shit," Mario said. Every now and then Mario told an anecdote, which Jade couldn't be sure was true. When the men's chairs scraped back against the floor, Juan reappeared.

Freddie said the word "shutters" to Juan, who shook his head. Freddie led Juan outside and pointed at the shutters on the back windows. Juan shook his head again.

"What?" Freddie asked, "shutters have no *llamo?*"

"So, what's the weirdest job you ever did before we worked together?" Mario interrupted.

Freddie explained how he'd constructed a casket for a man to rise from when his guests arrived at a Halloween party. He'd also been paid to make tombstones out of wood with each guest name painted in gray; then he positioned the markers across the front lawn.

"Mine was polishing suitcases with black shoe polish," Mario said.

"Who had you do that?"

"Deland." He coughed. "Woman said she'd give me a new job every week." He paused. "She still owes me over seven hundred bucks."

Jade went to her room at the back of the first floor and quickly changed into tights and a plaid skirt with a stretchy waistband. Although Ellen Sturges had told her not to leave the men alone in the house, Jade couldn't imagine them doing anything with her gone that they wouldn't do right in front of her.

She took the keys to the Geo the family let her use for errands and slipped out the side door without the workers noticing. As she left, she paused to listen to a story about a woman who'd missed her train stop on her way home from the city. She called the library to pick her up and take her to her car because it was on account of their book, which she'd been reading, that she missed her stop.

"They picked her up?" Freddie asked. In the pause, Jade heard the paint rollers and brushes sweeping against the dining room walls.

"They picked her up," Mario said.

Jade caught her breath in the car. With the younger children at a town recreational program followed by a visit to Ellen's mother, Jade had the afternoon free. As she drove she thought she might have had fun visiting grandmothers and grandfathers. Other than her aunt and uncle in Chicago, Jade had never known any of her relatives. At least Vivienne got cards, even if she didn't see all her cousins.

In her jacket pocket she'd stashed a piece of paper with the address of a women's clinic in Danbury. She'd called two of the 800 numbers in the Yellow Pages only to discover that they were fronts for the right-to-life movement. All this distance now between her and Vivienne, and still Jade couldn't escape the fanatical voices demanding rights for something no bigger than one of her front teeth. What about *me*? Jade wanted to scream.

Jade had almost been fooled by the voice at Safe Abortion. The female timbre had been calm, consoling, remotely motherly. The woman had spoken with just enough intimacy infused in her voice to remind Jade of a distant relative she'd never met but who understood her. For a few minutes, Jade imagined the woman could name her favorite color and television program and could even judge Jade's taste in clothing. The voice hadn't asked, but told Jade, "You're confused." Exactly. In the end Jade had to hang up because a tall man wearing a suit and holding a thick date book was waiting to use the convenience-store telephone. When Jade had called back, she'd gotten a different woman entirely, one not nearly as friendly.

Jade never made her calls from the Sturges house. The person on the other end of the line could have one of the phone attachments that showed a caller's number. Jade couldn't risk anyone calling back.

On the drive to the Women's Health Pavilion, which sounded like a huge tent at a big-deal picnic, Jade recalled its details. Member of National Abortion Federation, abortion to twenty-four weeks, state-of-the-art medical office, no age requirements, free counseling. That's what she wanted. Someone who'd understand that she needed to get on with her own life as soon as possible and not get all tied up in someone else's.

The single-level brick building was located on a busy narrow street, its parking lot and entrance tucked in the back. Although the structure didn't look any more threatening than an office building, it intimidated her. She knew she had to go inside. Like jumping into cold water, she just had to do it quickly and not think too long about the aftershock.

As Jade pulled open the gray metal door, a young man said, "Good afternoon. Name?"

"Sara Sturges," Jade said quickly, the phony name easily slipping out of her mouth.

"I don't see your name on my list," the young man said. He didn't appear more than a few years older than Rory. "Do you have an appointment?"

"Well, I don't actually."

"I can't let you go in then." He shifted his weight from one leg to the other.

"I just want some free counseling," Jade said softly. "Like it said in the advertisement."

"You have to call them first and get an appointment. Then

they put your name on this list." He turned the clipboard toward her as if she were a child needing a demonstration.

"Could I go in and make an appointment?" Jade was wondering when she could next steal away to take care of what was going on in her body.

"No, my instructions are not to let anyone in that's not on the list." He briefly told her about a recent bomb threat that had resulted in stepped-up security.

Jade reasoned that she could have made an appointment, gotten on the list, and *then* brought a bomb in her pocketbook, but she saw that she could get nowhere with the young man, who seemed anxious to return to reading his wrestling magazine. The simple confrontation had exhausted her. She didn't want to stand outside some 7-Eleven and call the clinic back, not with the wind whipping her voice and hair, the rush of traffic scrambling her questions. She wanted to go to bed.

A mile before she reached the Sturgeses', Jade stopped at the post office. She'd written another letter to her mother in Massachusetts, the third since she'd arrived, but none had been answered. It was frustrating to be this close to Rexanne and not be able to reach her. Rexanne had no phone, at least not listed under her own name.

The line in the post office was at a standstill. An elderly woman at the counter said, "I'm holding this place in line for my husband."

The woman directly in front of Jade said, "I only have two letters."

So did Jade. In addition to the note to Rexanne, Jade had written a chatty letter to Ellis and Vivienne. She gave a few new details about the Sturges children, but mostly she talked about how different the scenery was without all the fields and farms. She even admitted in writing that she missed Ellis and Vivienne.

"Madam, I was here first," the elderly woman said. Just as the postal clerk was about to intervene, an old man in a suit appeared. Carrying a box full of packages, he sidled up to the woman at the front of the line. Someone behind Jade groaned and a second clerk immediately began to serve the line that had grown to ten people.

"I need a couple of zip codes," the thirty-year-old in front of Jade said to the clerk, who immediately pointed toward a thick black book in the far corner of the room. "I was told you'd do that for me," the woman persisted. She wore jeans, a baseball cap, and a half-a-dozen thin gold bracelets.

The first time Jade had come into the post office, a customer was giving directives as the clerk wrapped a package for her. Jade never knew a place like Blue Field existed, where people expected, demanded, and received special attention with the most simple tasks. It would never have entered Jade's mind to ask the postal clerk to find her mother's zip code. There were chores you were supposed to do yourself, lots of issues you didn't want some stranger getting in your business about.

Actually, Jade had wanted to search for the number herself. No one had to know that Jade preferred to double-check the zip code to be sure her letters were getting delivered properly. It was like inviting an outsider who knew nothing of the relationship into the middle of a family argument. Like the time the rookie cop from Paradise barged in on Hank and Loreen's routine argument over Saturday television. Eventually, the screaming had turned on *him*.

After she purchased the stamps and posted the letters, Jade had a couple of moments of regret. Had the letter been too hard?

Rexanne—

Why don't you answer me? I'm in Connecticut. I came out here to talk to you. I'm pregnant. I wanted to tell you in person, but you've made this impossible. At least, you could call. I gave you the number, didn't I? Don't tell anybody!

Love,
Jade

Maybe Jade's mother had moved, the unopened letters accumulating at a wrong address like the scene she once saw in a movie. Maybe she'd died suddenly like Benjamin. It would be some joke on Jade if Rexanne had returned to Paradise, their two planes passing in the air within miles of each other.

Jade regretted sending the letter until she unlocked the Sturgeses' box and riffled through the stack of catalogs and bills and found nothing addressed to her. How could Rexanne be so cruel to turn her back on her only daughter? What could she be doing that was so much more important?

Jade not only wanted to find out what was going on with Rexanne, she wanted to know what her mother believed really happened to Benjamin. Jade and Rexanne had never discussed the particulars openly.

Jade was about to pull into the driveway when she spotted the handymen. Freddie beeped a long good-bye and even Mario lifted one hand in a wave. Ted's khaki-colored Mercedes was parked in front of the house. When Jade went inside and greeted him, he didn't mention her leaving the workers alone. She got the feeling that he often found his wife's precautions over the top. Ted worked most days in New York where he had a studio apartment, but at least one weekday he remained in his office at the house.

Ted Sturges was tall and lanky. Even if he was simply sitting around the house, he wore crisp shirts or sweaters that looked brand new. His face was smooth, unblemished, yet slightly rugged, his hair dark with a few flecks of gray above the sideburns. When Ted smiled, he still looked sad to Jade. He didn't talk a lot, but unlike Ellis whose silence was a barometer of general discontent, Ted seemed purposely quiet. He could have been saving all his words for his work.

Ted was a professional ghost, he'd told her, explaining that he wrote books for people with ideas or interesting lives. He listened to their stories or rewrote the accounts of people whose only writing credential was knowing the alphabet. Although he was devoted to his children, Ted Sturges seldom touched them. He wasn't the kind of person who relied on physical gestures to make a point. Jade had never even seen him put his arms around his wife. He was handsome, in a complicated, older man kind of way.

Jade went into the kitchen to start an apple pie she'd serve at dinner. She'd just rolled out the dough and fitted the bottom half in the glass pie pan when Carolyn and Vicky arrived home. She was surprised that their grandmother hadn't come into the house, but merely let them out of the car. Jade would like to have seen if Grandma Sleight was a kindly, softer version of Ellen Sturges.

The four-year-olds wore identical blue denim dresses, but different-colored tights. They had mousy brown hair, wide dark eyes, and high tiny voices that, in the house, never seemed to quiet. Vicky's straight hair was combed back in pigtails, which she reached back to touch every so often, and her bangs were blunt cut. Her little round face was freckled. Carolyn's hair hung down straight to her chin. The girls resembled each other around the eyes, but otherwise didn't look much alike. After helping them off with their coats, Jade poured each a plastic cup of white grape juice.

As Jade placed the apple slices in the crust, she promised the girls that when the apples grew and ripened on the tree near the garage, they could pick them and make a very special apple pie.

"Will you make it for us?" Vicky asked.

"Oh, your grandma could make it," Jade said, realizing she couldn't promise anything much more than a couple of weeks ahead.

"No, you," Carolyn said.

Jade concocted an outlandish story about getting a giraffe to reach up for the fruit. The girls studied her, their eyes full of curiosity.

When Jade had first arrived, the refrigerator was bare except for a quart of milk, a half-empty bottle of wine, a box of Pop-Tarts, and a few of the usual condiments. Ellen Sturges didn't object to the fruits and vegetables and juices Jade had suggested, but the woman didn't seem to appreciate a full refrigerator either. The three children did.

As the girls watched, Jade slid the pie into the oven. Because their mother never cooked, they considered Jade a magician. When he was small, Benjamin had been amazed when she'd baked cream puffs, carefully split them in half, and filled each with a spoonful of butterscotch pudding.

Jade followed Carolyn and Vicky up the curving staircase to their bedroom, where a pink canopy bed sat at either end, three windows and a flowered area rug between. Their own bathroom was situated off the far side of the bedroom. Positioned in one corner of the spacious room was an intricate dollhouse the size of a refrigerator lying on its side.

"This is the mommy's room," Carolyn said, pointing to the

study with its blue-flowered wallpaper and a tiny mahogany desk
at the window. The furniture in the miniature rooms could have
belonged to the wealthy; nothing looked brand new, though it
appeared solid enough to last generations. Jade noticed details—
decorative mirrors, ornate candlestick holders, wall-sized paintings—that would belong to no one she knew in Paradise.

Watching the girls' hands moving in and out of the rooms,
she envied them touching miniature chairs and tables and beds
before their own dreams had grown too big for the structure.
Before they understood how quickly important issues could
crowd any size house, ruin its charm. Jade liked the dollhouse's
upstairs bathroom best of all, its porcelain tub with claw-footed
legs positioned beneath a tiny stained-glass window.

Suddenly Jade felt a familiar wave of nausea and rushed
downstairs for Saltines. Ted passed her on the stairs. She heard
him calling, "Where are my little mermaids?" and the girls
squealing in reply.

By the time she went back upstairs, Jesse had arrived home.
He sat in front of a huge computer system in his room, a cell
phone in a leather case to one side of the screen. Jade had to
remind herself that the boy was nine years old.

"Jesse, it's time to practice," she said.

He ignored her and said, "My parents are buying me a new
computer and the twins will get this one."

"What do they need a computer for?"

"This," he answered, producing a flash of color on the screen
and a metallic-looking bumper car that he directed with his
mouse.

"Come on, Jesse," she said emphatically, despite the compel-
ling screen.

"Let me call Jeffrey first." He picked up the digital phone.

"Don't use that one," Jade said. "It's too expensive." Ellen had explained that the phone was a lifeline to her oldest child; she insisted that he call her at the slightest indication of trouble. Jesse looked at Jade as if he'd never heard the word "expensive."

"Come on," she repeated, and, after a few minutes, he turned off the computer and followed her downstairs to the music room where his oboe sat in the corner like a trophy.

Her every suggestion became a fight with the boy, who was small for his age. Jesse was defiant and self-confident, nothing like her brother. Benjamin had been easy to coerce. Rexanne used to say that whenever Jade would command, "Jump," Benjamin would ask, "How high?"

When Ellen finally got home, Jade served dinner and ate with the family. They crowded at the kitchen table because Ted said he couldn't tolerate the odor of paint lingering in the dining room. Jade thought of Mario's story of the woman and the Concorde.

"They're too white," Ellen said, gesturing at the next room.

"What?" Ted asked.

"The dining room walls," she said in a tone that meant he'd asked the most stupid question imaginable. After a few minutes of silence, she said, "I'll have the workers redo the walls."

Jade couldn't imagine what "too white" meant. She passed the stuffed lamb chops. Jade started to cut one of the chops into pieces for the twins. "Here, I'll do that," Ellen said softly. When Ellen stuck a piece of meat onto the fork, Carolyn, playing the baby, immediately opened her mouth. Vicky fed herself. Alternating between eating her own meal and offering food to Carolyn, Ellen spoke to Ted exclusively. She ended her story with, "Too bad he fell in his own house. He couldn't even sue anybody."

The statement led to a discussion of insurance and eventually produced a question from Jesse. Ted tried to explain. "Let's start with homeowners," he said, but abandoned the issue when Ellen suggested that their son shouldn't worry himself over insurance until he got older.

Jade appreciated that Ellen wanted to shield her children from difficulties as long as possible. Jade and Benjamin had been right in the middle of any problem that had to do with the farm or with Ellis and Rexanne's relationship. In Paradise there wasn't room or time enough after work to hide problems. Children there were exposed to every problem from the day they were born. Even wrapped completely in layers against the cold, a child could sense anxiety. Trouble always got through.

About the only time Ellen Sturges talked was at dinner. She seemed to unwind from the stress of the workday with a barrage of words. Or it could have been the martini Ted made her. Not to leave anyone out, he'd set three glasses of Sprite, each with a pierced olive, in front of the children. Jade drank a Coke.

During dessert Carolyn announced, "Jade will make a pie with those apples." The girl pointed toward the kitchen window, then looked at Jade.

Ellen said, "How nice."

Ted said, "From our apples?"

"Sure," Jade said. Ellis loved Jade's apple pie.

"You know, Jade, this half-and-half isn't quite as good as the brand you got last week," Ted said.

"You shouldn't have the stuff anyway," Ellen said. Jade didn't think Ellen ate so much as moved the food all around on her plate.

When Vicky started pouting, Ellen motioned for Jade. Just when Jade would start to feel comfortable in her place, one of the Sturgeses would lure her out of it, almost making her part of the family only to slap her away. Jade wouldn't have to put up with this treatment for long. She'd make an appointment and return to the clinic. She had some money saved. Then she could go anywhere. By herself. She wouldn't even need her mother, who, so far, hadn't been a bit of help.

That evening Jade felt bloated, anxious, and a little homesick in the huge house with its "too-white" dining room walls. She almost missed the scent of burning pastures in preparation for a new season. Her Connecticut room and attached bath were pale coral with a green and yellow flowered bedspread, a little too Viviennesque for her taste. And yet it was her own space, off-limits to the children. At the back of the house, the room was steps away from a little-used door to the outside.

If Rory were nearby, Jade could run off into the woods with him, or, on rainy nights, sneak him into her room. The rain would pound away at the windows, and wind would push the branches into each other while she warmed herself against his body. Jade couldn't imagine Ted and Ellen Sturges in the storm of passion. So much of what they said to each other was too subtle.

A light interior tapping, nothing like rain, startled her. Jade pulled on her robe, but by the time she got to the door, nobody was there. Somewhere upstairs deep in the house, a door clicked shut. Then silence.

Before her sat a grocery bag. She picked it up. Inside was a new Cuisinart. Jade unwrapped every blade and attachment, setting the many parts all over her rug. She read the instructions start to finish. Only when she'd carefully fitted every piece back into the box, did she notice the tiny green Post-it stuck onto one flap—"Thought you could use this."

"Act like they shit don't smell. Baby, everybody's shit smells. I don't care how many silver spoons you got up your ass."

Pearline talked constantly before and after night school classes in Danbury. Her Jamaican English accented with American slang entertained Jade almost as much as the stories. In two weeks, Jade knew the names and antics of Pearline's husband Stewie and the children still in Kingston; her friends and four children and two grandchildren she visited every weekend in Queens; her employer, Lauren Nash, a single parent of two who ran a bed-and-breakfast in Blue Field. Pearline was forty-five, but spoke to Jade as if they were the same age.

Among her many stories, Pearline had interspersed a recipe for jerk chicken, which Jade wanted to try for the Sturgeses. Jade had stuck the recipe in the special blank book Rexanne had given her, and later decided to copy the instructions on the first page. It was satisfying to finally have something written down.

The only bit of information about herself that Jade had shared with Pearline was that she was an au pair for Ted and Ellen Sturges. Pearline had said, "You better watch out. That woman went through fifteen baby-sitters in three months when Jesse was a baby. They loved that little baby so hard they didn't trust nobody with it." Pearline had pulled out a pack of gum, offered it to Jade. "Fifteen's not the record though. I'm keeping track." And then Pearline had gone on about baby-sitters and au pairs and the Connecticut mothers who hired them.

Pearline had a storehouse of intimate details about the residents of Blue Field, particularly women with young children. She told Jade she simply kept her eyes open and her ears pricked. But Jade suspected Lauren Nash was a gossip who flaunted her knowledge like Vivienne's friends. If anyone but Pearline had told her, Jade probably wouldn't have believed the behind-the-scenes details.

When Ellis and Vivienne phoned and reported the progress

of someone disking fields, or named a new kind of bean they'd heard about, or mentioned a property that had been sold, Jade was reminded how different Connecticut was from the world she'd left. Connecticut had that little hook on its western border like Nebraska's, but the similarity ended there. Vivienne didn't write letters, but she sent comic strips and announcements of goings-on in Nebraska, like a quilt show or horseshoe tournament, all neatly sliced from the pages of the local paper. Ellis had forwarded Jade's red woolen hat, the one he'd given her two Valentine's Days ago. Jade was surprised that those bits of familiarity gave her a twinge of homesickness.

If Jade really thought about it, Sara's makeup and noisy costume jewelry would look trashy next to the gaunt faces of her new neighbors, though maybe Pearline wouldn't think so. Sometimes in sleep, Jade mashed the details of both states together. She could be dreaming of her bedroom in Blue Field, but the bedspread or lamp or window would look like the one she'd had in Nebraska. Jade wished she'd left the promise of a baby behind in Paradise. Thinking of the cells dividing and aligning at breakneck speed in her body, Jade knew that the longer she put off returning to the clinic, the more complicated her life would become.

As they walked to their cars in the high school parking lot, Pearline was talking about a room she'd cleaned at Lauren Nash's bed-and-breakfast that morning. Guests had washed their two poodles in the bathtub and dried them with the inn's sheets. The ACC hotel management course for sure wouldn't prepare Jade for that kind of incident. She wondered if she should still pursue the program once she'd received her GED diploma.

"Oooh, that dog smell followed me all around the room," Pearline said, shaking her head.

Although Jade had noticed a robin that morning, the March

air remained cold. She pulled on her gloves as Pearline exclaimed how rich people treated their dogs like babies. "No one has that kind of time in my country," she said. "No one but the very little ones."

Pearline reported that the dog odor drifted into her own room at the inn where she lived. Her employer automatically deducted the price of the room from the weekly salary. The other inn employees, mostly Mexican men who maintained the building and grounds, lived together in a one-room outbuilding. Some of the men were illegals.

Jade felt illegal herself, undercover, out of place. She had said little about herself, and yet she had a lot to say. Pearline's dark face was without blemishes, had few lines, but her hands were coarse as a farmer's. Jade looked right into her nearly black eyes.

"I'm pregnant," she said, as if the one fact should explain everything about her.

"Don't think I don't know," Pearline answered immediately. "Girl, I got four babies back in Jamaica and four more grown ones in the Queens. I know." Pearline went on about how she was younger than Jade when her first baby was born.

Jade couldn't imagine eight children. One was enough to change your life completely. But maybe after one it didn't make all that much difference. Like when you went on a trip. Ellen Sturges said you needed as much paraphernalia for an overnight as for a week-long stay.

Jade wondered what else Pearline knew. Could this forthright woman leaning up against the Sturgeses' car tell that Jade had lost a brother? Did Pearline know why he'd died?

Pearline was gibbering about a stole that her employer no longer wanted. She said she'd admired the fur piece since the day she'd first arrived at the Bed and Bottle Inn. But instead of passing it on to Pearline, Miss Lauren had given it to her eight-year-old to play dress-up. During a temper tantrum, the child had jumped up and down on the shiny fur.

"It's nice that they send you to night school anyway," Jade said, thinking of how helpful the Sturgeses had been in locating the program and seeing that she enrolled quickly enough to graduate in June. Initially they'd been puzzled that she hadn't made plans to finish high school, but by the end of the week Ted had the GED details.

"At first I thought they send me so I can help the children with their schoolwork," Pearline said. Without criticizing, Pearline explained that Lauren Nash didn't have the time or patience with lessons. "Now I know Miss Lauren didn't want her neighbor to have a smarter au pair than I." Pearline mentioned a Bosnian refugee who was working for the woman across the street from the Bed and Bottle Inn.

Pearline would have gone on about her employer, about the competition between Blue Field neighbors in everything from hors d'oeuvres to mailboxes, but Jade brazenly directed the conversation back to herself. "So, do you know anybody who's had an abortion around here?"

Pearline squinted at Jade in the dark. The huge trees all around them were stark and still, though Jade knew they were coursing with spring.

"Girl, you can't go interfering with God's will."

"What about my will?"

"You gave it up when you slept with that boy who got you this way," Pearline was quick to say.

"Maybe it wasn't a boy," Jade said defiantly.

"No matter," Pearline said. She began talking about the father of her first child; he'd recently died. Suddenly Pearline became quiet. The uncharacteristic pause so startled Jade that she turned to look behind her.

Pearline took an audible breath. "You know there's women in this part of the world who would do anything to have a little baby like the one you don't want," she whispered. Jade cringed thinking of Vivienne and her efforts, which seemed to have infiltrated every crevice of the country. Pearline was describing the skinny bodies, the long faces and perfectly coiffed hair. She said some of the women looked remarkably like the horses they owned and rode. Going off on a tangent, Pearline told about setting up for a lunch Lauren Nash had given a few months earlier where figs had been served. "Only figs. Now they were done up really pretty on a big silver tray. But there were only figs. Figs and some kind of special water."

Jade said, "If they're so awful, why would I want to give one of them my baby?" She stopped. She'd actually said "my baby." As if the possibility inside her now had a form. An actual shape and weight.

And belonged to her.

In New England, where almost everything was foreign to Jade, the unborn baby suddenly felt like the only thing she was close to. She tried to get her mind around the idea of actually carrying a baby to term and then handing it over to someone who genuinely wanted it.

Pearline exhaled a high whiny sound. "Because you don't give it," she said, emphasizing the "give." "You get them to pay." Then Pearline relayed a series of anecdotes involving the incredible amount of money spent on fertility drugs, specialists, and adoptions.

"Miss Anna introduced her child to her friends with 'in vitro' like 'in vitro' was part of the baby's name. She was proud that all the money she spent produced a baby." Pearline coughed. "Most of the women are not this lucky." She deviated to explain her theory that being too skinny made you infertile.

"Want me to pay you a finder's fee?" Jade asked, laughing. She was thinking of Vivienne's real estate job, how when Hank had directed a buyer to her, Vivienne had shared part of the commission.

"What's that?" Pearline asked.

When Jade didn't answer at first, Pearline cleared her throat. Jade looked at her watch in the dark and started to go for her keys.

Pearline said, "You make a whole lot of money. And then God's not mad at you either."

5

april

It moved.

"You can't do this, Jade."

"I'm doing it," Jade said, surprising herself with her defiance. She cupped the receiver even though there was no one else in the house.

"Jade, we have to talk about this."

"You should have talked about it before now." Jade thought, But no, you were more interested in dead relatives than your daughter. Your daughter who made her way to a state right next to the one you're living in.

"I just got your letter," Rexanne said. She meant the *big* letter, the one Jade had mailed weeks earlier. When Jade questioned why she hadn't received it until now, she heard Rexanne's voice go soft. "I can't explain right now, honey." Rexanne's gentle tone, asking forgiveness, didn't soothe Jade's anger.

"Well, I just hope you know what you're doing," Rexanne said.

Jade paused. She had no idea what she was doing. She should have been her old self now. She should have been back to being by herself. But her body continued to change to accommodate the new life. She was tired most of the time; her head ached frequently; her waistline kept growing though she didn't think she looked overtly pregnant yet. She was constipated, her nose stuffy, and she easily lost her concentration, even over a simple recipe.

"Give me your phone number in case I need to talk about it."

"I can't do that, Jade."

"Why?" Jade practically screamed. Even Vivienne would *talk* to Jade.

"I can't explain right now. I'll call you in a day or two."

After she heard her mother take a breath, Jade hung up. The phone call had shocked her, made her assume a stand that before she'd only flirted with. Despite Rexanne's objections and the argument that Jade would be throwing her future away, Jade had now determined she would have a baby. Sell it to the highest bidder. Hand her baby over to a rich woman and become rich herself. Maybe the next letter Jade sent her mother would be from Paris. Or at least some place where people appreciated food.

The call wouldn't cost a penny; the Sturgeses didn't dock Jade's pay when she called long distance the way Pearline's employer did when she phoned Jamaica. Last week Pearline had reported that Lauren Nash advised her to buy a fax machine and send it to Stewie. As she described the possible new arrangement in her weekly communication, Pearline had appeared puzzled. "In the long run it'll be a lot cheaper than these hour-long phone calls," Pearline repeated without imitating Lauren. Jade thought Lauren Nash missed the point: Pearline loved to talk.

Jade understood her mother less than she ever had in her life. Two nights ago she swore she'd seen Rexanne on *America's*

Most Wanted—a cunning woman who bilked unsuspecting bachelors of their pensions. But only the actor resembled her mother, the actual woman far too heavy, her lips too thin to be Rexanne. And the crime wasn't Rexanne's style, but these days what was?

All Jade had gotten from her mother's two letters was talk of Nancy Jane. Nancy Jane. If Nancy Jane was so great, why hadn't Rexanne named *her* Nancy Jane in memory of the woman? And why hadn't Rexanne told her all these details before now?

"Ellis wouldn't have it," had been Rexanne's quick answer. She coughed. "And back then neither would I."

The first letter Rexanne had sent, which talked about her mother, Nancy Jane, read like the pages of Jade's history book. The dry details and dates, born in 1912, married in 1952, and other dull facts stretched across the pages in Rexanne's familiar handwriting. Jade had skimmed the incidents and comments for a mention of herself, questions about the Sturgeses, inquiries about Ellis, but found merely long-winded accounts of a woman she'd never met.

Only after she'd reread the letter a couple of times and received a second chattier one did Jade believe that Nancy Jane had been not only an actual person, but related to her.

She paused over the part about Nancy Jane's mother, Ann, "pooh-poohing" the city girls' high-laced walking boots and their tight skirts worn six inches from the ground. Many of Nancy Jane's friends left the farm to take city jobs and then send their meager wages home. "In those days mere children," Rexanne wrote, "left their warm beds to work in factories and shops."

Not Nancy Jane, who learned to ride by the time she was five. Soon she was riding a Shetland pony to round up the cows. Eventually, she could balance herself standing on his rump even when he was moving all-out. Nancy Jane hooked the pony to a cart and drove out to the field with stoneware jugs of water for the workers. Because Nancy Jane was an only child, she had to learn to run the tractor, to plant and harvest like the best of farmers. Nancy Jane never knew her father; Ann told the child simply that she didn't have one. All the while she planted or disked the fields or nursed ailing animals, Nancy Jane wondered what life was like outside the farm.

Jade understood that longing. Pictured the young woman, who maybe even had green eyes herself, dirt from the fertile earth tucked in her clothing and hands and hair, and beneath her fingernails. The scent of oiled leather, manure, and fresh-cut hay permeating her clothing. Rexanne said she'd read how the literati ridiculed smaller towns and rural life. Before she left Nebraska, Jade had never heard her mother use a word like "literati."

Nancy Jane's strongest memory as a child was the summer day in June, in her seventh year, when women got the right to vote. Nancy Jane stood in a kitchen full of women, all squeezed up close to the many skirts and aprons. She smelled chicken and potatoes cooking. Carrots sat in cold water waiting to start boiling as the women laughed and talked. A black and white dog in the corner lifted one back leg to scratch its underbelly.

"All this political freedom," Nancy Jane said, "disappeared with my hair." Without her mother's permission, young Nancy

Jane snipped off the long braid of hair that lay against the middle of her back. Ann had been furious, so angry she refused to eat with the girl for nearly a month.

Rexanne had filled in the background for Jade—short hair in those days was associated with radicalism and free love. For Nancy Jane, it came to mean the opposite; her mother never let her out of her sight. Jade thought that maybe the hair cutting had upset the mother, not only because of what it suggested, but because city girls wore their hair short.

Secretly, every night before going to bed, Nancy Jane cut at her hair so that it never grew a half inch after that first shearing. Eventually, Ann came to accept the fact that her daughter's hair had permanently stopped growing.

Jade admired Nancy Jane's pluck. She wondered why her own mother revealed the life as if it were a story, why she was telling these stories now, why she always said "Nancy Jane" instead of "my mother." She imagined Nancy Jane's hair brown like Rexanne's and a little curly.

On Wednesday Ted came out of his office well before Jesse and Ellen were expected home. The twins were watching Nickelodeon. As he searched the pantry and refrigerator for ingredients, Ted announced plans to make dinner. Jade offered to go to the store for him, but he said, "You take the night off, Jade. I'll do the whole shebang."

"You want me to go somewhere?"

Ted smiled. "No, Jade. I simply want to cook in my own house."

Blushing, Jade thought Ted's breaking into her routine must have to do with the men's group, which met on alternate Saturdays at the different members' homes. Two weeks earlier, six men had filed into the den, Ted shutting the door behind them. No one farted to get a laugh or talked about some neighbor who'd gotten a piece of cheese or peanut stuck in his throat. Ted's acquaintances, unlike her father's, talked quietly about books, about a national news issue Jade didn't fully grasp, about their workout routines. Later Ted made drinks and someone broke out cigarettes. After the men had all taken one, Ted asked Jade to run the pack under water so none of them was "tempted." Jade had hidden the cigarettes in her room. Now she couldn't remember one of the visitors' names. Ellis's friends were cruder and with the militia stuff probably no more in touch with the world, but every now and then she missed them.

While Ted was shopping, Jade stole upstairs to cut her hair. She'd been thinking about the connection between short hair and freedom every since she'd read about Nancy Jane. Even using a mirror, Jade had a hard time making sure the cut was even, especially in the back. She cut off only an inch at first, but eventually shortened her hair to just below her ears. She studied her face in the mirror—it looked fuller, softer. Not bad. But maybe that was as much a result of the pregnancy as the haircut. She wondered what Sara would think of the look. Or Rory.

A car door slammed. Ted was back with two grocery bags. Without noticing her hair, he began to prepare a mixture of spinach, leeks, pine nuts, and mushrooms, which he then spread down the center of a large pork tenderloin. He rolled the meat, and carefully tied pieces of cord around the roast. He wouldn't even let Jade cut the lengths of string. She could have shown him a more efficient way to peel and slice the potatoes and apples, but Ted would only have raised one hand to her like a school crossing guard.

Seated in the dining room, its walls now an off-white Ellen called linen, the family awaited Ted's culinary feast. Jade tried to tell him any meat that size would take longer than twenty minutes to cook, she didn't care how high you set the temperature. The potatoes and haricots verts (Jade's family would never harvest beans so early) had gone cold, and the meat was still not fit to eat.

Vicky whined, and soon Carolyn joined her. Jesse was making a bet with himself whether the dinner would be done before he reached a particular score on his Game Boy. He kept upping his goal. Jade tried to suggest microwaving the meat for a short time, so at least the inside cooked, but Ted wanted no interference. His expression was serious, and he wore a red apron that said, "Maine Lobster," in white letters across the waistband.

"Ted, let's just go out," Ellen finally said. Jade was surprised at how easily he agreed.

On the drive into the village, Ellen kept glancing into her vanity mirror at Jade's new haircut. "Looks very nice," Ted finally said. Jade watched the sky graying, the still bare trees dissolving with the day. Sitting with the children, Jade decided she should tell the Sturgeses that she was going to have a baby, that she'd offer it to an adoptive family. She wouldn't bring up anything about money. A restaurant would be perfect, a public place so no one would scream at her or worse, cry. She thought she remembered a scene from a movie where one of the characters said the only place he could break up with his girlfriends was in a restaurant.

Ted said that in another week the country club would reopen. Jade told him that in Nebraska, they had the Cummington Gun and Country Club. Ellen cleared her throat.

The waiter delivered frogs' legs to Ellen, chicken to the twins and Jade, shrimp scampi to Jesse, and a filet mignon pooled in red to Ted. As Jesse played with his shrimp, Jade watched Ted. She thought there had been a mistake; his meat was uncooked. But he poked his fork into piece after piece of the moist dripping steak and then buried it in his mouth.

"Great," he said after a few minutes.

"You like it that way?" she asked.

"Wonderful," he said.

Jade mentioned that the farmers she knew never ate their meat partially cooked.

"You're in Connecticut now," Ted said kindly. Jade thought back to the time she'd made sirloins for the Connecticut family. Cooking the meat all the way. Probably Ted had only been polite then when he said how much he enjoyed the meal.

"The steak comes from a cow," Vicky announced.

Ellen smiled.

"That's right," Ted said.

Carolyn asked, "Do you have cows on your farm?"

"Thirty-three at one time," Jade said. "This time of year the babies are born." She remembered Ellis with his arm around her the first time she'd watched a calf being born.

"Veal," Jesse said, and looked to Ted, who ignored the boy. Benjamin never competed with Jade on any level. In fact, he hadn't competed with anybody, but moved along a path all his own.

Jade answered a few more questions about her ex-farm. She felt the parents only pretending to pay attention when she described plowing and chiseling the rubbery earth in preparation for spring planting. She could almost hear an "Oh my" at her mention of birthing the calves. The Sturgeses never asked about her family, even after she'd just finished speaking with Ellis.

"They treating you all right?" Ellis asked the last time he'd called. After she assured him that everything was fine, Ellis told her about the Easter Ping-Pong drop. Dressed as the Easter Bunny, Hank rode out in the field and dropped a couple thousand Ping-Pong balls from the basket of a cherry picker. Kids could trade the specially marked balls for prizes at local stores.

Ted overtly turned the discussion to his new book project on Internet etiquette, which he was ghostwriting for a software developer. A sentence into his story, Jade lost interest.

In a recent letter, Rexanne had explained that farmers were excluded from the prosperity of the twenties, which most of the rest of the country enjoyed. Farmers had no hard cash in a world that was putting increasing value on consumables. On the plains, they broke more sod to make the same amount of money. Rexanne had gone into a lot of boring detail about taxes on farmland increasing, pastures being overgrazed, foreign competition, overproduction. The parts of the letter that had intrigued Jade were Nancy Jane's reactions to injustice.

> Nancy Jane was the first woman—and the youngest of either sex—to organize a blockade. Milk was literally spilled. "A farmer can't drop prices and produce less to even out his take," Nancy Jane said. "Beans have to be picked."

Jade got an image of her mother in the library poring over history books. Back when Jade was in junior high, Rexanne didn't even like helping with homework. Though some of the information *was* interesting, Jade couldn't imagine an adult acting like a student when they didn't have to. Jade couldn't wait to graduate and be done with it all.

When Ted ordered a second glass of wine, Ellen raised her eyebrows at him. Jesse pointed at an elderly man at a table of five waiting for his entrée. The man was silent, unmoving, his forearms resting on the chair. "Lincoln Memorial," Jesse said.

Nancy Jane had campaigned tirelessly for Roosevelt's election. She'd seen him in person, though Rexanne didn't mention precisely where. Could it have been Paradise when her young grandmother spotted Roosevelt carried to the podium, after which he adjusted his braces and ran his hand across his hair as unselfconsciously as if he were settling into his private dressing room?

Not all the details from the story Jade was reconstructing came from Rexanne's ten-page letters. Jade remembered some details from when she'd been young, back when Rexanne told old Paradise stories instead of imaginary bedtime ones. Fantasies about giant cats and secret underground passageways never matched the excitement Rexanne expressed when talking about her own history.

Nancy Jane organized share programs during the lean years when goods and services were bartered between farmers and the community. She became involved in the Federal Emergency Relief Act, Farm Mortgage Act, later the Bankhead-Jones Farm Tenant Act, the Farm Security Administration. She preferred being off from the fields promoting and protecting them and leaving her mother to keep things up. But with Nancy Jane spending less and less time on the land, the farm floundered. When the property went into foreclosure, neighbors bought and returned it to Nancy Jane and her mother.

The people reciprocated in this way, not for all the campaigning Nancy Jane had done on their behalf, but for what they could actually see—the trees. The tall exclamations in the land reminded them that they had stood up against oblit-

eration. After the dark blizzard of dirt had swept across the
earth, filling attics until they collapsed, blowing chickens off
never to be recovered, sifting through the briefest crevice to
choke animals and babies, Nancy Jane remembered trees.
She told everyone to plant trees to hold the land in place.
She urged the government to help with planting. Native cottonwood trees were easily propagated. One had only to stick
a cutting into moistened soil to see it grow four to six feet
the first year.

Jade's body, the promise of a new child, was almost trivial
next to all her grandmother's accomplishments. What could be
so hard to say when maybe everything her grandmother said at
one time raised not only people's eyebrows but their voices?

Ted was ordering a cafe latte, double decaf with cream. The
waitress scratched her head at the double decaf part. Overtly
irked, Ted said, "Just forget it and bring me a cup of regular
coffee."

"Decaf?" the waitress asked. She was young, her blonde hair
beginning to pull loose from the ponytail holder. She looked
tired.

"What did I say?" Ted asked and the waitress left. Ellis and
his pals might belch and reach for food and talk loudly at the
table. They wouldn't dab politely at their mouths with cloth
napkins. But she didn't think they'd intentionally harass a waitress either. They could tease with a vengeance—"Lookin' good
tonight, darlin'. When we goin' out on the town?"—but she
hadn't heard Ellis or his friends be mean to a woman. Not in
public anyhow.

Ellen touched the back of her husband's hand. Carolyn wiggled in her seat, stuck her tongue out at Vicky. Ignoring his
parents' reprimands, Jesse played his Game Boy right at the ta-

ble. Deep inside, Jade felt a flutter. For a minute she couldn't hear the oddly musical notes of the toy and the background clatter of dishes. She heard only her own voice revealing her secret. And then she said it. She imagined the entire restaurant going silent, everyone peeking over menus and each other's heads to study her.

"Baby?" Ellen said so softly she made it sound foreign. Like Spanish. A word she'd never heard before.

Jade didn't realize she was nervous until she actually pulled up the parking brake outside Marilou and Peter Driscoll's stone house. She was even more anxious than she had been on taking her first plane trip. Then Ellis and Hank had dropped her off at the Omaha airport. Hank's last words had boomed, "Remember, don't inflate the life vests *inside* the cabin," and then he'd laughed. Ellis had hugged her extra hard, then backed away, turning his head quickly to the side.

Now a light breeze lifted her hair as she got out of the car and headed for the front door, which was a deep blue, startling against the gray. Tiny buds were forming in the trees. Before she reached the door, it opened. Peter Driscoll, a short dark-haired man, extended his hand and enthusiastically called, "Marilou," but she was right behind him. She had curly auburn hair and was a few inches taller than her husband.

"You must be Jade," she said gently. Everyone was smiling and seemed to be holding their breath.

As the couple showed her into their large house, overrun with decorations, collectibles, and antiques in fabric, stone, china, glass, and metal, Jade realized that she hadn't known how tall the two would be. The Driscolls were seated the first time she'd seen them at the town's annual Firemen's Roast Beef Din-

ner. Jade had accompanied Pearline to the fund-raiser solely to
check out couples who not only might want her baby, but pay
well for it.

As the crowd of people had sliced into beef, stuck forks into
mashed potatoes, and talked over one another, Jade studied couples who had no idea that they were being scrutinized as potential providers for her baby, and as more immediate benefactors
for herself. Jade ruled out the Zimmermans immediately. Judy
threw her head back in a haughty laugh at the same time that
Michael smiled at a young woman at the adjoining table. When
Jade had discounted them, Pearline became defensive. "People
maybe have all kinds of reasons for acting the way they do," she
had said and jabbed at her beef. About the Joys, Pearline said,
"Don't ignore him. He's a lawyer." But there was an occasional
expression around his mouth that Jade didn't entirely trust.
When she hadn't responded, Pearline went on, "Their name
should have some bearing." Pearline had looked up and repeated, "Joy," as if Jade was an idiot.

When people started drifting toward the dessert table, Pearline had gestured at the Blacks. They were young and very good-
looking. Jade had been ready to say, "Yes," right then, but
Pearline was concerned that the couple was too cheap. "You
know she works at the Y office three mornings a week just so
Mr. can exercise for free." Jade could have thrown Pearline's
early comment back at her—maybe the Blacks had a reason to
be stingy—but she let it go.

In the end, Jade went with Marilou. Pearline teased it was
because Jade liked her hair. But Jade had watched the woman's
eyes, too, lined at the corners, anticipation and resignation so
rolled up together you couldn't tell which was predominant. It
was the look shared by less popular girls standing on the sidelines
at school dances.

Now Jade noticed the expression again as Marilou led her to the kitchen. Peter covered his anxiety by bragging about his occupation—"hatter to the stars." The kitchen opened onto the family room, which featured one entire wall covered with head shots of different actors and personalities. Jade recognized some of the faces. There were also group photos, one in which Peter stood next to a man in a leather beret and a woman wearing a large flowered hat. The latter Peter described as one of his masterpieces.

"Peter," Marilou said softly, shaking her head as if she heard his stories of the rich and famous nightly. Her eyes and forehead were marked with fine yet noticeable wrinkles. She wore no makeup.

Jade was startled by a light touch on her shoulder as Marilou guided her back into the large kitchen. Living with the Sturgeses, Jade had almost gotten used to an absence of physical contact with adults.

Marilou was pointing out a cake she'd made, dessert she'd take to a friend's house later that night. The large chocolate cake was fashioned in the shape of the trunk of a tree, complete with a knothole, the entire surface ridged to resemble bark. Though Jade enjoyed cooking, she imagined the cake had been a tedious task. As Marilou explained, without Jade's coaxing, how she'd used different-sized loaf pans and an extra-sharp knife to approximate a tree, Jade guessed that Marilou wanted to assure her that she'd have no trouble turning mere sandwiches into special shapes—maybe smiling faces—for a child's lunch.

Jade thought of the tree Freddie had told her one of his customers had wanted painted white to match the fencing at the front of his house. Mario had told Jade that was nothing and gone on to say that an entertainment lawyer was building an immense stone house on the outskirts of town. The man had had the twenty-five oaks and beeches on his property sawed down and replaced with a string of evergreens. "They think they can do anything," Mario had said to no one in particular. "They can," Freddie replied, the remark sending the two men bickering.

What Peter and Marilou showed her next put Jade in mind of Ellis. They walked outside about two hundred feet to an outbuilding the size of a two-car garage. A birdhouse constructed by Peter stood just beyond the entrance, "Retweet" burnished into the wood. Peter explained that he was "into woodworking as a hobby."

Once inside the building, Marilou spread her arms and said, "Well, this is *my* job." Against all the walls were animal cages of different sizes. Veterinary supplies, feeds, perches, stands, and toys filled the room. Huge skylights encompassed most of the ceiling. "I call it my animalarium," Marilou said.

The building would make a nice apartment. Pearline had told her that a number of women in Blue Field and surrounding towns had residencies for animals that had been hurt or abandoned. "The ladies compete," Pearline had said, raising her eyebrows. Jade pictured a band of unnaturally thin women rushing in the direction of a roadkill or en masse pulling a bird from a cat's mouth. She couldn't imagine Nancy Jane organizing those kinds of missions.

Marilou pointed out Pammie, a fawn with a broken leg. There were injured chipmunks and homeless cats with names like Katie and Al. A large brown rabbit that Marilou called Layla hopped freely around the room. When he thought no one else could hear him, Ellis used names like "sweetie" and "cutie pie" around his ailing animals.

"Are you a vet?" Jade asked, noticing a hypodermic.

Marilou shook her head at the same time that Peter said, "She dabbles."

"All my poor little babies," Marilou said.

"She's very caring," Peter said to Jade. Marilou turned and smiled awkwardly.

Marilou bent to pick up Layla, the rabbit, and said to Jade, "You want to hold her? Go ahead." The gentle way Marilou offered the animal made Jade's eyes water. As they walked back to the house, Peter was mentioning that he got one hundred channels on TV, but he was upgrading to three hundred. Marilou said the new service was called "extreme TV," or at least that's what it sounded like. But Jade was still thinking about all the animals. Ellis's preoccupation tending unfortunate creatures was less understandable to Jade.

Jade wondered if the story Mario had told of putting in a new ceiling for a woman who loved animals had been about Marilou. "Every time you turn around there's a gewgaw of a puppy or a bird or a squirrel with a smile on its face. So Freddie's kissing this woman's ass right in front of her whole bird-watching group, which is having a snack in the living room. He's saying his dog is like a regular member of the family. You can tell the lady is pleased as shit with him. Then we go upstairs and the ladies supposedly go outside to look at her feed some maimed eagle. The lady's poodle follows us upstairs. We're at the top of the stairs and Freddie must think the coast is clear because he says, 'You know what I like about these dogs? If you ran a stick up his ass, he'd make a great mop.' Well, downstairs somebody clears their throat. It's all over."

Moving through the large rooms of the house, Marilou pointed out her decorative details as Peter trailed behind. When they reached the bedroom, Jade saw that the visit had been a carefully orchestrated progression. The three paused outside the master bedroom, the house's headquarters of intimacy. The walls were white; the bedspread and rugs were white; and filmy white see-through curtains hung at each of the three large windows.

Pearline had told Jade that the Driscolls had at least three miscarriages. One of the other bedrooms must once have been painted in pastels and prepared for a baby who never came home from the hospital. Jade wondered precisely when the toys and clothes and shower gifts had been put away, the room repainted and redecorated to resemble an ordinary guest room. The picture of them transforming the room with hope and then changing it again into something purely functional touched her. And whenever she felt this vulnerable, she involuntarily thought of Benjamin.

"Well," said Peter, clearing his throat. "Let's go downstairs and have a little talk."

Marilou brought out coffee for herself and Peter, and an herbal tea for Jade. "You don't want to be drinking caffeine," Marilou said.

"How's Ellen Sturges handling the pregnancy?" Marilou asked to Jade's surprise. Jade shrugged. Like Jade's family and farm back in Nebraska, the pregnancy was a subject that wasn't discussed, as if it might go away on its own like a mysterious rash. But ever since the announcement, Ellen's Post-it notes had turned pink. Was Ellen worried one of the neighbors would lure Jade away? Was Marilou asking because she feared Ellen would want Jade's baby? It was all too confusing. Jade wished people here would put their concerns on the table.

Peter sipped at his coffee every couple of seconds, and the rest of the time glanced around the room as if it weren't one he knew by heart, one he'd helped design. Marilou didn't touch her coffee. She coughed periodically.

"I'm not quite sure how all this is done," Peter said.

"Of course you are, Peter. Remember Sally and Fletcher?" Marilou paused. "Frank and what was her name? That blonde with all the freckles."

Peter put up his hand as if to direct the conversation elsewhere. He glanced at Jade. "We'd be honored to have your baby, Jade," he said simply. They looked at her.

She had the power to change all three of their lives. Nancy Jane had changed lots of lives for the better, but at least Jade was making a start. For a second, she entertained dragging out the decision-making. Visiting another couple or two or three to see who needed her baby most. Marilou and Peter were silently pleading, probably praying. They could give her baby good clothes and toys, no hand-me-downs or handmade outfits. Summer camp. Private schools. College. And maybe when the child was grown, it would search the country for Jade, go on TV and ask for her to come forward just to thank her in front of the entire country.

Peter cleared his throat. "We'll give you whatever you want."

Although they were rich, the Driscolls didn't resemble any of the Blue Field people Pearline had told stories about.

"I think that would be very nice." Even as she spoke, Jade knew she sounded sweet, not like herself underneath.

The Driscolls took a simultaneous breath. Then they swooped down on her, the three of them embracing in the beautiful room filled to overflowing with breakables. When they finally pulled back from her, Jade caught Marilou dabbing at the corners of her eyes. Peter squeezed his wife's hand.

"Should we draw some papers up or something?" Peter asked. Jade replied that that sounded so businesslike.

"She's right," Marilou said. "We'll just take things step-by-step."

"What does the father think about all this?" Marilou said, gesturing on the last two words.

"He doesn't know," Jade said simply and set her empty teacup in its saucer.

"We have to iron out the details," Peter said.

Why don't you make him a hat and leave it at that, Jade wanted to say.

"Jade's the mother," Marilou said.

"We'll need his signature," Peter persisted. "What does he look like?"

"Later," Marilou said succinctly.

And whose signature would they go after?

Rory's. Rory, who'd loved her in an empty bathtub, the snow-covered third base on the high school ball field, the unfinished housing complex in Paradise. In his truck where once she fell asleep and woke to his warm breath at the back of her neck. She'd momentarily thought it was summer, the window above her bed open to a gentle push of air. Rory who made her forget every other man who'd entered her. At least for ten or fifteen minutes, he reduced those images to rhythmic noises in her throat.

But there were other signatures, too, names that could be scrawled along with her own, releasing all parental rights. In December before she started seeing Rory exclusively, there'd been Mike, who hadn't even combed his hair first; Carl, who'd come between her and the cold ground, his pants lowered to just above the knees, his belt buckle marking her thigh for days; Johnny, who'd clenched her so hard she feared she'd die in the very spot her brother had; Craig, who coughed or cried or maybe spit afterward, sounding like the engine of an old truck trying to turn over; and Mr. Donnelly, pummeling her in the room that held the paperwork in quadruplicate for each of her class-mates' futures.

Jade looked up at the couple, now more scared than she was. They knew the stories of girls and women who took back their babies and their promises; young fathers who changed their wild ways and wanted to marry and make their families whole; cus-tody battles, courtrooms replacing nurseries. She couldn't picture Peter and Marilou having sex; they seemed too careful. And their bedroom was too white. She wondered if once they got the baby they'd ever touch each other again.

And before. Had they loved with passion like you saw at the movies, or comfort like Jade had with Rory, or anger like many of the other boys. She had no idea what it felt like to love someone with the sole goal of having a baby. And what hap-pened to that love when nothing came of such lovemaking?

It found its way into wood projects and animal boxes and broken bird wings.

"How do you know you'll love my baby?" Jade suddenly blurted.

Marilou came to her as spontaneously as if Jade had just fallen. She put her arm around Jade. "We love it already," she said.

Peter looked away, but a few seconds later he spoke gently. "We'll take care of all the medical bills. We'll give you money so you can go on to college. Or whatever you want to do."

"Thank you," Jade surprised herself by saying. For a minute, they felt like an extension of her family that she'd never met.

No one back home could know what she was arranging. Not even Sara. If she slipped and said something and the details got back to Rory, her secret would be out. Maybe he'd get Vivienne to help him come after her.

"What's your doctor's name, Jade?" Marilou asked as she stood up.

Jade looked at them. "I don't have a doctor."

Marilou and Peter stared at each other, then at Jade. Marilou scratched at the tip of her nose.

"We'll take care of it," Marilou said, sounding like a deal had been finalized. "Peter will make a few phone calls." Peter nodded.

Through the picture window, Jade spotted a distant oak tree that had grown into the silhouette of a girl's face. It was huge.

Jade anticipated Rexanne's voice every night before she went to bed. The call didn't come. Ellis phoned weekly, putting Vivienne on at the end of the conversation. Finally, Jade received a thick manilla envelope. Despite her frustration with Rexanne, Jade had to admit the letters comforted her, simultaneously making her forget her predicament, while inviting her into the world that she'd descended from. The house was empty when she sat on the window seat in the dining room, propping herself against a couple of plump upholstered pillows. The manilla held a hefty business-size envelope marked "Read This First" and a soft package.

Jade unfolded the pages to find more details about Nancy Jane. Rexanne reported that when her mother was forty years old she'd met a man.

Daniel was a violinist who'd come to town, set up a tent in a fallow field, and gave concerts for an entire week in August. At dusk at the end of the workday, from beneath the muslin-colored cloth of the tent, the tender violin notes carried out over the surrounding fields ripe with crops. Nancy Jane left her house each evening to experience the incongruous music, rising like a dew of champagne above the fertile earth, baked hard by months of unrelenting sun.

He had dark hair, even darker against his white shirt, long fingers, and brilliant green eyes. During any one of his concerts, Nancy Jane stopped looking at him only long enough to close her eyes and picture herself in a bath, his music, warm water enveloping her. And yet, her fantasies felt like a luxury she couldn't afford what with the farm chores and her political work on behalf of the county and state's farmers.

Jade understood that as a young woman, Nancy Jane had worked the farm alongside her mother, Ann, instead of meeting up with people her own age. And later, the men who attracted her were from town. Sometimes embarrassed to be seen with farm girls, town boys met country girls after dark, behind barns, beneath tall corn where they couldn't be identified. Nancy Jane was anything but clandestine. Although she was admired by the time she'd passed the normal age of marrying, most of the local men were intimidated by Nancy Jane's accomplishments, if not her independent nature.

After his last concert Daniel carefully placed his violin in the velvet-lined case, then stood back and rolled up his sleeves, looking at Nancy Jane all the while. *His eyes were the color of the grass beneath our feet.* Daniel asked Nancy Jane if she wanted to dance. Despite the fact that she thought it was odd, frivolous even, dancing outside where work lay all around them, he put on a Victrola. Daniel took the lead in whisking her around beneath the tent as night came on. At the end of the record, sweaty and breathless, she helped him collapse his tent and secure it in the back of his truck. Then when everything was rolled up and stashed away, he handed his violin in its case to Nancy Jane. He picked her up and carried her to the truck. Later, she figured out that he'd given her the instrument to hold so that she wouldn't flail against his advance.

She took him to a local meeting of the American Farm Workers where she moderated a discussion on the benefits and dangers of a new fertilizer. And the following week, in Omaha, Nancy Jane spoke to the regional membership about the importance of farmers voting. She talked about price supports and how the growing mechanization of family farms would affect all their futures. At the conclusion of her speech, thunderous applause followed her from the front of the room back to her seat. While the audience was applauding, Daniel asked if she would marry him.

Whether her speeches flamed the wrong people or her sex alarmed some segment of the community, more pointed now that a beau accompanied her to different agricultural and political functions, or, as Daniel protested, his being non-Protestant disturbed the wrong people, they began to be harassed. One evening when Daniel was playing Prokofiev for Nancy Jane in the living room of the farmhouse where she'd grown up, a rock shattered the window. Later, when they'd cleaned up the mess and had time to reflect, Daniel asked, "Is it because he's Russian?" Nancy Jane smiled sadly.

They married quietly and lived on at Ann's house. The two women ran the farm, Nancy Jane along with some hired help doing most of the work. Daniel gave music lessons, sometimes traveling three hours to a student's house. And he handled the financial end of running the farm.

Two days after Nancy Jane discovered she was pregnant,

a cross was burned on their property. The aftershock was blame—Nancy Jane accusing Daniel of being Catholic, Daniel yelling that Nancy Jane was too outspoken for the community. As Nancy Jane's belly grew, Daniel began to accompany her to church on Sundays, and, at his pleading, she declined invitations to speak. Daniel continued to indulge his wife long after the baby was born, maybe as compensation for making her give up the political arena that had fired her life.

As she neared the end of the letter, Jade discovered that Daniel died a year after Ann did, when Rexanne was ten years old. Nancy Jane stayed on the farm in Paradise alone with Rexanne. But after Rexanne married Ellis and Nancy Jane saw that the farm would remain intact, she left for Massachusetts where her ancestors had originally departed for the west. Rexanne said that all Nancy Jane wanted was to return to Massachusetts, maybe to do the reverse of Willa Cather, to see how satisfying it felt to reach a foreign place in America. After Nancy Jane boarded the bus, known as "the Orient Express of the Midwest," Rexanne told everyone, Jade included, that her mother had died. She destroyed every photo she could find.

Jade hadn't known her grandfather's name until now. Daniel. Nancy Jane. Nancy Jane and Daniel.

Jade didn't know what to believe. Was her mother totally insane? She'd never met her grandmother. Rexanne and Ellis seldom talked about her. The phone never rang with Nancy Jane's voice. How had there been no grandmother letters or birthday gifts?

Did Nancy Jane know that Jade and Benjamin had been born?

Did Nancy Jane once feel as out of place in Massachusetts as Jade now did in Connecticut?

A social worker in Massachusetts had called Rexanne, and soon after, Rexanne left Paradise to take care of her mother. Not simply to escape the trouble in Nebraska. And not for some man. Rexanne revealed that she was living in her mother's house.

Apparently Nancy Jane recently said that once you got past all the rigmarole it was one straight line. She talked nearly every day about the Transcontinental Railroad as if it had happened to her. Nancy Jane mentioned her own grandmother, Isabel. Rexanne told Jade she'd never known her mother wanted to cross the country in a train, visit for herself all the little spots Roosevelt campaigned in. Maybe she'd wanted to go east so that she could then turn around and cross the entire country by train, follow the history of the Transcontinental Railroad herself.

In the letter Rexanne pleaded with Jade to forgive her, to do things differently than she'd done for her own mother. But Jade thought, I'm not the one; it's you, Rexanne, who's cutting me out, who won't come see me, who won't let me even call you. Who's told me all about Nancy Jane's past, but not that she's alive.

Jade carefully folded the letter. She was more frustrated than ever. What did all this mean to her? What was true and what was embellished?

Sinking back into the pillows, Jade opened the second item in the manilla envelope. She lifted up a small piece of cloth. A dress. A baby's dress. Tiny white roses and leaves were embroidered along the neckline and down the center. Pleats narrow as yarn lined either side. Three shiny white buttons, the size of pieces of rice pressed into a circle, were sewn at the back of the neck.

"Nancy Jane made this for me," Rexanne's note said. "I wore it as a newborn, but I never put it on you. That's how mad I was at her back then when she abandoned the farm."

Never even let me see it, Jade thought. What was she supposed to do with it now?

Jade ran a bath. She slipped into the water and tried to imagine her grandfather's seductive music. Before anyone got home, Jade would reread the stories now that she knew her grandmother was alive.

6

may

My new "boyfriend" rides his bike all over New England, not little trips between here and there, but thirty hours at a stretch. His father tells him it's amazing what diverted sexual energy can do to a kid his age. Sometimes Adam gets tired of diverting it, and then he comes to me. We fool around a little, but never take things too far. Mostly I just like to talk to him. It's the only way I've really been able to get inside Connecticut since I've been here, not counting Pearline, who's a whole different story.

Though there's all kinds of reports on male hormones, I don't think Adam rides because he's sexually frustrated. I think he takes off down an empty road at top speed because he's angry. Adam is Lauren Nash's nephew, and he complains about her as much as he does his parents, says he doesn't see how they and their friends are so much different from drug addicts. "They're looking for the quick fix that comes from acquiring material things. The only difference is that buying stuff isn't illegal."

I still haven't met Lauren, so I can't tell how tough he's being. Though if what Pearline says is true, he's probably got a point.

When Adam's riding, he can't stand the dog breaking his focus. So he bought this electronic collar gizmo for his dog, which keeps it from barking. Adam's going to Yale in the fall. He's got every CD that was ever made. I mean, he's not taking any vow of poverty to prove his argument.

And yet, I like him. I enjoy sitting with him and listening to music. He's got dark thick hair—maybe like my grandfather Daniel's—that dips into his brown eyes. I talk to him almost like I used to with Sara, leaving out all the makeup and clothing parts, which she could really go on about. He's the kind of guy I think Benjamin would have liked.

Sometimes we discuss the baby. I don't think there's a thing wrong with what I'm doing. But don't ask him. He'll tease that I'm on my way to eternal hot weather, the likes of which Florida has never seen.

We both agree that family values suck. The perfect little four-person unit that doesn't want its mother to work outside the house, boys to be gay, girls to think about boys until they know how to trap them into a marriage, or anyone to take away their guns. They might have to shoot their TV out if there's too much violence on it.

Sara thinks family values may have been what killed my brother. That's because I haven't told her all about me. I haven't told anyone. And I haven't told Adam about Benjamin yet. I can't take the chance of crying in front of him.

Ellis would go crazy if he knew how many Jews I talk to now. He says Jews took away his farm, which Adam says is total bullshit. Probably the thing I like best about Adam is how he makes me think. Like, for instance, he shows me how the lies about Jew bankers are nothing new. He might even be better at history than Rexanne.

If Adam were me, he'd have an abortion. But he's not me. And he's rich.

The weird thing is, he likes that I'm pregnant. He says around here it's like constantly thumbing your nose. I could tell his parents were alarmed when he introduced me. His father ran his hand back and forth along one side of the kitchen door frame, and his mother cleaned her glasses the entire time he told them who I was and who

I work for, which, in Connecticut, are pretty much the same thing if you're in the service industries.

I'm going to miss him when the Sturgeses take me with them to Maine next month. Adam says he'll ride his bike up, but considering the trip is a good eight hours by car, I don't think I'll see him much.

I won't see Juan and Freddie and Mario either. They'll be here looking after the house, taking Ellen's calls, laughing behind her back.

Juan's never said anything, but I know from the way he lowers his eyes that he wants to go out with me. Despite Freddie's commentary, Juan knows enough English to make a move, but it's not surprising that he doesn't. Lauren Nash has him on such a short leash, he practically has to ask her permission to go to the bathroom—which, by the way, is a toilet and slop sink in the middle of the basement of her B&B. No walls. No door. Juan and five other Mexicans live in one room smaller than Marilou's "animalarium." Lauren buys their food and booze, deducts it from their wages. Plus she tacks on a "delivery charge," at least according to Pearline. Lauren lends Juan to Freddie when groundwork or cleaning or repairs at her business slack off. Probably she gets most of the eight dollars an hour Freddie pays Juan. Juan with his darkest eyes and strong forearms.

I know why Whoopi Goldberg and Cher and all those other movie stars take working men as lovers. Those men use their hands. They could work on you for hours without tiring or even having to change positions. They hone you to a polished piece of wood, a focused point of desire, to become just your body so you forget every thought and problem, and then you lose your body, too, become liquid, rising and falling like a wave, sometimes gentle, sometimes crashing. They almost want to make something of you. Take pride in how you come out, I guess. That would be my guess.

I could talk about even this with Adam, except that I wouldn't want to get him started into trying to prove something.

Sometimes I have this fantasy. If things were way different, if I'd

known them both before, which one would I want to be my baby's
father—the one that makes me feel fine or the one that makes me
think I am fine?

"Oh, God," Peter said. "It's a little. . . ."

Marilou interrupted him. "It's such a cute little head," she said. Her voice was soft, excited. She put her hand on Jade's wrist.

Besides admiring the red hair and generally feeling sorry for her, Jade approved of Marilou's background. Her father had been in the hardware business; she'd attended public schools; she'd worked as a waitress when she was going to college. When Marilou had revealed these details on the third meeting with Jade, the sentences came out as a confession. Pearline had said Marilou was trying to explain that she didn't fit any more comfortably in the wealthy community than Jade did.

Jade lay on her back, her tummy smeared with slimy jelly. She felt scrutinized the way animals must in a zoo, except that the Driscolls were focusing on a monitor just to the side of her rather than staring directly at her face.

"Legs. Feet. Is that a hand?" Peter asked the technician. He simultaneously ran his own hand through his hair, then turned to Marilou. There was a long silence.

"Wow," said Marilou.

Jade didn't understand why the Driscolls were making such a big deal of the ultrasound. Jade had seen plenty of fetus shots on TV, and they all looked more or less the same. The technician glanced at Jade. She had black hair, even blacker than Peter's; she was young and efficient.

Jade avoided looking at the monitor. She didn't want to know the sex of the baby or see its tiny body parts. She didn't want to know about the pre-baby sucking its thumb like Sara's sister had once witnessed of *her* own baby. Those details were for the Driscolls. They, after all, would be the ones who'd be doing the feeding, the waking up in the middle of the night, the burping, and diaper changing. All Jade wanted was assurance that she wasn't having the twins she'd dreamed about two weeks ago.

Jade wondered if anyone had ever noticed an unborn baby with its hand outstretched, demanding right up front—food, protection, money. Growing up with the Driscolls in a house much nicer than the Nebraska farmhouse, it would never have to beg for money for a field trip and then feel bad when a stack of bills arrived in the mail. She just hoped Peter didn't make the child so many hats that the other kids laughed.

When the show was over, the technician directed the Driscolls back toward the waiting room. Jade asked, "Don't you get tired of looking at pregnant women all day?"

The woman, whose name tag said Doris, answered, "It's better than the hearts."

"Hearts?"

"Sure. They use ultrasound for lots of things besides babies." She sighed and said, "It's a job." With the crinkly white paper, Jade helped wipe the jelly off her middle.

"Take your time," Doris said when Jade slid off the table and reached to retrieve her shirt.

As she brushed her hair out and straightened her clothes, slid into her shoes, Jade thought not of the Driscolls, but the Sturgeses. While Marilou and Peter had become more animated around Jade, and more possessive of her, the Sturgeses had grown increasingly withdrawn. With Jade's plan out in the open, Ellen was more quiet than ever. Ted seldom ate dinner with the family these days, often staying in town to dine with colleagues or, when he was at home, carrying a plate to his office.

Last week, Ellen announced they'd be taking their annual Maine vacation earlier this year—right after Jesse finished school—and staying longer than usual. Jade's responsibilities would remain the same; she'd simply take care of the children in a different New England state. Jade wondered if Ellen didn't want to keep her away from the Driscolls the same way her own mother had tried to break up a friendship with a troublemaking schoolmate back when Jade was in fifth grade. Or the way Ann must have tried to protect Nancy Jane from hurt by disapproving of city people.

The Sturges children didn't appear to notice any change in Jade. When Jesse wasn't showing off for a friend or absorbed in a new computer game, he asked her not about the baby but about where she'd come from. A couple of times the twins had cozied in beside their brother to hear stories of Jade's farm. When Carolyn got caught up in the story, she sucked her thumb loudly until Jesse called her a baby.

Jade described details that Ellis had once imparted to her—how, at three weeks, the average pig weighs twelve pounds, the mother four hundred. "Cool," said Jesse. She'd told them that the superior teats were the ones at the front and the dominant males got those. Rolling on the floor laughing, Jesse had gotten the twins giggling. Jade told about listening to the six o'clock farm report every morning, dependable as sunrise. She described driving to dump corn, which the grain companies would then purchase. Jade relayed an incident of five years earlier: after she'd left the window in Ellis's truck open overnight, it filled with flies by the next morning. She'd thought Ellis would punish her, but instead acted as amazed by the phenomenon as she'd been.

The three sat mesmerized as if she were reading from a favorite storybook. They always asked questions—which animal smells worst—and she always answered directly, "Cows are cleaner than hogs, but hogs bring in more money."

"Here comes the wild turkey," she'd call and then chase them into bed. Jade momentarily wondered if Nancy Jane had run into many wild turkeys in her day.

"Oh, excuse me," Doris said, opening the door. "I said take your time, not move in."

"I just got daydreaming," Jade explained as she squeezed past her and out the door.

"I do plenty of that myself," Doris said. "About Powerball," she added.

"Are you OK?" Marilou asked as soon as Jade entered the reception room.

"Fine," Jade said.

"Well, then. I thought we might head over to the mall. Maybe you could pick out a few new outfits." Marilou looked Jade up and down. "You won't be fitting into those much longer."

On the drive to the acreage of stores and parking, Jade noticed how quickly some of the trees had gone green. The day before had been rainy, and now the greenery was everywhere. Some trees bloomed white; others were covered with deep pink blooms. She could smell lilac. In July in Nebraska, some days she thought she could hear the corn grow, it ripened so quickly in midsummer.

Peter and Marilou talked about high chairs, baby swings, bassinets, strollers, and cribs. Their enthusiasm was endearing, but Jade soon grew bored. Neither of them said anything about using someone else's baby equipment, handing down baby clothes, as was customary in Paradise.

Jade asked if Marilou had grown up with lots of pets. "No. In fact, both my parents were allergic. I never had a real pet until I met Peter." She quickly added, "I don't mean it like that," and blushed. She explained that they bought a kitten the first month they were married.

Marilou said that as a child she was always bringing home hurt animals. "My parents let me keep them just until they were better. Then I had to find homes for them. The real challenge was distracting my brother Larry from doing experiments on them." She told Jade about her latest ward, an opossum whose tail needed soaking in boric acid twice a day.

"The opossum is the stupidest animal in North America," Peter said.

Soon the Driscolls' dialogue became background buzz, as Jade thought back to Ann, the new character in her mother's letters—Jade's great-grandmother.

Ann was born a year after the Civil War ended. She was such a quiet, peaceful baby, Isabel took her as a sign of the times to come. *"I was an omen,"* Ann wrote in her diary. *"I became a memento, too."* She meant she was a keepsake from her mother's love.

Ann grew up in a bawdy house in town. When Isabel's husband Frank died in the war, Isabel supported herself with Bel's, originally intended as a simple inn when the Transcontinental Railroad was being built. But when the railroad workers wanted more than a good night's sleep in a clean bed, Isabel diversified.

Ann's childhood was surrounded by the scents of perfume and whiskey and dust; the clinking of jewelry at wrists; the thunk of boots hitting the floor, the squealing of bedsprings. The women of the house doted on Ann, but she stayed away from the men; they made her mother and her friends scream. For money, for pretended pleasure, for pure frustration. Ann stole from the prostitutes, the patrons, and eventually her own mother. Supplementing this money with her salary at a grocery store on Main Street, she bought a horse and some cattle and moved back to the family farm abandoned years earlier. The original house, with its front door open like a gaping mouth, Ann made her home. At first, she'd rented the land that had not been farmed since the grasshopper devastation. She rode through goldenrod, meadowlark song. Though repelled by men, she dressed as a man herself, looking remarkably like one of the drovers when she checked the plains to be sure no one had moved fence. Well out of sight of the railroad tracks, she worked the land and vowed never to get married.

There was so much land. No fences or trees, no rooms or ceilings, just land that seemed to stretch into eternity. She believed different soils had histories. Prairie soils were richer than forest ones because there were no trees to draw the nutrients out. The darkest soils were most fertile. *In places, sunflowers were the closest thing to trees.* The raggy grass moved like the sea she'd never seen.

Ann covered herself with buffalo skin instead of a man's body to stay warm in winter. She spent evenings on a bench behind her stove logging the day's events. In another book she wrote her mother's story. Her kitchen was in the basement of the sod house, plaster laid directly on dirt walls.

Jade wondered if Benjamin had inherited his love of the land from Ann. It was either that or Ellis telling him repeatedly, "Boy, you best respect what's right below your feet." She'd have to discuss this with Rexanne. Although Rexanne had included her phone number in the last letter, Jade decided to wait it out. She didn't want her mother to think she was desperate. Besides, Jade was more interested in talking to Nancy Jane these days. And Jade sympathized that Nancy Jane worked so hard for the farm that was now lost anyway.

Rexanne had found nothing in Ann's own handwriting to corroborate this tale, but she didn't discount it either.

Ann never slept with a man except for Frank James of the James Gang, who rode onto her land one afternoon and had his way with her. She was well over forty at the time, and supposedly never saw him or any other man again. When Nancy Jane eventually asked about her father, Ann said simply, "You didn't have one."

Ann died working in the garden she'd first planted the summer she was able to buy back the land the ancestors no longer farmed. She grew more than fifty kinds of wildflowers.

Lately Jade had been dreaming about her grandmother though she didn't even know what she looked like.

"You did." Marilou's voice broke into Jade's reverie.

"I did not," Peter replied. "I met him. That I'll admit. But I never did any work for him."

"Jade, you'll have to come over to the house next month when he's here."

Jade didn't know which star they were talking about now. She fantasized herself as Ann telling her mother that she was going back to live on the family farm. She blurted out, "I have to go to Maine next month with the Sturgeses."

Marilou looked at Peter. Peter took his eyes off the road and turned to his wife. A car honked behind them, and Peter immediately applied the brakes.

"Are you sure it's next month they're going and not July?" Marilou asked. Her hair looked particularly red and shiny in the sunlight. "The Sturgeses always spend July in Maine."

"This year they're going for three months," Jade answered.

"Three months?" Peter and Marilou said simultaneously.

In the long silence that followed, Jade watched trees and telephone poles flipping by.

"Jade, do you want to stay with us for the summer?" Marilou asked. Jade saw herself on a cot in the animalarium, one more wounded creature needing special attention before it was reintroduced into the world. Some of Marilou's wards had never been released.

"Who will take care of the children?" Jade asked.

"Maybe they could take care of their own children for once," Marilou snapped. Marilou's reaction made Jade think of what Pearline had revealed—there was an all-out war between career women with babies in day care and the stay-at-home moms. The stay-at-homes were self-righteous in their lifestyle, almost as rabid as Vivienne's right-to-lifers.

When Peter said, "Marilou," it came out in a croon.

In the maternity shop at the mall, Jade self-consciously whipped through the racks of dresses. There were plenty of bold colors and patterns that brought attention to the pregnancy. Threw it right in everyone's face, as Adam would say. Finally, Marilou suggested Jade stay in the dressing room and she'd bring dresses to her. Jade stripped down to her underwear, then slid the oversized clothing along her body.

"Let's see, let's see," Marilou called from outside the dressing room. Marilou tucked a piece of hair behind Jade's ear. "That's just adorable," Marilou said with longing. Meanwhile, Peter was holding up a hat and calling it "crap," as he pointed out the poor design and stitching.

If Jade had grown up in Connecticut with parents like the Driscolls, maybe she'd be used to selecting and discarding solely on the basis of whether or not some garment pleased you, not what it cost. In a Blue Field gallery she'd gone to with Ellen, there were bizarre bracelets made of dice and crucifixes, a martini glass with its base in the shape of an armadillo. Jade didn't know what people did with those kinds of items other than display them. Nancy Jane and Ann never had such impractical luxuries.

Jade felt she'd tried on a hundred dresses, rejecting them all for one reason or another. Suddenly, pulling a pale pink jumper over her head, she felt a kick. Not a flutter, but a decisive movement in the midst of a sea of indecision. Without thinking, she almost called out to Marilou. Jade took a deep breath, leaned against the dressing room wall, and held the moment all to herself. A kick. Definitely a kick. Most of the time she thought about the baby, it felt like it was in her head. But right now the baby was completely in her body.

"I'll take this one," she said, her selection based solely on wanting to be done with all the trying on.

"That's it? You only want one?" Marilou asked, surprised. Jade could hear Sara's voice, "Go for it, dummy. Take them for everything they'll hand over."

"Marilou," Peter pleaded. He looked tired and older than usual, his tirade against the store-brand hats exhausting him.

Marilou helped Jade unbutton the jumper. "I can do it," Jade said sharply. Sometimes it felt like Marilou owned her, another collectible to be dusted, admired, fussed over, and displayed. The Driscolls could make her way more claustrophobic than Ellis and Vivienne ever had.

On the calendar in the Driscoll's kitchen, all the doctor appointments and meetings with Jade were highlighted and September 15, the estimated date of delivery, circled three times in red. With Jade's sketchy, half-remembered dates, she wasn't sure August or October weren't just as likely.

On the way out to the car, Peter whispered to Jade, "Do you know how much I love that woman?" Marilou strode ahead of them with the package. Ellis had never made such a comment to Jade, and now she wondered if he still loved Rexanne.

"How much?" Jade asked, but Peter just shook his head. Jade thought it odd that he'd blurt out such an intimate detail. But the last two times she'd seen him, he appeared to go to a lot of trouble proving himself more sensitive than other Connecticut husbands. What bothered Jade was that he didn't simply clear the dishes, but announced the fact that he was doing it. Jade remembered the boys from high school who did the most bragging on their sexual prowess. Usually, they were the ones who were still virgins.

Jade drove with Jesse in the passenger seat. The way the sleeves of his Little League outfit stood out from his slender arms made her think of tiny lamp shades. His hair was sharply parted, and he held a bag filled with treats and a juice box, which Ellen had insisted on packing.

Kids got so much attention in Connecticut it was disgusting. To obtain what they wanted even three-year-olds learned to play their parents like musical instruments. Just before she left the house, Jade had spotted a brochure of adult education classes. "Raising the Exuberant Child." "Parents Are Teachers, Too." Jade had read the course description for one called, " 'No!' If this has become the number one word in your vocabulary, it's time to rethink the discipline issue. Come discuss this growing concern of parents before you pull your hair out." Jade couldn't imagine paying for those courses, but the parents produced their course registration dollars as nonchalantly as when grocery shopping.

Mothers could be so pathetic. Giving everything to a child who continued to take until the woman became small and frail enough to blow away. Jade had plenty of differences with Rexanne, but she'd never called her an idiot in public the way kids around here sometimes addressed their parents.

When Jade tried intriguing Jesse with the farm in Paradise, she could sense that he was concentrating on something else entirely. For those brief moments when he blocked out the provocative images of waving grasses and animal sounds, he reminded her of Benjamin. So focused on something beyond what lay right before him, her brother had appeared transfixed. She had loved his face at those times, intent on what she couldn't share, and yet, at the same time, she'd felt excluded, even if his preoccupation lasted only as long as a sneeze.

"Well, Jesse, here you are." As she pulled into the parking lot, she reminded him that Ted would be over in an hour when the game officially began.

"Later," Jesse said simply. Nothing like Benjamin. At first Jade had dismissed Jesse's aloofness as an inability to accept anyone else into the family. And later, she'd thought the announcement of her pregnancy that had made Ellen and Ted go numb, had merely rubbed off on their son. Now she saw that Jesse's remove was probably part of his personality that would become more and more pronounced as he grew up. What would she do with a child of her own who completely dismissed her?

Jade drove fast along the narrow tree-lined back roads on her way to pick up Pearline. Their classmate Tina had invited them to a barbecue north of Danbury. Pearline was waiting outside of her employer's Bed and Bottle. Wearing a large straw hat and brightly flowered red dress, Pearline looked out of place in the neighborhood, whose Main Street didn't permit shop owners to use a single color on their store signs. "Black and white only" was the ordinance in Blue Field's commercial district.

"Wow," Jade said as she leaned to open the door for Pearline.

"Wow me or wow the place where I work?" Pearline asked.

"Both," Jade said, though she was focusing on the yellow house intricately trimmed in white, the flower boxes at the front windows. "Pretty nice."

"Should be for what folks pay to spend one night," Pearline answered. She wore a strong gardenia-like perfume.

"Don't tell me," Jade said absently. Driving off, she spotted two Mercedes parked in the back.

"OK," said Pearline. "But I will tell you, you could probably buy a nice color television set for what it costs one night back there."

"You already have a TV, don't you?" Jade asked.

Pearline shrugged. "I'm just saying," she said. Pearline went on about Lauren's temper and a visitor's request that Pearline walk her dog three times a day.

"He was an *old* dog," she said emphatically and gestured to show how she had to lift his back legs up step-by-step to get him back to the room.

"You know what she said before I left?"

"Who?" Jade asked.

"Miss Lauren," Pearline said. "She said, 'What's that black spot on the ceiling?' And I said, 'But that's a fly.' And she said, 'Well, get it *off!*'" Pearline shook her head as Jade laughed.

When Pearline started mentioning names of people Jade didn't know, mostly relatives in Brooklyn, Jade drifted. If she owned Lauren Nash's business, she'd expand what was probably a small kitchen, convert the whole first floor into a restaurant where she'd make different specialties every night. Sara could play the piano. But the last time Jade had called, Sara talked almost continuously about the prom and what she'd be wearing. She didn't have any news about Rory.

"Pearline, I was thinking when I get my money from Marilou I might start the hotel management courses."

"Keep your mind on the baby. Least until it's born," was Pearline's advice.

"I know about that. But, I've got to make a plan." All her ancestors had had big plans.

Pearline ignored Jade and talked about the surveillance camera that many people used to monitor baby-sitters in their homes. "I wonder if Marilou has one for the animalarium," Jade said.

Pearline raised her eyebrows and changed the subject. "Juan's been asking for you," she said suddenly.

"Has not," Jade said, though she couldn't hold back a smile.

"Well, not exactly *asking*. But I can tell," she said.

"Just give me that jerk chicken recipe," Jade said.

"And what nice thing you do for me?" Pearline asked. She wore rust-colored lipstick.

When Jade didn't answer immediately, Pearline said, "Where's your book?" Jade took her right hand off the steering wheel and reached behind her.

"Don't be hittin' any bumps if you want to be able to read this," Pearline said. Jade pulled the steering wheel hard to the right, then immediately straightened it. She laughed.

Pearline said, "Lord alive, girl. What are you gettin' so riled up about? Juan?"

Tina lived in a condo with her sister, who was throwing the party in honor of Tina's earning her GED. About fifteen people crowded into the small patio area where a Weber grill was smoking. When Jade heard "Hey Jude," she got a twinge. Ellis had belted out that song in the new combine when Jade was a girl.

Within ten minutes after Jade and Pearline arrived, the crowd had doubled and spread toward the property's treed boundary, and the music had turned to Metallica. Tina finally noticed Jade, and as she came closer Jade realized the print on her friend's T-shirt wasn't flowers but handprints. Tina squealed, then hugged her and Pearline together. Tina had unkempt blonde hair that was almost white, a great body, and she always wore high heels. Jade teased Tina that except for not having the puffy lips, she could be mistaken for an actress on *Baywatch*. The heels didn't really go on the beach either, Jade admitted.

Jade and Pearline were the only guests from Tina's GED class. A small contingency of older women in pastel shorts and print tops might have been relatives. At least six other people had arrived on motorcycles. For sure, Ellis and Vivienne would have wanted to give Jade a graduation party.

"Belly up," someone called and offered Jade a beer. He didn't know.

No one could tell she was pregnant. No one but Pearline. The others were probably as oblivious as Tina.

"Great, thanks," she said despite Pearline's *tsking* behind her. In the end, Jade passed the beer to Pearline rather than drinking it herself.

"You think you're hot shit don't you, babe?" one of the motorcycle guys said to Tina. "You with your diploma." He was laughing as he put his arm around Jade's classmate.

"Bite me," Tina replied, and drew herself another beer. The group of pastel-dressed women had pulled into a tight protective knot.

Another biker Jade had heard someone refer to as "Moose" had a swollen stomach covered by a tight T-shirt that said,

"Take me drunk. I'm home." As he approached Tina he called, "Well, look at the horns on you." Tina just grinned and shook her head. To Jade the comment sounded like something one of Ellis's pals would have uttered, not someone from Connecticut. For sure, the bikers would have scared Benjamin. Would they have hurt him, too?

In the bright afternoon with the scent of smokey barbecuing meat puffing into the air, Jade knew she'd become more interested in herself lately than in other people's stories. She guessed it had something to do with Rexanne's detailing their history. Lots of Jade's ancestors didn't fit in any better than she did herself. Jade was even intrigued by her own conception. Would Rexanne ever tell her that story? Maybe her new curiosity had something to do with the pregnancy. These days *she* felt like a baby, contemplating everything that touched her. This new interest in her ancestors almost felt like a chemical reaction. Maybe it all had to do with hormones. Pearline was constantly advising Jade that hormones were to blame for moods and cravings.

"Well who's this?" Pearline asked and whistled softly. The tone of her voice brought Jade back to the present moment. Adam stood off to the side, scanning the crowd.

"What's he doing here?" Jade said, though she was glad to see him. He didn't fit with any group of guests at the party. Blue Field, Jade decided, was exclusive even in Connecticut.

"How would I know?" Pearline said softly. "Just because I work for his aunt."

"How come you're always wanting to fix me up with somebody when I'm already in trouble?" Jade asked.

Pearline winked and said, "Maybe because you *are* in trouble."

"Hey," Adam said as he approached, then, "I'll be right back."

When he returned, he had a juice for Jade and another beer for Pearline, but Pearline had already ambled over toward Tina.

"Guess I'll have to have them both," Adam said. Jade had never seen him drink two beers in a row.

Adam seemed to be from a foreign country. He had more control than any of the boys she'd known in Paradise. The guys in her hometown just wanted to get with women whenever they could. And when they weren't with women, they were drinking. Drinking and laughing about women.

One night a group of kids from Paradise had driven in four cars to a country club where they'd broken into the pool. Everyone had stripped off their clothes, underwear included, and lowered themselves into the water. Jade was one of five girls idling in the deep end of the pool in the darkness as the boys laughed and circled them pretending to be sharks. If Adam were with them, Jade imagined he'd swim up casually and start talking as if they were at a cocktail party. None of that goofy whooping and splashing.

"I haven't seen you in a while," Jade said.

"I was in Virginia. It was a beautiful trip, but tough, too." He took a swig of one of the beers. "They're all tough in one way or another." He described cherry trees blossoming against the pale blue sky. His spotter had driven behind in a van, where Adam slept for a few hours at a time. He was in training for a cross-country race that he hoped to qualify for.

"How are you feeling?" he asked.

"Probably better than you are," she answered. The training sounded grueling when Adam described the pain in his legs and arms, the exhaustion he had to get past, the way he had to push himself beyond what he thought he could bear. Ellis had once worked at least as hard on the farm.

"The Driscolls took me shopping for clothes," she said.

"Clothes?"

"You know. *Big* clothes."

"Oh, God," he said and raised his eyebrows sympathetically. "The Driscolls."

She sensed he wanted to add a detail, suggest something about the Driscolls. Everybody in Blue Field had inside information on someone else, like your family knowing the embarrassing moments of your childhood.

"Your date's here," Adam said, indicating the biker with the huge, T-shirt-covered stomach.

How could her great-grandmother not like boys the whole time she was growing up? Adam was cute and funny. Of course, there were the other kind of boys, like the ones who'd harassed Benjamin. But to deprive oneself of all of them was crazy.

Tina's sister came out of the house screaming that one of the cats had licked away some letters from the cake she'd made. "It says 'happy uation.'"

"Sounds sexual," Adam said.

Jade slapped him lightly on the arm. He snatched her hand and held it.

"What do you say we blow this joint?"

"What about Pearline?"

"Maybe she'll pick somebody up."

Jade slapped him again, then reminded him that Pearline was married, even had grandchildren though she wasn't fifty. Adam just shrugged his shoulders at Jade.

After she'd told Pearline she was leaving, Jade offered to secure Adam's bicycle on the car, but he insisted on riding it with her following like a spotter. It felt like years ago that she had gone on dates with Rory, stopping at the D.Q. for food. She could use a shake now.

By the time they reached his house, Adam was sweaty and

talking what Jade called his bicycle talk. The dog, Bonedaddy, stood back wagging his tail, not barking, as Jade listened politely to Adam's goals and distance records.

"Where would you go if you could bike anywhere in the world?" Jade asked.

"Mexico," he replied immediately. "I'd drive down the Baja and give all my parents' money away before I reached the bottom."

And where would that leave *you*? Jade could have asked.

Jade wondered if Juan was from the Baja or from mainland Mexico.

Adam left Jade in the living room of the huge house while he went off to shower. The side window looked onto an enormous swimming pool set in the midst of different deck levels and flower boxes. A garden just beyond was meticulously laid out with railroad ties marking off the sections for different vegetables, and a thick layer of mulch protecting the pampered plants from stray weeds. Everything in Connecticut was handled more carefully than in the Midwest.

Jade opened one of Adam's energy bars on the table nearest her. Though it was thick and chalky, she was so hungry she wolfed it.

"That was fast," she said to Adam, who stood before her, his hair wet and combed straight back, his knees and legs and forearms for sure still damp.

"What can I get you besides the energy bar?"

"A new life," she answered.

"Your life's just fine," he said.

"That's easy for you to say."

"Actually it's not." He put his arm around her. "When are you going to Maine?"

"Two weeks." Before revealing the Driscolls' offer, she wanted to make up her own mind.

"I'll be there every other weekend," he said. "It'll be great training." He sounded as if he were trying to convince himself rather than her.

"Were you an 'exuberant' child?" Jade asked, remembering the parenting course.

He just smiled at her. That wide genuine smile. Those perfectly aligned teeth.

All night Jade thought about Maine—whether she should go with the Sturgeses or disrupt their plans by remaining in Blue Field with the Driscolls. If she told Ellen and Ted she didn't want to spend the summer in their northern cottage, maybe they'd tell her they didn't need her anymore. And maybe that didn't even matter. She could stay with the Driscolls until the baby was born, collect her money, and leave the entire Connecticut world behind.

Vivienne told Jade that her cousin Robert had once sent her a Christmas card from Maine. The snowy scene featured a pair of moose. Ellis advised Jade to be careful around the water if she did decide to spend the summer on the Maine coast.

Jade played out different scenarios. Sometimes they included Adam and Juan. Her imaginary conversations drifted into dreams. Once she woke right after confiding in the Driscolls' rabbit, Layla, that she wanted to return to Paradise and talk the decision over with Sara.

The morning was dark green and wet as she drove toward the Driscolls'. The lacy trees intermittently formed a canopy that sunlight couldn't penetrate. At one point in the drive, Jade was racing toward a castle where she would be imprisoned until she gave over her firstborn child. Jade would become part of a fairy tale whispered to children before they fell asleep. People would think simultaneously of her name and motherhood relinquished. Some would consider her a hero, others a victim, and maybe a few a monster.

As was usual on her visits here, the boldly colored door opened before Jade could knock. Peter bent at the waist and, at the same time, made a sweeping gesture of gallant welcome. He stood aside as she walked into the foyer.

If the Driscolls had adopted *her*—and Benjamin—how much fun she would have had racing through the spacious rooms with her brother, playing instead of trudging off to do farm chores. What she could have prepared in the modern kitchen outfitted with every appliance and cooking gadget ever invented. She and Benjamin could have snuck into the massive attic for a secret meeting. And right now she might be thinking about college, maybe Vassar or Yale, instead of breathing lessons. But she couldn't imagine life without Ellis and Rexanne.

If everything were different, maybe Benjamin would still be alive.

Peter explained that Marilou had gone on an emergency call in Brewster, where three dogs had apparently crossed the highway together, two of them struck by cars. Marilou had a beeper for such emergencies and a Range Rover with a flashing blue light.

Although she knew the situation was totally different, Jade couldn't help but be reminded of Vivienne's "on-call weekends," which usually required canceling plans to participate in some rescue mission. On Ellis's birthday, Jade and Vivienne had just set out a special turkey dinner when the phone rang. Wearing a frilly yellow party dress, Vivienne had paced in the kitchen with the receiver tucked between her chin and shoulder, simultaneously stirring gravy and adjusting the heat on the stove.

By the time Vivienne hung up the phone, she was visibly torn between serving Ellis his dinner and driving off to Omaha to talk a confused woman into becoming a mother. Because the operators answering the hot line hadn't been able to convince the young woman caller not to have an abortion, "personal intervention" was required. Jade hadn't thought Vivienne needed to leave right then, but Vivienne argued that the prime time to win someone to your cause was in the heat of the decision-making process. "Tomorrow could be too late," Vivienne had said softly. "Tomorrow some feminist might have gotten to her." Vivienne said the word "feminist" as if it tasted bad coming out of her mouth. She heaped Ellis's plate with the hot food. "Two hours from now could be too late."

"What about two minutes?" Jade countered. "Maybe it's already over. Forget about it. Let's eat."

In the end, Vivienne had left, not even stealing a taste of her dinner. When she and her father were alone, Jade had been surprised that Ellis hadn't become perturbed, but said, "Isn't she great?"

Marilou's missions were visible—an animal struck by a car; an abandoned litter of cats; a deer with an arrow protruding from its flank.

"So, how are we feeling today?" Peter asked as he directed Jade into the living room.

"Good," Jade said. The Driscolls used the "we" word so frequently these days that it made Jade jittery.

When Peter went into the kitchen to pour her a glass of seltzer, Jade said, "Do you have any idea when Marilou's getting back?"

"Sorry, I don't," he called. His voice was huge in the big room.

"Do you know where the dresses are?" Peter had called Jade and asked her to come by because Marilou had bought Jade a couple more outfits to try on.

"We'll get to that in a minute," he said, placing the tall glass on the end table nearest her. A thick lime slice bobbed on the top of the fizzy drink.

He sat so close to her that when he lifted his beer to take a sip, she could smell it. She studied his face. He was older than Ellis, but she couldn't pinpoint his age.

"As long as we've got this time together, I thought you could tell me a little about the baby's father."

As Jade took in a quick breath, Peter lifted both hands in a gesture of surrender. "We just don't want any unexpected problems down the road," he explained.

"There won't be any," Jade said simply. "He doesn't know." She lowered her eyes. No one would know as long as Sara and Rexanne didn't reveal the secret. And at this point, Sara appeared to have forgotten about Jade's condition; the girl was so obsessed with the prom she didn't have space in her imagination to think about anything else.

"He doesn't know?" Peter asked, a look of incredulity spreading across his face.

Instead of sympathizing, of examining how a man desperate to be a father must feel if his own lover hadn't told him what he most wanted to hear, Jade said simply, "Can we drop it?" She came across more irritated than she actually felt.

"Do you want to watch a little TV?" Peter asked.

"No," she said softly. Why didn't Rory know? Was she afraid not of him taking over her life by insisting on marriage, but of him rejecting her completely?

"How tall was he?" Peter spoke softly, yet insistently. The tension in the air was almost visible.

"Listen, just show me where the dresses are, OK? I've got to get back before the twins come home."

"Taller than me?" Peter seemed to be holding his breath. His persistence frightened her.

For a minute, they all blurred into one face, one body—all the boys and Mr. Donnelly and even Rory. But no one facial feature or expression, no distinctive hairstyle or muscle group or even an identifiable piece of clothing came into focus. There was only a vague face, a male presence that imposed itself, like weather, to determine her mood, her plans for the day.

"Did he have hair like mine?" Peter was asking.

Suddenly she heard a plane, though far overhead, thunderous in its passing. The noise blended with her emotions to make her panic.

He bent even closer to her. "Jade," he said, "you are a beautiful pregnant woman."

That's it. Jade wasn't sure she'd thought that remark or if she'd actually spoken it. "I'd better go."

"Jade, I want the baby to know I love it before it's born."

"Mr. Driscoll, please," she said, standing up.

"Sometimes I feel like *you're* my wife." He put his arm around her and pulled her into his chest. Jade was surprised at his strength. She smelled a mixture of aftershave and something like glue, the combination making her think of money.

"Jade," he breathed her name into her hair.

She jerked back from him and ran to the front door.

"Come back," he called.

She tugged at the door handle, twisted a lock, then pulled it free and hurried to her car.

She was breathing hard and heading down the driveway when she glanced in her rearview. Peter was behind her.

She stepped hard on the gas and the car lurched forward.

Though Peter honked, she ignored him. Her hands shook on the steering wheel; she squeezed to steady them. As the trees and buildings flashed by, she breathed deeply. Then she couldn't see because she was crying. On approaching town she slowed a little, but noticed none of the buildings specifically. At Oak Street, she ran a red, then made a hard right and lost him.

It all came down to this: the sex. And maybe, except for Rory, it had all been one big mistake that continued to haunt her. It was as if she'd caught a disease that an antibiotic had never entirely knocked out of her system; she became reinfected again and again.

Maybe this was why her great-grandmother Ann avoided men.

The week before Benjamin died, Randy Hill had grabbed Jade after school. His hands were strong, his breath sharp. When she resisted, using the excuse that she had to meet her brother, Randy laughed. "Is that little twerp the only thing standing in the way of us getting together?"

She hadn't answered, but simply broke away. The following week Benjamin was dead.

When she reached the Sturgeses' house, no one was home. She slammed the front door behind her, grabbed the cordless phone in the kitchen, and locked herself in her room. Jade called the number that last week she'd vowed she wouldn't. Jade called Rexanne, who answered on the first ring.

"Mom? Is that you? It doesn't sound like you."

"Jade. Jade. Jade."

As much as she tried to hold it back, Jade cried openly now. In between sobs, she spit out the story of how the Driscolls had won her confidence, then how Peter's new concerns had turned sexual and spoiled the plans. She felt sorry for Marilou and herself and especially the unborn baby.

Rexanne seemed to take all the details in, then surprised Jade by proposing a plan so quickly. Jade would go to Maine with the Sturges family. Rexanne would visit her there next month and then together they'd decide what to do.

"Can we go cross country?" Jade asked. "On the train?" She felt like a child bargaining for treats. And she wanted to get as far away from Blue Field as possible.

"Maybe we can."

"Like the Transcontinental Railroad," Jade said. Rexanne didn't answer.

"Can Nancy Jane come?" Jade pleaded.

"Get your degree, honey."

"I have my degree."

"Just go along for another month, then I'll have myself together." She paused. "I'll tell you everything."

"A month?" A month.

"It's a complicated situation here, Jade."

After Jade finished talking with Rexanne she immediately pressed the numbers for the little rented house on Main Street in Paradise.

A month.

The phone rang six times. Jade pictured the small rooms downstairs, the smaller rooms upstairs, her bedroom on the third floor with the animal posters her father had given her. She was about to hang up when she heard his hello.

"Ellis?"

"Jade? What's wrong?" He always initiated the phone calls.

Jade couldn't answer. She choked back a sob.

"Baby doll, what's the matter?"

What she wanted to say caught in her throat. She thought of a car racing down the highway suddenly veering off into a ditch, coming to a hard stop.

Suddenly she knew she couldn't tell him, worry him with more problems. She felt like someone in an accident who'd gone into a coma and couldn't speak, couldn't send out the sentences that would describe feelings, couldn't even lift her arms.

"I miss you," she said suddenly. It came to her as an excuse, and yet she meant it absolutely.

"Oh, you're just homesick," he said, calming her.

She asked after Vivienne, and he responded. Hank had gotten his beans and corn in. Cassidy was trying a new pea this spring. With Wal-Mart opening over in Doral, Ellis was thinking of applying for a job, though he imagined they preferred to hire kids who were more familiar with computers. News of the rural details soothed her the way lying on her back and staring into a blue, cloud-filled sky could.

"There's no reason you've got to stay up there. You want to come home, you come on back."

"Thanks, Dad," she said. Jade never called Ellis "Dad." He was quiet then.

7

december

Before I could picture Ellis fitting the receiver into the phone on the kitchen wall, then checking in on his animal wards, then absently going back to look at his paper, he cleared his throat. Humphed. He must have sensed how needy I was at that moment, because my normally silent father was talking to me without hesitation. He told me all that I'd been waiting to hear. And then some. It came out like rain.

You know how I got this scar—the mark I told you was a snake baby when you were but a baby yourself? Not Dillon cracking me with a beer bottle at a card game like he jokes. Not the end of a firecracker blowing off to burn my nose and make Kirk a little deaf all in one swoop. Wasn't nothing like that.

It was a hoe, see, something a farmer should be smart enough to keep out of his face. The tool became a weapon so fast I didn't have time to put my hand up to stop the thing from landing in the middle of my puzzlement.

Rexanne fought me over that lake. Told her she should make her garden right inside the shelterbelt, but she said that location would be too shady. The spot where the lake now sits was the focus of arguments for months. Finally, she let loose on me. With all the land we had, it makes no sense that we both got so stubborn about the very same place.

Then all I wanted was a dot on the land, the best part of where our families' property joined, one area different from the work of the farm, nothing to do with crops. A lake wherecould teach my kids to fish. Or just sit and watch the surface reflect everything above our heads, bringing heaven a little closer.

Water is precious on the Plains. The strange thing was, I knew that spot had been a lake, was almost asking me to hollow and fill it again. A farmer knows his land by heart, understands it like his own body. The earth gave to the curve of a bowl as soon as I stuck my shovel in.

She tends to blame everything on the lake I made, but I can't believe you can pin all your trouble to one spot on eight hundred acres any more than you can locate ugliness in a person on a single scar. With a broken machine, that's definitely the case. But with people, and with nature, it's likely a combination of circumstances falling one on top of another, locking up like pieces of a puzzle, that causes a catastrophe.

Thought she'd get over it, come to see my point after the machinery pulled away and left my finished project beautiful and stocked with fish. But we never did much there as a family. Now and then, I'd sneak off to fish stealthy as a cheatin' husband, but always throw the catch back. I couldn't imagine your mother would clean and cook a fish caught from that water.

Even back then, she wasn't all that crazy about roasting any kind of meat. When you got bigger and she stopped cooking altogether, the food confused me. You made all these special dishes that tasted OK, but when a farmer works the fields and raises the animals, that's what he should be eating, not some weird concoctions that don't have any obvious connection to a day's work.

When the farm started losing money, she gave up hope instead of putting in more hours, like she always expected we'd fail and she now had a genuine excuse to cut out. After your brother died, she stopped going to church. Eventually, she gave up believing in everything. But I think she'd quit me way before then.

Didn't always show it in public, but I was crazy about that woman. In a way, I still am.

There's nothing sweeter than coming in from the field, the broad sunset behind me stretching all across the bumper crop. Her dress was fresh and pale yellow. You were in the next room trying to teach your baby brother to count; the fields were thick with summer and the work ahead. I pressed hard against her, my dirt-covered self marking her with the farm. I don't understand how someone could want more from life than a moment like that.

But she did.

See, mostly it's green Deere country out here, except for my Farmall, the bright red tractor that was my daddy's. The land that I came to farm was my daddy's land and Rexanne's family's. He worked some of Rexanne's land before we married. It made perfect sense that Rexanne and me, who'd grown up alongside each other, would get married, pool our land, double our wealth, raise a family right along with crops.

I disked and planted our fields with corn and soybeans and sorghum; mowed grass; painted buildings; picked weeds and volunteer corn and rocks. Harvested acre after acre year after year.

There's nothing nostalgic about hard physical work, at least not among ones who've actually done it.

When it rained or snowed, I walked our house nervous as a cat; fiddled; polished machinery; even counted buttons on pigs. The best part of a day when I couldn't be in the crops was looking in on Rexanne playing music in the barn and singing along as she fed the animals. "Crazy." "I Walk the Line."

When I rode my daddy's Farmall, the transmission heated up, warming my butt at the same time the sun toasted my head. I drove in the heat as long as it took to find the best place to enter a field. Big open spaces calm me. One time when I went to Chicago, had to fight myself from getting back in my truck, driving until I could see corn again.

Rode the Farmall to find where to put our lake. And after determining the location, I'd ride out every day and envision the water. I'd dismount, slide a couple of wood blocks, which I'd taken out there just for that purpose, behind the back wheels. Just imagining a swim after the heat of the day had soaked through filled me with contentment.

My neighbor Carlsen increased his acreage and not by moving fence. Didn't ever consider we'd need more land than my family's and Rexanne's combined. Little by little, I sold off acres to pay somebody or another. Every time I looked at Carlsen, I saw my own failure to maintain a farm. When he was late for a payment, I squeezed him for it. Lately, I've wondered if he, in turn, squeezed my boy.

There are a few simple rules in farm country. Only the strong survive is one of them. How did I hold out as long as I did? I worked every single moment I was awake.

A woman can't live on work alone. I know that now.

Heard all Rexanne's stories about her grandma running cattle like a man, but I don't hold by them. On a farm, the lines are divided between men and women. They're clear as crop lines. Women's work and men's work. Men and women.

Your brother never understood that point. Being different isn't always valued, or even tolerated in the country. A purple tractor? People just wouldn't go for it. You've got your John Deeres green as grass; your apple-red Farmalls; dark blue Fords; yellow like hot-dog mustard is JI Case. Anything else is asking for trouble.

Seeing all the animals should translate into natural human sex. Livestock do it in broad daylight. Spotted him watching a boar mount a sow, so I knew he knew what was supposed to happen. Even when we brought out the suitcase bull for artificial insemination, I thought he got the picture.

I was stupid. Before doing some reading, I thought he could take a pill or something to straighten himself out. Now I see it's all part of nature, like a bull that we say doesn't "take to cows."

It makes sense that a farmer would want his son to eventually manage everything he's worked for, everything the ancestors fought weather and Indians and even their own kind for. Had I known how things would have gone, never would have pushed the farm on Benjamin. We weren't a big enough family with a second or third son to take on the future. For a while, I thought that maybe you would want to be responsible, but I don't know why I ever thought that. Should have spent more time with you.

I don't blame you for going after something else. Miss you, but don't blame you. These days you have to find your frontier wherever you can.

Even Hank can't make a go of it anymore. Not with crops anyway. He plans to take in thousands and not by wholesaling corn. Said he'll hire a band, set up a petting corral, pull together tunnels out of hay bales for the little ones. For the older kids, he'll cut a maze through corn in the shape of a flying saucer, set up speakers to play music from *Star Wars*.

He'll charge admission. Loreen can make angel food cakes and her famous butterscotch meringue pie to sell. Takes pick-your-own and hayrides to a whole new level. That is, if it doesn't rain. Still have to worry about the rain.

Brad says he's going to start charging money to let people from out of town watch him castrate his bulls. Says he could make a bundle, probably more than I pulled when we sold off our entire farm and all its machinery. Now everybody's thinking of what they can do. Cassidy went on the Web and found out that some guy outstate has gotten into raising ostriches to replace turkeys for Thanksgiving. But who can fit them in an oven? And somebody else has set up an old Pony Express station on his property, and for souvenirs sells cheese in the shape of mailbags. Farming's nothing the way it used to be. Now it's Disneyland.

They say it's Germans more than farmers from New England want to keep their kids on the farm. Rexanne and me proved that out. I'm pioneer stock, too. Just don't make a big deal about that stuff the way Rexanne does.

Yes, I wanted my boy to take on the farm. But deep down, I think Rexanne wanted him to escape it. Go to college, get a job that didn't depend on weather. Maybe between the two of us, he got a mixed-up message.

He was always closer to your mother, preferring her kind of work, especially with the animals. Animals and that camera. Before he was old enough to go to school, the boy could practically deliver calves himself. He could sense when a cow was sick, kept illustrated records so he knew everyone's baby sister and brother. A camera hanging around his neck, he'd separate the cows in heat.

I was going to buy him his own horse. Twice had it all picked out and then we'd need the money for a new tractor, fencing for a field. Was always something. Even had a name I thought would be good—Moonbean, a mistake he made as a baby when every other word *did* have to do with beans.

He could go through the names of corn easily as reciting the names of his family. So I couldn't believe he wouldn't want to touch the seeds, dirty himself with their dust, poke at the ripening ears. But he'd get in another world when he was cultivating and could wipe out a whole row of corn. Remember him running the tractor into the shed the day after he'd pulled up a whole strip of lawn with the Farmall.

Showing him everything, I hoped there'd be one thing he'd like so much that he'd gladly take on the entire life of the farm. Like I had the lake, and before that, the idea for the lake. Come a point, I would gladly have given him the lake if it would have made a difference.

But time and again he'd stop short of letting the farm take him over. Cassidy made this special prod to get worms for fishing. It was a golf club rigged with an electrical cord and a rubber handle that stuck into the ground. As soon as you plugged the thing into a socket, worms wiggled to the surface. The boy liked gathering them up after I pulled the pole out of the ground, but would he bait my hook?

He did stand up to me. I'll give him that. Knew I never liked chickens for their mess and their noise. He went out and picked twenty chicks—white leghorn banties—paid for them with his own money.

I've thought this out enough times that I know now what I

wouldn't believe then. He didn't belong on the farm.

Rexanne was the one there when his first tooth fell out, when he went on his first day of school, bought the Indian bead craft set I said was for girls. It wasn't that I wasn't interested. I was working. That was all I knew to do.

She wasn't there when he died. None of us was.

We might have gotten out from under our financial problems if he hadn't died. Rexanne seems to think he would never have passed if there was any way we could have saved the farm.

Hate to think of people tromping all over our fields to play some silly game, our farm reduced to pure entertainment.

One of the problems is that a farmer's wife isn't a farmer's wife altogether these days. She works in town part-time to keep things together. Should have accepted this. I let our son work outside.

One day a week he helped a man who wouldn't join the ESSOP, a man whose land bumped up against my fields. I've given this consideration. I think Carlsen saw Benjamin's disposition. The ESSOP recognized it, too. And looking back on it, I see I was the one set Benjamin up with Carlsen.

In the natural world, animals weed out the infertile males, leave the weak to die.

It was the ESSOP that told me, some man I'd never talked to up close. Met me in the field and hit me with the news. Don't even remember his name now, only him saying, "Best you're away from here now." I ran to our house, changed my shoes and didn't even have time to tie them before the rest of them came over to console me.

People stopped talking about the accident way before I'd settled the incident in my mind. People forgot about what had happened, while I still thought about it every single day.

I wanted to go over the details again and again until they made some sense to me. Life was unreal; every step felt part of a dream. But I didn't say anything; I *couldn't* talk. It was like I'd lost my voice.

And I had a mountain of questions. How did he suffer? Why did he suffer? Why couldn't the happenstance have fallen on me? Instead, what found me was this news—you have no control over the weather. Anything can happen.

It had.

I had nightmares. Developed this tic of glancing over my shoulder to be sure no one was behind. Dillon said I acted like somebody who'd just got back from Nam. At first, he thought this was funny.

The nightmares brought back things I'd done as a kid, terrible stuff—throwing a cat in a thresher, sticking a firecracker down a live rabbit's throat just to see the consequences. Rexanne didn't believe these stories I told on myself.

She forced me to go to this group therapy. "Don't give me any of that psychology crap," I told her. And she told me anything was worth a try.

At the first and only meeting I attended, everybody had a story about losing a child. They called themselves a support group. You've got your victims of mass murders, serial murderers, suicides, drunk drivers. And you've got me who doesn't have a clue what his son's a victim of. All I know is that I should have been able to save my own boy.

Maybe the men looked at my boy like a horse with a bad leg, an animal in pain.

I've tried to make good by the animals now.

· · ·

The night of the accident I went into his room and gathered up all of his belongings—his clothes and posters and shoes. His hat and camera and pillow. Part of me just didn't believe. Part of me thought he'd need his things wherever he was. And then when I had this huge nest of belongings together, I blacked out.

Cried every day without letting anyone see. Got lost in the cemetery once my eyes were so full. Even when I was dressed and on the road, in my head I was lying in bed.

I still can't stand the thought of snow on the grave. Brush it off before it builds up. He once told me the cold seeps into your shoes like water. Last January when the stone was covered with a coating of ice, I scraped it so hard I scarred the rock.

I know I told you an angel was watching over him, but it was me.

Was me who made a boy who stood out.

It was me who cut a lake into an acre that should have been farmed, made it shine in sunlight like a jewel anyone would envy.

three

8

june

At first, I thought they were coming after me. I pictured Peter in pursuit, constantly watching, trying to grab me when the Sturgeses weren't looking. On the phone, at a rest stop, on the back lawn that empties into the ocean, hiding anything that's said.

I wonder if their marriage is crashing as I look out on Maine trees, lush for so few months it's hard to believe. Or their relationship could have been disintegrating for years, and they thought a baby would repair it. I wonder how much he confessed, how much he blamed me.

What calmed me were my father's words. And Rexanne's tales of women I've never met.

In Connecticut, what looks like shelterbelts don't intentionally protect the land, but hide neighbors' business from one another.

The first time I heard the five syllables of "infidelity" was in my parents' kitchen. It was filled with smoke. Rexanne didn't smoke then, but that day she and Hank's wife, Loreen, puffed cigarette after cigarette, and in hushed voices talked about men. Loreen cried; Rexanne comforted her. Then the beer came out and they weren't so quiet after that.

Yesterday we had an intense storm. Severe weather still makes me think of consequences. I can't help myself. The corn might be broken, beans get too wet. . . .

I've told anyone in New England who asks that my farm looked like a patchwork quilt. That's a lie, but I know they want to believe a pretty cliché more than a description close to the truth, which reeks of pigs, rotten corn, and the dreams of a farmer's children.

At night I imagine I live in another time. The crisp white sheet tucked around me could almost be a dress, long and full for a wedding. The air is cool, and crickets screech with the beginning of summer. In darkness, the darker backdrop of pines points skyward.

I'm flung on the bed by a stranger who wants me to love him. He begs me. I become Isabel about to give birth to a daughter as the Transcontinental Railroad is being built just outside this room. Rexanne has told me that Isabel's screams were almost hidden in the rhythmic sounds of spikes driven into rail, her long, high notes striking above the assurance of progress. Theirs the melody, hers the variation.

You only hear old stories of strength and survival, never the anxiety—the instant when events could have gone differently. Maybe because histories ignore the actual moment of decision-making and hold only the details of an outcome do I choose them over my own life.

My body is as full of the past as the future. I've told Rexanne that I want to meet Nancy Jane.

Even at six months, Jade didn't think the average person could tell she was pregnant. Like they wouldn't know that she'd lost her brother just from looking at her. Yesterday when Jade wore her spandex pants beneath a tunic top and long vest, Ellen had complimented her. Jade figured the remark really meant that Ellen felt more comfortable with Jade's condition discreetly covered. Today Jade could probably even fool Rory. So long as he didn't touch her. Run his hands along the hard swell of her middle.

She hadn't unwrapped any of the maternity outfits Marilou had bought for her, and now considered sending them all back, like returning wedding gifts when the ceremony was called off. But then she pictured Marilou opening the packages, maybe regretting for a moment that she'd never grow large enough to wear them herself.

Jade's room wasn't situated in the back of the Maine house as in Connecticut, but between the children's rooms. With her windows open, she could hear the girls talking fantasy stories and, on her other side, Jesse poking away at the keyboard to his computer. Outside, Ellen planted pink and yellow and purple flowers in a garden outlined with rocks. Ted, for sure, was reading the newspaper on the front porch as he did every morning after breakfast. And back in Nebraska Ellis and Vivienne would be eating waffles with peaches and walnuts the way they did every Saturday. Jade could go for a waffle.

Walking barefoot along the wooden floor, Jade passed bedroom after empty bedroom; there were eight on the second floor alone. "Long as we don't have to heat them, I don't care if we have fifty," Ted had said to her. The house was never used in the winter, though the Sturgeses had discussed the possibility of one year opening it up for a New England Thanksgiving.

The huge old house was impeccably maintained, the wooden staircase sweeping, the living room fireplace heavy with marble, the kitchen small yet functional, the dining room grand. Vivienne would love to have this as a listing, even if it never sold. If Daniel had been wealthy, he might have taken Nancy Jane to an impressive mansion like this one. But then she would probably have felt hypocritical so removed from the farm.

To think that Jade had once imagined the "cottage" as a log cabin. There were windows of all sizes, each with a different stunning view. The dining room looked out on a long border of evergreens. Off in the distance lay the ocean and a "sea house," positioned close to the tide line. That building, with its high, beamed ceiling, wraparound porch, and full kitchen, was sometimes used for parties, but mostly for changing before and after a swim.

Jade had brought all her belongings to Maine, even the Cuisinart. At first she'd worried that the family would suspect her of taking off. But they'd been so preoccupied with their own packing and sorting, no one had said anything about the room Jade had stripped back to the way it had looked before she'd arrived in Connecticut.

The terra-cotta kitchen tiles were cool against Jade's slightly swollen feet. She picked up the phone in the small sitting room off the kitchen. Ellen never minded Jade using the phone, but she didn't approve of her talking to Pearline. Jade could almost see Ellen worrying that the two were scheming.

Pearline had phoned yesterday with "an urgent situation," but their conversation had been cut short with call-waiting.

"Let me tell you the story," Pearline said now. "Don't say no."

"No," Jade answered.

"This woman has no husband," Pearline said.

"You mean no ex-creepazoid like Peter?"

Pearline made a funny sound, almost a grunt. "She *was* married," Pearline said, "for twenty years."

Before Jade could conjure up the particulars of divorce, Pearline was quoting, the potential mother. "I told myself good marriages don't have to show anything. Good marriages don't have babies. It is romantic thinking there's just the two of you and that will be the end of the line. And then he died and changed everything."

If she were in the mood, Jade might have been taken in as Pearline described the woman's house and job, which she would quit to raise a child. Constantly instigating meetings with boys or prospective parents, Pearline was only trying to help. Maybe she imagined one of her own grandbabies sacrificed to the rich, the child taken in and fed a steady diet of entitlement.

"She said that? 'I would like a beautiful baby'?" Jade asked.

"She meant that," Pearline said.

Jade had seen Pearline's room at the bed and breakfast only once. There was a single bed without a headboard, a crucifix hanging above. Holy pictures, which looked like the Tarot cards she and Sara had once played with, were stuck over most of one wall. In one corner of the ten-by-twelve space sat a digital clock bigger than the television. Two side-by-side doors opened onto a tiny closet and a private bath with a rusty shower stall.

A large coat closet in the parlor of the B&B connected the business of the inn to Lauren Nash's living area. Pearline had shown Jade how louvered doors pushed into that room, which at first glance appeared to be a museum. The dark oversized furniture, the area rug in a cheetah design, the maroon and golden wallpaper, Jade thought hideous.

"Pearline," Jade said softly, looking around. "I'm thinking of maybe keeping the baby."

There was a long silence. "Maybe," Jade added, then mentioned that Rexanne would be rescuing her before long. It could be a mistake; Jade knew she might end up hating the responsibility of a baby, but right now it was all she had.

"This woman lives down the street. I could keep an eye on the little baby," Pearline said, ignoring Jade's announcement.

If it hadn't moved.

If it had just stayed still for nine months, maybe she would have been able to believe it was like an appendix or a spleen that could be removed, and within a week you were pretty much back to normal again.

Pearline asked whether Ellen might want the baby now. "What if that is why she does not like me talking with you."

That possibility sounded too much like a fairy tale. Jade hung up the phone just before Ellen came in from gardening. Ellen pulled off her large straw hat encircled with a light blue and white sash.

"This place is great," Jade said.

Ellen said she and the family had been vacationing in Maine for the last five years. "We rented one year in the Vineyard," she said as she turned the tap at the kitchen sink. She took a long drink. "The master bedroom was this horrible shade of pink."

Despite the fact that Jade pretty much ran the Sturges household, she felt inconsequential whenever she stood near Ellen for more than a few seconds. She was shocked when the woman leaned her back against the sink and asked directly, "Jade, who's the father of your baby?"

With the blunt question, Jade suddenly saw Ellen efficiently at work in her law office. Asking direct questions, recording answers in anticipation of a hearing. Before this, Ellen hadn't mentioned the Driscoll arrangement, hadn't so much as blinked when Jade left those prospective parents behind and helped pack the SUV for Maine.

Because Ellen was so unexpectedly forward, Jade's initial re-action was to reciprocate and reveal the whole story and all its ugly details. Boys on their knees in the dirt; boys crawling off her exhausted; she taking their hard bodies into her mouth, into her body; boys calling at all hours of the night; boys crying and cursing her. The dirt on their fingers getting lost in her black hair. And she, Jade, in the safety of her own room, gulping air to calm herself, not letting a drop of emotion out in front of any of them. Especially not Mr. Donnelly.

But she panicked, looked around. Jade spotted the local paper laid open on the chair. A man about Ellis's age, but handsome, polished; he had a mass of black hair.

"Andre French," she said.

"Don't be silly," Ellen said.

"I'm serious."

Ellen leaned forward and put both hands on the table. "What are you saying, Jade?"

"Andre French is the father," she said, surprised at her growing confidence.

"How could that be? He's, he's a violinist," Ellen said. Silently Jade filled in the unspoken words—"and you're the product of a broken farm." Jade imagined Ellen propped in bed that night as she spoke without looking at her husband, "What would someone like Andre French see in Jade?"

"He must resemble Andre French." Ellen looked around the room.

Jade would never have mentioned this guy's name if she knew Ellen would make such a big deal. She could have said any name, and yet, she'd wanted to pin the responsibility to a real person, even one she didn't know. Especially one she didn't know.

Jade concocted an elaborate story about a concert in the school auditorium to celebrate the 150th anniversary of Paradise. She mentioned that Andre was born in Nebraska, then borrowed a few details from her grandmother's life. Nancy Jane had literally been swept off her feet by a violinist. His long slender fingers, eyes that seemed to catch every detail surrounding him.

When Jade was finished, Ellen stared at her as if really seeing her for the first time. She tapped Jade's belly lightly. "You might just have a little prodigy in there."

What if it were *all* a story? What if none of the details Rexanne had told about saving the farm, and organizing farmers, and falling in love with a violinist were true?

And where the fuck was Rexanne?

Ordinarily, a Post-it note would have been stuck to the door to remind the family of items not to forget on their outing to the Lobster Festival, the list detailed in impeccable handwriting. But Ted had told Ellen to cut it out with all the notes. "We're on vacation now," he'd said.

As she made up the final bed, Jade heard the family gathering in the foyer below. "Go on ahead," Jade called. "I'll catch up with you." When the front door closed against the children's voices, she flopped onto Ellen and Ted's bed. The fresh sheets were 340-count thread, all cotton, and about the softest thing Jade had ever felt. A pattern of tiny white dots, only slightly brighter than the background white, covered the cloth. She'd never heard of sheets being so exorbitantly expensive. As soon as she'd helped Ellen unpack, Jade had taken them out of the packages and washed them, as instructed.

In Nebraska, sheets were no big deal. Her family had ordinary ones of poly and cotton, mostly poly; percale, they said, to make it sound fancier. The only time Jade noticed laundry was when Rexanne hung it in the sun instead of shoving it in the dryer; all night the sheets would smell of sunshine. And great-grandmother Ann probably didn't even have sheets.

Jade's sheets in Maine were soft, but nothing like the new ones on Ellen's bed. She hoped that one day when she slept with a man she truly loved, she could buy one set of expensive sheets. Smoothing the bedding, Jade was glad of a few moments to herself. With the entire family underfoot most of the time now, they made her claustrophobic. Even in her grandmother's day when women worked without all the time-saving tools that chopped and dried and washed and sorted, there were precious times alone. A woman could let her mind go blank without a group of people to constantly answer to. Jade had to practically wipe every one of their asses they'd become so dependent upon her. Jade, where are the paper towels, the lightbulbs, the bread, the shampoo . . . ? Jade, what time is it? Jade, did you see what I did with the Metro section of the paper? Caring for a baby couldn't be any more work than this.

After she'd tucked the nubby white bedspread over and under the pillows, she decided to call her mother. Counting out fourteen rings, Jade tried to see the small Massachusetts house Rexanne had never fully described. Jade hung up. She thought Rexanne should have come for her by now or, at least, have called with an excuse.

Because the front door had swollen with humidity, Jade pulled it shut hard. She walked down the long stone driveway. In the distance, a man was cutting the field-sized lawn with a gas-powered push mower, the buzzing following her as she headed toward the lobster festivities. There were crafts demonstrations, contests, a flea market, an outdoor lobster feed, all culminating in the lobster parade. The town sponsored a lobster festivity each month of the summer, with the largest one slated for August.

Off Main Street at the town pier, an audience of locals had gathered for the lobster-boat races. Fishermen in jeans and T-shirts squinted as they looked skyward. Even the children mingling among the fishermen, and a smaller group of wives and girlfriends were waiting for something to happen.

Jade caught the eyes of a young woman about her own age with deep olive skin and very dark straight hair. For a minute,

Jade thought of Juan. She smiled then walked over and said, "What's going on?"

"The races are delayed," the young woman replied. She went on to explain that the fog in the cove made racing treacherous. "No visibility."

"But people drive in the fog," Jade said.

"That's nothing like this." The young woman walked away.

Jade waited at the pier for about half an hour with the townspeople, who took bets on whether the sun would come out, burn off the fog, and set the scene for a clear morning of lobster-boat racing. The locals leaned against their trucks and cars. Every once in a while, a hearty laugh broke against the hazy air. A couple of people eyed Jade, but she was fairly at ease blending into the scenery of parked cars and bad weather.

Jade anticipated the girl coming back over and introducing her friends more than she did a change in the sky. But soon the young woman stood with her arms folded against her chest and stared off into the gently lapping water, all gray and full of hopes being dashed. When Jade finally left, she passed Back to the Past, a chic antiques shop sure to interest Ellen. A bumper sticker, "If it's snowing, I'm going," was plastered onto the three different vehicles with Maine license plates. Maybe the locals liked to boast that the best time to be in Maine was not when all the vacationers spent their summer dollars. In the warm damp air it was difficult to imagine snow, the entire town covered over in white and not a trace of the summer people. But at a gas station, there was a sign for snowmobile repairs.

Now Jade walked behind a dense trail of people heading for the flea market building and food tents. A brown van lettered in yellow with "United Family of Christ Christian Sunday School" pulled up just ahead of Jade and parked. The first girl to step out of the vehicle wore a tight T-shirt with the words

"Show Me the Money" splayed across her large chest.

The Snow Harbor festival was a mix of outsiders standing right alongside the year-round residents. The artist of a life-sized moose sculpture was explaining how the installation had been constructed entirely of local trash. Jade wanted to ask if the cans and wood and plastic had been found locally or made locally.

A series of panels mounted with other artworks surrounded the giant trash moose. A set of antlers had been varnished and painted to replicate an eagle. She carefully studied each of the works, challenging herself to distinguish the discarded thing from which beauty had been made. Her favorite was a freestanding abstract beehive constructed of hundreds of frozen orange juice cans. Finally, she focused on the artist himself, not particularly good-looking; other than his beard and height nothing to distinguish him. And yet, surrounded by his work he commanded attention. An elderly woman in khakis and a white tailored shirt examined the works, asked questions, stood back.

The Driscolls had befriended Jade only because she could give them something they couldn't produce on their own. And yet, she felt sorry for Marilou, who'd already bought a car seat for the baby, the top-of-the-line model that Jade had helped pick out.

Jade admitted to herself that lately she wanted to contact Rexanne not to see how she was doing, but to garner more details about Nancy Jane.

Following the arrows and signs indicating the flea market and crafts fair, Jade found herself in front of a low stone building that was part of a school. The interior of the large space was filled with tables manned by at least a hundred vendors. There were knickknacks, potholders in the shape of lobsters and fish, handmade baby bonnets and blankets, jewelry, books, dolls made of corn husks, animals fashioned out of seashells. One table featured Creative Mud Flaps for trucks. Another displayed five-foot molds for making alligators and dinosaurs and lobsters out of snow, as well as the traditional snowman. Nontoxic paints were included in the package. Jade avoided a promotion that might have been a Yankee version of the ESSOP.

Ellen and Ted stood by two tables covered with lighthouse lamps. Ellen gestured at the different wooden lighthouses while the middle-aged vendor waited patiently for their decision. Ellen and Ted were fighting. Their arguments were never the explosive events that had taken over the farmhouse in Nebraska when Ellis and Rexanne would get into it, but a low-keyed bickering that didn't go beyond words.

"Why, Jade," Ellen said, her voice now soft.

"What do you think would look better in the sunroom?" Ted asked. "This large one or the one with the little red light?"

Ellen shook her head. Her thin lips tightened into a line.

"The seagull on this one is bigger than the man," Jade pointed out.

"Right you are," Ted said. He put two fingers to his forehead. "I hadn't noticed that." The proportions of the figures at the base of the different lighthouses suddenly became a new point of contention.

"Why don't you gather up the children and get them some food? We'll join you in a few minutes," Ellen said.

"They're right around here," Ted said. He pointed to the left. Ellen asked the price of a custom-made lamp, which would incorporate seagulls, people, and boats in correct proportions.

When Jade turned to find the children, she spotted the young woman from the pier.

"Your parents?" the girl asked.

"Are you kidding?" Jade said, glancing back at the two making such a big deal over a stupid lamp. "My employers."

The girl stared at Jade. "My name's Robin," she said. Her teeth were straight and white, her dark skin flawless. She invited Jade on a trip across the harbor the following evening with some friends.

"What do you do there?"

"Drink," Robin said.

Before Jade could ask why she was being invited, Robin said, "My brother thinks you're cunnin'." Jade wondered if the brother looked anything like Robin. "See you later," Robin said.

Jade waited in line with the Sturges children as they chattered about the meal choices. Two hundred feet off, seven separate fires blazed beneath the schoolyard swing set. Propped over each fire was a new full-sized metal garbage can. Jade heard someone in front of her explain that the lobsters were boiled in seawater in the containers. She would note this secret preparation in her book.

"Oooh," said Carolyn, simultaneously licking her lips. Although they'd been at the seashore less than two weeks, already the children's hair was sun streaked. Vicky's face was heavily freckled.

"Garbage can pans, yuk," Jesse said. "I'll take a hamburger." He'd bought one of the Snow Shapes molds and was studying the description of a "snowman shoot-out" on the back of the box.

Vicky opted for a hamburger, too, but Carolyn decided to join Jade and eat lobster. Jade was helping the girl open her lobster at the picnic table Jesse had selected when Ellen and Ted showed up. They took seats across from each other. Jade pulled the shell back the way the host on a television cooking show had. Then she gently broke off the small legs. Jesse watched the process intently.

"Everybody having a good time?" Ted asked, checking his

watch. Jade bit into an ear of corn, dripping in a delicious butter sauce. In Paradise, the corn would be forming on the tall stalks, the first ears growing plump. Sometimes Jade would pick an ear and eat it raw, right in the field.

Ellen pushed her corn aside and poked at the coleslaw with a plastic fork. Jade concentrated on the perfectly cooked lobster meat. Sliding her finger up into the shell, she scraped around for bits of flesh she might have missed. She wondered if Rexanne ate lobster and fish now or if she was an even stricter vegetarian than she'd been when she left Nebraska.

"Another one, Jade?" Ted asked. "Go ahead."

Ellen stared at her, then looked down at Jade's middle. Ellen hadn't touched the Jell-O dessert that came with the dinner. Jell-O was featured at every public feed Jade had gone to as a kid. One Fourth of July, Ellis suggested that Rexanne make a map of the USA out of Jell-O. And she had, even delineating the boundaries of the individual states. Jade wondered when Jell-O was invented—how long her family had been experimenting with unique ways of preparing it.

As Jade waited in line for a second lobster, she noticed a contest in the distance. Three men sat on separate blocks of ice, each the size of a mini-refrigerator, the kind she'd seen in the RV Rory had taken her to. In Nebraska at a local fair one year, Jade had watched a gristle race. A huge platter of gristle, sheared from the beef that had been served to all the neighbors, sat at the head of a long table. After someone dished the warm greasy mass onto individual plates, the contestants raced to finish. A man Ellis and his friends called Little Whitey nearly choked. Just remembering the whole spectacle almost made Jade gag. She decided she'd rather sit on a chunk of ice for an hour than eat chewy fat. Jade would have to ask Nancy Jane if there was time for senseless competitions in her day. Suddenly someone was lifting a red steamy lobster out of a strainer and gesturing at her plate. She got a second ear of corn, too, just to demonstrate to Ted how it was to be eaten. He'd tried to shear the kernels from the cob with a feeble plastic knife.

"Fresh enough to flop," someone behind her said.

When Jade returned to the table, she could tell Ellen and Ted had been talking about her.

"I wonder what it would be like to have four children at the table," Ellen said.

Jade stared at Ellen. Here she would go days without speaking to Jade, without talking to anyone, and then she'd come out with a remark that could stop a horse. Ellen had denied Jade's pregnancy from the beginning. Her only overture so far had been driving Jade to the gynecologist for a checkup a few days before leaving Blue Field. She'd waited for Jade in the car.

Pearline was a seer. *Maybe Missus will want to keep the baby for herself.*

As Ellen looked toward Ted, Jade figured that she'd told her husband about the phony violinist-father. It was easy to fabricate a story people wanted to hear. More than legitimate details, you needed confidence.

The lobster parade began well before sunset, the loud sustained honk of a fire engine sounding the start of the festivities. People lined on either side of Main Street craned to see the vehicle heading up the parade and the marching band that followed. Carolyn and Vicky wiggled and jumped. Even the usually cool Jesse seemed rapt with the approaching spectacle.

"Here it comes," squealed Vicky.

"It's only a fire truck," Ted said, though he was smiling. "We have those in Connecticut."

"A *new* fire truck," someone standing behind Jade clarified. Ellen turned and grinned politely.

It felt as if an hour had gone by before the first vehicle, outfitted with red and white crepe paper streamers and more than a dozen firemen hanging to its exterior, passed by. By then the children were already looking beyond the truck to a Barney knockoff, huge and orangish-red, who tossed individually wrapped hard candies at the crowd.

A woman who raised goats on the outskirts of town came next, flock in tow. She wore a long gathered dress and a faded red sweatshirt. With only her voice and a long stick, she directed the animals along the street. "How come they don't run away?" Carolyn asked Jade.

"How come you don't run away?" Jade answered and both of the little girls laughed.

"I could make them run away," Jesse said, glaring at the twins.

"Calm down," Ted said. "Hey, who's this?" He pointed at a costumed pink pig waving emphatically.

"Miss Piggy," Carolyn screamed as she gripped Jade's hand.

"Miss Piggy wears clothes," Vicky answered.

"I wonder what the general theme of this parade is," Ellen said. She was studying Carolyn holding Jade's hand.

"Fun," said the woman behind Jade. Jade caught the woman shaking her head at Ellen.

"Freebies," said the man with her, just as the pig sent a handful of plastic necklaces into the air.

An organization promoting racing dogs as pets came next. Each person in the group held the leashes of at least four animals. They stopped to let the onlookers pet the dogs. "That's McGinty," the woman who'd stopped nearest Jade said of a thin gray dog. "That's Sammy," she said of a white dog that Vicky was trying to hug.

A man handing out pamphlets on the dog adoption program said, "They're all retired and looking for good homes." With his gaunt face and very thin arms, he reminded Jade of one of the dogs.

"What's retired?" Vicky asked,

"They don't work anymore," Jesse answered, looking at his father.

"Like Mrs. Christopher?" Vicky persisted. She fingered a plastic purple necklace.

"No, not Mrs. Christopher," Ted said, smiling. "She doesn't work because she's rich."

"Are we rich?" Carolyn asked.

"OK," Ted said. "Let's just watch the parade now, shall we?"

Numerous cars, some convertible, some obvious racing cars, were interspersed throughout the parade. Pickup trucks decorated with stuffed lobsters, young women in red bathing suits, a few elderly men waving drove by. Groups of policemen strode in undisciplined formation. Jade saw nothing to remind her of Nebraska. Those corn and harvest festivals every summer and fall focused not on different agendas, but solely on the crops. Tables of baked goods and relishes, debates on the upcoming weather, and sometimes farmers trying one another's home brew, even that made from corn.

Adam could outride any one of the guys in the Maine cycling group that paraded down the road next. Jade couldn't wait for him to visit; he was someone she didn't feel defensive around and have to constantly apologize to. Yet, she couldn't imagine anyone pedaling all this way to see her. As he sped along roads, uphill and down, would he notice billboards, road signs, and wildflowers, or would he have a single-minded picture of her propped in front of him the entire time he pedaled? When Jade thought of Adam, she didn't automatically see his face. Instead, an icon of a silhouetted guy on a bike racing along a tree-lined road popped into her head.

A large flatbed vehicle announcing "Class Reunion" appeared with seven old-fashioned desks, an elderly person sitting at each one. The year of the individual's graduation from high school was propped on the different desks; the oldest person had graduated in 1916.

Jade quickly calculated Nancy Jane's graduation year: 1930. All of the people in the parade were older than Jade's grandmother. But not her great-grandmother. Jade didn't know if Ann had even gone to high school. Devoting her life to the physical work of the farm, how would she have been able to focus on a run-on sentence or memorize how many pounds of grapes were produced in a country thousands of miles away?

"That's my great-grandmother," Jade announced to Vicky as she pointed at a small gray-haired woman at the 1925 desk. She was exhilarated identifying with what was right before her, even if it wasn't true.

There would have been a small one-room building with a potbellied stove for heat. Jade imagined the students sharing books in dim light as a humorless teacher absently struck a ruler against her open palm.

The woman behind Jade who'd responded to Ellen's comment about the theme of the parade laughed. "Miss Cromwell never married."

Jade snapped, "That doesn't mean she didn't have a baby." Suddenly Jade couldn't hear anything; she felt as if everyone at the parade were staring at her. But that moment of self-consciousness passed with the float of elderly students. In truth, in the big picture, not that many people cared about Jade's pregnancy. But, in earlier times, people kept watch over one another probably as closely as Ellis's ESSOP. An unmarried pregnant woman would have been punished in some way.

The finale of the parade featured a large metal crate pulled by a tractor. In the cage, which looked like one meant for a dog, was a man dressed in a lobster costume. The crowd laughed and pointed. Carolyn covered her eyes. The man opened one side of the crate, stood up, and pulled off his lobster head, his fuzzy hair standing straight up.

"Remember me?" He appeared to be looking directly at Jade. She thought it was the man who'd won the ice-sitting contest. She hoped this wasn't Robin's brother.

Without telling the Sturgeses she was going out, Jade left the house. The night was cool, the sky bright with thousands of stars, shards of something bigger. But by the time she reached the pier the sky had dulled. She heard the water before she saw it, then all around her water lapped at blackness. The first time she'd seen the ocean, an hour after the family had unpacked, she was amazed at the shimmering expanse of blue. After returning from a trip to California, Sara's brother-in-law Terry had described the ocean by saying that if you stared long enough you'd think it was summer wheat. Every field had borders, but this water appeared contained by nothing.

At the pier about twenty-five people milled around, their cigarettes spotting the air like fireflies. A beer can hissed open. Robin sidled up before Jade had even begun to search for her.

"I'm glad you made it," Robin said, the darkness camouflaging her eyes and hair. Jade thought of a fish swimming just below the surface of Ellis's pond, only movement pulling the body into view.

"Isn't there too much fog to go out?" Jade asked. She was glad she'd worn a jacket.

Robin shook her head. "Don't worry about it. We won't be racing now." Two other women immediately came forward, and

Robin introduced them as Sally and Chris. Sally was light-haired and sort of cute; Chris was plain with very large breasts. Sally lit a cigarette.

The three chatted among themselves, Robin the fastest talker, the most dramatic. Every phrase she spoke was emphasized with her arms as well as her hands, each word setting her body in motion. She was nothing like Sara, nothing like anyone Jade knew.

Without a formal announcement, the group split in half and began boarding one of two lobster boats. Robin leaped into one, then turned and offered a hand to Jade. Her father a lobsterman, her mother a Penobscot Indian, Robin had ridden in lobster boats all her life. With the sides of the painted wooden boat only a couple of feet high, a passenger could easily topple out if the driver slowed sharply or hit unexpected rough water.

Jade made her way to the front of the boat where a large kid the others called Deeber was fooling with control switches. He set his beer on a ledge and took the steering wheel. "Adios, Padre," he hollered to the other boat. The boat lurched forward, its headlights picking up the cove. Jade grabbed at a bar-level surface and wedged herself behind it.

The two boats sped out of the harbor, their engines exploding the quiet. Deeber used his walkie-talkie to communicate with the boat behind him. *"Wooo whee,"* he yelled. The rest of the kids echoed his enthusiasm.

"I thought you said there wasn't going to be any racing," Jade said and tried to smile.

"He looks like a crazy man, but Deeber knows this harbor like the back of his hand," Robin said as she touched Jade's arm. "I've never seen him get balled up."

With the exception of short bursts of the headlights, it was totally black. The boat continued slicing through the summer night, the dark immediately closing up behind them. After a while, the second boat hung back, and Deeber contacted it intermittently with a few competitive words.

Robin pointed out the radar system, the line that indicated their precise path to the next harbor. "What's that?" Jade asked, indicating marks on the lighted map.

"Rocks. Places we want to stay away from," Robin answered, her voice projected over the roar of the boat's engine. She went on to tell how once when the boat had gotten caught up on a ledge, they'd had to wait the night out for help.

"Yikes," Jade said, imagining dampness and unfamiliar sounds sinking into her as she anticipated first light.

"That was before Deeber had all this new equipment," she said, pointing toward the dashboard's lights.

"Don't worry. I'll take care of you." Her stare dropped below Jade's face. Like Pearline, Robin knew before Jade could figure out when to tell her.

Jade trusted that Robin had the practical know-how to pull herself out of any predicament. She was the kind of person who understood danger without allowing it to consume her. Ellis would call Robin "spunky." Although Robin had said that she worked in the local paper mill, Jade couldn't picture her vivaciousness stomped down by a routine workday.

Deeber called for another beer, which spurted when he opened it. The entire landscape could have been paved over for all she could see of it.

"Jade, this is Samuel," Robin said. Her brother was tall with black hair and the similar dark good looks as his sister, but none of the animated gestures. He nodded at her.

"Where the fuck are you going, Deeber?" Robin called. At the expletive, Samuel shut his eyes.

"Enjoy the ride," Deeber answered. Samuel mumbled that he

thought Deeber was lost just as the boat behind crackled across the radio, "Where we headed, Deeb?"

"Up your ass," Deeber hollered. But before anyone became seriously worried, the far lights of their destination appeared. Jade thought the lights looked like tiny stars about to land.

"I told you," Robin said. "Deeber just looks like a Masshole." Robin lit a cigarette. "You could blindfold this lobsterman and he'd find the way to his favorite bar."

When the two boats docked, everyone filed off. There was laughter; empties were kicked, new cans opened, cigarettes lit. With Samuel and Robin on either side of her, Jade let herself be led along the street thick with "people from away," as Robin called them, and brightly lit shops. The moon, almost three-quarters full, now hung like a beacon to a foreign place. If she wanted to return to the Sturges house right now, Jade would have no idea in which direction to walk.

The people around her were pulling out ID. In Nebraska Jade knew which bar she could sneak into; she'd forgotten the rules here, wasn't prepared to be carded. When had legal drinking ages been instituted? She couldn't imagine anyone bothering Nancy Jane. Jade quickly looked to Robin, who said, "No problem." From her jeans pocket, Robin pulled a small stack of cards. She flipped through the out-of-state licenses until she found one without a picture. "This will do."

"It says I'm twenty-nine," Jade said.

"Don't worry about it," Robin said.

Once inside the club, the group of lobstermen and their dates spread out, like liquid spilled onto the floor, gradually trickling off in different directions. But within a few minutes, Jade found herself, along with most of the people from the two boats, standing at a long, high wooden table in the club's courtyard, which was decorated with hundreds of tiny white lights. The lights hung on trees and were strung along the top of the brick enclosure.

"What'll you have?" Samuel asked her.

Copying some of the others at the table, Jade ordered a Narragansett beer. Samuel smiled at her and said, "Nasty Gansett." Sara had mentioned that her sister drank dark beer when nursing her baby; Pearline, though, would disapprove. When she raised the glass to her lips, the pungent alcohol repulsed her. Because Samuel was watching, Jade held her breath and took a tentative sip. No one but Robin knew she was pregnant; even her slightly swollen ankles were concealed by long jeans. Jade couldn't help but think of drinking beer in Rory's truck back before she'd ever thought of moving to the east coast.

"Isn't this a pisser?" Samuel asked. He set his own beer in the space between them and Jade did the same. She surveyed the crowd, the built-in wooden levels that could be sat on or leaned against, used either as tables or chairs.

Deeber was telling a joke about someone who went on a job interview dressed as a parrot. "Polly want a job," Deeber said. Over the laughter that followed, Jade heard part of the punchline repeated—something about 911.

"Here we go," Samuel said. He pointed at a waitress carrying a wire container full of test tubes. The different liquors were golden, tan, green, a few bright red.

"This one's cinnamon," Robin said. She bought a Jack Daniels and downed it.

"I think I'll pass," Jade said.

"I'll buy it for you," Samuel said. "It's only three-fifty."

Jade shook her head. Robin winked.

The table of lobstermen and town women continued to buy drinks and laugh. Someone pointed out a black man at a nearby table, made a remark. Tuning out the different discussions, Jade

watched how easily they spent their money. Robin had explained that the workday began at four in the morning when
they pulled and set their traps in the dark. They worked until
noon. Afternoons they took their catch—bugs, the men called
lobsters—to the cooperative, and then repaired their traps or
boats. Sometimes they fished, too, catching halibut for the local
restaurants. In winter a few of the men wore wet suits and dove
for mollusks, which a Japanese distributor purchased with cash.
When Jade asked if the locals got tired of eating "bugs," Robin
said lobstermen couldn't afford to eat lobsters themselves.

Ellis and probably Nancy Jane and Ann took the best crops
to market. Beans picked too early or too late were designated
for the farmer's table.

Samuel covered Jade's hand with his and she let him keep it
there. Robin wasn't with any man in particular.

There was an outburst at the end of the table. A friend of
Samuel's named Jack bent toward a man wearing a pale pink
polo shirt. The stranger held up his arms in surrender, simultaneously explaining that he was merely talking to Chris, one of
the two women Jade had met back on the pier. He confessed
that he had no idea Chris was Jack's girlfriend.

"What's your name?" Jack demanded.

"Paul," the man answered in a lowered voice as if admitting guilt. Jade thought of her brother then, picked on and
beaten up.

"Your ass is suckin' wind," Jack said.

Samuel and the others tried to calm Jack, but couldn't erase
the lines of anger from his forehead, eyes, and mouth. Jade wondered how she'd sneak away if the fight got out of control, and
how she'd get home if the lobstermen became too drunk to drive
the boat. Deeber already looked bombed.

"Get the fuck out of here," Jack yelled. "Gut bucket," he

called after the departing man. Jack said, "I have to piss so bad, my back teeth are floatin'." Jack was led off with his fellow lobstermen to the men's room. With Samuel gone, Robin came around to Jade's side and explained that Paul resembled a vacationer who'd been discovered the day before trying to catch lobsters in Jack's territory. "That's a big no-no," Robin said, explaining that the lobstermen marked their territory with specially colored buoys.

Chris shook her head and took a swig of her drink. "The guy was just talking to me for Christ's sake," Chris said. She was studying nights to become a manicurist and had a six-year-old son from her first marriage who now adored Jack. "Kee-Reist," she said on an exhale. "I hate it when this happens. It gets everything started," she said. Then she looked around, knocked one of Robin's cigarettes from its pack, and lit it. "He can't stand it when I smoke," Chris said defiantly. Chris had pretty eyes, but her reddish hair was strawlike. She looked a good ten years older than Jack. Robin told Jade that Jack was sure to take his anger out on Chris when they got home.

What if Daniel had struck Nancy Jane when he'd gotten jealous of her popularity in the farming community. From all Rexanne had told her that didn't seem likely, and yet time had a way of softening ugliness. For sure, Ellis had never touched Rexanne or Vivienne. But she wondered about her father's friend Dillon.

After the men returned, Jade had a couple of dances with Samuel. During a slow one, he pulled her tight. Peeking over Samuel's shoulder, Jade saw Chris trying unsuccessfully to get Jack to dance.

On the boat ride back, the passengers were subdued. Only Samuel had gotten a second wind. He hung off the side of the boat and hollered, probably to impress Jade. Then he worked his way up to the front of the boat where he stretched out below the windshield. He lay on his back, eyes closed, as the boat sped toward home.

"It's not their baby, is it?" Robin asked. Even a little drunk, Robin was expressive, her hands flying out from the sides of her body as she spoke. "I had to ask you."

"What do you mean?"

Robin wanted to be sure that Jade wasn't a surrogate mother for the Sturgeses.

"No, no," Jade said emphatically. She didn't mention that at one time she'd thought of selling her baby to the Driscolls.

"Good," Robin said and looked up at the sky. Just before they docked, Robin told such a complicated story of surrogates that Jade couldn't keep the chain of events straight. The upshot involved two people, unaware that they were siblings, having sex.

Samuel offered to accompany her, but Jade walked home alone. Crossing the damp lawn, she made her way toward a small light deep in the house. After quietly opening the heavy side door, she crept through the unlit rooms. Before she reached the staircase, she heard Ellen's voice, high and strained.

"Your mother called."

"My mother?"

"Your mother," Ellen repeated, though *she* seemed more like the mother waiting up for Jade instead of leaving a Post-it note.

Jade instinctively anticipated a reprimand, questions of her whereabouts, then grounding for the next couple of days and nights. But she quickly reminded herself that Ellen was her employer.

Ellen said, "She wants you to call her back."

"Now?" It was three in the morning.

"She said she wanted to talk to you," Ellen said, then she got up and went to the stairs. She was wearing a yellow-and-white seersucker robe.

In the kitchen Jade dialed the number in Massachusetts that she now knew by heart. Rexanne's voice was deep and sleepy. "Jade, your grandmother died."

The announcement surprised Jade. She wanted to say, "I always thought she was already dead so it's no big deal." But it felt like a big deal. And Jade wasn't sure why.

"What happened?"

"She forgot everything. She even forgot how to swallow."

"When did this happen?"

"It's been sort of gradual," Rexanne said. She coughed. Rexanne confessed that she'd had to move Nancy Jane into a nursing home and that was where she'd died. For weeks Rexanne had been cleaning out the house in preparation for selling it.

Jade listened to the silence between her and her mother. In the distance, peepers screamed into the black outside.

"I've got my eye on a car that I'll pack up with everything I want to keep. We can start a new life. You, me, and the little baby." Rexanne paused. "Jade, I'm coming to get you."

"I've heard that before," Jade said.

9

july

By now, one good shot of me and most people know what's going on. I can still fool a few of them. Ellen's gardener, who Robin calls Purple because he wears purple socks or a lavender T-shirt or violet shorts, tells me just about every day that the Maine air must be stimulating my appetite, fattening me up.

My breasts are the shocker. Rory wouldn't believe how big they are.

With all its moving around, I can't help but think about the baby. Yesterday it was hiccupping.

One minute I want out, and the next I'm trying to figure what it will look like. I want it to be a boy, but I think it's a girl. I could ask one of the doctors that Ellen takes me to. But, what's the sense of knowing the baby's sex when you don't know for sure who's the father?

The baby could have such curly red hair I won't ever be able to shake the image of Mike digging his feet into the hard dirt around us. His face turned all serious concentrating on something beyond either of us as he went on jerky and urgent like some tractor on the fritz.

Or blue eyes like Rory's eyes, bright with the promise of a different kind of life, yet nothing else about him unique enough to drive him from the place where his parents set him down.

Or what if the baby gives me away by growing into a fussy kid who stacks toys the way Mr. Donnelly tidies his piles of papers?

The baby could connect with the song, "Joy to the World," coo at its silly lyrics, hum its melody when she's older. Conceived at the moment the song burst into the barn with a presence of an actual person coming upon me and Alvin, pants down to knees. Bits of straw everywhere I could see.

I dream about sex a lot these days. These aren't pleasant dreams, cloudy with kisses or passion. They're dreams where I'm attacked, forced into positions no body could ever get into on its own. In one of them, two Mexican boys hold me down in a car wash, the soapy strips snaking over my terrified body.

The dreams are worse than any of the other recent side effects— varicose veins, puffy ankles, leg cramps, and Ellen constantly at me to drink more water. She's bought me a special water bottle holder I can sling over my shoulder. But I don't.

The baby could have Nancy Jane's drive to change the rules and carry on her last crusade to make life easier for farmers. Though I never met her, I don't like to think of Nancy Jane dying and her causes forgotten.

Sometimes you see little girls that look as though they got every single gene from the mother. I doubt I'll be so lucky. Still, I picture the little baby with my green eyes and dark hair. Sara told me a baby's hair can fool you. Sometimes it starts black and then all falls out and comes in another color, maybe blonde. I don't want the baby to look like any boy I know.

So I'm waiting. Sometimes I feel all I've ever done is wait. Wait and wait. For Benjamin. For Rexanne. For Ellis. For Nancy Jane. For stories of Isabel. And now for the baby. The baby's the one I can't imagine. Even more than Benjamin.

I still expect to see him. The way he always looked to me. The body in the casket wasn't anyone I knew.

Jade expected Rexanne to sleep in her first morning in Maine, the air crisp and scented with evergreen. But she slipped down-stairs and into the kitchen before Jade finished setting the break-fast table. When Rexanne arrived late last night, Ellen had shown her to a guest room prepared by Paulina with fresh flow-ers, towels, and bars of soap in the shape of starfish and seashells. Jade had hoped the new cleaning lady would be as fun to talk to as Pearline, but only the names were similar. Rexanne had exclaimed that the room was lovely as a hotel.

Then she made a fuss over Jade's haircut, which everyone else had long since grown accustomed to. Rexanne promised to even up the ends. Unlike Nancy Jane, Jade hadn't touched her hair since initially cutting it. In fact, Jade thought it had almost grown out to the length she was used to wearing.

"What's on the menu?" Rexanne now asked Jade.

"Eggs Benedict," Jade replied without looking up from her preparations.

"Fancy," Rexanne said, running her hand through her short hair. Jade couldn't get used to her mother's cut, much more dramatic than her own. Since Jade had last seen Rexanne, her long brown ponytail had disappeared; the new cut looked frosted in places. Sometimes Rexanne had parted her hair in the middle and left it hanging straight down her back just the way, she said, it had looked all through high school.

Jade had thought she'd be happier to see her mother, but somehow Rexanne jammed Jade's feelings together; the blend of old farm life and new au pair life annoyed her.

"My favorite cook," Rexanne said brightly, though her eyes looked tired. Her nails were bloodred and a cell phone was clipped to the waistband of her slacks. Rexanne's nails had never been anything but natural, though every once in a while, sitting in front of the television with the family, she'd absently buffed them to a high shine.

"Are you still a vegetarian?" Jade asked.

"Yep," Rexanne answered. "Still can't touch the damn stuff." She cleared her throat and immediately produced a cigarette.

"I don't think Ellen will go for that," Jade said, nodding at the smoke.

"No problem, sweetie. I'll take it outside."

When Rexanne returned, Jade could detect the slight odor of smoke, which, if she concentrated on it, would make her gag. The cigarette had energized Rexanne. She had a slew of questions—How was Sara? How was Ellis? Was Ellis still living with "that frilly woman"?

Defensive of her father, Jade gave cursory answers, then posed a question of her own. "Who are you expecting to call?" Jade stared at the cell phone. Everyone in Connecticut, even the children, had one, but she never would have expected it of her own mother.

"Tom," Rexanne said succinctly, as if Jade should know what that meant.

Before Jade could gather any information on the mystery man—was he a boyfriend, some cousin Rexanne hadn't told her about, or somebody else?—the twins appeared in their pastel nightgowns. They stared at Rexanne. While Jade was still making introductions, Carolyn suddenly squealed and ran at Jade. Vicky laughed, and the sunny kitchen filled with the little girls' enthusiasm.

"Let me help!" Vicky called. Jade told the child to find the bread. The girls began arguing over who would assist until Jade assigned Carolyn to set the table. Silverware clinked around the little girls' voices. A few minutes later, Jesse showed up, followed by Ellen and Ted.

Jade still hadn't gotten used to their noise first thing in the morning. As soon as the family hopped out of bed, they switched on the television, landing headfirst in the problems of the world. In Nebraska, where everyone was up even before the sun, the beginning of the workday was almost reverential. Jade used to drink her juice or coffee without exchanging half a dozen words with Rexanne or Ellis or Benjamin. Then she walked out to the barns, the darkness stifling any commotion. Sometimes she felt she was still deep in her dreams as she absently fed the animals or milked a goat or gathered eggs. Only when the sun appeared and she was eating a hearty breakfast did Jade talk with her family, radio voices in the background droning on about grain prices.

When Rexanne and Ted shook hands, Jade thought she saw him study the red fingernails. Her mother's right middle finger featured a whitish icon that Jade guessed was either an astrological sign or possibly an open book. She didn't ask.

"So, what do you do?" Ted asked. Jade thought the question sort of blunt, though he *was* working on a new book. Every time he started a project, he went into reporter mode, questioning everyone around him. Once he even startled Jade by asking what she planned to do with her life.

Rexanne put her hands on her hips. "I'm in transition at the moment."

Ted smiled and said, "Know the feeling."

The family filed into the dining room. None of the adults spoke until Jade brought the eggs to the table. As soon as Ted complimented Jade on the melon soup, Ellen said, "I love the Fosters dearly, but I can't believe Judy would serve wine that wasn't sulfite-free."

Catching Rexanne's attention, Jade prayed that her mother wouldn't roll her eyes the way she always had at Ellis. But Rexanne sipped at her soup, then gracefully put her spoon aside to take the platter of eggs from Ted. When the dish came to Jade, she portioned some to each of the twins. Sitting side-by-side, Rexanne and Ellen looked like different species. With Rexanne wearing lipstick and a bright turquoise blouse, Ellen appeared to have been bleached a couple of shades lighter. She wore no makeup; her hair was very blonde, her clothes all whites and beiges.

"Oh, excuse me," Ellen said, turning to the others. "Judy Foster is one of the women from my Mensa Moms group back home. She happens to be vacationing about a mile from here."

Although she was certain Rexanne wanted to know what in the hell Mensa Moms was, Jade hoped she wouldn't ask. Jade would explain later about the group of high-IQ mothers who shared ideas for making their children grow up smart. Connecticut women didn't get together to quilt or to exchange gossip and recipes while their children attended meetings of Future Farmers of America or their husbands rallied for an ESSOP event.

"How are the courses going, sweetie?" Rexanne asked gently. Jade cringed.

"Oh, she finished up and got her GED," Ted said, not without a hint of pride.

"I don't mean that," Rexanne answered, as if graduating from high school were as routine as brushing teeth. She put her fork down and flicked her new hair away from her eyes.

"Oh?" Ted said and glanced at Ellen.

"Next year me and Carolyn go to school," Vicky announced, her mouth full of toast.

"That's very nice," Rexanne said. She took a taste of egg, *mmmed* at Jade, swallowed, and said, "ACC. Associated Correspondence Campus."

"Oh," said Ted again. He smiled the way he did when one of the children used the wrong word in an endearing way.

Looking down at her plate, Jade was sorry that she'd ever confided her plans for the hotel management course. Neither Ted nor Ellen admitted to Rexanne that they knew nothing of Jade's interest in the program. They politely let Rexanne go on about the school and its "highly qualified instructors." When Jade had first come to live with the Sturgeses, they'd told her almost immediately that they'd both graduated from Yale.

Jade finished her breakfast without talking. She honed in on different conversations, but mostly she hoped Rexanne wouldn't incriminate her further with her own past.

All the time Jade and the children cleared the table, Ted and Ellen and Rexanne discussed vegetarianism. Jade left the dining room as Rexanne said, "It got so I couldn't look one of my hogs in the eye."

Then her phone rang and Rexanne's voice became high and cheery, so unlike her last days on the farm. As she carried the phone from the dining room table, her voice trailed into the next room. Jade knew that Ted and Ellen were subtly exchanging looks. And at the next meal, Jesse would want to bring his own phone to the table.

Jade sat down in the kitchen. She was sweating. The family was back upstairs by the time Rexanne got off the phone and breezed into the kitchen. She put her arm around Jade. Then she quickly withdrew it to pick up the blank book with the leaf-green, textured cover that had been her parting gift. Rexanne flicked through the pages.

"I'm glad to see you're using this," she said, then stopped. "What have you got written in here?"

"Recipes," Jade said. "I needed to look up my melon soup entry to remind myself how much honey to use."

"Recipes?" Rexanne said. "I thought you'd . . . I don't know. I thought you'd be writing something more personal in here."

"Recipes are personal."

"OK. But I was thinking more like your feelings."

Sometimes Jade thought she didn't have any feelings, couldn't cry if she wanted to. She hardly heard Rexanne going on about how badly she wanted to find a diary of her mother's, how delighted she'd been when she'd read Ann's.

"Why didn't you tell me I had a grandma?"

"I just didn't mention it." Rexanne slid a pack of cigarettes out of her pocket, lit one and tapped it against a saucer she used as an ashtray. Jade didn't reprimand her.

"What was I supposed to think?"

"Jade, sweetie, I can't tell you what to think." With each puff of the cigarette, Rexanne went deeper into the past. She talked about how angry she'd been with Nancy Jane. Jade felt reluctantly tugged down a long dark tunnel, and she had questions all along the way. But Rexanne didn't stop babbling long enough for Jade to form a significant question. Finally her mother stubbed out the cigarette. Jade opened the window over the kitchen sink.

"Why did you leave us?" Jade asked, looking out the window, away from her mother's face and the bright fingernails. She was remembering how tightly Ellis had held her when Rexanne had driven off from the farm.

"I was afraid the rest of us would be killed." Jade heard Ellen's and Ted's footsteps directly overhead, and the lighter patter of the children down the hallway.

"And you didn't care if *I* got killed?" Jade's own voice, loud and accusing, surprised her.

"You know I tried to take you with me."

Jade felt her emotions punched all around the kitchen.

"All of my friends said, What's wrong? You're not over that yet?" Rexanne described the different prescription bottles she'd not taken a single pill from. She reminded Jade that she'd stopped going to church. Maybe Rexanne's latest changes—the hair and cell phone—were symptoms of that same loss.

"I could forgive Ellis many things," Rexanne said. "But not for not crying."

Normally Ellis did leave pain festering in his body, gurgling in his gut with a beer, pounding in his head with a headache, maybe letting only a fraction of it out when he pulled the trigger on a gun along with his buddies.

Jade instinctively wanted to stand up for her father, to reveal all he'd confessed so that Rexanne would understand. But, respectful of Ellis's confidence, Jade let the impulse pass.

"Why didn't you write?" Jade asked instead.

"Didn't you get the letter I sent you last week?" Rexanne reached into her pocket for another cigarette.

"I mean after you left."

Rexanne blew a series of smoke rings into the air above Jade's head. "I wrote. I think Ellis probably didn't want to show you."

Jade rolled her eyes at her mother.

"I wrote," Rexanne reiterated. "Not at first. But after I got settled in Massachusetts I wrote regular." She said that she had called, too. "He wouldn't talk to me. And every time I asked for you he said you were on a date."

A date. Maybe with Rory they were called *dates*. But the rest of her encounters were hardly dates.

"I've got to get these dishes cleaned up," Jade said.

"Let me help you."

"No. This is my job," Jade answered and Rexanne obediently sat on a bar stool.

After scraping the white plates, Jade loaded the dishwasher

then wiped the counter surfaces with antibacterial dish detergent. As an accompaniment, Rexanne hummed a song that sounded like "Crazy." They'd talked about the past, but Rexanne hadn't mentioned a word about what the two of them would do tomorrow. Or the day after. Where did Rexanne want to take her? She looked settled right here in the kitchen.

Ellen came into the room, tilted her head back. She was sniffing out the smoke. "I'm off to town," Ellen said softly. "The girls might need help getting dressed."

"Who was smoking?" Jesse asked from the doorway. His oversized clothes made him look huge. Rexanne raised her hand, wiggled her fingers, but didn't apologize. Jesse looked toward his mother.

When they'd gone, Rexanne said, "That boy reminds me just a little of Benjamin."

"You've got to be kidding," Jade said.

When Adam arrived in Snow Harbor, it was the first time he'd gotten off his bike in seven hours. Ted had laughed, admitting that he didn't even like being in a damn car for seven hours, let alone working his legs into a frenzy. Ellen shook her head, but she was smiling. Jade pictured Ellen's pastel notes posted to different parts of Adam's body—wash here, bandage this, dry this, presoak the cotton. . . . Ted had been the one to invite Adam to visit in Maine. Although he no longer rode, he enjoyed talking about bikes; he'd been an enthusiast during college.

Adam hadn't looked exhausted, but happy to see Jade. And when he'd kissed her gently on the cheek, everyone went silent except for Vicky, who giggled. Jade felt moisture from his lips making a visible imprint. It was then that Rexanne had suggested that Adam settle not in one of the many spare bedrooms directly above, but down at the sea house. Ellen had appeared relieved, not put out, at the idea.

Jade didn't think that Rexanne's recommendation had a thing to do with privacy. Rexanne had probably counted on the opposite—the distance between the main house and the secondary one would dispel rumors, discourage romance. In fact, Jade snuck down to the sea house at every opportunity.

The ceiling in the main room was so high that whoever cleaned the cobwebs from the beams would need a ladder. Pine beams stretched the length of the room. The main room, two bedrooms and kitchen were painted pale yellow, the shingles a grayish-blue, and the wraparound porch stained the color of oak. Because Adam tended to distance himself from other people, the place fit him perfectly.

But Ellen and Ted didn't let Adam feel too independent down by the waterfront. Throughout the day, one or the other intermittently popped in to check on a lightbulb or a spare roast in the freezer or the supply of beach towels. At the purr of the approaching battery-powered vehicle, Jade would prepare herself for the intrusion. The Sturgeses never interrupted an embrace or a kiss. But they tromped all over a discussion Jade and Adam would be enmeshed in—turmoil in the Mideast; the tyranny of corporate sponsorship of sporting events; the stupidity of 90210. And, most heated of all, his diatribes against the waste of the wealthy. She wondered if Nancy Jane had gotten so verbally worked up about farming issues when she was alone with Daniel, or if she saved her orations for the crowds.

Now Jade and Adam sat on wooden armchairs on the porch. Adam talked with the same fervor Jade imagined he pedaled his bicycle. As he was mentioning a country she'd never heard of, she studied the regular slap of the ocean, its distant crashing softened, yet not stilled, by the harbor. A passing breeze was refreshing in the heat of the late morning sun.

Adam brought her an orange juice. "I forgot to give you this," he said, handing her a soft package covered with brightly flowered paper. "It's from Pearline."

Jade sipped the juice then tore off the colorful wrapping to find a pair of support hose that Pearline had once told her would ease the pressure of her swollen legs. Tucked in with the stockings was a piece of paper that held three names, complete with addresses and phone numbers, and Pearline's comments. "Single mother who lost her baby," "Rich yet happy couple," and finally, by the third name, "The answer to your predicament."

"Pearline's a good woman," Adam said, "but she's beholden to those Connecticut assholes." He made a sweeping gesture with his right arm, then went on to explain that Pearline felt his aunt had saved her from the poverty that had taken over her country like a disease. He believed Pearline had exchanged that poverty for another kind of oppression. Before Jade could empathize with Pearline, she heard the puttering of the golf cart. "Here they are again," she said. But minutes later it was Rexanne who walked onto the porch.

She wore a short, sleeveless pink dress and white sandals. In the light breeze, Jade noticed her mother's nipples protruding against the soft cotton. Rexanne brushed her hair from her face.

"I've got tuna fish," Rexanne said brightly.

"It's only eleven-thirty," Jade said.

"Well, we don't have to eat right this minute," Rexanne said.

Adam pulled up a seat for Rexanne, a low multicolored webbed chair that was meant to be sunk in the sand.

"Isn't this gorgeous?" Rexanne said. "It's a shame to think of leaving." Jade didn't know if she was referring to herself or to Adam or to all three of them.

Small ripples, aftershocks of the distant waves, caught the sun as they made their way to shore. Jade silently watched the water as if it were the opening scene of a newly released movie.

When Rexanne unwrapped the sandwiches about an hour later, Jade was surprised at how good hers tasted.

"It's the dill," Rexanne said and smiled. After a pause, she added, "Are you going to jot it down in your book?"

Jade looked away from her mother at the same time that Adam said, "What's the book?" Rexanne explained briefly about the gift that Jade had misused. As she spoke, she worked her feet out of her sandals. Rexanne's toenails didn't match her bright red fingernails, but were a deep metallic blue.

While Rexanne spoke to Adam, Jade watched her face lighten. She'd never seen her mother act coquettish around one of her friends. In fact, she'd never seen her mother flirt at all. The practicalities of running a farm didn't allow frivolous departures. In Nebraska, even the radio wasn't purchased for the music that pulsed through it but for the daily gravel-voiced report of grain and livestock prices.

"Food's important," Adam said. "And great food. Well, what's better than that?"

Jade thought it odd that Adam was championing food, which normally he thought of solely as fuel for his bicycling body. Adam pushed back in his chair slightly and announced that he was going for a swim. When he went into the house to change, Jade felt Rexanne's eyes on her. If they were back in Paradise, if Adam were Rory, Jade imagined her mother would say, "He's cute, Jade." But today Rexanne said nothing.

Within seconds, Adam reappeared, not the least bit self-conscious in a black Speedo suit. He was slender and tanned and muscled, particularly in his calves. The hair on his chest and forearms was very dark. Jade watched as he walked gingerly down the porch stairs, stepped around the smooth rocks on the beach and up to his ankles in the water. Not so far down the beach, Jade spotted two young people on a blanket. Each held the other's face. Then the girl stroked the boy's hair. They laughed and talked and pulled into one another until their blue-jeaned legs became tangled and Jade couldn't tell whose legs were whose.

Hearing a splash, she turned to follow Adam's figure stroking long and regular, farther and farther away. Her mother was gone, too. Jade walked around to the other side of the porch in time to catch Rexanne in the golf cart slowly cutting across the huge lawn. Rexanne was waving to Purple, trimming a mass of bushes at the top of a hill.

Adam stepped out of the water and onto the porch. His foot-prints stained the floorboards and trailed into the bathroom. While Adam was changing, Jade heard someone at the door. It was Robin.

"Hey," Jade said. "How come you're not working?"

Robin explained that she'd gotten the afternoon off. One of the owners of the paper mill had died the day before and the mill closed at midday. "Out of respect for the dead guy," Robin said.

"Why not the whole day off?" Jade asked.

"They told us Mr. Fingerhut wouldn't have wanted to lose a full day of production just because he died."

"Unbelievable," Jade said. Robin and her coworkers could use somebody to champion them.

"I saw you from the beach," Robin said. She had a six-pack of beer in one hand and a bag of thick pretzels in the other.

As she came into the room, Robin said, "Who's the guy?"

And then, as if on cue, Adam appeared in jeans and a fresh white T-shirt, which stuck to him in places where he hadn't dried off completely. Robin offered him a beer.

She turned to Jade. "I brought this just for you," she said, producing an alcohol-free beer Jade had never heard of.

Adam asked if Robin had met Rexanne. "Who's Rexanne?" Robin asked. She pulled her chair up close to Jade. Jade revealed how Rexanne left Paradise, and Ellis had taken up with Vivienne. When she mentioned her mother's mission of uncovering the stories of their ancestors, Adam said, "Important work." Then Robin told the story of her own mother being shot by another lobsterman in love with her.

"Wow," Adam said. Robin said she'd never really felt a part of either of her parents.

As Adam and Robin traded embarrassing stories of their upbringing, Jade couldn't truly grasp why he felt ostracized. The only thing she could point to was his intelligence. She wondered if it had been the same with Nancy Jane, the bright young woman who caught her stride only after leaving the farm.

When Jade returned from retrieving a couple more beers, she noticed Adam and Robin sitting very close, her hands a whirl of emotion trying to make a point. Adam was explaining his theory that everyone had two sets of parents—the couple who bore and raised you and another two people you chose as adoptive parents. The chosen parents were ones you sought out because their opinions jibed with yours; you weren't just jammed together because of the gene thing. You weren't obligated to love them.

"So who are your chosen parents?" Jade couldn't resist asking. "The Sturgeses?"

"You don't know anything," he said, getting up and going out to the porch. Jade knew that Ted and Ellen had taken an instant liking to him without word one being spoken. Jade also knew that she would always resent Adam's money and social standing, even though most of the time he spent with her he was trying to forget about it.

After a few minutes Robin said she was leaving. "Want to go over to the Clam Hut? It'll be a corker," Robin said.

"I really don't feel like it. Sorry," Jade said. Some days her body was a tremendous weight she was pushing around from room to room. Robin called to Adam, who waved from the porch.

When Jade sat back down with Adam he was explaining that contrary to what most outsiders thought, wealthy people weren't lazy or inept or cowardly. Intrinsically recognizing their own limitations, they *couldn't* start from the bottom and make it. Jade didn't totally grasp his argument. If he really believed that, she didn't think he'd be so hard on people with money. She always had to ask him a lot of questions to absorb his ramblings. But she did sense that he was confessing something about himself, and felt obliged to reciprocate.

Although the sky was still a light gray, the moon was becoming visible. Jade's heart picked up speed as she rehearsed how she would tell him.

"I had a brother," Jade said.

"You never told me you had siblings." He turned to her, his face silhouetted against the fading backdrop of sky and sea. A flock of birds cut black forms through the air.

Jade bent away from him and looked down the beach as she revealed a few details of Benjamin's last year.

When she paused, Adam asked, "How did he die?"

Jade shook her head, widened her eyes.

Rather than admit that she'd botched any interrogation by moving the body, she shrugged her shoulders. "No one knows," she said.

"They didn't investigate?" Adam asked. Jade shook her head again.

Adam put his arm around her. It was warm against the cool sea air blowing their way and the tide creeping closer to the front steps.

"When I was a boy, I made this safe in my bedroom wall?" He described cutting through Sheetrock with a steak knife, and installing a fireproof safe. Having seen safes in the movies, he'd always wanted one of his own. Because his mother thought he wanted to start saving money, she hadn't gotten angry at him for destroying the wall. Instead, she bragged about her juvenile banker to all the members of her reading group.

"From time to time she'd ask me how much money I'd accumulated. I always told her it was a secret. She never pressured me to show her what was inside. Thank God. Because what I kept in the safe wasn't money at all, but pictures of naked women."

Jade laughed. Was Adam using this story to come on to her? Before she'd decided for sure, Adam bent to her, kissed her hard. The phone rang. It was Ellen asking if she was sure they didn't want to come up for dinner. Jade said no, she was pooped. Rexanne got on the line and said there was a good movie on at nine.

When she hung up, Adam took her by the hand and led her into the room where he slept. Everything he did was gentle, yet very determined. He pulled down the nubby white bedspread on the single bed, turned down the sheet, sat on the edge of the bed while drawing her to him. He peeled off her T-shirt, unhooked her bra, while looking into her eyes the entire time.

When he finally lowered his hands as well as his eyes to her belly, Jade became self-conscious of her size. He ran his hand so lightly over her middle that she barely felt it. He pressed his ear to the swell of her.

No one had ever made love to her this way. Like real slow music. Even when their pace quickened he watched her, touched her face softly, was careful not to put his weight on her.

Afterward, she ran her hand along the sheet, the pillowcase. She didn't think the material could be more than 200-count.

They dressed in silence and then walked along the beach. Adam said, "You probably should leave these jackasses. Raise your baby somewhere far away from them."

The moon now lit the sky, the gentle lapping of the water becoming less and less visible. Adam's dark features were getting lost in the evening. Down the beach, a group of people had a fire going.

"It's probably almost time for *Killer Cops* or whatever that movie is your mother wants to watch."

"Probably," Jade said. She said the stars made her think the sky had been bitten in lots of places.

"That's weird," he said. "But I like it."

Jade stopped, turned to Adam, and held his face, stroking his hair like she'd seen the girl at the beach do to her boyfriend. But he didn't respond by taking her finger in his mouth the way the boy had.

It felt like just the other day that Jade was wrestling over whether to leave Blue Field for Maine with the Sturgeses or to stay behind with the "hatter to the stars" and his baby-needy wife. Tomorrow she would take off with Rexanne for Chicago.

Jade had a friendly discussion with the Sturgeses. Ted had

said he understood completely that Jade would want to be with her mother now. He'd done all the talking while Ellen stared at some point above Jade's head.

"Andre French isn't the father," Jade finally said. "I don't know why I said that."

"That wouldn't have mattered," Ellen said.

"Really?" Jade said.

"I don't think so," Ellen said. She paused. "It would have been nice."

Then Ted had patted Ellen's hands folded tightly in her lap and suggested that Jade return to Blue Field when she was ready to settle down, making both her and her mother sound like foolhardy teenagers.

"And if you change your mind, that's OK, too. You can turn right around without giving it a second thought," Ted said. He insisted that he wanted to tell the children *after* she'd gone. His mouth had twitched when he referred to the children.

Ellen had touched Jade then, put her cool fingers on Jade's wrist and squeezed. "Call us if you have any trouble," she said.

Jade had gotten used to the family, even its snobbery, its wastefulness. Just last week they'd bought a large rug and hired two men from town to install it in the garage because Ellen thought the cement floor was too cold for the children's feet. "Hey, man. Try not to scratch the bike," Jesse had said to one of the workers. The Sturgeses parked their car on a rug nicer than any rug in Ellis's house. Jade had laughed when she relayed the story to Rexanne, but she didn't let Adam know, because the incident would have infuriated him.

With Rexanne upstairs packing while the Sturges family watched television in the sunroom, Jade took her time with the after-dinner cleanup. She dried pans and silverware, then concentrated on swiping around the sink and stove.

She'd talked to Ellis before dinner. It was harder to tell him that she was leaving with Rexanne than it had been facing Ted and Ellen. Ellis humphed, then went into new details about the ESSOP. Cassidy now had four phone lines and a fax machine to disseminate information to the growing membership.

"What does he need four lines for?" she asked, though she really didn't care.

"Oh, he needs them," Ellis said, keeping the conversation away from Rexanne. But, at the same time, every sentence he uttered seemed, in some way, relevant to her. "Be careful," he finally said. The hardest would be telling her father about the pregnancy. She had no idea when or how to do that.

When she first heard the tapping sound, Jade thought a squirrel was scrounging on the porch. The noise persisted. It was Robin knocking lightly on the kitchen window.

"I just wanted to say good-bye and good luck with the baby." Robin would have left for work by the time Jade and Rexanne hit the road in the morning.

Jade suddenly wanted the whole scenario to change, for Robin to insist that they could remain friends, stay the whole year in Snow Harbor. But Jade had seen the town only during the weeks when a temperate climate seduced "people from away"; she hadn't spent a winter in Maine. Maybe Robin could go with her, becoming part of her future the way Jade had once counted on Sara. Adam, too. A train of friends crossing the country.

"My ancestors are from here," Robin blurted.

Jade paused as if she was thinking that over, but really she was just letting herself give in.

"I used to clean this house," Robin said. "When it was owned by the Ward family." Robin widened her eyes. "It's an incredible house."

"It's big," Jade said. "And there's that great view of the ocean from upstairs." She heard herself sounding like Vivienne, pointing out the best points of a prime real estate offering.

What could she offer Robin other than simply freedom? Like Rory, Robin accepted her given boundaries. Jade's ancestors hadn't been so complacent.

Not that long ago, all Jade wanted was to go off with Rexanne. How quickly her emotions had shifted so they were no longer pointed along the straight lines of a tarmac road.

"Adam's still up," Jade said. Robin turned to look in the direction of the sea house. Two small squares of light stood out like paintings.

"Have you told him good-bye?" Robin asked.

"Sort of," Jade said. She should let him try to talk her out of going, but she was afraid he'd want to sleep with her again. And she wouldn't be able to say no. And then she'd feel bad that they weren't more crazy about each other.

"Go down and say hello," Jade said.

"I don't know," Robin said. "He rides that bike like a horse."

Though she wasn't sure what Robin meant, Jade smiled. Hearing her mother in the hallway, Jade quickly hugged Robin and, with both hands, closed the door gently. Robin's hair smelled of pine.

"All packed, honey?" Rexanne asked.

"Not exactly."

"Well, get a move on. I'll finish this up for you." Rexanne promised Jade that in Chicago they'd visit La Roux, once Nancy Jane's best friend.

That prospect should have excited her, but Jade could only stare at the tiny lines sprouting from the corners of her mother's eyes. A clean glass pie plate sat on the counter. Jade would never make that pie from the Blue Field apples that she'd promised the twins.

"Why so down in the mouth?" Rexanne asked. "We'll have a regular adventure." Jade sighed. "Oh, sweetie," Rexanne said. Spotting an open bottle of wine, Rexanne took a juice glass from the nearest shelf and poured herself a glass. She tasted it. Then she emptied two packets of Sweet'n Low into the burgundy liquid, stirred with her finger, and took another sip.

"I've got a story for you. In fact, I was going to save it for our trip. But I think I'd better tell you now."

Rexanne looked up at the ceiling, then toward the refrigerator. Her lipstick had worn off, and when she pushed her hair from her face with one sweep and held it back, she almost looked like the Rexanne Jade had known in Nebraska.

"I'll be right back," Rexanne said. She returned a few minutes later and motioned Jade outside with her. The sky was black to one side of the large house yet full of stars. On the right, an incomplete piece of moon changed shape with passing clouds. Hearing the children's voices inside the house, Jade looked toward the large lit room. Rexanne guided Jade onto the lawn. They stopped at a bench near one of Ellen's flower gardens.

"To tell you about your great-great grandmother Isabel, I really need to tell you what I know about her father first."

Jade was ready for a story that would take her away from the subject of her own leaving.

Rexanne smacked a mosquito. Then she said that Isabel was born on a small farm in Massachusetts which was sold by the time she was school age. The family moved to Boston where Benjamin, her father, found work as a carpenter. Rexanne interrupted her story to say that when she'd gone to Boston for the first time two months ago she couldn't believe how old it looked. "You could just picture horses and carriages pulling up to the brick houses on Beacon Hill." She added, "It even smells old."

"What does that mean, 'smells old'?" Jade asked, but Rexanne ignored the question.

The family stayed in Boston until Benjamin caught what was called "Western fever," the emotional flu of the day that left a person restless, sleepless, agitated, and mumbling about the world becoming "too civilized." Too crowded. Luticia, Isabel's mother, had no desire to abandon Boston. She was not bored with spinning flax that some of the neighbor women complained of. She'd already left her family farm to follow her husband's wishes. But, in those days, a wife obeyed every decision the head of a household made even if it were spoken under the weighty stupor of alcohol.

Rexanne produced a flashlight the size of a pen and a couple of pieces of paper that she read from.

I remember leaving home. It was the day on which I began my diary. Every departure from the community was treated as a death with all of the townsfolk turning out for a large dinner and send-off. I was thirteen. I could not imagine so many people attending my funeral.

"Let me see that flashlight," Jade said.

"Later," Rexanne said, going on to explain that although Isabel saw how tearful the departure made her mother, she soon looked on the new lifestyle as a camping trip that would go on for months. She couldn't believe they'd actually left their house behind and had nothing to return to.

It was spring when we left, after a difficult winter in Boston. The air was crisp and I could smell the earth, which for so many months had been covered by snow. All my father could talk about was the Pacific Ocean. I did not understand this fascination. Every summer we saw the Atlantic Ocean. We stretched out at its shore, swam into its waves, raced along its edge. "Pacific" held no meaning for me. My father's dream caused nothing but tears in the family. There was much terrain to cover before reaching the other ocean. My father mentioned mountains and forests and deserts as my mother shook her head and said, "Indians." "Sickness." "Bears."

Long after our wagon left town, I still heard crying. I thought this crying was in my head, that perhaps it would not leave me. Soon I discovered this noise was not crying, but the squeaking of the wagon wheels. For most of the trip, it felt as if I was dreaming. My mother and father and five brothers and sisters and one sister-in-law and two young men, who traveled along to help out, were spread among three flat-bed wagons. To see what distance we traveled, my oldest brother tied a rag around one of the wheels of the cart. We took turns counting the rotations.

My father had planned the trip for many years, down to the water barrels hanging off the side for gathering rain. One of the wagons he specially made had two stories and beds built in. We brought flour and ham and sugar and coffee, blankets and clothes. Dried codfish, beans, bullets, and guns. And we brought ten saplings because my mother heard tell that there were no strong trees in the west.

Rexanne stopped reading to say that Isabel listed everything in her diary, even Benjamin's threats that the transplanted trees wouldn't grow west of the Mississippi. The main reason the girl documented the journey was because Luticia felt Isabel needed to keep reading and writing now that she wouldn't be in school. Isabel was the youngest of the children.

Benjamin had looked for the best oxen for a month before buying his. During the long days on the road, Isabel thought up names for each of the twenty-five animals. She slipped food treats to Banner, her favorite. Once after they'd passed through a valley of yellow and blue wildflowers, she stuck flowers under his yoke.

On some occasions we saw the leavings of the travelers before us. It could be a slightly warm campfire, a container of trash. But other times, we spied furniture—a chest of drawers, chairs, a huge wooden table—abandoned to weather in an effort to lighten the load. These reminded me of bones. They were the skeletal pieces of a house. "See there," my father said repeatedly, to strengthen his argument with Mother, who had wanted to transport her mahogany bed out west.

Summer was nearly over by the time they reached their midpoint of St. Louis. When they came to the end of trees and saw the tall grasses, Rexanne said it must have looked like a premonition of the ocean. They took the Oregon Trail, headed for the Platte River to guide them through the state, but settled in Paradise, Nebraska, when Luticia died. She'd caught pneumonia during a particularly violent thunderstorm and finally gave out on the high plains that would become the family's home. Benjamin, of course, blamed himself for his wife's death and set to putting down roots in earnest. He never mentioned the Pacific Ocean again. The trees from back east were planted and Isabel watered them regularly.

Rexanne paused in her story to emphasize that when the

family reached Paradise, there was no hotel, no place to bathe and rest. There was merely a piece of land on which to build a future. Rexanne said people today didn't have the guts to change their lives the way their ancestors had.

Jade considered that if Isabel could do what she did, what was the big deal in getting in a car with Rexanne? There were McDonald's every few miles, cell phones, radios.

"One question," Jade said.

"Shoot."

"Why did you name him Benjamin if you didn't want anything to do with Nancy Jane?"

"Jade, I named your brother after the character in *The Graduate*."

"Dustin Hoffman?"

Rexanne nodded. "The real question is, how did I know to call you Jade?"

"What are you talking about?"

"I'll tell you when we get on the road."

Jade wanted to press her mother for details, but the cool moist air had penetrated her sweatshirt.

"Well," Rexanne said. She stood up and struck her thighs with the palms of her hands. "We're all set, kiddo. I've got this ATM hooked to my savings."

10

august

I forgot what a bad driver Rexanne is. Not bad in the way that some people get talking and sail right through red lights. She can focus. In fact, she's way too focused if you ask me—on stuff that doesn't have anything to do with traffic. She'll say, "What in the hell does the guy in front of us have on his head?" She'll move up to within inches of his back bumper, give it some gas, but then hang alongside until she's satisfied she knows what's what.

I never want to be the person who cuts her off. She's up their tail like nobody's business. Doesn't care who they are. After a trucker wouldn't let her get over to make her exit, she kept up honking so long, the guy finally raised both hands like he was being held up. Then she flipped him off and stepped on it. "So, how's my driving?" she turned to me and asked. She's not like this with people any other time, just when she's behind the wheel.

Now Ellis is a good driver—defensive, careful, courteous. No matter how angry or upset he is, he never takes his feelings out in a car.

With me, I don't think of the other drivers as people. Just crap you have to deal with to get from one place to another.

For the longest time, that's the way I thought about the baby. I couldn't categorize it as an actual person. It was more a feeling than

a body with a head and fingers and toes, something that was wrong
with me. A flu. And all I wanted was Rexanne to spread a cool
washcloth across my forehead like she did those times I got a fever,
so that by morning I'd be back to normal.

Sometimes I thought about whether it would be a boy or girl, and
I tried on the different possibilities for father, but I never truly believed
I'd have a real baby. Just like I didn't imagine I'd ever have breasts,
and then there they were. I thought they were little bruises on my
chest the way they felt all tender at first.

The ancestor stuff is totally different. When I finally understood
they were once actual people, the last one of them died.

But I can't pinpoint exactly which night my feelings changed about
the baby. I guess it was after Rexanne and I mapped out our route
to Chicago. The morning we left Maine with a plan, I started to
worry. Would her head be too big? Would she have all her fingers?
Would her eyes be permanently crossed? Would she be slow, even
retarded? Would she learn to walk or join the heap of Jerry's kids on
TV? Would she be normal? Would I want her to be normal? Would
she be gay? Would he be gay?

What if something goes wrong like something's always gone wrong
with my family?

When I was a little girl I worried about the chickens, the cows,
even the beans. Sometimes I thought I was the only member of our
family who was concerned about whether we could pay our taxes.
But after Benjamin died, I saw there was no reason to worry. It was
all so far beyond us, I might as well relax and take what comes.

I think I would have gone on like that, letting time and boys roll
right over me if it weren't for the baby. The baby's changed everything.
The baby's made me start to worry all over again. It's like my mind's
turned completely around. All this baby stuff has me curious like I
probably was when I was a little baby myself.

Jade had imagined a leisurely drive to Chicago, but Rexanne pressed on at a steady fifteen over the speed limit, stopping only when Jade complained that she needed food or the bathroom.

"You can't have to go again," Rexanne said.

"I've got a baby sitting on my bladder," Jade said.

"Forgot. Sorry." She squinted. "Fish my sunglasses out of the glove compartment, will you?"

The RV Rory had shown Jade would have been perfect for this trip. Jade could have lounged in the back, read magazines whenever she wanted, gone to the bathroom every ten minutes without having to make a big deal of stopping. Prepared lunch on the tiny stove, while making calls on Rexanne's cell phone— to the Sturges children, to Robin, to Pearline. To Ellis and Vivienne. Maybe to Adam. And all without leaving the air-conditioning.

After a while Jade grew bored with the monotony of the interstate and started bugging her mother to finish telling about Isabel. Midway through New York State, Rexanne flicked off the radio and picked up her story.

Rexanne said that the first season in Paradise, Isabel's family probably planted peas, beans, potatoes, maybe prairie peas, spiderwort, and phlox. Between the time they settled in Nebraska and Isabel married, diary entries became sketchy. Rexanne thought without Luticia to prod her, Isabel didn't have much interest in recording observations. Jade suggested that it had more to do with the fact that during hard times, Isabel had needed a place to store her emotions.

"Oh, there were plenty of difficult times ahead," Rexanne said. "Not to mention blizzards and twisters."

Isabel was just sixteen when she married Frank Taylor against her father's wishes and moved to a new farm. Frank was ten years older, tall and kind. They built their own house with long

strips of prairie sod chopped into pieces the size of bricks. Sometimes flowers bloomed on the roof. Isabel grew to like cooking
for him, mending his clothes, and reading him stories at night
after dinner though he was always asleep before she reached the
conclusion.

"How do you know Frank was kind?"

"She said it in her diary," Rexanne said.

"She said 'kind'?"

"Can you just listen?" Rexanne asked.

"OK," Jade said as if she'd just won a point.

"Can I continue?" Rexanne said.

She was married less than a year when Frank, along with
most every man in Nebraska, joined the Union Army and set
off from home. Though Isabel could take over some of the farm
chores that Frank had patiently demonstrated, she couldn't handle the entire farm herself and was far too proud to ask her father
for help. Coming from a big family and spending her youth in
a city, she grew intensely lonesome in the middle of a huge plain.

And frightened. There were stories of savage Indians on
horseback and armed with every conceivable weapon—guns,
bows and arrows, tomahawks, scalping knives. Before long
she'd dug a secret room in the sod house where she could wait
out Indian raids. Isabel slept with the handle of an axe in her
left hand the times the Indians built fires on the outskirts of
town and sang all night. The songs made her think of howling
coyotes.

She became angry at her husband for leaving her, angry at
the war, angry at her hard-hearted father who'd shut her out of
his life. Sometimes she mistook the night birds' calls for Indians
laughing and covered her head with the straw-filled pillow.

Jade felt the baby kick. The baby wouldn't let her forget
about her body for more than a few minutes at a time.

While the Civil War waged on, groundbreaking ceremonies took place in Omaha for the building of the Union Pacific. Isabel went with some of the women from town and two of her sisters. She heard from one of the railroad workers that Frank had been killed and would not be coming home.

For the next couple of days she stayed on in Omaha, asking stranger after stranger for details of her husband's death. But no one had a thing to tell her except that he was gone and she was young enough to start over. More than one of the men winked at her.

In Paradise a wolf started following her around the farm. He grew so tame that she could pet him. She called him Frank, and for a time she believed that he was the spirit of her dead husband, keeping watch over her. She fed him; he slept at the door outside her house. She read stories aloud at night with the window open.

But a neighbor accused the wolf of raiding his henhouse and shot the animal. Shortly afterward, Isabel sold the farm and moved to Omaha where she used the money to open an inn at the beginning of the railroad, the "real road" the man at the bank called it.

She met Tak just as construction began on the railroad. He was small, about her size, and had straight black hair. He was from China. He'd crossed the sea, lived in San Francisco, was the best worker on the Central Pacific, then crossed half the country to reach Nebraska. Rexanne didn't know if the Union Pacific had lured him away, or he'd simply happened upon Isabel's inn.

He wore floppy blue cotton pants and shirts and worked methodically, seldom taking breaks. Though his English was excellent, he seldom spoke to the other workers. With the dynamite, he was a master. He could set it, light it, and run off to safety with such speed the others were amazed.

Laying rails, straightening, leveling, spiking, tamping.

Isabel was impressed with how brave he was. She became his lover almost immediately. In her diary she wrote that she hoped by sleeping with him she'd receive some of his strength. Instead, she grew weak with love. She wrote page after diary page for Tak. With Frank she'd felt comfortable, safe, warm. With Tak she felt on fire.

"I wish you could read it," Jade interrupted. She wanted Isabel's actual words, not her mother's interpretation of them.

"I can't read and drive. Besides, I've read it enough times that I won't leave out a single syllable."

"Let me drive then," Jade said.

"Just listen."

Rexanne said that Isabel sneaked into Tak's room every chance she got. When the other workers taunted him for his clothing, she altered Frank's clothes to fit him, chopping a foot off the length. But the others, mostly Irishmen, ostracized Tak as much for what he did as for what he looked like. The bosses held up Tak as an example of what was expected of each worker. The harder Tak worked, the more hostile his comrades became.

The affair was discreet. No one knew. When Isabel could have made it known by giving him the excuse he needed to fend off the workers' accusations that he stole a horse, she said nothing. She could have said that the horse was taken in the hour that Tak was beneath her, breathing in her deep breaths.

Isabel saw how the others, the ones with the roughest mouths and hands and who had more to do with whiskey than wielding tools cut their eyes at Tak. Their rumors, their name-calling made her love him more. Tak sounded like a noise, not a name. A secret sound she loved to hear herself say over and over again until it became rain.

She'd only just learned of her pregnancy when she heard

about Tak's accident. He died in the explosion, never to worry what they would do with a baby between them.

They said there was nothing left of him. When no one could find his body, she thought, for sure, the other workers had sabotaged him.

She thought of Tak to the exclusion of her business. With the war over, few wanted to stay at an inn without accoutrements, despite Isabel's occasional tasty meals. After her baby, Ann, was weaned, Isabel gave herself over to the sweaty bodies, the hardened arms and legs. She changed her name to Bel.

Isabel sold her inn and started a new one farther west, closer to the point where the men were laying track, a mile a day, three strikes to a spike. The building with its sod base and cloth covering looked like a huge prairie schooner, a large version of the ones in which her family had originally traveled west. She didn't grow rich on the sweat of the workers as the railroad did. But she was able to support herself and to hire on a couple more women.

The hell-raisers dominated the settlers, at night filling the town with fighting and whoring and profanity. Every day as the clanging of iron echoed out across the plain, the men in the forward positions vulnerable as they encroached on Indian hunting grounds, Isabel searched for a piece of her lover. She wasn't content with strangers' advice that he was dead as she'd believed when Frank was missing. She looked for the gold ring that Frank had once given her, that had fit Tak's baby finger. She looked for Tak's dark eyes, his tender toes. She looked for any part of him to be sure that he had really happened to her.

She didn't look at her daughter. Rexanne stopped her story to light another cigarette. "It's a disaster for a child if the parents love one another too much."

"My baby should be in pretty good shape then," Jade said,

surprised that she'd actually used the phrase "my baby."

Isabel moved west another time, following the progress of the railroad. But that town, too, disappeared after the track was laid. Even though the general store and liquor store and gambling hall were abandoned, Isabel stayed on. Saturday nights became an entertainment for old-timers who remembered Bel and men passing through on their way somewhere else. Eventually the town was a stop on the railroad line, which Isabel herself never rode. She only listened to stories of the men who rode it and built it. To her, a machine screeching across the plains, making clouds of its own, was the end of something.

"Did Isabel have any other babies? From other men?" Jade asked.

"I'm not sure."

Jade wondered how Rexanne was sure of anything, how much what Rexanne told her varied from what was actually written down, how much what was written down varied from what truly happened.

Ann left to reclaim part of her grandfather's farm, the original Paradise land then owned by a great uncle who'd moved on to Colorado. The rest of Frank and Luticia's family had moved farther west as well. Ann started a life apart from her mother. Shortly after, Isabel died in an Indian raid, her body, too, never recovered. Ann didn't search for more details because she didn't understand a woman who believed there was nothing dumber than a cow. Ann spun wool for relaxation, not for sharing stories with other women. She could shoot better than boys. She caught rabbits and found the eggs of prairie chickens. The railroad brought wood, which Ann bought to make a real house. And the railroad took her crops to market.

When Rexanne had finished with the story, Jade asked, "How do you know all this?"

"Research." Rexanne explained that she'd been following leads and visiting libraries for months in Massachusetts. "Plus the Internet."

"They never found Isabel's body?" Jade asked. Rexanne shook her head.

"There was a folktale." Rexanne briefly detailed the story of Isabel finding Tak and the two of them moving into an abandoned mine. Jade thought the theory intriguing, but Rexanne dismissed it. "Rubbish," she said.

"How could I have known to call you Jade? Back when I had no idea of our ancestry. Before I knew diaries existed?" Rexanne cleared her throat. "I thought I called you Jade because it was one slip of a letter that made you stand out. So easily you could have been Plain Jane, but you were precious to me."

"How long have you known all this?" Jade asked. The sky felt wobbly. One incident could create a chain of people that went on and on.

"Not so long. I put things together the last couple of months. I've still got some stuff to figure out."

"Me, too," said Jade. She was thinking again of her brother. She wanted to know if Rexanne had researched that story. But Rexanne simply shook her head.

Until they neared Chicago, Jade couldn't lure her mother into much of a conversation even when they stopped and the heat suddenly pressed on them like someone had dropped it from above. And when the weather nearly smothered her, all the other stuff did, too, especially leaving Robin and Adam, Vicky and Carolyn. Her body as well as her head felt terribly uncomfortable. She whined. Rexanne bought her a lemonade and hurried her back into the car.

Cranky with all the traveling, Jade asked what was the big deal with visiting La Roux. Rexanne reminded Jade that the woman had grown up with Nancy Jane in Nebraska. Jade finally coaxed her mother into saying, "I want to find out why everybody left town. La Roux went to Chicago and your grandmother to Massachusetts." She lit a cigarette.

"Why do you think La Roux will tell you?"

"She's old," Rexanne said. "Nancy Jane's dead. What can be the sense of holding onto information?"

"You never know," Jade said.

"Oh, you know," Rexanne said, pointing at another mileage sign to Chicago. Then she was quiet again.

Jade looked past the sign, at the skyline featuring a huge mall similar to others they'd passed since Massachusetts. Her ancestors had never encountered any real stores as they pressed through the elements, moving directly along the ground, taking turns walking beside the wagon. Inside Rexanne's car, with the air conditioner going full blast, you wouldn't even know it was summer.

With a convention in town, hotel rooms in Chicago were hard to find. The only vacancy was in a small expensive hotel touted as European style. Rexanne said, "What the hell," and snapped her American Express card on the glossy check-in counter. "We'll go high on the hog for a couple of nights," she whispered to Jade.

Dark polished wood and brass filled the small lobby of the Taunton. In a cozy sitting room off the lobby, deep green and rose upholstered chairs were angled at a large marble fireplace.

"Classy," Rexanne said when she came up behind Jade and peered into the room. "But you must be used to this. Being with the Sturgeses all this time."

"Nope," Jade said. A richly appointed, as the Sturgeses said, room was always a surprise. Jade couldn't imagine ever having the time to coordinate colors and fabrics and shapes to make such a pleasing picture.

Outside, a man sat on the curb behind a sign that read, "Free Advice." Jade considered for a minute if he recited adages like, "If you find yourself in quicksand, never struggle." Or did he answer questions. What would be better—having a baby girl to continue the line of women in Rexanne's history or a baby boy who might look like Benjamin?

When they opened the door to their room, Jade plopped onto one end of the king-sized bed while Rexanne poked around the room. Rexanne unlocked the hospitality bar, setting glass clinking against glass and metal. She held up a miniature bottle of vodka. "You want a Coke or anything?"

"Not one that small," Jade answered.

"The Cokes are regular size," she said. She squinted at the can. "Yep, twelve ounces."

Rexanne returned to rifling through the minibar as Jade gulped her Coke. "You don't want to know how much these cashews cost." Rexanne displayed a fancy container full of huge nuts.

Rexanne surveyed the room. "Why wasn't I ever as happy to open the door of my own house as a clean hotel room?" Jade didn't answer. She was thinking whether the baby could get tired before it was born or if only the outer shell of the mother wore down.

Rexanne sat on a corner of the bed. "Next time you know what I'm going to do? I'm going to polish the brass—if I'm ever so lucky to have brass—and wipe the mirrors, turn the place spotless, so I only have to do what hotel housekeeping does each morning. No unmade beds for me. No, sirree. I'm going to treat my refrigerator like a hospitality bar, stock it with expensive treats and drinks I can't afford to eat and drink."

"What about milk?" Jade asked. "Where would we keep plain ordinary milk?"

Rexanne ordered room service for dinner, a rosemary chicken plate for Jade and eggplant Parmesan for herself. A young man pushed the meals into their room on a table covered with a pale pink tablecloth. At the center of the table sat a tiny vase with two white carnations. The server removed the metal coverings from their meals, setting the thick odors of garlic and onion loose on the room. Rexanne made a big issue out of writing an extra tip on the bill. As soon as he left, Jade pulled a chair up to the table.

"Isn't this fun?" Rexanne asked.

"Mmmm. How are we going to pay for it?"

"Jade, I spent the first half of my life getting worked up over money every turn I took. I'm just not going to make myself crazy anymore. That's why they've got all those cards. You don't even have to see the money."

Not seeing money was exactly what had bothered Ellis. He argued that if he gave someone a stack of cash for a tractor, he knew precisely where he stood. The way it went, his life had turned into paperwork, so many lines of numbers he couldn't make out what he owed from what he was worth.

"Where do we head after Chicago?" Jade asked. Though she knew the idea was crazy, she wanted to direct her mother back to Ellis, urge them to repair their relationship, use all the credit cards and ATM cards on themselves.

"First, we have to see La Roux, your grandma's best friend. I need to bounce a few ideas off her."

"Can we see Aunt Ethel and Uncle Conroy as long as we're here?"

"I don't know if that's such a hot idea," Rexanne said. She wiped her mouth with the stiff cloth napkin, which matched the tablecloth. "Maybe we'll stay here awhile." She called room service to pick up their dishes.

"This hotel?"

"Not this hotel. But Chicago," Rexanne said.

"What's awhile?" Jade asked. By simply planting herself in a new location instead of forging onward, Rexanne believed something positive would inevitably happen to her. Jade, on the other hand, had it in her mind to go all the way to the West Coast. To California, which Isabel's father had originally dreamed of, to San Francisco where the other half of the Transcontinental Railroad began. She and Rexanne had gotten up momentum now, traveled through Maine and all of northern New England, across the breadth of New York State, skimmed along the southern edge of a few of the Great Lakes. But they still had most of the country to go.

Jade filled out a hotel postcard to Adam.

"He's a nice young man," Rexanne said.

"He's OK."

"Jewish?"

"Uh-huh."

"What'll your father say?"

"I'm not going to marry the guy. I'm writing him a postcard." She ran her palm along her middle.

Rexanne started talking again about why La Roux and Nancy Jane had left Paradise. "I'm guessing it had something to do with a man. Except that Nancy Jane was no spring chicken at that point."

As intriguing as Rexanne's stories were, Jade wanted her mother's attention.

"Where was I conceived?"

Rexanne stopped talking only momentarily. "I have no idea," she said.

Jade wanted specifics. Was the setting for her beginning a rose-colored bed a shade darker than the tablecloth in front of her?

Rexanne sighed. "Jade, your father and I had known each other since grade school. When we grew up and got married, we were so crazy for it, we jumped each other every chance we got. Even out in the field. Sometimes we were so exhausted from the farm we could hardly lift our forks to feed ourselves at night, and yet we found the strength to make love. It's impossible to know which time because there were so many. That's what I'm trying to say."

Rexanne stood up and pulled the heavy curtain back. "They call this the Gold Coast," she said, opening the window and blowing smoke against the heavy summer air and the sounds of traffic. But Jade concentrated on a field, Ellis and Rexanne rolling into one another in the soft, barely damp earth he'd just plowed. Could it have happened in a motel room? For sure no place so fancy as this spot in the Taunton.

Jade wished she'd paid more attention in science, particularly to the sections on genetics. Then maybe she'd understand how the Chinese part worked. Was it a strand, a pinpoint? What exactly had belonged exclusively to Tak, making its way down the line to her black hair? And why hadn't her brother inherited any of the traits of that ancestry?

"What about Benjamin?"

"What?"

"Do you know where he was conceived?"

"Absolutely," she said. "Benjamin was planned."

Rexanne looked straight ahead and didn't say anything more. Jade considered whether Rexanne had kept track of her temperature on a notepad by the side of the bed the way that Vivienne had, whether Ellis had looked at her routinely with hope.

What did it mean that the child who was planned for, desperately wanted, was lost? So quickly. What greater danger was Jade in, she who'd been conceived in haste, by chance, with no thought for the future? Or had her very beginning made her stronger? The parts not coaxed together, but joining of their own tough will, their need to survive at all costs because no one else was thinking of them.

She thought of the trees purposely planted in strange soil and others propagated by wind and insects and animals.

"I wanted both of my babies very much," Rexanne said.

"What do I put on the forms?"

"What forms?" Rexanne said.

"You know, forms that say 'white' or 'African American' or 'Asian American' or 'other'?" Other. Before finding out about Tak and how complicated a lineage could be, Jade had pictured a dwarf as "other."

"White," Rexanne said sharply. "Don't get carried away."

La Roux Homer lived downstate, not far over the city limit, on a street of small identical brick houses. She had been born two hours after Nancy Jane, the town doctor in Paradise proceeding to La Roux's farm immediately after he'd delivered Nancy Jane.

La Roux was tiny, pretty even, and looked amazingly young for someone over eighty. Sara's great-grandmother never left her bedroom, where the single unmade bed against the wall was surrounded by stacks of old newspapers and magazines.

"Hello, hello," La Roux called. She had whitish-blonde hair and wore lipstick, a purple skirt, and a feathery white blouse that made Jade think of a bird. Wisps of fabric stood out from the fancy blouse that could easily have belonged to an exotic dancer.

La Roux hugged Rexanne and Jade. She stood back, looked Jade over, turned to Rexanne. "You never told me you were about to be a grandma," La Roux said. "Congrats!"

Instinctively, Jade looked around for the twins before remembering that she'd left that responsibility in Maine.

"Won't be long," Rexanne said, going for her cigarettes.

"Oh, not in here, honey," La Roux said, putting her hand on Rexanne's. "Smoke don't bother me one bit. But Bambi puts up a hissy fit."

Jade immediately lost her awareness of her own body when she spotted the large gray and white cat sitting beneath the archway to La Roux's dining room. He swung his tail emphatically.

"See? Don't even want me talkin' cigarettes."

The room was full of knickknacks with a menagerie of animal figurines on nearly every surface. One end table featured woodland animals—a squirrel, a deer, a wolf—another, creatures from the sea. Everything was out of proportion. Photos of La Roux were interspersed among the different animal groupings. "That was taken just last year," La Roux said proudly of a picture of herself in a white bikini. The lamp to one side of the photo had a blue shade trimmed top and bottom with little white balls the diameter of pennies. Jade jumped when something brushed her leg.

"Barney," La Roux admonished. "Don't go scaring my guests." Barney was a white rabbit not quite the size of the cat. Another woman appeared in the doorway and was introduced as Tara.

Tara wore no makeup. Her movements were stiff, her expression blank and fixed. The straight hair parted down the middle and pulled tightly into a ponytail looked like Rexanne's photos from high school except that Tara's hair was gray. When Tara left to prepare drinks for the women, La Roux identified her as her brother's granddaughter who'd come to Chicago to get over a divorce. Tara had stayed on with La Roux in "Chitown." La Roux pronounced the name as if all the residents were bashful.

"Nancy Jane never mentioned you having any children," Rexanne said.

"No. Just Bambi and Barney. They're plenty for me."

La Roux said, "Don't worry about Tara. She doesn't like my lifestyle. But then, I doubt she goes for anybody's." La Roux worked as a breakfast waitress for a short-order cook and spent her money on face-lifts, tucks, and general cosmetic improvements. Jade imagined herself watching a cult movie instead of sitting inside an actual woman's house.

"I say it's nobody's business," La Roux said directly to Rexanne. Jade imagined Rexanne contemplating what La Roux and Nancy Jane had in common besides the coincidence of their birth. But before Rexanne could ask a question, La Roux retrieved a hula hoop and held it about three feet off the floor. "He could go much higher before he got so big," La Roux said.

Jade wished Ellis could see the size of this cat.

Without any coaxing, Bambi ran across the room, jumped through the hoop and then looked at La Roux. "Tara, where's the Lickin' Chicken?" A hand came around the corner to deliver a small red canister with a drawing of a cat's face on the front. The whole routine, right down to the presentation of the treats looked choreographed.

La Roux sat on a stool and lined five yummies on the rug. Bambi faced her, the treats between them. "OK, you can have one," La Roux said. "Just one." Bambi immediately hooked one of the treats and pulled it toward him, ate it, looked up.

"That's the most amazing thing I've ever seen," Rexanne said.

"Wave to Mama," La Roux said. The cat stretched, put both paws on La Roux's knees, then swiped at the air with one of its paws.

Bambi proceeded to box, say his prayers, play dead, and open the cabinet under the kitchen sink on command. Rexanne exclaimed after each of the tricks and even Jade had to say, "Wow," a couple of times.

"What does the rabbit do?" Jade asked.

"He watches," La Roux said. "He's the smart one." She paused. "And he loves up to his mama sooo good." La Roux lifted the animal and kissed the top of its head.

Rexanne invited La Roux to go out to dinner, but the woman shook her head. Too many people used animals as an excuse not to go fifty miles from home, Jade thought.

"I'm sorry," La Roux said. "My tail's just not twitchin' today." She sat down.

"You're doing fine," Rexanne said.

"Yeah," Jade said, waiting for Rexanne to segue from pet tricks into a discussion of why La Roux had moved away from Paradise.

As soon as Tara left to run errands, La Roux said, "Your mother and me were pals when we were little kids. Then she got involved in all that political stuff." She slapped at her knees. "We were always competitive." The old woman explained that being born on the same day used to make her think Nancy Jane was her twin. Jade wondered if La Roux worried that her own death was near; Rexanne had written to her right after Nancy Jane died.

La Roux sipped at her tea, touched her neck occasionally, as if assessing it for cosmetic improvement, and reminisced. Anticipating the cross-country trip, Jade couldn't always concentrate on La Roux's stories, despite the fact that they involved Nancy Jane.

When Rexanne leaned forward and knocked over a china squirrel, Jade looked at La Roux. La Roux admitted that Nancy Jane had causes outside of Paradise, political agendas to improve other people's lives, while La Roux's project had been herself.

"I don't see what's wrong with that," Rexanne said, though Jade sensed her mother was only humoring the woman. Even La Roux didn't seem convinced. When Rexanne asked the big question, La Roux was ready.

"I left town because of a married man."

"A married man?" Rexanne asked.

"A married man who broke my heart. All the time I knew him, he was married. Knew he didn't love his wife. Just didn't know he loved someone else in addition to me." La Roux succinctly explained that after he died, she left Paradise.

"He had one arm, but boy did he make do with that one arm." La Roux explained how the man from Texas could hunt and sail.

Jade heard Rexanne catch her breath. And shortly afterward, Rexanne made an excuse about needing to get on the road. "Where do you stay?" La Roux asked. "Still in Paradise?"

"No," Rexanne said. "Not Paradise."

Before she'd gotten to the car, Rexanne had one cigarette going in her mouth and an unlit one in her hand. "It's amazing," Rexanne said.

"She could make a lot of money with Bambi," Jade said.

"La Roux and Nancy Jane were seeing the same man. Neither of them knew, I mean, they each knew there was another woman. They just didn't know their best friend was it."

Jade hadn't considered that those kinds of affairs went on in the old days. And she couldn't imagine her *grandmother* having an affair. But then, Isabel and Tak had been a complete surprise, too. Somehow, though, Nancy Jane's past felt a little more real after meeting her contemporary.

Rexanne said she thought La Roux would have more stories about Nancy Jane's life, particularly the twenty-some years between leaving the farm and her death. But, apparently, Nancy Jane hadn't kept in touch with anyone from Paradise after she'd left. Rexanne wondered aloud if Nancy Jane had started seeing the man before Daniel died or after.

"How did he die?" Jade asked.

"Who?"

"The one-armed bandit."

"Nancy Jane said it was an accident, but she wasn't more specific than that." But Rexanne confessed that she didn't know how much of what Nancy Jane had last told her was reliable. Jade's grandmother deteriorated dramatically during the time Rexanne had lived with her.

"Sounds like a segment for *Unsolved Mysteries*," Jade said.

"I should write a book," Rexanne said.

Jade thought about trains. Sleek, fast-moving engines gliding across the country toward a destination in California no one in her family had seen. She visualized the different cars in bold, primary colors, like the toy train Benjamin had adored.

Rexanne said the Transcontinental Railroad didn't exist anymore. According to her, it was all Amtrak with no more reverence for the romantic past when the country was first connected by rail than bungee jumping had for committing suicide. She said, "What's your hurry?" and "Why don't we just linger in Chicago a bit. I'd still like to take La Roux to dinner and see if we can't pump her for a few more stories." But Jade didn't think the hanging back had much to do with La Roux. Rexanne seemed to be waiting for something else.

Jade kept at her mother. A baby wouldn't postpone being born until Rexanne got off her butt. Rexanne's motives were revealed the third afternoon at The Three Bears Motel, a run-down two-story building attached to a popular working-class bar outside the city. The room was decorated with an orange plastic curtain at its only window and dull, marred paneling on the walls. The back of the door looked as though an actual bear had tried to claw its way to freedom. Alongside the bed, a patch of rug was patterned with cigarette burns where countless people had fallen asleep smoking.

Jade wished they'd stayed in the fancy Taunton Hotel second. That way this place might not appear to be such a dump. When she reminded her mother about the ATM card, Rexanne said, "We don't want to go crazy and max anything out."

Rexanne's cell phone rang. She walked outside with it, leaving Jade in the room with a view of a black pickup, its entire hood lettered with "Have a Good One." The truck hadn't moved in three days. Rexanne laughed. From the smeared window, Jade watched Rexanne writing something down.

"Where are we going?" Jade asked after they'd checked out.

"It's a surprise," Rexanne said. She wore makeup and had applied a fresh coat of strong-smelling nail polish.

"Does it have to do with Benjamin?" Jade asked.

"What?"

"I have a feeling we're not headed for the train station."

"Drop the train shit, Jade," Rexanne said. Her voice sounded tired rather than angry. "Besides, what in the hell would we do with the car if we got on a train?"

"We could leave it with Aunt Ethel and Uncle Conroy."

"Aunt Ethel? My God, Jade."

Jade didn't really want to see the couple and their bakery, which might remind her too much of Benjamin. And yet she'd go if it would mean taking the train to San Francisco. She'd do anything. Jade remained quiet as Rexanne criticized Ellis's brother.

Beyond the Chicago suburbs, the grass was burnt in places, the trees coming closer and closer together, then breaking apart to accommodate large stretches of warehouses or small farms. Isabel and her family might have passed this same way when they set out for the west from Boston.

"I think you can at least tell me where you're taking me," Jade said.

"A friend's house," she said, and at that pulled onto a gravel road. A few minutes later, she parked in front of a white trailer on cinder blocks at the end of a line of similar ones. Two dark green plastic chairs sat on the small metal porch.

Rexanne honked. A man opened the door and smiled.

Although it must have been seventy-five degrees, Jade's hands were cold. She pressed them along her cotton skirt when she got out of the car to follow Rexanne.

Tommy was taller than Ellis, darker, and younger. He had an openness about him, the opposite of Ellis with all his humphs. Tommy was the sort of guy who would fire a gun with his eyes closed; Ellis would memorize the target before he ever closed his eyes. Tommy's eyes were light blue and his nearly black hair was caught up in a stubby ponytail.

"Come on in," he said, ushering them in front of him as he held the door. He knew Jade's name without Rexanne making an introduction. The enthusiastic way he opened his doors and closets reminded Jade of someone who wasn't used to entertaining guests. There were no posters or paintings on the walls, no photos or knickknacks balanced on tabletops, the starkness of the rooms the opposite of La Roux's over-the-top decorating.

"How long have you lived here?" Jade asked.

"Eight months," he said, before going off to get them drinks.

"Where did you meet him?" Jade whispered to Rexanne, who shook her head and smiled.

"I ran into him in Massachusetts," she said softly. "We've kept in touch."

If a lightbulb could have gone on over Jade's head, it would have been as large as the sun. "You tricked me," Jade said.

Rexanne smiled. "I didn't trick you."

After Tommy delivered an iced tea to Jade and a gin-and-tonic to Rexanne, he went out to the car to bring in the suitcases. In their minutes alone, Jade had a ton of questions to ask her mother.

"You didn't want to visit Chicago to find out about Nancy Jane. You wanted to hook up with . . ."

"Tommy."

"Tommy."

"I had both things on my mind, Jade. The Tommy thing wasn't firmed up until yesterday."

The wood paneling in Tommy's living room wasn't as dark as The Three Bears. Every third strip of wood was light pine. Jade concentrated on the panels, counted them. The sofa and matching armchair were a pale blue and green plaid.

Rexanne and Tommy hadn't kissed or even hugged, but that was because of her. When Tommy returned with the suitcases and Rexanne got the door for him, Jade could almost feel her mother refrain from touching him. Jade held off going to the bathroom as long as possible. Rexanne kept pushing her hair back from her face. The moment Jade was out of the room they'd

go at each other, the way she and Rory used to as soon as Ellis
and Vivienne went upstairs to bed.

A push-out window the size of a piece of notebook paper was
positioned above the tub; Jade couldn't have squeezed out if
she'd wanted to. She sat on the toilet and stared into the mirror.
The vanity, which came within inches of her knees, was covered
with the same pattern of willow trees as the walls. At every
corner, the paper was peeling.

Tommy and Rexanne brought pizza home for dinner, and the
three ate it in front of the television. As soon as she finished
eating, Jade went in to bed. She left the light on awhile and
stared at her surroundings, a room that looked like it had served
as a workplace before its hasty conversion. A brand new pink
and yellow bedspread covered the single bed; Jade could smell
the fresh-from-the-package fabric. A makeshift work table on
the other side of the room was crammed with a carburetor kit,
wood glue, a staple gun, and some other tools she'd never seen
before. This was the only room in the trailer that was filled with
the cluttered evidence of living.

To the right of the room's one small window hung a collection of key chains. A rabbit's foot, a cowboy boot, a fishing lure,
a calculator. There must have been a hundred. Even the room
with the double bed, its headboard padded vinyl, where Tommy
and Rexanne would sleep, was stark as an average motel room.
Belts flung over the mirror above the white chest of drawers
were the only evidence that someone slept and dressed there.
As she drifted off to sleep with the light still on, she thought,
This must be what my baby feels. No idea what's ahead. No idea
how long it would stay.

The next morning Tommy made scrambled eggs and bacon
for breakfast. Rexanne looked as though she might take a piece

of the bacon, but, in the end, she passed. Tommy drove Jade and Rexanne to his place of business, a cement building, with a couple of floor-to-ceiling skinny windows, in front of a larger cement warehouse. Tommy was an importer and processor of materials for exotic cowboy boots. A collection of finished boots stood in a glass cabinet beside his desk.

Tommy pointed out boots made of eel, alligator, boar, elephant, lizard, deer, goat, and stingray. He announced that several of the boot styles retailed for more than two thousand dollars.

"What kind of cowboy buys stingray boots?" Jade asked. For sure, none of her ancestors wore fancy boots. She was hoping Tommy would have been something like a cook.

"Lots of stars buy these boots," Tommy said, not without pride. He glanced at Rexanne. "Quit leanin' on those cigarettes so hard," he said to her, and she immediately looked around the office for a place to snub out her smoke.

Tommy had calls to make and a shipment to sign in, so Rexanne took his truck and headed to a nearby mall with Jade.

As Rexanne put the truck in gear, she turned and said, "Well, how do you like Tommy?"

"He's all right."

"Guess what his middle name is?" Rexanne asked. Jade thought of Sara's enthusiasm when it came to boys.

"I can't guess," Jade said.

"It's Ben. Thomas Ben." Rexanne made a right following the highway signs. A light rain was misting the windows and turning everything gray.

"He likes children," Rexanne said.

"I'm not children," Jade said.

"That's not what I meant, honey. He wants a family."

"Great," Jade said. Everybody wanted a family but her, and here she was with nearly all the pieces for one of her own.

"Jade, I'm trying to tell you Tommy wants us to live with him. All of us. You, me, the baby. I've thought it all out." She paused. "I've thought about you." She gripped the wheel. "I know I've given you reason to doubt it, but I do think about you all the time."

"Good," Jade said unenthusiastically.

"I mean it. He wants us to be a family."

"He wants me to live with you two?"

Jade had thought of Tommy as a fling, a stage, a lover who disintegrates into an occasional car ride, not someone you structured your life around. Suddenly, Jade missed her father.

Jade didn't say anything as the street signs for places she'd never been popped up and then folded back into the rearview and disappeared. Rexanne pulled into a large shopping mall and parked in a handicapped spot.

"I'm not handicapped," Jade insisted.

"Then I am, OK?" Rexanne said and grinned.

Jade couldn't understand where Rexanne's abandon had come from, mainly where she'd gotten the confidence to leave and keep starting over again.

With the exception of one day of Christmas shopping and one afternoon before school started, Jade couldn't remember a time when she'd bought clothes with Rexanne. In all the years Jade was growing up, Rexanne was disinterested in outfits for herself or the embellishments of jewelry and makeup. Jade couldn't believe Rexanne now wanting a fancy watchband. But Rexanne's old practicality showed itself when she suggested Jade buy a couple of larger bras.

Despite the fact that it was the middle of the week in the middle of the day, there were a fair number of shoppers strolling from store to store, idling in front of displays and chowing down at the food court.

"You let me know if you get tired," Rexanne said. "That's the thing I remember about being pregnant with you. I'd do a couple of little things around the house and then I'd want to lay down and sleep for eight hours. Me who was used to working dawn to dusk."

"You're usually more sleepy in the beginning. Before you hit the second trimester," Jade offered.

"Oh, I was exhausted right to the day I delivered. Maybe I'd been wore out for so long, my body finally felt it had a legitimate excuse to shut down for a couple of hours at a time."

Actually Jade was tired, but she didn't want to admit that to Rexanne and hand her an excuse not to go cross-country.

The two sat down at a table apart from anyone else at the food court. Rexanne came back with a grilled cheese for herself and a chicken sandwich for Jade. Nothing special, no spice she challenged herself to discern, nothing to note in her book, yet the sandwich tasted great.

"I never thought I'd be anything but a farmer's wife," Rexanne said suddenly, as if confessing to something.

Jade took a sip of her bottled water.

"I got pregnant with you, Jade, and everything fell into place." Rexanne bit her sandwich. "For a while," she said, her mouth not completely empty.

As Jade ate, Rexanne talked about what it was like to have a mother who'd made something of herself outside of Paradise. Expecting that her daughter would get straight As, Nancy Jane never complimented Rexanne's schoolwork. Rexanne suggested that maybe Nancy Jane had been trying to protect her, not getting her hopes set on some goal she couldn't carry all the way through. "Who knows? Maybe she was jealous of me growing up in a time when you *could* have a kid and a career."

"Maybe she was just mad at you for making everything stop for her," Jade said.

"Maybe," Rexanne said. She lifted her chin in the air as if smelling that possibility.

"Did you leave home because of Tommy?"

Rexanne shook her head at Jade. "It was me. It was all me," she said, confessing that she'd never slept with a man but Ellis until she left Paradise. "Even when I found out Nancy Jane was sick. It was still about me. A whole new world opened up when I got out of town," Rexanne said. Rexanne started to talk about men.

"I don't really want to hear this," Jade heard herself saying, as she pushed her empty plate toward the center of the table. She picked at the French fries Rexanne had left on her plate.

"I think I was angry with Ellis for not protecting Benjamin any more than I had. For not making my life any better than I'd made it myself being the wife of a farmer." Rexanne sighed. "At least that's what the shrink said."

Her mother had been to a psychiatrist. It was routine as buying milk for residents of Connecticut, but not for Rexanne. Jade guessed the psychiatrist stuff happened in Massachusetts, too.

Her mother had so many secrets, she might know something more about Benjamin. Jade chose her next question carefully. "If you wanted to forget Benjamin, why did you pick a man with his name?"

"I don't know why, but it makes me feel a little good, OK?" Rexanne stuck her fork into a fry and left it there. "Sometimes these things happen, baby." Rexanne reached across the table and took Jade's hand. "You OK?"

"I don't know. My tail's just not twitchin' today," Jade said. When Rexanne didn't respond, Jade said, "It's a joke."

• • •

Jade concentrated on the train clicking along the track. Starting in her feet, the regular sound bumped up through her body, smoothing out to match her breathing. Click, breathe; clack, breathe; click, breathe. After a while, she tried to forget about the sound; she didn't want to hyperventilate or have the rhythm stick in her mind like some goofy song.

Jade was on her way back to Paradise. To Ellis. At Union Station she'd followed signs "To all trains," then tagged along with the crowd of people filing into the cars. From the platform, she hadn't been able to see either end of the train it was so long.

The train would cross the Missouri on the way to Council Bluffs, where in Isabel's time the Union Pacific had begun racing westward until it caught up with the Central Pacific. Her hands resting on her middle, Jade watched the bushes and lush crops caught within the borders of her window like a living photograph.

Yesterday, she'd lost it. She'd gone along with all of Rexanne's plans, her poking around for ancestral information, waited for her in Connecticut and Maine. Jade felt she'd been patient. But Rexanne could have told her about Tommy, warned her, *asked* her, for God's sake, if she wanted to move in with a man who fell somewhere between their ages.

Tommy tried to be helpful, even going along to pick out a crib. But at one point when all the choices about the baby felt yanked away from her the way they had with the Driscolls, Jade panicked. Jade had said something like it was her baby and not Rexanne's. Rexanne had probably only been trying to protect Tommy's feelings by pointing out that other people just wanted to help. And then that evening in the kitchen of Tommy's trailer, the whole issue of father came up like somebody had shot a gun in the air—Jade saying Tommy wasn't her father, far from it; Rexanne saying Jade could have told Ellis about the baby so he wasn't so shocked; Jade saying, "Hold it right there."

Rexanne admitted that she'd told Ellis what was going on. Jade said Rexanne had no right. Jade had thought Rexanne and Ellis no longer talked. Rexanne said that Ellis was still her husband and Jade's father. Then Rexanne changed the subject, asked who the father of the baby was. Expecting the query for weeks, Jade had a story all ready about Rory. And she intended to tell Ellis a different version—the boy was from Connecticut, making it look as though she'd been corrupted after leaving the safe confines of home and gone east, instead of it happening the other way around. But she was so riled about Rexanne telling Ellis the baby news, Jade admitted that she didn't really know— or care—about the baby's father. Rexanne slapped her then, across the face.

In the end, after tears and apologies, Tommy had made lemonade while Rexanne called Nebraska.

Jade saw how Rexanne and Tommy pulled away from each other whenever she came into a room, how Rexanne wanted Tommy to want a family. Jade didn't dislike him. Using only herbs and egg whites, he'd prepared a special omelet for her and Rexanne. Jade promptly noted which herbs in her book of recipes. Despite his ponytail, she'd initially judged Tommy as a conventional meat-and-potatoes man.

When Rexanne handed over the phone, Jade said, "Daddy, I'm coming home."

"That's my girl," he'd said, no questions asked.

Jade didn't talk about the baby or the fight with Rexanne. She told Ellis only that she wanted to play candy checkers with him when she got to Paradise. He once bought chocolate-covered cherries—white ones and dark-chocolate ones—and they'd lined their respective colors on either side of the board. They ate the ones they'd captured, the cherry juice oozing down her chin.

"How long has he known?" Jade had asked after she'd hung up. Rexanne had shrugged, sent her hand through her hair. Jade thought of her previous phone conversations with Ellis when he hadn't mentioned the situation, talking instead about advertised water fights or a pioneer picnic or a new animal he'd rescued.

"He's your father," Rexanne said.

"A father," Jade said, "not a weapon." And when Rexanne had looked at her genuinely puzzled, Jade said simply, "He doesn't need to know *everything*." Rexanne didn't understand that flopping the truth down in the middle of the table like a prize goose wasn't always the right decision.

That's my girl.

He wanted her. No matter what was up with her or Rexanne or Vivienne, Ellis still loved her. Jade wasn't sure her mother was capable of emotion that unconditional. When she saw Ellis, she'd tell him Rexanne didn't know anything. The baby's father was from Connecticut, maybe a rich boy who rode bikes instead of getting a job, who'd ridden away from her right after he met her. She wouldn't give a name.

When Rexanne and Tommy dropped Jade at the train station earlier, Rexanne handed Jade her cell phone in case there was "the slightest problem." Tommy told her to "take 'er easy."

Now the land just outside the train rose and fell in small hills. Jade touched her middle, and, as if in response, the baby moved.

When the train stopped, Jade didn't pay attention to the name of the station. A thin, middle-aged man in a short-sleeved tan shirt took the seat diagonally across from her. He opened and closed the briefcase on his lap a couple of times before turning to a man sunk into his seat reading a magazine. The tan shirt man began asking questions, eagerly awaiting an answer only to deliver a new question—whether the train was on time, how often the man rode the train, what his destination was, where his home was. It went on and on, like a dog repeatedly pushing a ball on someone's hand, and the man nearest the window probably just home from a day's work, worn down by the demands of supervisors and clients and the troubles of his fellow workers.

The women to Jade's left were yakking nonstop. One of them said, "Cheese? I love cheese. I put cheese on everything. I should have been a rat." The woman closest to Jade was recounting a story of how she *almost* got a butterscotch candy stuck in her throat. The other wasn't even trying to connect the candy story with what she wanted to discuss—how much it would cost to pave her driveway. Someone else was discussing the three *P*s of cold weather—plants, pets, pipes. "Bring them inside or wrap them."

For a moment, Jade wished that she could blather right past all the issues she'd eventually have to mention to her father. Fields of mature wheat passed by, crops blowing into one another as the sky dulled with the end of the day. Just as Jade was falling off to sleep, she thought she heard someone mentioning the Transcontinental Railroad. The route of the Union Pacific had originally followed the Platte River. How hard the men had worked back then, under grueling conditions and long hours, how dangerous their work exploding stone, fitting steel like huge fillings in the enamel-hard earth, pounding the metal until it sang out. Jade tried to picture Tak in his floppy blue outfit, his chest and back sweaty when he first spied Isabel, who was pretty and headstrong.

The railroad workers had slashed and dug and planted track along the river, making one town after the next. Jade wondered if, crossing hostile Indian territory without cranes or bulldozers, Tak had laid the ties or placed the heavy rails, driven the spikes or aligned the track. Or if he did each of these tasks at some point during the long and exhausting project. Did Isabel cook for him, envelop his bruised limbs with kisses when each night he returned his worn body to her? Did he sleep heavy and still as the tracks freshly laid or did he move against her all night long? What were their conversations in candlelight? In darkness?

There were too many stories Rexanne's research couldn't begin to unravel. Right now Jade wanted to hear the jabber around her transformed into a conversation between Isabel and her lover. Jade wondered how different their everyday words would be from these passengers'. What would her ancestors have thought if they could have glimpsed in a flash their descendant making her way home on a fast night train? Paradise unconnected by roads, railways, and telephone lines was unimaginable.

Returning was probably the right thing, not just the only thing left to do. Maybe a person *should* stay right where they were planted, like crops rejuvenated themselves. She would talk things out with Ellis, make plans to put the baby in the little room upstairs by hers, the one that always seemed as if it belonged to Benjamin even though he'd never slept there. She could get her ACC degree and then, with or without Sara, a job running a restaurant in a nice hotel like the Taunton in Chicago.

She could even call Rory if she wanted to go the traditional route. Get married, gently lead the baby into her old life, advising which mistakes of hers not to make.

Or she could do something less predictable.

Something she'd always wanted to do. Something everyone around her had grown too soft to do.

She could follow the approximate path of the Union Pacific until it hit Ogden, Utah, and became the Central Pacific.

All she had to do was stay on.

Jade had nearly sixteen hundred dollars in her wallet, money she'd saved from working for the Sturgeses.

Ellis would have left early to meet the train. She pictured him at the station, on the platform, shifting his weight from one foot to the other, sifting coins deep in his pockets through his fingers, shaking them as her arrival time neared. He would be thinking of what his daughter would look like pregnant; maybe he'd be remembering his wife pregnant with *her* and how much hope he'd had back then. Maybe he'd be thinking how this life kept going on and on despite every failure, every good intention. He might humph to himself.

It would be too sad watching him waiting for her, his face concerned when she didn't get off. She wondered if he'd be in his militia garb.

Jade dug out the cell phone Rexanne had given her for emergencies. She hit the tiny power button, heard the purr of connection that shot out far beyond the train. When the green light flashed slow and steady to indicate that she was in range, she carefully pressed each of the keys of her old phone number. It rang. She pictured the wall phone in the kitchen, the animals recovering in cages beside the refrigerator.

"Hello." It was Vivienne.

"Is my dad there?"

Jade held her breath for a lecture on the pregnancy, but none came. Was it possible that Ellis hadn't told her yet?

"He's just leaving to pick you up. Where are you?"

"Can you go get him? Tell him I'm not coming in tonight." Jade paused. "Something's come up."

"Are you OK?" Vivienne's concern sounded genuine.

"Fine. Just get him. Tell him I'm fine."

"OK. You hold on. He'll want to talk to you." Jade heard Vivienne's high voice calling her father, then the screen door slam shut, the name "Ellis" called again. Or maybe she'd said "Ellie." Jade thought she heard him answer. Then the phone crackled and went dead.

december

I couldn't get off the train.

Except for the day when Benjamin and I decided to run away to Chicago, I've never felt so confident. Only this time I would go all the way. I needed to reach a place my ancestors had set their sights on and then been distracted from for generations. Ride at least close to the tracks they'd laid yet never traveled. I knew I had something to finish. I felt it. I believed in that feeling with my entire body.

I had dinner in the dining car and took a room in a sleeper car. After I got settled, I called Ellis back. I hoped he'd say something like, "That's my girl," to what I'd just done, but what he actually said was, "I knew you'd tell me in your own time." He was meaning the baby, not the trip to San Francisco.

I didn't go into the father stuff with Ellis because he didn't seem concerned with that part, other than wanting to be assured that the boy was white. He must have figured the boy, whoever he was, wanted out. A couple of times Ellis asked how I was feeling and when he'd see me. He said after San Francisco, I should come back to Nebraska. He had his own pioneer stories, he promised. He said Vivienne was already planning a flower garden for next spring on a swatch of land that runs alongside the Main Street house. He put Vivienne on the phone then and she gave me the phone number of her cousin in San Francisco. The one who sent her that cool Christmas card.

And then, even though I was still pissed with her, I called Rexanne. I didn't want her to call Ellis and get him all whipped up. She went mental when I told her I wasn't getting off in Nebraska, said she was going to meet me at some point along the route and drive me back to Chicago. Then all of a sudden she was worried about me traveling alone being as pregnant as I am. She relaxed a little when I told her I'd be staying with a cousin of Sara's. That's actually the cousin of Vivienne's. Vivienne hasn't seen him since they were kids. I can tolerate pretty much any geek for the one night I plan to be in San Francisco.

Rexanne said she was going to make an appointment for me to see a doctor as soon as I get to San Francisco. I told her to calm down. The baby's not going anywhere. Now it's more like squirming because there's not much room for a kick. Feels sort of like my own muscles moving around.

Finally, I just listened. Felt her voice rush over me as the square of darkening scenery in the train window flipped by like a film from someone else's life.

We left Omaha at midnight. Until now I hadn't thought of it as the midpoint of the United States, but only as the nearest big city. When we moved through Nebraska, it was so black it might not even have existed.

You have to be in the place that fits you. Otherwise, you try to change the place itself and that can be a disaster. After December—Benjamin's December—I had to leave before I destroyed what little was left of our spot in Nebraska. By the time I got up the courage to actually go, so much of our life together was already part of the past.

Years ago, the strong sod turned to dust, and it was all our doing. By forcing the short-grass prairie to bear fruit unnaturally, it decomposed—not underground the way our dead do, but right before our eyes. The earth flew into eyes and mouths, along the parts in hair, crept under toenails. It fought its way into each house through the slightest crack. Every opening could be shut, bolted, reinforced at the seams with cloth, and still the dust of old mistakes had returned and settled by morning. For months, every breath our ancestors took was filled with dirt.

Jade, how did I know to call you Jade?

I found part of our past in my mother's house. Ellis wouldn't understand how someone you haven't talked to going on twenty years would be worth abandoning your nest for. But Ellis understood less and less of me the longer we were together. That doesn't make any sense, but it's true. Believe me.

Though it was July, I found her sitting in her living room in a thick winter coat, gloves, and wool hat. She said a fella was on his way to pick her up and take her home. Of course, no one showed up.

Nancy Jane degenerated even more after I arrived. Maybe *because* I came and she could finally let her guard down and allow someone to take care of her. I hate to tell you all this, but it's part of her story. I found sandwiches in the coat closet, and on the floor beneath the dining room table—place mats, which she insisted discouraged bugs from crawling up her legs when she was eating.

She used to know the difference between a piece of toast and a paperback book. She made a life saving the farm, as well as the land and livelihood of thousands of other farmers. The woman who organized farmers and helped pass farming legislation had, at the time of her death, a wallet covered with—I kid you not—fifty rubber bands, which she thought would foil robbers. Her theory was that the thief would snap his fingers, drop the wallet, and run away.

Sometimes, especially in the morning, she was perfectly lucid. She told fascinating stories of holding off the supply of milk and produce to drive the prices up. She remembered the color of a shirt she was wearing over fifty years ago. When she called me Ann or Mommy I felt myself a coconspirator in her recreation of history.

Remembering the time of the Lindbergh flight, Nancy Jane said she was alternately studying the moon and her mother's stomach big as the moon. When Lucky Lindy went all alone on a voyage, everyone hoped for him—rich and poor, stockbroker and farmer. I don't know what she could have been remembering; she has no brother or sister that I've heard of.

There was so much history in Massachusetts, I panicked that I wouldn't hear all the stories before she made no sense *all* of the time. I woke at night sweating in a little town incorporated more than two hundred and fifty years ago. A mile from her house was a green and white church that belongs on a postcard.

I think I kept my mother a hostage in her own house just to listen to the stories about myself and my relatives. Just to hear her mistakenly call me Ann or Isabel. Listening to anecdotes, deciphering the handwriting of the past, squinting at double columns of minuscule type on frail paper, this is what I struggled with: how much is really true to what happened and how much is what we want to be true no matter *what* actually happened?

The funny thing is, the more I've found out about my ancestors, true or imagined, the worse it's made me feel. In comparison, my life is dull as hay.

When I was born, they rushed Nancy Jane to the hospital. In the whirl of paperwork and procedures that followed, my name was misspelled. And I kept it, the only thing about me unique.

What had I done but stay put? Spread my life out exactly where I'd been dropped? My own mother was part of history; my grandmother ran an entire farm herself; my great-grandmother was Isabel. And hers was the best story. A story of true love.

Jade, I hit a woman in a historical museum on Cape Cod. I didn't have permission to go in. I had only the premise that our family divided in the middle of the nineteenth century, my great-grandfather heading west to farm the land, his brothers going in the opposite direction to sea. I wanted to understand how a shipmaster could spend a lifetime leaving his wife and children.

Patiently I told the woman at the desk that I wanted to verify my history, but she wouldn't bend. I needed to sort out which of Nancy Jane's stories were fancy, which factual. The woman I confronted had no concept of living with someone who was losing her mind right in front of you. She said, "Rules are rules."

And then something came over me, as they say. It really did. The energy I felt became a presence, an actual body almost, right in front of me, then it settled on my face, traveled all the way down to my feet. Those three words pressed at me like the enemy. *Rules are rules.*

I've never felt so alive in my life as when I struck that woman. The only other time I got so physical was over Ellis's lake. For the half-hour before she came to and the police arrived, when I rampaged through the library in search of my past, it was like I was on drugs. I was euphoric. I had a genuine mission.

I don't remember much after that. They put me in jail for

trespassing and assault. The librarian was a volunteer, her husband an attorney. Their kid drove a sporty car with a bumper sticker that read, "My parents went to Europe and all I got was this stupid car."

That's why I couldn't come to you right away.

Jail wasn't so bad. I knew right where everything was. Everything had a place and every person did, too. There were no shoes stashed behind milk containers in the refrigerator, newspapers in the toilet tank, little boys under water. Even the vertical bars in each of the cells separating people one from the other made sense.

I did worry about my mother, that she'd hurt herself without anyone to walk behind her and turn off the stove, lock the door, untangle her hair. Ultimately needing to be home with her got me out of jail.

In jail, I had a lot of time to think. And now I know something crucial: the greatest crime is a life that hasn't been tasted. Nancy Jane had a passion for politics, and Ann for the land, and Isabel for a man.

Nancy Jane was self-taught, her love of public life a dream realized. And though her career was cut short, she knew what she wanted, went after it, and put her mouth on it.

All I've been is the wife of a farmer, helping in the fields, canning vegetables and relishes. Gradually, I began to hate the things the barns and fields produced; I couldn't stand even the touch of meat. Some of my revulsion came after we lost Benjamin, but it was growing even before.

In jail, I vowed to change my life. I thought of how I used to fall asleep in the movie theater in town when Nancy Jane was off with her political life. I was so small I had to stand on the seat to see the pictures. To this day, I love movies. I think

I love them because they are other people's stories and not my own.

When I was released from jail and returned to Nancy Jane's house, it was a mess. She was sleeping on the floor between two tablecloths. The whole place could easily have burned with her in it. Most of her lucid moments had disappeared over the days I waited for my future to be determined.

The social worker helped me find a nursing home. I visited her every day and probed for details, but some days she wouldn't speak at all. Wouldn't even open her mouth for a piece of chocolate.

It took weeks to clean up the house. And no matter what I did, the place still smelled like Nancy Jane decaying, her past and mine, blown away.

How did I know to call you Jade? How could one slip of a letter from Jane to Jade be so prophetic?

In the beginning, it's like nothing else. You'll see. You'll see when you have the baby. It almost makes you believe this will be what your life is about. This can save you. Make up for all the passion you never had, or become the passion itself.

But it doesn't. Those early years when you've memorized even the scent of your child, when you know every bend and marking of the little body, disappear and you find yourself asking, "How could I produce someone so unlike me?" Before you know it, your children don't need you anymore. Oh, they say they do or pretend they do, but they can make their way just fine without you. You can't protect them any longer. Your job is done.

I couldn't protect your brother. God knows how careful I was with him when he was a baby. He was so delicate, I had to hold his head in the palm of my left hand and wash him in no more than two inches of water. There was a pale blue washcloth I remember soaking up the water with, then squeezing it over him. I remember thinking he was smaller than a roast I'd make for company, his tiny arms and legs and fingers stiff then flailing.

He was a true joy, a boy to take on the farm, to make sense of all the hard work we'd put into it. He was all Ellis could dream about.

Benjamin needed attention each step of the way. He had allergies to the hay dust. Every other day at school he puked. The janitor who was called in to clean up the mess got tired of his own routine line, "What'd you have for breakfast, kid? Ice cream?"

Benjamin was a good boy. Good in school. Brilliant in school plays when every other child came off as an amateur by comparison. In 4-H he showed cattle, raised vegetables, won prizes for his dahlias. He shied away from sports, and much to Ellis's disappointment Benjamin didn't enjoy farm work, not even making the stone boat to clear the land of rocks. He hated vaccinating the pigs, came in crying every time Ellis forced him to. To keep himself from crying, Benjamin sang to the cattle that were to be sold.

Still, he swept the barn cleaner than anyone in the family, anyone who ever lives there, I imagine, ever will. He loved to iron. But, day by day, our dreams of him perpetuating our life-style dropped away. And yet, somehow that made Benjamin and me closer. There was an uncanniness to our relationship Ellis envied. Benjamin could be helping me with cleaning or sorting one thing or another and he'd just know what to put into my hand without me saying a word. Sometimes in the middle of a chore when we were working closely, I'd feel I actually had four hands.

Benjamin was always hanging on to me until I got him that camera. Then I saw the thing more than his eyes; he took photos of everything. We never did find the camera, even after we cleaned out his room.

One day when he was still in grade school I caught him with another little boy from his class. They were supposed to be feeding the chickens, but they were having a contest out back of the barn to see who could pee the farthest. After that, he was careful never to even let me see him dressing. He wouldn't allow anyone to spot him without his shirt on.

He loved to dress up. One of my biggest regrets—more than setting him, as an infant, in the combine when Ellis was sleepy—was the Halloween he missed because he had to keep picking corn. Racing to get the last of the crop, we needed every hand available, even Benjamin's tiny ones. He didn't complain, but I knew his heart was broken because he wouldn't be able to put on his costume for another year. They's why I let him wear his Casper mask in the fields that evening. Ellis said we were crazy, but Benjamin just picked and picked, stopping now and then to lift up his mask for a taste of fresh air.

That was the day that I realized I had no expectations for him. Never had. He was small, so tiny as a newborn I suspected he'd die like a runty piglet. In a way, I guess, I never believed he'd actually live through infancy and childhood. I think, too, that I may have been disappointed. And the saddest thing is that Benjamin probably knew this before I did. I wanted a big strong boy to show Ellis what was what, somebody from my family's farming stock to take hold of the line from our ancestors, who staked out land for us to love.

Over time that land changed. Sod houses became wood; meadows and pastures turned to wheat fields and cornfields.

Barns cropped up and fell down. Each new boundary became another line or wrinkle in the face of the plain.

Jade, I don't want to be one of those women who polish a scar until it shines like some piece of jewelry with their constant worrying it. And moaning over the original wound at a convention of other scar bearers. You make a mistake and you go on with your life. A scar's a scar. You can't take it off; you learn to accessorize around it until you think you can't see it anymore.

And yet, sometimes I think the only emotion I've ever truly felt has been guilt.

Hours before he died, I sent him down to the lake for fennel. The "little garden."

He was upset. He confided that you wanted him to go to Chicago with you. He didn't want to go. He didn't want to disappoint you, but he didn't want to leave. In truth, I think, he didn't want to abandon Carlsen, who'd come to depend on his help. Ellis and I were both concerned that he spent too much time with that man.

I told you the "little garden," was our secret spot—yours and mine—but I had something there for Benjamin, too. He discovered the garden the day he died. How could I exclude him from the best place on the farm? Did I think if I told him about it, he'd never want to leave?

I imagined that the place was where Isabel had stood as a girl when her father said, "Here. Right here. This is where we will stop. This is where we will start our future." And I guessed, though I have no way of knowing for sure, that the spot was where Ann had grown beautiful flowers and died among them.

It's lovely, the only slight rise in land for miles around. It was there that I planted my garden. Everyone said the vegetable garden was spectacular. On nearly half an acre I planted all the standards, of course: tomatoes, cucumbers, squashes, green and yellow beans, a huge patch of potatoes, and carrots. I put in asparagus and strawberry beds, blackberries, three varieties of peppers. And I planted melons and pumpkins and spinach. Every morning just after feeding the animals but before I made breakfast, I tended my garden. I plucked weeds and watered seedlings the whole time you grew inside me. As the plants grew strong and tall, I imagined you sprouting arms and fingers and eyelashes.

Sometimes in the evening when I'd stand back from my work, all in tall neat rows, interspersed with sunflowers and wild-flowers and zinnias, all I could think of was a painting. A work of art I had to dabble with every day.

When Ellis got it in his head that we needed a lake, Benjamin had just started kindergarten. I don't know where the idea came from, but it hardened into a wall in his head. When we sat down together at dinner, the lake was all he'd talk about. I just couldn't get excited about a man-made body of water, wasn't convinced it would be worth the work. But Ellis was so enthusiastic about the thing that I finally said OK. That was before I found out where he intended it to be located.

Right over my garden. The one spot in the world that was all mine. The square of beautiful diversity compared to miles of monotonous field crops. We got into a terrible fight. When I look back, I think now that that damn lake was the start of all our trouble. A jinx on our life.

Oh, Ellis picked out another spot for me that he said was better because it was nearer to the house, but the new plot wasn't even close to being the same. And I never forgave him.

Secretly I put in a few prized plants at the site of the original garden for you and your brother as a memorial to what I'd once had. Raspberries and parsnips. And fennel. Plants that had never been native to this land. Fennel was for Benjamin. The day he died I sent him for fennel. I thought it was time he knew himself. I wanted him to bring it to me so I could say its Italian name to him—*finocchio*—homosexual.

Maybe he figured it out. Maybe he knew what I thought I'd be telling him. Benjamin was a smart boy. And right in sync with me. Him with his fingers smelling of fennel. Maybe the discovery that I knew hit him with such a blow it knocked him over. There was a bump on his forehead no bigger than the pit of a prized plum.

four

september

Soon as I get feeling bad about leaving Rexanne and Ellis behind, I spot something amazing. They've got these train cars with an upstairs. The windows on the sides curve up into a ceiling. Sometimes it feels like you're swaying a little, but you can see the entire world almost. When we pulled out of Denver, I was up there thinking about Isabel traveling by wagon. And then, all the silos and fields and cattle, the "amber waves of grain" behind me went out of my mind.

    I've never seen mountains so big they're scary, so big they make me the size of a speck of dirt. Except for when the train's moving slow going up an incline, we could be flying.

    With all its dips and hills and hollows the land can almost look like a body. But with none of a person's problems. And then the form rolls away to become another shape entirely.

    I worry about Rexanne worrying about me, telling Tommy, and him shaking his head and secretly in his mind saying he never wants any damn kids of his own. I agonize about eventually facing Ellis with a giant belly and poor Vivienne with her thermometer still by the bedside. And then the train goes through a long dark tunnel that takes my breath away. Of course, these days that doesn't mean much with the baby all pressed up against my lungs. When its feet wedge into my ribs, I have to stretch to pop it out of that position. Every once in a while, I wish I could jolt it from me altogether that easily and go on traveling all over the world.

But there's cool stuff just ahead. Tunnel after tunnel, some a mile long, with a surprise at the end of each one. Spotty evergreens, earth reddish brown, even now snow at the mountaintops. Broken rock. A river.

You can't see Promontory Summit, that spot where the two railroads met to make a finished path straight through the country. How weird is it that you actually have to get off the train and drive? I hear the museum's not that great, no big deal to let you know that a spectacular accomplishment finished there. In four years, men set down nearly two thousand miles of railroad through mountains and Indian territory and blizzards. And some minuscule bit of me was part of that achievement.

Chiseled rock formations come in faces and figures, not unlike clouds. A hat, a nose, a wing. Yellowish like landed sunshine. Brush low and dry.

When I grab a sandwich, I think about Ellis eating back in Paradise saving a bite for the animals, and Rexanne bringing vegetable burgers to Tommy's office.

Now it's desert.

When the train arrives in San Francisco, I can say I've reached my destination. I'll head back to Ellis until the baby's born. Can't do much sight-seeing in this condition. And everybody all in your face about it.

For a reason I can't explain, I'm thinking way back to my tin dollhouse, the roof peaked and three floors high. It was nothing like the elaborate handmade one that Carolyn and Vicky played with. Mine was tin. At least I think it was tin. All the decorations and some of the furnishings were stamped right onto the metal. The fireplace, curtains, rugs, paintings, even the knickknack shelves were part of the walls. There were a few actual pieces of furniture—a pedestal *sink, a pink bathtub, a couch. Those mostly got lost. But the house itself was indestructible.*

When Jade first woke, she thought that she might be in Isabel's inn in heaven. Four tall metal posts protruded from the comfortable bed, and gauzy white lengths of material hung from a canopy. Last night when she'd gotten into bed, she'd forgotten to pull the drape across the multipaneled picture window, and now sunlight bleached the white room even brighter. A long skinny window looked onto a rock garden. On the far wall was a fireplace, its mantel exquisite with fresh pink and white flowers.

What Jade had spotted when she'd first gotten off the train was a far different scene from this bedroom in Vivienne's cousin's house that would eventually become Robert's B&B. When she'd passed a group of homeless kids, Jade thought she heard one of the girls say, "My family sucked." For a minute, Jade wondered if that squalid life on the street was what she deserved, not the pretty upstairs room and spotless bathroom down the hall.

Jade opened her door and heard the other guest complaining to Robert that somebody had read his complimentary paper. "The pages aren't tight," the guest squawked. Jade closed the bathroom door on Robert's animated response concerning "The San Francisco Comical."

Robert was tall and thin, someone Sara would point out as gorgeous. When Jade had first met him, he'd looked her over, pointed at her middle, and said, "Honeymoon suite," while his partner, Denis, tried to nudge him into being more polite. She instantaneously forgot that he was related to Vivienne.

Though she'd been exhausted when she arrived at Robert's house, she listened politely as he explained that after losing three computer jobs in four years because of mergers, he was in the process of going into business for himself. Because Robert had no Pearline to help him, he planned to do everything himself including changing sheets. When renovation and decorating were completed on the two upper floors, the B&B would have a total of eight rooms. "B&B" made Jade think of snooty Lauren Nash.

"So how *is* Vivienne?" Robert had asked. Jade shrugged her shoulders and said she seemed happy with Ellis.

As Robert talked, Denis remained attentive even when Robert revealed *his* story. Denis was a copyeditor for a book publisher. He had dark perfectly straight hair, golden brown eyes. With his slightly stocky body, mustache, and average face, Denis was the kind of gay man who, as Sara would say, "could pass." Except that Robert had a big mouth. When Robert stopped talking, Denis snuck outside for a cigarette. Both men were somewhere in their forties.

Robert liked interesting things to happen to him so that he had first-person stories to tell. With only word-of-mouth referrals for the two guest rooms Robert had completed so far, he had already garnered a storehouse of entertaining anecdotes.

"And how did she sleep?" Robert asked as soon as he spotted Jade.

"Great," Jade said, reaching for a glass of juice on a flowery tray at one end of the dining room table. A massive collection of salt and pepper shakers was arranged in a hutch in one corner of the room. She spotted a pair of covered wagons that might have resembled the ones in which Isabel had traveled West.

Producing a plate of homemade breads and jellies, he asked, "So, what's on the agenda?" Without waiting for her to answer, Robert announced that she might want to visit Muir Woods. Robert had a gray and white cat called Poindexter that jumped on his lap as soon as he sat down. Jade couldn't help but think of Butterbean back in Paradise.

Mr. Dagney, the other guest, was "planning an excursion momentarily," Robert said in an exaggerated drawl, then winked. Robert said, "I'm driving."

When Jade hesitated, Robert said, "Oh, he's fine as long as his paper is tight."

"It's not that," Jade said, awkwardly pushing back from the breakfast table, the cloth napkin, the pretty mint-green place mat. With the possibility that the slightest activity could become a physical ordeal, she wanted to save every bit of energy for the trek back to Nebraska.

"Oh, come on," Robert said. He promised to take her to the train station afterward. Jade couldn't wait to see the Pacific.

Jade insisted on riding in the backseat of Robert's Honda Civic. As Robert and "Dag" chatted about the city, Jade knew that she should phone Ellis with the exact time she'd be returning home. He'd told her Vivienne could use a little notice in order to prepare a special welcome-home dinner. But San Francisco was wild. Jade watched restaurant after interesting restaurant flash by the window. She'd never seen so many chic "eateries," as Ellen Sturges called them, in such close proximity. When she was staying in Connecticut, Jade hadn't once gone into New York. And even Chicago was nothing like this.

Robert took what he called the long way to their destination, driving down narrow streets, turning around at the bottom of dead-ends just to offer a glimpse of an extraordinary view, or old earthquake damage, or simply a building he admired. As they went up and down hilly streets, now and then spotting the water, Jade felt pushed through a huge outdoor museum. She marveled that little about San Francisco was flat. The Civic dipped and curved along roadways. Jade caught glimpses of a colorful flower garden, or an intricately decorated front door, or an elegant stone terrace. Dag didn't complain about the diversions.

If Isabel had had the money to take the new train her lover had helped to build, if she'd reached this city and met his family, would Jade ever have been born? She tried to envision a San Francisco without cars and modern business. It was almost possible at Muir Woods.

Jade told Robert and Dag to go on ahead. She walked slowly, deliberately, through the quiet shaded park that was cooler than she'd anticipated, and moist. The trees were huge and the farther she walked, the larger the redwoods appeared to grow. The garden of trees became increasingly spectacular. This was no scrawny band of trees, transplanted for privacy or protection, but a dense and fertile breeding ground for the largest, the oldest. Some of the trees were fourteen feet across; one was at least a thousand years old.

Tak could have seen this very same tree. It was possible.

The other people around her spoke in such hushed voices, they could have been visiting a cathedral. Bending her head back as far as she could, Jade looked up. Even pictures she'd seen in a library book with a man standing alongside the giant trees were no preparation for the immensity in front of her. She reached out to touch the bark.

"What did the city look like a hundred years ago?" she asked Robert as they waited for Dag to come out of the souvenir shop.

"Do I look that ancient?" Robert said.

On the way home, Robert parked facing the water for a few minutes. It didn't appear as rough as the ocean in Maine. "Are you sure you want to go back to the cornfields already?" Robert asked.

· · ·

Every night for almost a week Jade dreamed of trains, the long sleek metal slicing through time and all kinds of terrain. Sometimes she was inside the train, other times running alongside trying to keep up; once she idled above the train. From that vantage point, it looked like an immense silvery river snaking along the ground.

Each night before she went to bed, Jade thought of her great-great-grandfather Tak laboring over the rock and earth and metal, completing one more segment to change the country forever. She didn't know what the monotony of that kind of labor felt like. Nebraska, at least, had lots of flat parts, but there were other problems when wind and anger tore across the prairie. Probably Tak wasn't so ennobled by his task as anxious for the immediate reward of Isabel's sweet-smelling bed. Did he think about the future, the possibility that they could be a family?

Each morning that Jade woke she thought it would be her last in San Francisco. With the due date imminent, Ellis started to nag her to return so she could be cared for by the local doctor. Once Vivienne picked up the extension and said, "Honey, you've got to take care of yourself. We're all set up and ready for you." She'd made up a temporary bedroom on the main floor so that Jade didn't have to deal with all the stairs.

Rexanne bugged her, too. Robert routinely handed Jade the phone and mouthed, "It's that mother again," and Jade would be giggling by the time she grabbed the receiver to endure Rexanne's reprimands.

Although she'd known the two men only a short time, Denis had told her that she reminded him a little of his sister. The only member of his family that he mentioned, Cecile was both independent and vulnerable. She was a licensed massage therapist with her own business. Jade was comfortable around him almost immediately.

Denis didn't talk about homosexuality. The only comment he'd made to Jade was, "At least my marriage lasted." And that was after two Chardonnays. His three brothers had been divorced a total of seven times. Robert and Denis had been a couple for twelve years. Robert was tougher to win over. Initially she'd thought he'd be the first to accept her, especially with the Vivienne connection.

For the last three nights Jade had made dinner for the two men in exchange for what Robert called "the weekly rate," which amounted to the cost of two nights' lodging. Jade knew they were giving her a break because they felt sorry for her, though Denis insisted that this was the slow season. Last night after she'd gone to bed, she'd heard a mumble of raised voices and envisioned her name flicked around their room like flashlight.

Jade surprised the men each night with a different specialty from her book of notes and recipes. Tonight she made a simple meatloaf with garlic mashed potatoes, the garlic her contribution to standard fare prepared by farming families for generations.

"I know why they call it comfort food," Denis said.

"It's nothing but good home cookin'," Jade replied, sounding like someone's grandmother. For sure, Isabel hadn't spoken that way, though maybe Ann had.

When she'd made an exotic layered pasta dish the night before, she'd said, "I know what you're thinking. You're thinking, 'What does a dirt ball like me know about cooking?'" She'd paused, caught her breath. "Hey, not that long ago I lived in Connecticut." Robert had raised his eyebrows dramatically, in mock impression.

"This is fabulous," Robert said of the meatloaf. He winked at Denis.

Denis asked what her plans were for the future.

"You know," Jade said, "I was thinking of taking this course through ACC..."

"What's ACC?" Denis asked. He set his fork aside.

"Associated Correspondence Campus," Jade said. Denis and Robert stared at each other.

Both of them told her the program was a waste of money. They dismissed her plan before she'd had a chance to describe the cover of the brochure featuring an attractive woman wearing sunglasses and standing in front of a pool talking to two men in suits. Behind them, a hotel rose like a cliff, its roof not even within the frame of the photo. The turquoise pool was surrounded by lush flowering plants and white chairs. The pictures inside the brochure showed long tables in a banquet room.

"Well, I'm sorry I didn't go to Yale," she said.

"Hey, you don't always have to go to school," Robert said.

"Jade, you don't need that bullshit," Denis said, not unkindly. He put his hand on hers. She wondered why he cared. Lately, complete strangers would walk up to her, touch her belly, mumble prayers, reveal stories of their own pregnancies. It could be unnerving with people she'd never met assuming they had the right to enter her life just because some new one was jutting out ahead of her.

"Take it easy with the wine, Denis," Robert said.

"I'm fine."

"Two glasses is fine. Three glasses is trouble," Robert said. Robert fussed over Denis, monitoring his smoking and drinking like a mother. Robert had confided that Denis was diabetic and used to be a mess.

"Jade, what do you want to do more than anything else?" Denis asked.

"I don't know. Make great food?"

"Perfect," Denis said. He wiped his mouth with the pale blue cloth napkin.

"Chef Jade," Robert said. He stood up and did a pirouette.

"Cut that out," Denis said. Robert made a face, stuck out his tongue. "I'm being serious here," Denis said. Robert hummed around them, trying to distract Denis.

"You could have your own restaurant," Denis said. "Eventually." A few minutes later, Denis slipped out onto the porch for a cigarette. Robert pretended not to notice, while Jade helped clear the table.

As soon as Denis returned, he said, "Now the next question is, what are you going to do about the baby?"

As Robert poured cinnamon coffee, Jade capsulized her exploits on the East Coast. She mentioned options considered and rejected. Robert was intrigued at the mention of "the hatter to the stars."

"Probably I should stick to my plan to go back to Paradise," Jade said.

"Paradise, how precious," Robert said.

Denis sighed, sipped his coffee. "What about the boyfriend? Where's he?"

For a second Jade considered concocting another story about the father. But she said simply, "He doesn't know."

"He doesn't know?" Denis asked.

"Well, I guess I'm not sure I know either," she said, lowering her eyes.

"What?" Denis said. But then the phone rang. Saved by the bell, Jade used to say to Sara when one of them was called on unexpectedly and the end-of-class bell drowned out any need for an answer. School now seemed like something she'd done in a dream years ago, though it hadn't even been seven months since she and Sara had gone to classes and dances and games.

It was Ellis again, telling her to come home. Telling her that Rory was going out with Sara now; Jade realized that was the reason she hadn't heard from her friend in so long. At least now Sara would never tell Rory about the baby. Ellis promised that everything would be all right if she'd just come back to him. But then Vivienne got on the extension phone and asked to speak to Robert. Robert said little, but stared at Jade the entire time he was on the phone with his cousin. After he'd hung up, he said, "All I know is that she always sends the funkiest Christmas cards."

"She's not trying to be funky," Jade said.

"Hey," Robert said, "she's concerned about you."

Denis said, "What's the scene with your daddy?"

Before she could reply, Robert peeked into the room and said, "Sounds cute."

"Robert!" Denis said.

"I'm trying to be funny, dickhead," Robert said, walking out of the room.

Jade revealed the news about Rory and Sara. Then she talked about the ESSOP. She paused, remembering that La Roux and Nancy Jane had had the same lover. When she started to tell Denis how the one-armed man had been seeing both women, Denis steered the conversation back to the present.

"Do you think of yourself as a kind of runaway?" Denis asked.

Jade just stared at him. She thought of the kids at the train station.

Denis told her he'd left home at twenty-three. For a minute she wondered why he couldn't be the father, not because she was in love with him or anything like that, but because he was kind and appeared as if he'd do all he could to set her life right.

While Robert sulked within earshot in the next room, Denis

told Jade that lots of people could be considered runaways. He told her that his grandparents in Europe had swallowed the promises of the Milwaukee Railroad and emigrated to America, then taken a train to Montana. They left most every possession behind, never saw their families again. Ahead of them lay only hard work to make the barest of promises come true. Maybe they could get a crop to come in on the arid soil, but they'd never get rich.

"I left home after college because there was only that thankless work ahead for me," he said.

Jade talked a little about Nancy Jane, who'd done her best work for the farm when she was away from it; about Isabel, who'd left the farm to save herself; about Rexanne, who'd left the farm to find herself. Ann had stayed and forged her own way.

Robert came into the room. "I haven't seen my family since I left Dallas fifteen years ago." He was uncharacteristically somber. "I used to have this fantasy that Vivienne was the only one in my family who supported me when I came out."

"She doesn't know you're gay," Denis said sadly.

Jade wondered aloud if the people who'd left the place where they'd been raised were doomed to never fitting in, or if they left home because they knew all along that they didn't belong there. Denis shook his head at her questions.

Stuart, the new guest, suddenly appeared in the kitchen. He was wearing a royal-blue robe and bright green slippers. "Can anybody get a little hot cocoa around here?"

"Later," Robert said, standing up and ushering the man out.

"Back to the baby," Denis said. "If it were me, I'd probably give the baby to my parents and start my life out here."

"You don't know about my parents," Jade said.

"Your dad seems to want you back home," he said.

"Yeah, but he's living with someone who's big into right-to-life." She paused. "Sorry, Robert," she called.

"Does she like babies?"

"She wants a baby desperately." She paused. "But how can I drop a little person into the middle of all that craziness?"

"How does anybody deal with anything?" Denis said. "Plus we're wired to be resilient." He paused. "Look at you."

"Look at all of us," Robert said. "I think Jade should keep it."

"Jade's seventeen years old," Denis said.

"Oh, yeah," Robert said.

What if the baby turned into a cute little girl like Vicky? What if Jade never found out anything about the baby?

What to keep, what to leave, what to value swished past her like the images of landscape in the train windows. She sat within the safety of these two men the way the train car protected her from the elements. She wanted details to be decided. Suddenly, she wanted to say something to get them to stop talking about the baby. She said, "My brother was like you."

"What do you mean?" Robert asked as he searched the cupboards for cocoa.

"My brother was gay," Jade said, looking Denis straight in the eyes. She'd never uttered that phrase before.

Robert turned to look at Denis. Then Poindexter, from out of nowhere jumped in his lap.

He died and we lost the farm and my mother left and I got pregnant. Tragedy after tragedy heaping into a pile until it got so high everything just crashed to the ground.

Denis put his arm around her.

"I thought maybe you knew. Maybe that's why you've been so nice to me," Jade said.

"That's not why," Denis said at the same time that Robert

said, "*How* would we know?" Denis went on to say that the world was made of two kinds of people—those who keep things running and those who take it to new and different places. Robert, he said, kept things running. Denis thought of himself as someone caught between the two. But Denis believed that Jade had the potential to become someone very special. "Maybe I'm wrong," Denis said, "but maybe I'm not." He paused.

"I'll say this, Jade," Robert said. "You've got balls."

"Was it an accident?" Denis asked. "With your brother."

Dr. Barnabas told Jade she was too close to delivery to travel any distancee. He reprimanded her for coming out to San Francisco by herself, frowned as he told Robert she should have made an appointment to see him immediately.

"She said she went to a doctor her mother had spoken to," Robert said. He cleared his throat.

Jade picked at a hangnail. She had lied to Rexanne, too, telling her she'd been to a clinic, that everything was fine.

Before they left the office, the doctor set a date to induce. "We can't let this go too long," he said simply. Then he suggested that Robert coach her with breathing exercises.

Jade wanted to know what would happen if "it went too long," what they did in the days of her ancestors when a baby refused to come out into the light of a strenuous workday.

Robert thought that Jade should have the baby in San Francisco and then her mother could fly back to Paradise with her. "She'll qualify for the weekly rate, too," he said.

"What about Ellis?"

"Frankly, the militia stuff scares the hell out of me," he said.

In the car Robert said, "Jade, I've been thinking. You might like to meet a friend of mine who owns a restaurant. Let him give you a tour of his kitchen."

"Robert, right now I just want to lay down until Tuesday when all this is over."

"I understand that, but I think Travis's restaurant will take your mind off your condition."

"I doubt it."

Robert said he'd drive her by La Trattoria, and if she didn't want to go in, well that would be that. "At least take a look at it," he said.

"Robert, it's not that I'm not interested. But I'm going to have to crawl in on all fours."

"We don't want that. Somebody might throw a saddle on you."

First, he took her on a detour across the San Mateo Bridge, which was incredibly long. When they finally got to the end, velvety green hills spotted with darker green trees made her think of an unmade bed, a blanket not smoothed of its wrinkles. Then the restaurant came into view, and Jade couldn't be sure if the place itself or the pressure of the baby was changing her breathing. La Trattoria was situated at the top of four graded terraces surrounded by gardens of herbs and flowers. The awning of the restaurant was turquoise, the building itself pale yellow. She began objecting that there was no way she could handle all the steps when he somehow drove up and around the back of the building, stopping at the front entrance.

Travis stood in the doorway as if expecting them. Unlike most of Robert's friends, Travis was huge, with a massive chest and large forearms. She followed him around the restaurant, which he explained had once been part of an estate. The two largest rooms shared an immense marble fireplace.

She turned, but Robert wasn't behind her. "Where's Robert?"

"Oh, he had to run home. The plan is that I'll take you back to his place when you're ready to go." He made a sweeping gesture with his arm in the direction of the kitchen.

"What plan?" Jade asked, confused.

"He had to meet the electrician at his house," Travis said, then quickly escorted Jade into a room full of gleaming stainless steel.

"This is the heart of the beast," he said. A line of large copper-bottomed pans hung above them. Before Jade could form a question, Travis asked, "Don't you love this kitchen?"

"It's beautiful," she said, and for a minute imagined herself among the utensils, pots, foodstuffs, totally absorbed in creating meals people would return for again and again. But it was intimidating, too. Jade lumbered through the kitchen, bumping into one of the stoves, knocking an empty box to the floor. She smelled onion, spotted a huge pot filled with water and peeled potatoes. Travis showed her his computer system, which cataloged his recipes along with length of preparation time and necessary ingredients. Each step was numbered and detailed. He printed out a recipe for grilled swordfish, then motioned at a chair.

"Travis, I should get back. Even reading exhausts me these days." She put one hand on the table, leaned her weight into it. In less than a week, her body had begun defying her simplest wishes. Sometimes she found it a challenge to get out of a chair for a cup of tea. She wanted to ask Travis how he got started, how he secured his initial investment, who his teachers were, but she was too overwhelmed to listen.

"Here's a little snack and then we'll hit the road," Travis said. He set a fruit-topped pastry in front of her along with a glass of apple juice.

"Did you make this?" she asked.

"Absolutely," he said. "It's all prepared here. Even the mayonnaise for tuna fish. I'll be right back," he said. When he went into the kitchen, she heard him giving instructions to one of the cooks who'd come in the back entrance. Jade hoped Travis wasn't an employer like Lauren Nash in Connecticut. Probably he wasn't, but you couldn't always tell with people at first.

Jade studied the empty dining room that before long would be filled with customers drinking and eating, laughing and talking, celebrating. The click of strangers' footsteps wouldn't pass by, but would enter the rooms full of inviting aromas—garlic and onion, pastries baking. . . . Jade couldn't imagine pulling it all together to serve fifty or a hundred dinners. Outside, the gardens were lush and thick. She wished that she remembered Rexanne's special garden where the lake now stood.

"I'll be right with you," Travis called. He wanted to change his shirt. Jade was glad she wasn't on her way to the hospital. Before they emerged from the garage, they had to wait for a worker to finish screwing around with Travis's car antenna. They'd driven less than a block when Travis pulled to the side of the road to phone the restaurant. Then he got out of the car to make a second call and finally jutted back into traffic.

Jade's first reaction when they parked across the street from the white house with the yellow trim was that Travis was at the wrong address. Pink and pale blue ribbons and crepe paper streamed from the fence, almost hiding the newly installed bed-and-breakfast sign. Balloons were stuck all over the front door. She heard voices, laughter, more commotion than when Ellis had his friends over on weekends.

Suddenly, Robert opened the door, hugged her. "Surprise, surprise." She looked back to Travis, who shrugged.

"You knew about this?" she asked.

"Knew about it? I helped to plan it," the big man said.

"I've never done a baby shower before," Robert announced. "Come on in."

The living room was full of people, mostly men, even the doctor who'd earlier advised Jade about inducing. Denis put his arm around her. "Now you know why Robert brought you break-fast in bed this morning." He paused. "He didn't want you to see all the food in the kitchen."

Denis led her past pastel flowers and candles, pretty dishes filled with candies, fruits, huge shrimp, platters elaborately mounded with vegetables and cheeses, and introduced her to their friends. They'd invited Jade's friends, too: Sara, Rexanne, Adam, Robin. But none of them had shown. Robert said he'd even invited Ellis because he knew he wouldn't come. "And Vi-vienne," Robert interjected. Over the course of her stay Jade had confided stories about all of them. They'd even called Pearline.

"She's a trip," Robert said.

"It was all right there in your book," Denis said. "Among the recipes."

"I snooped," Robert said.

"I can't believe you did that," she said, staring at Poindexter peeking at the commotion from beneath an armchair. Denis said that Ellis and Rexanne hadn't thought much of the party idea. All both of them wanted was her headed back home. He went on to report that Adam thought a shower would be great, but he was in the middle of a cross-country bike race and probably wouldn't be able to make it in time.

Jade had an insane wish. That Nancy Jane, Daniel, Ann, Isabel, and Tak could be here. Her hormones must have been getting the better of her for that idea to have popped into her head.

"I can't believe I put a party together on such short notice," Robert was announcing in between compliments.

Robert touched her lightly on the arm, directing her attention to a huge man coming out of the bathroom. The man was even bigger than Travis. "Look at the photographer," Robert said. "He's filled."

Jade giggled. "Photographer?"

"Of course. We've got to document this party," Robert said.

Photographer, and she thought of Benjamin. Then Ellis. Suddenly she remembered that her father had mentioned gathering up Benjamin's belongings, including his camera. She would call Ellis and ask if there was film in the camera, tell him to develop it. But right now an elaborate array of food was spread over every inch of the large mahogany dining room table. Some of Robert's salt and pepper shakers were interspersed around the serving dishes. Jade spotted slices of the *timpano* she'd made for Robert and Denis.

"You set out my leftovers," Jade whispered to Robert.

"Are you kidding?" he asked. "That was fabulous. I had to share." Robert proceeded to ask a thin blonde man what he thought of the dish. The man made a sound between a purr and a growl. Someone else said, "You'd better keep her, Robert."

"There's nothing like living across the street," another man said.

Jade heard a very handsome man in jeans and a white T-shirt saying, "I don't eat shellfish," to a platter of huge shrimp. "It's too much like insects. I can't even look at a shrimp."

Men were talking and laughing no matter which way Jade turned. The entire first floor of the B&B was decorated in pastels. A four-foot cardboard baby bottle was stuck to the bathroom door.

She sidled up to a woman who'd been introduced to her as

Meghan. Meghan looked older than Rexanne and wore her hair so short Jade could see her skull. Meghan filled her in on Fitzgerald and his lover, Gabe, who was known to throw punches when he'd had too much to drink. When Fitzgerald got closer, Meghan said to him, "Where's dream boy?"

Fitzgerald laughed. "I made him wait in the car."

"Like a dog," Meghan said. Then she laughed. The photographer snapped a picture.

Every so often Jade heard a relevant song. When "Having My Baby" boomed into the room, a few of the guests sang along. She tried to picture Rexanne and Ellis in this mix of people and noise. Pearline would be fun, but she'd have her share of comments. Sara would think the men were unbelievably good-looking.

"How are you?" she asked a young man Denis introduced as Ramon.

"Telling the T," the man said.

Denis didn't explain. He pointed at the photographer, who was saying, "Ninety-eight percent of my profession is knowing how to mesh and flow into the party mood."

Robert said, "Let's stick to the two percent."

The photographer turned and said to Meghan, "Come on, give me a hug."

"Jesus," Robert said. Denis told Robert not to worry. "What I want to know is who recommended him?" Robert's voice was unnaturally high.

Two men Jade recognized as guests who'd checked into the newly finished room on the second floor stood in a corner arguing about birth plans. The taller of the two men said that it was a good idea to go into the process with a plan in mind— whether you wanted "a block," a midwife, or a doctor to coach you; what kind of music you wanted playing in the background.

"A plan?" the other man said. "There's no planning this. You can pretend like you've got some control over the outcome, but you're damn lucky if the baby comes out whole." He said he had two kids. As Jade neared, both men stopped talking and looked at her.

"Presents, presents," Robert announced, clapping his hands emphatically above his head. To Denis standing next to the sound system, Robert said, "Take it down a notch."

"Nice segue," the taller man said. He wore a gold band on every finger of both hands.

Jade heard the photographer say, "I was born that way. What's your excuse?"

Robert ignored the comment and bent close Jade. "Denis was afraid you'd have the baby before we could get the shower organized." He directed her toward a seat in the corner of the living room. The usually tastefully upholstered chair was decorated with garish golds and silvers, blues and pinks. It sat atop a platform covered with a lacy skirt. The mirror hanging nearest the chair featured an outline of a baby drawn with lipstick.

"The seat of honor," Robert said and dramatically motioned her to sit down. "Turn that off," Robert yelled. "Baby, baby, don't get stuck on me," was blaring.

As the room quieted and Jade squeezed her way to the throne, she thought that her life to this point had been preparation. All that she'd learned about her ancestors, the trouble that had come to her family. Even Connecticut had taught her how rich people lived, what was chic to eat.

"Hey, don't go getting sweet on us," Denis said to her.

"Presents, presents," Robert repeated, and another man, one she hadn't yet met handed her a gift. The multicolored animal wrapping looked like the pattern from a baby's quilt. She slid the paper off, pulled back the top of the box to discover a silky, long white nightgown.

"This is beautiful," she said.

"For the hospital," the man who'd been introduced as Herbert said. "You might have a cute doctor."

Next she opened a small package that contained a hand-crafted hair clip. She unwrapped a shoe box full of condoms.

"Not funny," Robert interjected to the crowd.

"It's funny," Jade said.

An argument started in the back of the room then accelerated, other voices joining in. Someone said, "When you're ready for reality, let me talk."

"Quiet, girls," Robert called. He gestured at the troublemaking photographer.

Rexanne hadn't told Jade how the women in their past welcomed a new baby, if there was a party or a get-together, if Isabel and Ann and even Nancy Jane merely kept their fingers crossed, didn't talk about the impending birth in case there should be a problem.

A mountain of wrapping paper sat to either side of Jade's chair. Denis handed her a large package wrapped in glittery pink paper. She opened the box to discover a leather suitcase from him and Robert. The room went quiet. Jade shifted in her seat.

"It's for the hospital stay," Robert quickly clarified. Denis came forward and kissed her on the cheek. A couple of people clapped.

"You go, girl," someone said to Denis and laughed.

Gradually the guests drifted toward the dining room where Travis served cake. Denis had gone outside to reprimand the photographer, and Robert had followed Denis. On the way out, Robert nagged Denis about having too much to drink.

Jade stayed in her seat a few minutes longer and looked back over the packages. She'd only been to one baby shower, Sara's sister Molly's. She remembered Molly opening wrapped pacifiers, holders for baby bottles, playpens, baby outfits, bibs. When Molly had opened a card that said "Congratulations," and on the inside, "See you in twenty years," she'd started to cry. No one had presented Jade with a gift that indicated she'd be keeping the baby for long. Or even that she was having a baby.

"Come on, sweetness, this way," someone said.

"This party is a bigger kick than Jesse and Paul's wedding," someone else said.

Jade stood up, then worked her way to the cake, an elaborate tiered centerpiece with multicolored frostings and Jade's name in script at the center.

She felt different.

It took her a minute to realize that the baby wasn't wriggling. She took a deep breath, then stood still, waiting. She touched her middle, pressed gently with her fingertips.

"I think something's wrong," she said loudly.

"Where's the doctor?" Robert said.

"Just left," Denis said, moving toward her and motioning at the door.

To no one in particular Jade whispered, "It's not moving."

13

october

There were days when I wished that there would be no baby, no future. The day of the party wasn't one of them. Probably the first time I believed everything would be all right was the afternoon of the shower.

But when the baby stopped moving, time stopped.

Denis smoked all the way to the hospital. Robert even got going. They lit one cigarette after another, tossing them out onto the road, where they turned up sparks and fell away. Denis told me that while Robert was rushing me into the emergency room, he parked the car then wandered aimlessly. He wanted to be anyone in the parking lot but himself. "You," he said to the parking garage attendant, "I'll be you."

Anyone but the friend of a young woman losing her first child.

I didn't want to be myself. For sure, I didn't feel like myself. I wanted to be Isabel before she lost Tak. I wanted to be able to warn him of the danger ahead.

Inside the hospital, metal and whiteness rushed by. I could have been on a train ride through the polar regions.

Doctors swarmed everywhere. They performed an emergency cesarean.

I thought we lived in a house with steep eaves, with holes at each roof juncture just small enough for a bird to enter. One flew in and *grew to a size that couldn't get out, not even by the small door I came and went by, stooping every time. Each of us took a broom, its handle the yellow-orange of a standard school pencil. We took turns swatting at the bird, which was huge and healthy. We smacked and bashed it. We beat it against the wall. Because it was too large to ever leave that house.*

Things aren't always what they seem. Leaves fall with the sound of footsteps, but there's no path.

The baby cried and I cried. I cried for two days. Something made me keep crying even with the healthy little baby girl right in front of me.

Denis took off work, and the two of them scurried around the house making tea, delivering Brie and smoked salmon treats at any time of the day.

My world's no longer flat. Even my tummy's not back to flat. They tell me that will take some time, but I'm not holding my breath.

It was nothing like love at first sight.

Jade had heard stories, from Sara mostly, that a baby could change a girl's outlook totally. Jade didn't see that happening. The birth thing was amazing, but not transforming. Nothing like that. When did the maternal instincts kick in?

Baby paraphernalia filled Jade's room—a whole new world of bottles and diapers and powders and wipes. Delicate sweet odors to cover the nasty ones. Clothing the size of a doll's. Interspersed among necessities were gifts—stuffed animals, flowers, and then all the presents she'd opened at the shower. She'd need a U-Haul to cart everything away.

She handed Roberta Denise back to her mother, adjusted her nightshirt. "This isn't working for me, Ma."

"Don't worry about it, darling. I'll make her some formula. You can try again later."

"I'm just not into it," Jade said as Rexanne took the baby to the other side of the room. Rexanne wore a silky red-patterned skirt, which stood out among all the pastels.

Rexanne suggested the soreness from the incision was making Jade cranky. Just the use of the word "cranky" convinced Jade that Rexanne was treating her like a baby, too, not like the new mother she was supposed to be. It wasn't only the lingering pain, but everything—the exhaustion, the hair loss, breasts the size of grapefruits and hard as melons. She was relieved that the birth ordeal was actually over, but in another way she couldn't believe that it had actually happened so quickly. Like a sudden Midwestern storm that blew up violently, thrashed around the fields and farmhouse, then ended so abruptly it was hard to convince someone who wasn't there that danger had passed through.

Immediately before the doctors tried to resuscitate the baby in utero, Denis and Robert were forced to leave her. Robert was screaming, creating a scene. Denis tried to calm him and reassure Jade at the same time.

The shaving. The catheter. The funny-smelling cloths surrounding her belly. And then she went to sleep. And in sleep, someone unzipped her and whisked the baby out. The nurses coaxed her from bed ten hours later. But she was too weak and hurting to even lift the baby.

Somehow it was unimaginable that a new human being had come out of her body. Though she knew she was supposed to, Jade didn't feel a special connection to the baby, even after all the commotion, the very real possibility that the baby could have died. She guessed that the baby wouldn't have survived if it had been Isabel's.

"Touch her little lips with your nipple," Rexanne was saying. Jade took the baby who started to cry.

"Let her calm down first," Rexanne suggested. Jade ran her hand lightly over the baby head covered with the finest hair ever. The baby screamed.

"Relax, relax," Rexanne said to Jade as much as to the baby.

"I can't," Jade yelled.

Rexanne took the baby back and cursed the hospital for giving the sugar water bottle, spoiling her for sucking hard enough for breast milk. After feeding the infant a partial bottle, Rexanne presented Jade with ice packs for her breasts.

"It's no picnic any way you look at it," Rexanne said. "When I was feeding you, my nipples got so sore they cracked. They were bleeding."

"I don't need to hear this," Jade said, putting her hands to her ears.

Rexanne was jabbering about how you started with five minutes on each breast, then gradually built to fifteen. "Being stress-free is the key," Rexanne said as she went downstairs.

In the short time that she'd stayed at Robert's, Rexanne had dug in so well that she was as much a part of the house as the fireplace. She slept in one of the third-floor rooms that wasn't ready for paying guests because Robert hadn't finished decorating. He had to get the wallpaper up, and he had plans for new curtains and area rugs. Jade wasn't sure how much Rexanne paid, but she likely took some of what she owed out in trade. Every once in a while Jade would come upon her mother vacuuming or putting the breakfast dishes away. The other day Rexanne had raked the tiny front lawn. All Jade had left from her months of au pair work was $356.

"Hi, Mom." Robert was calling to Rexanne.

"Oh, Robert," Rexanne said, chastising him. "That shirt looks terrific on you." Jade pictured Robert looking down at his shirt, smiling back.

Jade heard Robert's quick steps, then the rapid-fire rapping on her door. At her "Yeah," he peeked in and invited her to go to dinner with him and Denis. "Let's go grubbin'," he said.

"Tonight?"

"You bet."

Two hours before Denis was to drive them to Travis's restaurant, Jade tried on clothes in front of the full-length mirror on the back of her closet door. She pulled out a couple of outfits from before she'd blown up into a baby machine. Although the clothes fit better than when she was overtly pregnant, Jade felt overweight. Fatzilla. She wondered how long it would take for the old stretched-out skin to spring back into place. Maybe the baby would turn her into a mall walker, one of those women who briskly strode the length of the mall before its shops opened, the excess flesh pounding along, swinging by, visible against stretchy sweats.

A dark oversized shirt and black leggings at least camouflaged her added girth. But her face looked plump. Rexanne let her borrow a clear plastic bracelet that Jade thought too young for her mother. Jade combed her hair, which seemed to be falling out like she'd been radiated.

Denis drove, smoking all the way, and Robert didn't bother to nag him. The men seemed to have made a truce: Denis no longer pretended to sneak outside, and Robert didn't pretend that he didn't see Denis go out for a smoke.

"This time you'll get a full-blown taste of what Travis can do," Denis said, as they pulled into the restaurant's parking lot.

"Sans surprise party," Robert added. He wore a brightly striped jacket and salmon-colored pants. In spite of his outlandish outfit, the other diners appeared to be looking at Jade. The first time since the hospital, people were staring at her and not the baby.

"Plenty of breeders here tonight," Robert said. Denis explained that Robert was referring to heterosexuals.

"Maybe they think we're a couple," Jade whispered to Denis.

"They can tell you're a fag hag, sweetness," Robert said and gently squeezed her arm.

Travis appeared at their table, bowed deeply. "Well, young lady, you look much different than the last time I saw you."

Jade still couldn't believe that Travis was gay. He was big boned and had the deep voice of a Pavarotti. She'd watched him on TV when she'd been with the Sturgeses. In Robert's case it was obvious, but there were other men like Denis, men you wouldn't suspect. Robert had even told her about straight men in San Francisco who tried to pose as gay because gay was so much hipper.

Jade wondered how long it would have taken before people could tell Benjamin was gay. Before everyone knew. When he was growing up, getting beaten up, she never really thought about homosexuality being the cause. She'd simply thought of him as "different" with a capital *D*. Like she'd always considered her straight black hair a standout among her mostly fair-haired classmates.

She considered Isabel and Ann and Nancy Jane. There didn't seem to be any gay men back then, but there must have been. Why hadn't Rexanne run into any stories of gay men with all her research? All of the digging hadn't turned up one bit of information that explained Benjamin's death either.

"Jade's deep in thought," Denis said.

"Thought schmought. She's in her mommy mode worrying about Roberta," Robert said.

"Am not," Jade answered. The baby was in Rexanne's competent care.

"Soft drink, or something harder?" Robert asked.

"Water," Jade said.

Travis brought out a smorgasbord of exquisitely prepared appetizers: pea pods filled with crab; rice crackers daubed with a mushroom pâté; dates rolled in bacon.

"Fabulous," Robert said with nearly every bite.

"Try the salmon imperial," Denis suggested.

Instinctively, she dug in her oversized purse. "I've forgotten my book," she exclaimed. She wanted to make a note about the pea pods.

"Just enjoy the food, Jade," Robert said.

"He's right," Denis added. "Sometimes it's important to stay in the moment, if you know what I mean."

"I know what you mean," Robert said.

Denis rolled his eyes. "You know what the greatest crime is, Jade?"

Before she could even think of an appropriate answer, Robert chimed in, "Life without butter." He went on to explain that if he were on death row, his last meal would be a tub of melted butter and an array of foods to dip in it. He mentioned shrimp, lobster, warm bread, then threw up his hands. "Somebody stop me," he said loudly.

Without reprimanding Robert, Denis said, "If your interest is food, you've got to center your whole life around that." He quickly worked into a discussion of La Trattoria and how wonderful it would be for Jade to get some training in Travis's kitchen. Then he added that working in the kitchen she might discover that it *wasn't* her calling. Something else might be. It was perfectly acceptable to try out different options. "It's easier to fail when you're not living in your hometown," Denis said.

"Travis thinks you're terrific," Robert whispered.

Jade didn't feel terrific. She felt confused, overwhelmed with all the baby stuff, with Rexanne right in her face like a hyperactive dog. Other times, particularly when handling the baby, Rexanne touched Jade.

"What about the baby?" Jade said. The baby, at least, was proof that she could do something.

Both men sighed simultaneously.

"You're too young to be a mommy, Jade," Robert said. From the quick response, the confidence in his tone, Jade understood that the men had already discussed her situation.

"We love you, Jade, but. . . ." She didn't hear what Denis said next.

A waiter refilled Jade's water glass. Denis spoke. "There are women lined up all over America ready to be mothers, but you shouldn't be one of them. Not yet, anyway."

"Not that Roberta Denise isn't adorable," Robert added.

Jade wanted to ask the big question—why couldn't Robert and Denis take the baby, and all four of them live together.

"Don't think we didn't think about adopting the baby. We talked about it just about every night since you went into the hospital." Denis stopped talking to take a sip of his Pinot Grigio. "But we're not the right parents for Roberta. We don't know the first thing about raising a girl."

"I would," Jade surprised herself by saying.

"Jade, you're a baby yourself," Denis said. "Well, not exactly a baby. But how would it work?" He repositioned his water glass, then looked at her earnestly.

"You and two queens bringing up baby," Robert said.

"I don't think so," Denis said sadly.

"Try the mousse, Denis." Robert went on to explain that

there were plenty of prospective adoptive parents. Denis insisted that Jade shouldn't exclude every couple in the United States because of a few "extremes" in Connecticut.

The main course arrived. Travis had recommended the salmon risotto for Jade. When she tasted it, she didn't think she could ever prepare anything as delicious.

"What do you think, Travis? Could you use another pair of hands in the kitchen?" Denis asked.

"Not yours," Travis answered. "And not wild boy's," he said, nodding toward Robert. "But if you're talking about the young lady's, well that's another story."

When Travis left and made his way to a table near the fireplace where a young couple ate lobsters, Robert asked Jade why Rexanne kept flirting with him. "That's just how she is now," Jade said. She ordered white chocolate whip for dessert.

On the drive back Jade was quiet. All their suggestions swarmed through her mind like a thick cloud of bugs she couldn't see beyond. Robert said he'd known Travis to promise more than he delivered on. Still, it was a possibility. Denis added that Jade needed to be prepared to do years of grunt work before she'd get to the point of preparing menus.

When they reached home, before Jade had even checked in on the baby, she phoned Sara, who answered on the first ring. "Are you still on the West Coast?" Sara asked. Jade heard a familiar sound, her old friend lighting a cigarette, inhaling. Jade wondered if she'd start smoking again herself, now that she was no longer pregnant.

"Yeah. Why don't you come out?" In the silence that followed, Jade said, "Just for a visit?"

"Like when?"

"Now," Jade said. "Now would be good." Jade said that the train ride was awesome.

Sara inhaled again, then said, "It's just such a busy time right now."

"What's so busy?" Jade asked. She pictured Sara in a bright pink sweater, heavy eye makeup.

"I'm getting married."

Jade bit the inside of her mouth. "Married?"

"It's not what you think."

"What do I think, Sara?"

"It's not to Rory."

"Who then?"

"Rory's brother."

"His little brother?"

"He's not so little."

They talked about Jeff for a few minutes, about school, about people Jade hadn't thought about since she'd left Paradise. Then Jade gave it one more shot. "Come on, Sara, come out before you get married. It's beautiful out here." She twisted the phone cord around her wrist the way Robert did. "Come on. What is life without butter?"

"Jeff *is* the butter, Jade."

Ellis showed up at Robert's B&B on Tuesday. The first thing he mentioned wasn't the adventure of a first plane ride, but Rexanne's hair.

"Looks pretty good," he said to Rexanne, and Jade could tell he wanted to touch it, especially the frosty parts. He humphed. Because Jade's own haircut had almost grown out, Ellis didn't notice it. Ellis said, "Where is she?" He scanned the room. For a minute, Jade had forgotten about the baby.

Since Denis had called to announce the birth, Ellis had phoned Jade every day. He'd ask Jade how she was feeling, if she was eating, what she was eating, and he'd always dwell on when she'd be returning to Paradise. And then he asked for news of the baby. When he'd first spoken to Jade after the birth, he'd said, "Sure glad everything worked out." Denis had FedExed the hospital pictures, but Ellis wanted descriptions, sounds. If he called when the baby was awake, Jade put the phone to Roberta's tiny face so that her gurgles and gulps could travel the miles back to Nebraska. Sara had warned Jade that granddaddies were the biggest spoilers.

When Denis took Ellis's suitcase, a brown vinyl one that looked brand new, Rexanne went off to see if the baby was awake. Jade was glad her father wasn't wearing a camouflage outfit, but a plain olive-green T-shirt.

At Jade's prodding, Ellis told her his plane was late boarding because some of the seat cushions had to be changed. Jade described the seat-belt extender she'd seen used on the flight to New York.

Ellis had sat next to a girl about Jade's age. "She must have had twenty magazines with her." He mentioned *Rolling Stone*, *Muscle and Fitness*; most of them Jade had never heard of. A man who read *The Businessman's Bible* for the entire flight sat in the aisle seat to Ellis's left. Ellis said he'd have to ask Vivienne if she'd ever heard of that book.

"Reminds me," he said, rooting into a paper bag. He pulled a camera out of the bag before finding what he was looking for. "This is from Vivienne," he said. The bag felt light as a package of cotton balls. Jade unwrapped a pair of white hand-knit booties and matching hat. "Made it herself," he said not without pride. The ensemble was a tasteful white, no bows or flowers or frills. A second bag from Vivienne held a basket containing a pacifier, two pink bibs, a tiny teddy bear, and, for Jade, lily-honey bubble bath.

Even with the special excursion fare, the trip had been too expensive for both Ellis and Vivienne to fly to San Francisco. Jade had tried to convince Sara to come with her father, but in the end Sara said that she was saving her money for the wedding.

Ellis walked over to meet Rexanne at the bottom of the stairs. "Here she is," Rexanne said. At first, she was reluctant to hand over the baby. But Ellis found a chair and Rexanne positioned the baby in his arms.

"Here's the little baby doll," Ellis said. She did look like a doll framed between his large forearms. The ESSOP guys would have some time with Ellis if they saw him now. Jade hoped that Ellis wasn't hurt that she'd named the baby Roberta Denise and not Elicia or some other feminine variation of Ellis.

"She's so fair," he said. Jade thought she detected relief in his voice.

"When you were in the plane, didn't it make you think of the Mystery Farm Contest?" Jade asked. She thought of the silos pushing toward the sky, the regular planted rectangles. Ellis didn't hear her. He was staring at Roberta Denise. And Robert was studying the "Sine Pari" tattoo on Ellis's forearm.

"Come on in, Daddy." Jade knew it was him at her door—the soft, hesitant knocking, the pause, the second knock.

"Is Roberta up?" he asked, immediately looking toward the bassinet.

"Just waking up." Jade got the baby out of bed, and while she changed her, Ellis retrieved a bottle.

When he returned, Ellis sat in the rocking chair. As soon as Jade handed her over, the baby stopped fussing. "There's my little girl," he said.

"I thought I was your little girl," Jade said halfheartedly.

"No, you're my big girl," he said.

Ellis still wasn't wearing the militiaman getup. Today he was dressed in a simple short-sleeved pale blue shirt. She pictured him tentatively poking through the racks at Wal-Mart to find something appropriate for the trip.

"When does she start on food?" Ellis asked. "I forget when you and your brother did that."

"Oh, I think it'll be a few months yet," Jade said. She wondered if she'd still have the baby then.

When Roberta finished eating, Jade held her while Ellis took a picture.

"I didn't know you took pictures," Jade said. He mentioned that he'd taken photos from the window of the plane. "Doin' a lot of things you don't know about," he said and smiled.

"Like?"

"We got this weekend wagon train." Ellis described a chuck-wagon cookout along the Oregon Trail not too far from Paradise. Vivienne put up signs promoting the event in her real estate office. "No modern pressures. That's what we advertise." He said the tourists really went for it. "When steaks were steaks," he said and laughed.

Next Ellis thought out loud about plans for an outlaw tour. "We've got Sam Bass," he said. "And everybody else who passed through."

"Who the hell's Sam Bass?" Rexanne asked, coming into the room without knocking. Rexanne always forged in, the task at hand taking precedence over anyone's privacy. The interruptions annoyed Jade less than they had in Chicago.

"Hey, Rex," Ellis said. His voice sounded a little defeated, as if he somehow knew her energy would outmatch his. "Sam Bass was the first and greatest train robber in the U.S. of A.," Ellis said without taking his eyes off the baby.

Jade's mother and father tolerated each other better than Jade could ever have anticipated, considering the explosive way they'd broken off their relationship when Rexanne had started packing.

"Carlsen remarried his ex-wife. Looks like he's going to sell his farm," Ellis said to Rexanne.

"Let me have her," Rexanne said. She put the sleeping baby to bed.

As soon as Rexanne had left, Ellis said, "You get up in the sky and look down on all the farms. Makes you wonder how anybody knows what belongs to who." Ellis absently rubbed at the scar on his nose. He reached into his shirt pocket and handed Jade a packet of photos. "This was what you were asking about."

Jade's hands felt clammy when she took the photos from her father. There were eight in all: one of Carlsen in his kitchen; several of the pigs and cows; a close-up of Jade smiling, holding a fistful of Monopoly dollars; one of Rexanne in the living room, in the background out the window her garden finished for the season; finally the sunset over Ellis's lake. For a minute, Jade thought he'd shot the photo just before he died. But the camera wasn't with him then. The picture could have been taken anytime that fall. In the photo of herself she looked so much younger. It was before any of the boys had touched her.

"There aren't any of Benjamin," she said.

"He was taking the pictures, Jade."

Of course he was. And yet, somehow she thought there would be clues if not actual evidence in the last roll of film he'd shot.

"Just let it go, honey," Ellis said softly. He put his arms around her. "Give me another chance, Jade," he said, his voice breaking.

"What?"

Ellis pulled back, looked away. "The ESSOP's cooling down these days. We're too busy trying to make money over the weekend." He cleared his throat. "Which is not to say we aren't prepared."

Somehow he did seem less volatile than when she'd seen him last. Jade thought of an old photo of her and Rexanne and Ellis. She hadn't seen it since they'd lost the farm. In the picture, Ellis and Rexanne leaned up against the front of his truck. Jade was propped between them like a live oversized hood ornament. Her parents were young, hopeful, and smiling because they had no idea of what lay ahead.

"I have time now to be a father," he said. "When you and your brother were tiny the farm consumed me."

"It's OK," Jade said softly.

Ellis cleared his throat. "These fellas are right nice to you," Ellis said.

"Do you like them?" Jade asked.

"They're OK," he said. "I don't need all the damn carnations in my room, though." Robert had prepared an arrangement of fall-colored mums and set out a bottle of Chardonnay in anticipation of Ellis's arrival. He'd joked to Jade about incorporating a handgun in the arrangement, but Denis hadn't found the comment funny.

Jade and Ellis left the room, shutting the door gently behind them. Ellis was talking about Crystal, a blue jay with one wing, that he'd rescued. He explained that he'd taught the bird to say, "Crystal want cookie." The bird was caged in the dining room away from the usual charges.

"I didn't know you could teach a blue jay words," Jade said.

"That bird is something else," Ellis said. "Patience. You need patience. Animals and children both need patience." He put the palm of his hand against the back of his neck.

"Remember when you had the hawk?" Rexanne said, meeting them at the bottom of the stairs. That bird had lost its flight feathers when Ellis found it. She went on to reveal how they had to send away for frozen rats for its food. Rexanne laughed when she said, "We used to order them by the bag. I forget, was it fifteen or ten large rats to the bag?"

"Vivienne got a thermometer with a blue jay on it. Pot holders, too. You know how she goes overboard," Ellis said to Jade.

"My Tommy's coming out next week," Rexanne said. "Soon as he finishes with this major account in Evanston."

Rexanne and Ellis simultaneously looked upstairs toward Jade's room.

"Maybe I'll make lasagna tonight," Jade said. They both liked her lasagna.

"No meat," Rexanne said.

"No meat," Jade said.

"Jade, I've got some photos to show you," Rexanne said. Ellis went off to watch TV.

"I coaxed these out of La Roux," Rexanne said. The small black and white face of Jade's grandmother was blurred in both of the shots that Rexanne presented. Her hair wasn't nearly as dark as Jade's. Then Rexanne produced one she'd taken with a single-use camera just before Nancy Jane died. The photo was of an old woman, her mouth agape, eyes dull.

"It was after the ministroke," Rexanne explained. Jade wished her mother hadn't shown her this picture.

"Will you ever move back to Nebraska?" Jade asked. With the farmers diversifying, the empty storefronts in Paradise might reopen. Tourism could build. Ellis had mentioned turning an unused silo into the world's largest kaleidoscope.

"Oh, sweetie, it's like wack-a-mole out there. You get one thing taken care of, and another trouble pops up right beside it. There's no getting ahead where we lived." Rexanne went on to mention that she was thinking of going to work for a genealogical publisher in Chicago.

"They offered you a job?" Jade asked rather than arguing for all the changes in Paradise.

"Not exactly. Not yet. But I'm optimistic." Superstitious about jinxing the possibility, Rexanne dodged Jade's other questions about the job.

"What about Roberta? What would you do with Roberta if you got that job?"

"Women deal with day care every day all over this country, Jade." Rexanne paused. "Besides, I didn't know you wanted us to have the baby."

"I want you and Ellis to have the baby." Start all over again.

She lit a cigarette, even though Robert was sure to reprimand her for smoking in the house. "That's not going to happen." Rexanne said that no matter how much they knew differently, kids always held out the irrational hope that their estranged parents would reunite. "I held out hope for the longest time myself," Rexanne whispered. "For me and Ellis."

At dinner, Robert, Denis, Rexanne, Ellis, and Jade sat around the mahogany dining room table. Baby Roberta was perched in her carrier on the floor between Jade's parents. Two Chinese brothers were the only other guests in the house, and they'd come in just as Jade was removing the lasagna from the oven. The men were visiting from mainland China and had stopped and watched as Jade set the table.

"Dinner?" the more handsome of the two had asked.

Jade hadn't known how to explain the bed-and-breakfast arrangement. She'd said simply, "Breakfast. The room includes breakfast. Not dinner." Then she'd turned to Robert and said, "Will you tell them?" He'd said, "I don't know how to begin. It's probably easier to let them join us."

Tonight was the first meal they'd all had together. There was an endless list of topics to stay away from—the militia movement, firearms, gay bars. . . . If Jade asked after Hank or Cassidy, Dillon or Brad, her father might stray into dangerous territory.

"We should get some more pictures of Roberta," Robert said.

"Professional ones," Denis said. "As long as everybody's here."

"Use the guy from the shower," Jade said and laughed.

"Let me repeat myself," Denis said. "Professional."

"Ellis could take the pictures," Rexanne said. Everyone looked at him.

"Could," Ellis said, staring at the baby. "Who's the guy from the shower?"

"*Baby* shower," Jade said.

Rexanne took the conversation back, away from all the business at hand. It was a relief for Jade to hear about people who'd died before she was born. Jade sliced into the lasagna. The first piece out was always the most troublesome. She set that less than perfect one aside for herself.

"Ann was quite a character," Rexanne said. "She ran the farm by herself. Roped cattle better than any man." As Rexanne talked, Jade worried that Ellis might take Ann's accomplishments as a criticism of his own inability to hold onto the farm. Denis and Robert might think Rexanne was alluding to the fact that Ann was gay in order to impress them. Every word became a complication. With all the digging, Rexanne hadn't been any more successful in turning up an answer for Benjamin's mystery than Ellis had been after developing the last photos.

Denis was stressed, too. Earlier she'd heard him confiding to

Robert as she tossed the green salad. He'd barely met his latest editorial deadline. He poured himself a glass of Merlot before anyone sat down.

"That's your second," Robert had reminded him.

"Look who's counting," Denis said in reply.

Denis confronted Rexanne about her habit of throwing the past up as an antidote to what was going on in the moment. With Rexanne mucking around in the distant past where no one at the table had to account for anything, it was sort of like watching television.

"I thought you'd want to hear about an independent-minded woman," Rexanne said.

"I'd much rather hear about you," Denis said. "Anyway, how can you be sure what went on a hundred years ago when you're not certain what really happened two years ago?"

"Merlot, anyone?" Robert asked, directing the bottle away from Denis. The Chinese men were talking to each other, gesturing at the lasagna.

"There's not too much to tell you about myself," Rexanne said. "I was a farmer's wife. I ran away."

"You can say that again," Ellis said, digging into his salad.

"What's that supposed to mean?" Rexanne turned to him.

"Whoa," Robert said.

"Wrote a note for me on a paper plate," Ellis said. He humphed and continued to eat.

"There's a *lot* to tell," Jade said. Everyone seemed to be jumping on Rexanne.

Denis stated that the past wasn't all it was cracked up to be. "Did your mother tell you about dust storms?" Denis stared at Rexanne. When Roberta fussed, Rexanne automatically got up to prepare a bottle.

Denis turned to Ellis, "You probably don't know about the

Vigilance Committee that took over San Francisco back in the mid 1800s." Robert, who was normally the one to incite rousing conversations among his guests, put his hand on Denis's. Pulling away, Denis went on. "I don't know why you want to bring up the past. Our ancestors wanted nothing more than to forget about it and go on. My ancestors were dirt farmers. You think they want me spreading that info all over the place?" He asked no one in particular how anyone knew what anyone else thought at a particular time. "Your own history is clouded with the romance of an unreliable memory," Denis said. He looked over at Jade's parents. "I bet you both remember things completely differently."

"Probably so," said Ellis. Jade sliced her father another piece of lasagna without him asking. She looked over at Robert who grimaced briefly to mean that Denis was out of control.

"So much for reliable memoirs," Robert said, but nobody paid attention to him.

"Your family history isn't your destiny," Denis said. "It's unknowable."

The Chinese men were talking more loudly, maybe arguing themselves.

"You know I was reading about this new drug that helps you remember things. The issue is that you remember all the positive things very clearly, but forget the negative ones," Robert said.

"The brain is amazing," Ellis said.

"Yeah, but look what's telling you that," Denis said.

There was a pause, then everyone at the table laughed.

Jade knew Tommy had arrived before she saw him. "Fabulous," she heard Robert exclaim. The next word she picked out was "boots." Her mother's boyfriend could be wearing anything from green ostrich to sharkskin with embedded jewels. Tommy had been planning to spend a couple of days in San Francisco, then fly back to Chicago with Rexanne, but Jade suspected her mother had asked him to come sooner rather than later now that Ellis was in the picture.

Roberta fussed in her bed. Jade now, almost instinctively, turned the baby on her side and patted her little back until she was once again breathing steadily. When Jade opened her door, she heard Robert showing Tommy around the house, even point- ing out the salt and pepper collection. Jade's favorite was the set of boobs positioned in a base the shape of a woman's torso.

Tommy strutted through the impeccable house, more confi- dent than usual, possibly to keep the pervasive gay culture at bay. Tommy had never been to San Francisco before, but he'd heard plenty of stories. Rexanne had confided that she'd had trouble convincing him to visit her in the city of brotherly love.

"Isn't that Philadelphia?" Jade had asked, but Rexanne had brushed the question aside.

Rexanne had talked about how she and Tommy could make a perfect home for the baby in Chicago, but Tommy hadn't even asked to see Roberta Denise. Jade stared at the sleeping baby, totally unaware of how she'd upended all their lives.

Jade came into the living room just as Rexanne was intro- ducing Tommy. "Ellis, I'd like you to meet . . . my friend," she said. She clicked the long nail of her forefinger against her thumb.

After humphing, Ellis extended his hand. "Tommy," he said, repeating the name. Tommy wore a charcoal V-neck sweater over a white T-shirt. In the sunlight his eyes looked even more blue than Jade remembered. His butt was too skinny; he made Jade think of a carney.

"Jade," Tommy said and kissed her lightly on the cheek. "How are you doing?"

"Just fine, if I could drop another ten pounds." She put her hands on her hips.

"Well, I'll let you get settled in," Robert said to the new guest. Robert had assigned Tommy a space of his own in the attic. There was a single bed in the room and fresh flowers, but the top floor hadn't yet been renovated.

"Does anybody need anything?" Robert asked, explaining that he had to go out to select paint for the third-floor bathroom. He assured them that Denis would be returning home shortly. Tommy picked up his suitcase.

"Earplugs," Rexanne said. "I could use earplugs. I don't know who was doing the snoring last night, but it sounded like motorboat races."

"Jade, could I talk to you a minute?" Ellis asked.

She knew what was coming. Her father had flown to San Francisco to take Jade and the baby to Nebraska with him. To rebuild a family? Or to rescue her and Roberta from liberals and Jews and gays? Late last night when she'd sneaked downstairs for a snack, Jade heard him pacing in his bedroom. Even an ex-farmer became anxious being away too long from the place where he'd been raised.

"Have to prepare for pheasant season," he said, mentioning that it started at the end of the month. Ellis thought that leading Nebraska hunting weekends could be a big moneymaker. "Possibilities are endless," he said. He mentioned turkeys, antelope, deer. Bow and arrow, muzzle-loading rifles, modern firearms. "Like to kick it off with pheasant. See how that goes over."

"Is this legal?" Jade asked.

"Have to check it all out," he said, surprising her.

"Mr. Nebraska," Jade said.

"That's not bad," Ellis said. "Hank can have his haunted barn and farmyard jamborees. Pig races on the hour." He paused. Ellis said he could take photos of the tourists up against Nebraska scenery.

"Want to change the baby?"

"Sure," he said.

Jade fussed around the room and tried not to think about her decision. Ellis had pretty much convinced her that returning to Paradise was the right way to go. But a second later, she'd know there was no possibility she could leave San Francisco. It felt perfect for her, especially with the possibility of work from Travis.

"So what do you think of your mother's beau?"

"Oh, he's OK I guess." She tried to make her voice sound matter-of-fact. "Too young though."

"Jade," he said very softly.

"Shhh," she said, not wanting the questions to turn to her. He humphed, then smiled at Roberta.

"Let's try these," she said, pulling out the booties and hat Vivienne had made. "Wait a minute." Jade scrounged around in her suitcase and found the white dress not much bigger than a man's handkerchief that Rexanne had sent Jade in Connecticut. She tried to smooth it out with her hands. The tiny white buttons at the back of the neck were hard to secure. Ellis helped her.

"Where'd you get this?"

"It was Rexanne's."

"It was Rexanne's?" He touched the delicately embroidered flowers. "I never saw this."

"It's a little wrinkly." She tugged at the material. "But so's the baby." As she fooled with the dress, Ellis ran his hands back and forth over his forearms.

At first Jade thought that the baby looked like no one she'd seen before. Red and crying, her face constantly scrunched up with wanting food or sleep, Roberta didn't seem a part of anything Jade knew. If anyone, Jade thought the baby resembled Denis. And she teased him about that, saying she should have named the baby Denise Roberta. Denis said his being a father would have flabbergasted his family. "You just want the baby to look like me because you think she'd be safest with me," Denis had said.

And yet there was no telling who Roberta would look like as she grew up. If Jade returned to Paradise, she would constantly worry that one day her child would develop a quirk to associate her with one of the jackass boys she'd known and discarded. A distinctive laugh, a cluster of freckles, an interest in jazz, any detail that would bind Jade to one man forever. Or maybe a telltale detail wouldn't show up for generations.

The doorbell rang, and, remembering that Robert had left, Jade hurried to answer it. There were no empty rooms.

"Coming," she called.

Jade opened the door on Adam. "My God."

"Hi," he said meekly. He wore a T-shirt and shorts, but was sweating. "Sorry I'm late, but I called that number in Chicago and the man told me you were still here."

"Late for what?"

"For the shower."

"The shower?" She paused. "Yep, you're late."

Adam explained how he'd ridden in a cross-country competition. He'd been intending to arrive before the party, but he'd hurt his leg and gotten held up in Colorado.

Jade ushered him into the house as he talked about the light-ning storm he'd ridden through.

"You rode cross-country."

"I did. I wanted to do it straight. Without stopping for more than a few hours at a stretch. But like I said, I screwed my leg up pretty bad. I stayed with my cousin in Colorado." He paused. "She pampered me."

"Why didn't you call me?"

"I thought you'd tell me not to come." Adam wiped at his forehead. "Besides, I wanted to surprise you."

He'd driven across the entire country on his bike to see her. Sort of. There was the race and all. Still, it was unimaginable. It was something her ancestors might have done in pursuit of a new life. Not as recreation.

"You could have flown." She was glad to see him, and yet he confused her. Her subservient Connecticut life no longer fit her here in San Francisco.

"I don't fly," Adam said simply. "I ride my bike."

"Well, hello again," Rexanne said, coming into the living room.

Adam apologized for his appearance. "Do you think I could get a glass of water?"

Rexanne went into the kitchen at the same time that Ellis appeared with the baby. "We haven't met," Ellis said.

As the two shook hands, Jade said quickly, "Don't go getting the wrong impression." She took a breath. "I was going to have the baby before I met Adam."

"I don't know if that's good news or bad news," Ellis said to Adam.

"How come?" Jade asked.

"Depends on whether I end up liking him or not," Ellis said.

"Wow," Adam said, now concentrating on Roberta. "God, she's so tiny." The baby's hands flailed at the white hat Vivienne had made.

"They usually are," Rexanne said, appearing with a drink. She studied the baby's dress. For a minute, Jade thought her mother was going to cry.

"Wait a minute. Aren't you supposed to be at Yale?" Jade asked.

"I blew it off until next fall," Adam said. Ellis glared at him, then instead of humphing, loudly expelled a burst of air.

"Let's sit on the porch," Jade suggested. She led the way, the others following her, including Tommy who'd taken off his boots and now wore flip-flops. It was three in the afternoon. On her way out, Jade ran into Denis.

"More company?" Denis asked.

"You could say so," Jade said, and made the introductions.

"Can I hold her?" Adam asked.

Rexanne poked Jade. It was a gesture that meant, "Don't toss *him* back. He likes babies."

Ellis handed the baby over, but kept his eyes on Adam the entire time. "Wow," Adam said again. "Jade, what are you going to do with her?"

Everyone went quiet.

"What?" Adam said, looking around.

Denis unfolded extra porch chairs, then he and Rexanne went for glasses and more drinks. Jade tried not to consider herself, but only the little person in Adam's arms.

Rexanne and Tommy weren't the ideal choice. Rexanne might be hurt at first, but she was just getting her own life on track and didn't need the distraction of mothering all over again, particularly with a younger boyfriend who seemed to have no interest in babies. Then there were Jade's hosts. Though Jade disagreed, Robert and Denis had outright told her they couldn't be parents.

She wished that Ellis weren't with Vivienne. Still, the woman was desperate for a baby. Vivienne genuinely cared for Ellis. And if she had a child of her own, she might not meddle in so many other women's choices.

Roberta made everyone smile. It was amazing how a baby evoked such optimism. But Ellis fell hardest. Around Roberta he was a man in love.

Keeping Roberta herself would mean Jade accepting what she'd been born to. Losing herself in a landscape of other losses. Jade thought of the cracked linoleum meant to look like brick on Sara's sister's kitchen floor.

But she could act as Roberta's sister.

Jade could always intervene and rescue Roberta if Vivienne got out of control. Sara could keep her eye on the situation. It was possible that Roberta would be entirely different from Jade; maybe she'd love farm life like Ann; maybe she'd want to buy the family land back. With a good restaurant job, Jade might be able to help her do that.

Denis delivered beers and glasses of wine as Adam talked about his bike ride west. He described the intensity of the ride, his spotters driving close by in a van. The van was equipped with speakers that spouted loud-driving rock and roll so that Adam didn't lose his focus. He concentrated on the road ahead. Jade wanted to ask if he ever thought about her, but it sounded too corny, especially with everyone around.

"At one point I was four or five hours away from seventh place."

Jade said, "Incredible." She bent forward and squeezed his hand. Adam didn't seem to notice that this part of San Francisco was as wealthy as his hometown. But he would. She asked him about Robin and Pearline and about the Sturges children.

After answering her questions, he went on to describe how a cold rain was a nice distraction, how the coaches pushed him to stay on the bike, and then he mentioned his fall. "I would have been too depressed if I didn't make it all the way, even considering that I was no longer in the race." He said next he wanted to bike down the coast. "I have a friend in L.A. I could lay up there." He couldn't wait to ride the length of the Baja.

"Hold her like this," Ellis instructed Adam. "Want to feed her a little more of the bottle?"

"Sure," Adam said, looking up at Jade. Jade wiggled her fingers in front of the baby's face, then touched her hand. Ellis snapped a photograph. When Roberta grasped Jade's thumb, Jade got a prickly feeling at the back of her neck. For an instant, she was back with Benjamin—the first time Rexanne had let her hold her brother. When he'd squeezed her thumb, she felt it all the way down to her toes.

Jade fantasized about living with Adam and the baby, the three of them a family. His parents might even support them until Jade got her career going. But that financial arrangement would make Adam furious. And the baby wasn't his. She couldn't pretend that it was. In a weird way, it didn't feel like hers either.

Jade liked Adam a lot, but she recognized she didn't have near the feelings that Isabel had for Tak, maybe not even the feeling that Sara had for Jeff. She hoped that some day she'd meet a man who would evoke that intensity.

"Looks like we have a full house," Robert called as he came up the walkway to the B&B. "Well, look at you," he said, pointing to Adam.

"I'm with her," Adam said, pointing to Jade. Robert laughed.

"Everybody's with her." He stared at the baby. "That outfit. It's so retro."

"Robert," Denis admonished.

"Kidding," Robert said.

"I think a couple of you will have to bunk together," Denis said. Flustered, Robert said he wished he'd finished all the renovations in September as he'd originally planned.

A sudden hard rumble made the hair on Jade's arms stand up. The wood flooring shook.

"Off the porch," Robert said.

The baby started to cry. Jade took her back from Adam. She'd just made her way down the steps when Denis said, "Don't worry." After another few seconds, he added, "It's over."

"How do you know?" Tommy asked.

"I've lived here twenty years," Denis said. "I have a sixth sense about this stuff."

"So that's an earthquake," Ellis said.

"That wasn't such a big deal," Adam said. "But I'm glad I wasn't on my bike."

"A shiver is what I call it," Robert said.

"You learn to live with it," Denis explained in an exhale.

Jade kissed the baby and handed her to Ellis where she belonged. "Mr. Nebraska," she said.

"Now talk the talk," Robert said to Ellis and clapped him on the back.

Jade took the porch steps two at a time. "I'm going to start dinner." Although it was still early, Jade felt like eating.

"What does everybody want?"

"I could maybe go for a hamburger," Rexanne said. Ellis stared at her. The baby did, too. Jade turned to look at them all, standing there on the lawn—Rexanne, Ellis, Tommy, Adam, Denis, Robert. In the second before they moved to join her, she thought of trees.

14

december

Last night there was another shiver. No big deal except that it got everybody out of bed. Robert had on a pair of lime-green boxers that you could practically see in the dark. One of his favorite salt and peppers, a tiny blue and white windmill an old boyfriend had sent him from Holland, slid off its shelf and shattered. Denis said it couldn't be helped. Robert got teary and said the little figurine was just too beautiful for this world. Whatever.

The earthquake gave me weird dreams. Normally stuff gets all scrambled up, but this one was truly wild.

Benjamin was Isabel's baby in my dream.

I think it was sort of like she'd adopted him. The strange thing was, she wasn't my mother. But she was talking to me like she was. She and Benjamin were in Paradise in the yellow farmhouse. She was younger than Rexanne and very pretty. But wise like Denis can be. Sometimes it even felt like I was the one talking. Totally bizarre. Lots of the dream was way too strange for me to translate into words. Mostly I remember how safe her voice was, how, as she held my brother, she told me not to worry. And I trusted her altogether.

You set out with all good intentions.

You want only what everyone wants—a better life for yourself and especially your babies. That's what my father wanted when he snatched us away from the farm I was born on, then dragged us out of Boston and put us on the trail west. What I thought was crying in our wake was a squeaky wheel on the wagon we rode off in. Tears became nothing more than rain.

And then, events you don't anticipate happen.

My mother died. I planted her trees at the spot where we'd begin the new life. Trees from the east. A purposeful arrangement, more like a bouquet of flowers than the haphazard scattering of nature. Later some of them would catch on, thicken with practicality and take a name of their own—shelterbelt.

Because no one ever reaches the exact spot they set out for, they demand all of the place where they are.

We picked rocks from the fields that would grow our food. We made piles and piles of those protrusions in the way of our smoothing the land into production. The grueling work made us hard. We learned to pick out other details that didn't belong. Sometimes those differences were as obvious as a face—a Chinese man among European immigrants. Other times they hung just out of view—girlishness on a boy.

December is the telling month. If you haven't set in for winter by then, you'll never make it.

We planted the winter wheat and waited.

There was no wrapping paper like back east, no little trinkets for holiday gifts. Our first Christmas in Nebraska, I gave my father a packet of twigs.

In December, the morning sky is dark blue, the fields pale with hoarfrost and patches of volunteer corn. The top layer of ground thaws by midday, but underneath it's frozen solid. December is called Moon of Frost in the Tepee.

We learned from the earth to steel ourselves against intruders. Against separation. We weaned calves in December. The mothers bawled like heartbreak, the babies catching on later and joining the ruckus when they realized what had happened. And we sorted the others for slaughter.

It must be done. It all must be done if you are to survive.

But the preparations are no guarantee. The weather will do what the weather will do. The land will do what the land will do.

Because you work hard against the coming snow, choose carefully, believe that each huge full moon will predict a morning, you don't accept an accident. You don't believe that what happens isn't part of your doing.

Guilt becomes one more job in the field. You learn to use it to leave yourself. You eat guilt for every meal, wipe your lips, and wait for dessert—more and more of it.

Did they kill my Tak or was it circumstance? Did he just give up? For the longest time, I thought *I'd* killed him. I'd brought him into my dangerous life where men rooted out differences like weeds.

I never found him, and no one found me. I didn't die at the hands of Indians. With them, I made a new life, a clean life. When I first came to them, they put me in the sweat house three times a day for one week. There my obsession with discovering proof finally dripped from the pores of my arms and legs and neck and chest.

They taught me that love doesn't die; it's transformed. *You* transform it.

Sometimes it's hard to recognize the connection. Because you continue to do what you've always done—take a blank sheet of ground and plant the same crops in rotation. Rain sun winter summer seeds crops . . .

We blame ourselves for tragedy, but not for love. It happened, not *he* happened. When I met my Tak, I didn't think he was an accident.

I know he was a gift.